THE FAMINE WITCH

STEPHEN BLACK

Quill & Crow

THE FAMINE WITCH
BY STEPHEN BLACK
PUBLISHED BY QUILL & CROW PUBLISHING HOUSE

Cover Design by Fay Lane

Interior by Cassandra L. Thompson

Printed in the United States of America

ISBN (ebook) 978-1-958228-50-0

ISBN (print) 978-1-958228-52-4

Library of Congress Control Number 2023921024

Publisher's Website: www.quillandcrowpublishinghouse.com

This book is dedicated to the victims of the Great Hunger, 1845-1849.

Above all else, I want to thank my wife, Fionnuala, and children Adam, Hannah, and Rebecca for putting up with my constant day-dreaming and keyboard tapping. Looks like Daddy came good, after all.

Publisher's Note

Please be advised that some of the material may be sensitive in nature. For a full list of potentially triggering content, please see Appendix B. For a glossary of the Irish terminology used throughout this book, please see Appendix A.

Preface

The Famine Witch is a work of fiction. The story and its characters were born in my imagination. Maggie Malone and her brother, Jinks, did not walk the streets of Belfast in 1847. However, when writing the book I sought to make its background and context as historically accurate as possible.

While much has been written about the devastating impact that the Great Hunger of 1845-1849 had on the southern provinces, less is known about how the northern province of Ulster fared. Indeed, many still believe today that this part of Ireland was relatively untouched by the famine and disease that ravaged the rest of the island. My research, prior to the writing of this story, discovered that this was far from the case.

In early 1847, a set of political, economic, and social circumstances existed that created the 'perfect storm,' plunging one of the industrial jewels in Queen Victoria's Empire into a spiral of turmoil and unrest. A starving rural population flooded into Belfast after the 1846 potato crop failed that autumn, adding to already cramped living conditions. This created a perfect breeding ground for typhus and dysentery to sweep through a population already weakened by extreme hunger.

This situation was exacerbated by an economic decline that resulted in many mill and shipyard workers losing their jobs at a time when every penny was precious. Political unrest and sectarian tension added to the simmering powder keg; there were bread riots and the hospitals and work-houses were unable to cope with the dead and dying. The town's grave-yards overflowed with bodies.

This was the backdrop to the story that took place in my mind. A dark, foreboding story that told of vengeful witches and bloodthirsty demons, yet nothing compared to the real horrors that befell the people of Belfast in 1847. A year that came to be known as Black '47.

- Stephen Black, Belfast, 2023

Prologue

A QUICK DEATH

THE TOWN OF BELFAST IN THE PROVINCE OF ULSTER,
FEBRUARY 1647

She frantically scanned the crowd, searching for him amidst the clamoring throng as the cart edged toward the square. She was greeted by wave after wave of hatred, rolling off the townspeople like steam from a bubbling pot. Bellowing obscenities at her, their ruddy cheeks and rotting teeth a united mass of hatred and spite. She blinked as a globule of viscous spittle struck her cheek before nodding and smiling at the source of the phlegmy missile, a woman by the name of Jones. She had treated pains in her joints the previous winter and waved away any thought of payment, given the woman had recently lost her daughter to a savage sickness that had indiscriminately swept through their small, insular community.

The man who she most wanted to see her die was nowhere to be seen.

"Hang the whore," bellowed a burly farmhand. The same farmhand who has tried to drag her behind the tavern on more than one occasion when deep in his cups. His unwanted attention had eventually reached the ears of the local sheriff, who was forced to have a quiet word in the young man's ear, warning him to cool his ardor or face a weekend in the stocks.

Hypocrites, the lot of them, she thought, refusing to be cowed by their ire as the cart neared her final destination, the driver gently coaxing his two disinterested dray horses forward. They snorted in protest but plodded on, the crowd reluctantly parting on either side to allow them clear passage. On and on, the cart swayed laboriously through the packed streets, the barrage of insults, spittle, and various other missiles intensifying as she finally relented and looked away, her emerald green eyes blazing with fury at their betrayal.

All because of him.

She would not afford them the pleasure of her tears, instead kneeling in the cart and allowing her striking red hair to mask pale, delicate features. Then the tears came, freely and with ease. Tears for the family she had begged not to come to the gallows. Their hearts had already been broken once during their all too brief farewell at the *gaol*; she would not make them endure that torment again.

The cart jolted over the uneven track, and she was flung forward onto her knees, her plain skirts absorbing most of the impact but not enough to avoid a set of skinned knees. She steadied herself and smiled sadly. Skinned knees were the least of her worries at the present moment.

"Halt."

The steely voice of the sheriff pierced the crowd's cries, bringing an unsettling silence over the dense throng. They had arrived. She looked up and, as the driver dismounted and shuffled toward the rear of the cart, caught her first glimpse of the gallows where she would draw her last breath. The *gaoler* had advised her, the previous night, to jump off the block and hope for a clean break of the neck. The more fearful allowed themselves to fall, resisting the inevitable, more often than not rewarded with a prolonged death, choking on the end of the rope for all to see until their bulging, bloodshot eyes and purple visages announced they were no more.

The mundane mechanics of death. At least she had options, unlike the five young women who had already met their demise at his bloody hands.

She was to be the sixth.

The irony was not lost on her, as the driver unlatched the cart's rear door, and two burly bailiffs manhandled her down onto the wet, damp earth. A light drizzle had started to fall, and she struggled to find her feet as they hauled her through the crowd, who had found their voices again, sly kicks and nips sending her on her way to the steps at the base of the gallows.

Above her, the sheriff awaited, his stern, impassive features in stark contrast to the skittish priest, a slight, hawkish man who looked as if he would rather be anywhere than mumbling a few half-hearted prayers to accompany her into the afterlife.

"Witch."

The first taunt was soon joined by a chorus of others, comforted by the anonymity of the mob. No doubt former classmates and neighbors were involved, all caught up in the frenzy that had spiraled out of control following her arrest two nights ago. A jubilant cacophony, as they had their answer now, no longer having to cower in their homes at night, convinced that a demon prowled the streets, ripping to shreds their young women and gorging itself on their hot, pumping blood. There wasn't much left when he was finished with them.

Even the most superstitious had accepted deep down that the assailant was most likely a mad vagrant, as opposed to anything of an ungodly nature. But then, the strange sounds had been heard at night, emanating from the sprawling woods to the west of the hamlet. A young lad had discovered large, unsightly cloven prints on his wanders at the forest's edge, and the locals had seized upon this uncorroborated account with gleeful abandon. Before long, a horned man had been observed cavorting with several, as yet unidentified, naked young maids before deflowering them in the most scandalous of manners.

Scare them enough, and they will believe anything.

She stumbled again as they hauled her up the uneven wooden steps, hastily constructed when the mockery of a trial had hurriedly concluded. The magistrate had made his mind up long before she had been brought before him, and even had she been afforded an opportunity to plead her case, it would have been a futile exercise. For they now had their witch, their *cailleach*, caught in the heinous act by the night watchmen, hunched over the poor, sobbing wench who would testify that, yes, it was Fionnuala O'Kane, the cunning woman, who had grabbed her from the shadows and held the blade to her throat, drawing blood and whispering in her ear that she would waken in a fiery chamber beneath the earth, there to be tormented for all eternity by the Dark Lord and his legions.

The minds of young girls were so malleable these days.

She let out an involuntary groan at the sight of the hangman, the priest's babbling inanities filtering into the background, where they reverberated with the now distant shrieks of the mob. A man of normal build and height, his face covered with a scarf to protect his true identity, when called upon to perform this grisly act. He could have been the blacksmith or the baker, it mattered not now. He stepped toward her and placed the noose carefully around her neck, his eyes betraying a glint of compassion before stepping back again to allow the pompous sheriff to take center stage.

That's when she saw him.

To her right and towards the back of the square, a section of the crowd had surged forward, eager to get as near the platform as possible for the final act. It was his bald head that caught her eye first, pockmarked and coated in a thick layer of sweat, above twinkling, beady, black eyes that were relishing every second of her approaching demise. He smiled a crooked leer that did nothing to improve his ugly features. A stout, short, nondescript lump of a body that contained a monster who would have butchered his sixth had she not stumbled across his path two nights before.

That was when they had spoken, and he had informed her of his real identity and intentions.

She would be his sixth now. The sixth was always the most important, he had told her. His smile became a grin, and he raised a finger to his bulbous lips as the sheriff asked if she had any last words before she departed to meet her Maker.

"Last words. Aye, I have a few. I curse this town and the foolish men who have brought me before you today. I curse the travesty of a trial I was forced to endure, and I curse every one of you who has turned your back on me. I, who sought nothing more than to help the newborn and dying—"

"Hurry up, girl," snarled the sheriff, but he shrank back slightly as her already startling emerald eyes burned with an anger that few that day would forget. He mumbled his displeasure at the continued delay but fell silent, like every other soul on that drab February morning.

All bar one. He kept smiling. Their eyes locked for a split second that stretched for eons, and the future of the tiny hamlet of Beal Feirste was sealed in that instance.

"And I curse the beast who should stand here, the one whose hands will forever be tainted by my blood."

She turned ever so slightly from the grinning monstrosity in the crowd and nodded imperceptibly to the hangman. The lever cracked, and she stepped forward into the abyss, a quick death that disappointed many watching on.

So, it began.

The Hunger

The stillness overwhelmed Maggie, and she embraced it, relishing every precious second of blissful calm. She caught her breath, scared to exhale, afraid that the drab mechanics of another day would disturb this fleeting peace she desired above all else. A desire that would never be satisfied for long.

Next to her, Jinks stirred and turned, nestling into his sister's back like a newborn pup seeking the comforting presence of its mother. She winced as the rattle of his phlegmy breathing penetrated the quiet of the tiny room they called home. She reached behind her, fumbling blindly until she found his painfully thin arm. Wrapping it tightly around her waist, she burrowed deeper beneath the mound of threadbare blankets, their only protection from the biting cold. An incessant cold awaited them at daybreak, when the gnawing hunger would drag them reluctantly into another day of mundane horrors.

The hunger. It was all they knew now.

Maggie gasped as the first raking pang possessed her, instinctively drawing both knees into her chest. She wrapped her little brother's arm tighter around her midriff, riding the pain until it subsided, leaving only a numb, nagging emptiness. They hadn't eaten in over a day, and the urgent

7

need to find sustenance shattered her false tranquility, like a hammer cracking the surface of an icy lake.

They needed to eat. And soon.

She tentatively raised an arm above the blankets, the chill of the bare room gripping her exposed flesh. February in Belfast was never pleasant, but this winter had been the hardest of her nineteen years on God's earth. 1847 promised to be a year like no other, a year where the suffering stretched out in front of her like a barren road, littered with the blanched bones of the dead and dying. The newspapers Maggie had read were already calling it Black '47. She knew that the town was on the edge of collapse.

And then there were the dead girls.

She shuddered and grasped the bowl that lay by the bundle of damp, filthy straw they called their bed, raising it to her parched, aching lips, guzzling the water as if it had just flowed from the purest Alpine stream. It was stale, but she knew that a few mouthfuls would placate her protesting stomach and keep the constant hunger at bay long enough for her to function and stumble into the waking city in search of a proper breakfast. It had to be done, dead girls or no dead girls.

Three dead in the last month. Butchered and left for all to see, their innards spewed across the cobbles.

Maggie shook her head to dispel the images, struggling to focus on more practical matters. Breakfast? Such a grand word. For her, it conjured up memories of better times, bright days filled with naive hope and a full belly. Warm crusty bread fresh from Elliott's Bakery on North Street slathered with thick, creamy County Down butter. All washed down with strong, sugary tea that only her mother could get just right. Not too strong and not too weak, with a splash of milk to set them up for the day ahead. She would hug them tight and fuss over Jinks, wrapping him in layer upon layer of warm woolen clothing before ushering Maggie and him out the door to school.

Maggie shivered, propelling the unwanted memories to the furthest recesses of her exhausted mind. Sometimes the loveliest thoughts left the deepest wounds. Mother had been dead for almost three months, taken by the hunger and sickness that haunted their every step. Buried in a pauper's grave not two feet deep, the cemetery at Friar's Bush was fit to burst with the famine dead. While the elitist newspaper editors applauded Belfast as an industrial giant, untainted by the malaise that had ravaged other parts of the country, the people on the streets knew the dire reality. The town was choking on the sweet, pungent stench of death. In the hospital, at the workhouse, on the very streets she walked. No amount of fancy words could paint over the mounds of bodies, ungainly tangles of limbs clothed in filthy rags. 1846 had been bad for Belfast, but nothing compared to the terrors of the past two months.

Their throats sliced from ear to ear, their blank, unseeing eyes a silent testimony to their bloody demise.

Bloody Hands.

That's what they called him.

The hunger had clawed its way north, slowly at first, then gaining speed as the failure of the potato crop in Counties Down and Antrim had filtered through to a disbelieving public. Field upon field of blighted potato stalks, a sickly, pestilential stench that had swept lives and livelihoods away like a tsunami striking a fragile shoreline. Prices rose, businesses failed, and a gradual, creeping panic took hold of the population. It had gripped hard and held firm. Neighbors who once would have given their last penny to aid one another, brawled in the street over a crust of stale bread.

It arrived at Maggie's front door the evening her father came home and told them there was no more work at the flax mill for him due to dwindling demand. He had sunk into his chair that night a broken man, his pitiful military pension not enough to feed them. A proud man who had survived the horrors of Quatre Bras and Waterloo as a raw teenage recruit, he was finally defeated by a two-line letter from an uncaring employer, blandly stating that his services were no longer required. Maggie lost her father that day to the bottle. Shortly thereafter, she lost her mother as well.

She turned awkwardly, her back aching. The thin layer of straw offered little comfort from the cold stone floor, nor did the only skirt and blouse she owned make any difference. She faced her brother, his thumb wedged firmly between thin, pale lips. He sucked on it greedily in his slumber, no doubt dreaming of his mother's rich broth that used to warm their hearts and stomachs on bitter winter days like this. Maggie tenderly stroked an unruly black curl back from his gaunt features. He was in dire need of a haircut, but what little money they scraped together could not be wasted on trips to the barber.

Father had staggered home two nights ago and she had rifled through his pockets as he'd snored loudly, muttering and cursing from deep within whiskey-infused dreams. To her surprise, she had recovered a sparkling shilling from the folds of his waistcoat. Too drunk to fritter it away on the booze or whatever wench had sat perched on his lap in the *shebeen* that night. Maggie's face twisted in fury at the thought, disgusted by her father's neediness and abject dereliction of his paternal duties.

She had taken the shilling, much as it had galled her. Pride had to be swallowed if food was to follow. Maggie had not been raised a thief, but the pilfered coin fed Jinks and her for another day, rather than lining the pockets of that fat pig, Jimmy Mulligan, who owned the *shebeen* her father favored in Smithfield. Now, however, that shilling was spent, and their father was God knows where.

"He's probably lying frozen in a gutter somewhere, covered in muck and *shite*. Best place for him," muttered Maggie, forcing herself from beneath the blankets, exposing her frail body to the withering cold. She was naturally slim, but the hunger had taken its toll, near translucent skin stretched over sharp cheekbones beneath a mountain of dark, impenetrable curls that she had inherited from her mother, and her grandmother before that.

An arctic gust swept through the sole cracked window. Maggie shivered again, squinting as she stretched, her pale blue eyes peering outside at the cramped courtyard. A weak shaft of moonlight illuminated the narrow entry that led out onto Bank Street, where the first sounds of the town waking filtered along its moss-streaked walls. Carts rattled over the cobbles as those fortunate to be employed rose from their beds to face the day.

Dead girls or no dead girls, life went on for the living.

All that mattered now was making it through another hellish day. Maggie wrapped her dead mother's shawl more tightly around her shoulders. It was all she had left of the woman who had brought her into this damnable world. Fine Irish wool, worth a shilling or two if she ever sought to pawn it, like they already had so many of their earthly possessions. But she wasn't that desperate. Not yet, anyway.

Jinks lay sprawled out where she had left him, oblivious to the growing din of the city around them. He could sleep for another hour, she thought, an hour's less misery for his tiny frame to endure. Leave her time to say her prayers and count the stones lined up along the windowsill. Twenty-six in all. There used to be twenty-seven not so long ago.

She pondered them through the grimy pane of glass, perched in a row. For all to see. Yet nobody ever seemed to pay the slightest notice to them. All the more surprising given some of the busybodies that lived on the court. One way in and one way out. Four walls of rising tenements that even the rats turned their backs on. Over three hundred souls crammed inside, often several families to a room. Only her father's standing as an old soldier saved them from the ignominy of having to share their pathetic quarters with another family. The landlord had lost his brother at Waterloo and taken pity on them.

It was another hour until dawn and another six after that until the soup kitchen on Howard Street opened. She juggled the potential scenarios in her head, as she shuffled towards the flimsy wooden door that opened into the communal hallway. Jinks could queue, allowing her time to head up to Smithfield in search of their father. He, more often than not, could be found in one of the sordid *shebeens* there, ever since he had been unceremoniously thrown out of his local, Kelly's Cellars, for brawling with another patron. Maybe she could head over there early and beg a few pennies off an amiable drunk before he sobered up.

She suddenly tensed, every hair on her body standing to attention, her hand suspended an inch above the doorknob. Something wasn't right, it was as if...

She spun around just in time to catch a shadow crossing the window outside.

They said he drank them dry.

She blinked, unsure as to what she had just witnessed. Someone had been standing outside, their back turned to the cracked window. Concealed by a dull hooded cape, but she had glimpsed a loose lock of red hair before...before...*she* had vanished. Yes, Maggie had never been as hungry in her life, but hallucinations? Could it have been her? The Black Lady? In answer to Maggie's prayers for protection from the hunger and the maniac stalking the drab streets of the town she was forced to call home.

Two hundred years since he had last stalked them.

The scream dragged her back to the present. It was a high-pitched, mournful wail that would haunt Maggie's nightmares for the rest of her days. She grasped the handle and flung the door open, hurtling down the hallway and out into the courtyard. Eileen McDowell was on her knees in the muddy yard, an excited terrier whipping about her in tight circles, yelping into the vacant skies.

Eileen cradled the tiny form of her infant son, Albert. The infant son she had buried less than a week before. Maggie raised a hand to her mouth, frozen with shock. The screaming started again. It would be a long time before it ended.

The courtyard erupted in a cacophony of sound and frenetic movement. From all sides, the residents of Carson's Court flooded out of their cramped homes in search of the screaming's source. They were a community, and togetherness was all that had dragged them through these last two harrowing years. When one of their own was in need, they all rallied around.

"In the name of God, Eileen, what's the matter?"

"Eileen, love, are ye alright?"

"Oh sweet Jesus, it's the wee baby."

The bedlam subsided to stunned silence as, one by one, the sorry sight registered in their frantic minds. Mary Doherty dropped to her knees to console the heartbroken mother while Joseph O'Neill, the carpenter, whispered to Eileen before gently prising the dead child from her arms. He turned quickly, the infant still wrapped in a funeral shroud, but not before Maggie caught a glimpse of blue-tinged lips and a tiny dirt-encrusted mouth. Not six months on this Earth and condemned to a shallow grave at Friar's Bush. The eleventh member of their community to have been taken before their time by the hunger.

"It's all my fault," wailed Eileen. "If I had only been a proper mother and been able to feed the child."

"Hush now, Eileen, I'll be hearing none of that talk," replied the Doherty woman in a firm, but caring, voice. "You did everything you could for the wee one. Now, you have to be strong. You've six other mouths to feed, alive and in need of their mammy." She gestured towards a nearby gaggle of children, the oldest no more than ten years of age. They stared open-mouthed at their distraught mother, unable to process what had happened.

The soothing words of Mary Doherty triggered a reaction from the other women in the courtyard, and they descended on Eileen in a flurry of sympathy. The children were ushered away to other homes, where they would be fed and watered until their bereft mother could mind them again. Nobody asked as to the whereabouts of her husband. Another soul lost to the demon drink, another victim of the cloud of despair that now hung over the town like a cloying shroud.

"It was Pickles, wasn't it?"

Maggie blinked and forced herself to return to the present. Jinks stood by her side, suddenly materialized from nowhere. He never ceased to amaze her. His mop of dark curls sat atop a pale, haunted face. Eight years old, and his chocolate-brown eyes had seen enough pain and deprivation to last several lifetimes. It wasn't right. He deserved better; they all did.

"Shush. Don't let the wee ones hear. They're upset enough as it is." She grabbed his arm and turned sharply, marching her brother across the courtyard towards their own door. The little dog was now occupied with gnawing on a dead rat nestled between its front paws.

Maggie shut the door behind them and stood in the dank hallway, her eyes narrowing to slits. It was a trick she had picked up from her mother whenever she had wanted to put the fear of God into her errant children. Maggie had found she could utilize it to equal effect whenever answers were required to difficult questions.

"John Joseph Malone, you had better tell me what you know, or I'll tan your backside—you see if I won't."

The introduction of his full name left Jinks in no doubt as to the sincerity of his sister's words. He shuffled uncomfortably, aware that Maggie was prepared to wait for as long as it took for the truth to be revealed. Jinks sighed; the game was up.

"I snuck out last night when you were sleeping. Me and Tommy Reilly went up to the cemetery at Friar's Bush. We wanted to see our mammies. I miss her, Maggie."

Maggie bit her bottom lip, battling to keep the tears at bay and retain her aggrieved demeanor. Her heart broke, but she couldn't go easy on him. A graveyard was no place for a young boy, especially a graveyard in the heart of a town crawling with drunks and other undesirables after the weak sun dipped below the horizon.

Especially with him back hunting.

"Jesus, Jinks. How many times do I have to tell you, you're not allowed out after dark? There's a madman out there—I've told you all this a hundred times. Do you want to be the death of me? To put me in Friar's Bush like Mammy?" Her angry facade petered out as the mournful expression on the little boy's face tugged at her aching heart.

"Come here, you wee runt. Give your big sister a hug and tell me what happened."

Jinks eagerly launched himself into Maggie's open arms, delighted he had earned a reprieve and would escape further punishment. She had never lifted a hand to him, no matter what mischief he'd got up to, but he'd been on the end of many a tongue lashing from her. He had once told her that he would prefer a cuff round the ear and be done with it, rather than the lingering dismay that he had disappointed his big sister.

Maggie laughed, a light, melodious tinkle aimed at warming his heart and stilling the worry she knew was never far from his juvenile mind. She steered him into their room off the hallway. It was all they had, it and a smaller enclave where their father slept on his increasingly infrequent visits.

They fell in a giggling heap onto their bed. The previous summer, Jinks had announced he was too old to sleep with his sister and had based himself in the far corner of the room opposite Maggie. But as the nights had gotten progressively longer and colder, she had more often than not awakened during the early hours to find him huddled next to her, sharing his warmth. Those were the best times, the nights when it was just the two of them, and they didn't have to endure the deafening snores of their father.

"So, tell me the truth and no lies, or I'll skin you and hand you to the butchers on Hercules Street."

Jinks gulped, and it was all Maggie could do to keep a straight face. He was a handful, but she had his measure. The giant, mustachioed men who worked in the meat industry always frightened the young boy whenever they had to venture onto the town's main thoroughfare. He winced, as the thought of a razor-sharp cleaver coming down across the back of his neck convinced him it was time to tell all.

"We were just mooching about. Tommy found a penny on the ground by the gates. I was trying to remember where Mammy's new home was when Pickles tore past and up the path. I reckoned he was missing the wee baby and wanted to see him, so we followed him."

Maggie nodded, not certain she wanted to hear the rest of the story. She had been there when they had dug her mother's grave. The coffins were meant to be buried six feet deep in single graves, but the rising number of dead meant that the gravediggers were putting two, three, and often more bodies in the graves on top of each other. Some poor souls were lucky if they had six inches of earth covering their mortal remains. She knew what was coming next.

"The wee skitter ran like the wind but I'm fast, faster than Tommy, so I kept sight of him. By the time I reached the baby's grave, he was going crazy, digging in the dirt. We thought he was just playing, so we left him to it, as I'd worked out by then where Mammy was sleeping. I never thought that..."

His words tailed off, and he began to pick at a loose strand of cotton on his favorite blanket. Not that he would ever admit to owning a favorite blanket.

Maggie sighed sadly before pulling him into her chest. Jinks was still a boy but was getting taller by the day. He was a fine child, not an ounce of badness in him despite his mischievous ways, and she would do everything in her power to ensure he remained on the straight and narrow path. It had been her mother's dying wish before she had closed her eyes for the final time in this very room. A wish Maggie would see through to fruition, no matter the price.

"The wee dog was just trying to help," she murmured in his ear, stroking his unkempt hair. "He saw how sad Mrs. McDowell was and was trying to cheer her up. But God had already decided to take the baby to Heaven, so he has to go back there now."

"Is he, though?" sniffed Jinks through the first trickle of tears. "Or are they going to put him in that box again and throw him in a stinking hole with all the other dead babies?"

"No, Jinks, no, the men will make sure he goes straight to Heaven this time." She struggled to contain her own grief and find the words required but stumbled on. If she stopped now, she doubted if their shared tears would ever end. "God saw him and decided he was too good for this world. He took him back to his true home. No more suffering."

She felt Jinks shudder in her arms, tensing at the words.

"Is that why he took Mammy? Because she was too good for this place?"

"Yes. I think so." Maggie sensed she was venturing onto dangerous ground, like an unsteady skater tottering out onto a frozen lake, unsure as to the thickness of the ice.

Jinks raised his head and fixed her with a puzzled expression, tear-streaked cheeks glistening beneath the everyday grime that coated the town's inhabitants.

"Then why won't he take us too? Why can't we be with Mammy? Are we bad people?"

Maggie's heart threatened to burst all over again, and it took every ounce of resolve to consider the question before calmly replying.

"God knows you are a good boy, and He will take you when the time is right. But He has plans for you and me. Great plans."

"Plans?" Jinks visibly perked up at this news, the suggestion of a smile creasing the corner of his mouth. "Does that mean we're special, like the angels?"

"Exactly," replied Maggie. "You're the most special boy in all of Ireland, and God is going to look over you, wherever you go and whatever you do. You're going to be different from all the other men. You're going to change this country for the better."

"Promise, Maggie?" There was a hint of doubt in his soft voice now.

"I promise."

She wrapped her brother in the tightest hug that her dwindling energy could muster and whispered a silent prayer for forgiveness. It was a lie but a well-meaning one. She only hoped it was true. Fate could do what it wanted with her, so long as the most important person in her life survived. She closed her eyes and buried her face in the boy's shoulder. He would not see her tears.

A second later, the hammering on their front door started.

An Ill Wind

S he watched as the ship lurched to its starboard side with a sickening crack, another section of the topsail mast ripped free by the relentless squall. It twisted and spun into the angry gunmetal-gray clouds before dropping and becoming engulfed beneath the roiling waves. A smile flickered across her previously impassive features as she savored the developing disaster beneath her gaze.

"Damn it, hold the line, or this storm will take the lot of us," roared the captain, unaffected by the battering downpour as it lashed against his face.

"We're trying, sir," replied his first mate, struggling to stay on his feet as the ship was sucked downwards again into another cavernous trough.

"Then try bloody harder if you want to see land again."

She watched keenly as years of discipline, sometimes brutally administered, kicked in, every man sticking to his task. She danced through their minds to see there was no panic, just a steely resolve to survive the storm and live to recount the tale to their doting grandchildren by a warm hearth with a cold mug of ale in hand.

The witch knew, for that was what they called her, that bad weather had delayed their departure from Liverpool for several weeks until the owners had finally lost patience, worried that their human cargo would die in the English port, depriving them of a weighty purse. The captain had grumbled; it was madness to brave the Atlantic in these conditions, but in the end, he was left with little choice. They had herded the wretched migrant cargo on board and crammed them belowdecks, half of them riddled with fever, the remainder a little more than pallid scraps of flesh stretched tightly over emaciated frames.

They treated her people like scum, worse than animals. They would pay for that, she thought, steadying her stance as the tempest intensified around her. The ship descended into another cavernous trough before emerging again, only her protective wards keeping it barely afloat.

"They paid me to deliver these vermin to Philadelphia, and that's what I intend to do," muttered the captain to the heavens as he angrily stalked the foredeck, immune to the buffeting winds. Less than two days out, and the winds had strengthened, thanks to her, lashing the deck with a scathing downpour that scoured the crew's skin and battered their bodies.

"Damn it," he growled. Philadelphia was a pipe dream in these conditions. "Hanrahan," he bellowed above the squall. "Set a course for Belfast before we're torn apart. If we drift any further north, we'll never see our coin." He squinted through the gloom at the still distant lights of the city, its harbor their only hope.

She smiled again. *Hope.* Such a fleeting, elusive concept.

"Aye, sir," shouted his first mate. "Belfast it is."

"Bloody Irish," snapped the captain as he stormed back to his cabin. "They'll be the death of me."

Belfast. The town where she had died.

She took it all in from the barren headland, invisible to the crew and passengers on the floundering ship. They could not see her, but she was amongst them, her aura a swirling presence that feasted on the panic and fear of every man, woman, and child on board. She inhaled the stench of sweat and urine on the cramped passenger deck, its foul aroma tickling her nostrils. It was manna from the heavens, a gift from the gods—the final act of an epic production she had been relishing for centuries.

This city would pay for its crimes. She would see to that.

She closed her eyes and reached out across the waves again, unseen by the sorry creatures that shivered and shat beneath the foredeck. The sickness raged within many of them, turning their pathetic bodies into lumps of feverish flesh. Once unleashed upon the city, the disease would be rife within days. The people of Belfast, already weakened by two years of cruel deprivation, would die in droves.

She would have her vengeance.

The wind whipped across her angular features as she tucked a loose strand of flaming red hair behind her ear; the remainder of her russet mane contained in a tight braid that snaked over pale, slim shoulders, cascading to the small of her back. A simple, but elegant, black dress was in stark contrast to sparkling, emerald eyes that blazed across the watery expanse. She swayed slightly, releasing another surge of the ancient power that resided within her. Tendrils of magic crackled and surged across the raging lough, wrapping their archaic runes around the stricken ship in a protective arch.

None of the miserable souls on board the Samhara knew that she had saved their lives. For now. As far as they were aware, the miraculous lull in the storm that had allowed the captain to gather his senses and steady the ship and crew was a gift from God. The brutal gale subsided, and the clouds cleared, a fresh westerly breeze filling the remnants of the sails and pitching the vessel towards land at a brisk rate. Hardened veterans slumped to their knees and gave thanks as others openly wept and hugged one another. Even the captain felt his normally thunderous eyes moisten before composing himself and focusing on the job at hand. Belowdecks, families huddled together and prayed, while those too sick to raise their heads merely mumbled quiet words of thanks.

She turned, her work done, and strode purposefully off the headland, skirts glistening as the dawn dew coated the hem of her dress. Below and to her left, Belfast awoke. Tired and hungry, but there was still a functioning port where business continued. The rich were still rich, she knew, largely untouched by the famine that had ravaged the island in recent years. Their order books remained full, and the money that should have been released to aid the poor still loitered in fat bank accounts, tied up in red tape and bureaucracy that even the most skilled accountant was powerless to untangle.

"They may enjoy it while they can," she murmured, her voice laced with disgust.

She sneered, looking down on the descendants of the good guardians of Belfast who had judged and persecuted her so many years before. She recalled the hatred they had screamed from their lofty pulpits and council chambers, their venomous words fanning the flames of suspicion the last time misfortune had struck the town. Even her own family had fallen for their lies, betraying her to the mob. And for what? Being different? Having an opinion? Not being afraid to stand up to the bullies, to speak against the daily indiscretions and travesties inflicted on good, honest people by an uncaring and corrupt patriarchy?

For catching a murderer in the act?

They had hung her for that.

All because of him. Bloody Hands.

She stopped, impervious to the last cruel shafts of freezing rain that raked across the exposed outcropping of stone overlooking the town. Flickering lights spread across the sprawling streets as its inhabitants woke to another day of struggling to survive. She sighed, smirked, and raised her face to the clearing skies before speaking, her voice clear and ominous above the wicked winds.

"This will be a day like no other, a day that will reverberate through the ages. I will scar you and all who walk your filthy streets for generations to come. This ship will dock, and I will allow its diseased cargo to seep into your hovels and taverns. It will spread like wildfire, and there is nothing your fine medicines can do to stop it. The rich and the poor will die side by side, the finest doctors in the land unable to curb the fever I deliver on you now."

She smiled again as the damaged vessel limped toward the shore, horns blaring to alert the port authorities of its imminent arrival. She would stand witness over Belfast and watch, as they had once watched her swing from the end of a rope. There would be no mercy shown, no shards of pity would pierce her unctuous heart. It was but a shell now, they had bled her dry and cast her into the void. Yet, still, she lingered, parents telling errant children tales of her dark deeds. She was a legend, a myth...a fairytale that few believed. The Black Lady, *An Bhean Dubh,* an abomination who heralded ruin whenever she visited their homes.

If one was to hear her haunting dirge during the night, they awoke the following morning to the death of a loved one. Few had heard, and fewer believed, yet for those who did practice her craft in secret, to proclaim their faith in public would lead to certain imprisonment. She presided over them, permitting their irregular pilgrimages onto the mountain, where her *cailleach* spirit lingered. She would appear to them occasionally, letting them know that she thrived, teaching them the truth of what had passed and what yet was still to come.

"I will spare those who believe in me, but only them," she spat, every word dripping with raw contempt. "As for the rest, I will revel in the suffering and agonies that are to come your way."

When the time was right, she would reveal her true nature, and Belfast would know the architect of its demise. She would walk amongst them, watching as they cowered at her feet. Those still alive would be sorry that the fever had not taken them. The graves would overflow, their bodies piled high on the scorched and barren earth.

"I curse these people, today and forevermore. They will never be at peace." She turned her back on the city. It was done. Her voice rose, a haunting melody in the old tongue, her words drifting across the mountain like choking ash towards the slumbering town.

Two hundred years since she had breathed her last. Two hundred years exiled on a barren mountain, trapped in limbo, awaiting his return. For he was back. She could smell him, almost taste him. He needed his six and the killings had started again. Three already. A blood penance that he saw as his right. Every two centuries he came, destroying all that stood in his path. Just as he had destroyed her.

But this time she would be the destroyer. Him and his damned down. They would suffer and perish for what they had done to her.

She once had a name; a job, a family, a lover. She recalled a man who had once gazed into her eyes and lovingly murmured that name. But now, those same eyes raged with a dazzling fury that could no longer be contained. She would walk these streets again, and they would know her true form. No more whispered asides or furtive glances.

The Black Lady had spoken.

Now was her time.

Favored By The Gods

Maggie flung the door open, spoiling for a fight before she had even set eyes on who was causing the commotion. The hour was still early, and the courtyard was deserted again after the drama surrounding Mrs. McDowell.

"Is the man of the house in?"

The sneering voice belonged to Billy Thompson, a snake in human form. Shiny black eyes, like volcanic pebbles, were the dominant feature in an otherwise nondescript face, a permanent five o'clock shadow masking his features. He leaned back, thumbs tucked inside his waistcoat pockets, an arrogant smirk tempting Maggie to slam the door in his face. She bit her lip, knowing that would be an unwise move.

"If you're looking for my father, I would suggest you enquire at one of the *shebeens* in Smithfield. He rarely resides here anymore."

Thompson nodded sagely and scratched his stubbled chin before grinning to reveal a mouthful of rotten teeth. Maggie grimaced as his foul breath threatened to overwhelm her. She took a step back, and he seized the opportunity, shouldering past her into the hallway, followed by two henchmen who had been lurking outside with him.

"What do you think you're doing? I told you he's not here."

"Begging your pardon, Miss, but I'd still like to conduct an inspection of your delightful abode." The sarcasm dripped off Thompson's lips like sour honey. "You two, check in there," he barked at his henchmen.

The two thugs disappeared into the room, where Jinks sat cross-legged on the straw floor. On seeing them, he jumped to his feet, chin jutting out in defiance. *He's the man of the house now,* thought Maggie sadly. The two oafs merely laughed at the scrawny waif before conducting a cursory search of the cramped quarters, which measured no more than ten feet across.

"No sign of him, boss," grunted one of them to Thompson, who leaned lazily against the doorframe, picking at a filthy nail with a blade he had produced from his overcoat.

"I don't tell lies," hissed Maggie, glaring at him with unconcealed contempt. "If you want him, then you'll not find him here."

Thompson lunged forward, grabbing Maggie's wrist before she had a chance to react. He twisted it behind her back in an awkward position that left the young woman gasping in pain. Jinks jumped forward in defense of his sister, but was whisked off his feet by one of the other men and unceremoniously dumped onto the floor. He scuttled into the corner of the room, helpless to assist Maggie who now found the point of Thompson's blade pressed firmly against her throat.

"I do admire a girl with a bit of spirit," he whispered in her ear. "But there's a time and a place for everything and now is not the time. Do you understand? Bloody Hands might be back, but I'm not averse to cutting disobedient girls up either."

He applied a fraction more pressure to the blade and Maggie groaned as it pierced her skin, a thin rivulet of blood trickling down her exposed throat. All she could do was nod weakly in reluctant compliance.

Not all monsters worked in the shadows.

"That's better, sweetheart," gloated Thompson, relishing the power he held over the young woman. "Now you tell your *auld* man that Mr. Brogan wants what he's owed and he wants it soon. Alright?"

He released his grip and roughly pushed Maggie back into the room. She stumbled and fell, and Jinks bounded forward to partially break her fall. The cold stone floor still removed a layer of skin from her palms, as she crawled into the arms of her brother. The tears came easily now.

"No point wailing like a stuffed pig. Just get that drunkard father of yours to pay his debts. Or I'll be looking for payment from you on his behalf." Thompson glowered at her, impervious to the suffering he was causing.

"We don't know where he is. Why don't you listen?" shouted Jinks, his voice frail and frightened.

"I don't care," roared Thompson, taking a step into the room. Jinks flinched backward, all too aware of the pain an angry man could inflict with a belt or boot. He had been on the receiving end of his father's intoxicated rage on more than one occasion.

"I'll get the money for you," spat Maggie, defiant despite Thompson towering over them with a raised fist.

"That's better." Thompson coughed, a raking gasp, before depositing a mouthful of phlegm onto the bundle of blankets at his feet. "Pretty wee lass like you shouldn't have much trouble earning a few shillings down Smithfield tonight. That's if *he* doesn't get you first. I'll be back in two days. Don't be disappointing me."

He gave them a final disparaging glare before turning and striding out of the room. His two companions followed suit, leaving Maggie and Jinks curled in a collective ball. The little boy sobbed quietly into the sleeve of Maggie's blouse, trembling like a terrified puppy. She clung on to him, fearing that if she let go now, she would unravel entirely and find herself locked in the Asylum, what was left of her mind in tatters. She could not afford to do that, she had to be strong, for if Jinks was left on his own, he would be in the workhouse or the graveyard before the winter released its icy grip on the town.

"But...Maggie. We haven't a shilling to our name. What are we going to do?" Jinks wriggled free of her embrace and wiped a sleeve across his tear-streaked face, eager to prove to his big sister that he wasn't afraid.

Maggie sighed and stared wistfully out of the little window that now offered a meager square of light, the gloomy dawn heralding the arrival of another unforgiving day.

"Don't worry, wee man. I'll think of something. I always do."

I need a miracle, she glumly thought.

It had been a miracle.

In almost forty years of seamanship, across every ocean on the globe, the captain had never known a day like it. He had given himself up to the seas, convinced that his ship and crew were doomed, condemned to be ripped apart in the storm that had held them at its mercy.

It was then that the violent clouds had cleared, like Moses had parted the Red Sea, allowing them a safe passage into the lough. Inexplicably, the wind had abruptly changed direction so that it was directly behind the Samhara, filling the remaining sails and propelling them towards the port at a rate of knots that beggared belief.

Unnatural, unheard of; something wasn't right, he could smell it in every nook and cranny of this stinking town.

"More ale, Captain?"

He lifted his gaze from the near-empty tankard, dragged away from thoughts of their extraordinary arrival in Belfast to the bustle of the gritty inn he had hurried to the second his feet touched the dockside. Several tankards of foul, strong Belfast ale had steadied his nerves and allowed him to dissect the events of the morning in microscopic detail. He was by no means a religious man, for a life at sea soon knocked that out of you, but if there was indeed a God or Gods, then the Samhara had been favored that day. Favored, or cursed.

"Aye. And a whiskey with it."

"Right you are, sir." His first mate began to weave through a mass of bodies towards the bar, where the scowling landlord awaited him.

"Wait," bellowed the captain over the chatter. "The cargo. How many made it?"

The first mate turned, uncertain how to frame his answer. The captain's temper was legendary in nautical circles, and he had spent the last ten years of his career at great pains not to invoke such wrath.

"It's not good news, sir. Maybe you should have that whiskey first."

"Either you tell me now, Hanrahan, or you find yourself a new boat. The choice is yours." His raised voice earned a few turned heads but, on realizing who had spoken, the other drinkers thought better of becoming involved and returned to their conversations. This captain had a reputation, a none too pleasant one at that.

"Over forty of them have the fever. We can't be certain though. The men won't go into the hold. The stench is..." Hanrahan paused, unable to put into words what the crew had told him. He was a big man, but he shrank to nothing before his furious employer.

"Useless bastards. I'll make sure they never work a ship again. Find me a doctor and get one of the town guardians down here now. I'll be damned if I'm going to sit in this filthy hole, waiting for the scum of Connemara to breathe their last."

"But sir..."

"But nothing," roared Captain Jeremiah Morgan, rising from the table in a menacing lurch. Five foot nothing tall and almost as wide, with a graying beard covering his expansive belly, he still put the fear of God into every man and woman in the bar. A stunned silence settled; its patrons afraid to move, lest they draw his vexed attention.

"Get them down here now. The Samhara sails tonight for Philly and any scoundrel too sick to travel is not stopping on my ship. Even if I have to tip them into the lough myself."

Hanrahan nodded and turned, pushing through the watching throng toward the door. He knew better than to continue the conversation, only hoping he had enough coin in his purse to convince the relevant citizens to drop what they were doing and cater to the captain's demands. Jeremiah Morgan was used to getting what he wanted.

Morgan settled back into his straining chair and stared darkly out of the inn's window to where his pride and joy sat at harbor, safe and sound despite the storm that had threatened to rip it in two. Repairs were ongoing and he knew that, for every day they sat idle in port, money would be lost. His job was to have the Samhara in Philadelphia by the start of the spring, irrespective of how many of his human cargo perished on the voyage. Once there, he was to collect a consignment of grain to bring back to Cork, where the real hunger gripped the island. He had witnessed first-hand the horrors of Skibbereen and Milltown, where the bodies lay rotting where they fell on country lanes and blackened potato fields stretched for as far as the eye could see. These fancy Ulster folk knew nothing of such want and deprivation, with their thriving shipyard and linen mills. They would take his diseased cargo off his hands and to hell with the consequences.

He took a sip of ale, the froth coating his well-oiled beard. Tomorrow, they sailed.

Maggie had left Jinks sleeping, exhausted by the visitations of Pickles the dog, and Thompson and his thugs. Before departing, she half-heartedly attempted to untangle the mass of dark curls, a deep brown that verged on black when left unwashed for any length of time. Her flimsy comb had made little headway, so she had stepped out into the silence of the courtyard. She washed her face in a communal barrel that had captured the latest downpour from the bleak, unfriendly skies. You might well starve to death in Belfast, but you would never die of thirst.

A steady drizzle was falling as the murky half-light revealed Carson's Court in all its dubious glory. Maggie dried her pallid face with the sleeve of a frayed brown blouse that she had been wearing for at least a week. It was hard to keep track these days. She pulled the shawl tighter around her shoulders, thankful for its reassuring warmth. When wearing it, she always felt a little taller, a little braver than normal. She would need all the fortitude she could get this morning.

She hitched her skirts and frowned. The soles of her leather boots were in dire need of a cobbler's attention, and her feet were already damp. They would have to do, and she was fortunate compared to some of the hapless children who flitted barefoot through the town's maze of alleys and courts. They were ghosts before their time. She pulled a flimsy linen cap down over her own untamed curls and focused her attention on the row of stones that adorned their narrow windowsill. Checking that nobody was watching, she hurried towards the sill and lifted one, savoring its smooth, cool surface against the palm of her hand. It soothed her, allowing the worries of the morning to slip through her fingers like grains of sand on a faraway tropical beach.

She swiveled and closed her eyes, resting the stone against the doorframe of their humble abode. Focusing on her breathing, she sighed and relaxed as a familiar, comforting heat radiated outwards from the stone, spreading across her hand and along her pale, bony forearm.

"Blessed Lady, guard this home and all who dwell within its walls. A spell of protection here I cast, a ward of might to hold it fast. So mote it be."

She inhaled deeply, relishing the wave of peace that permeated her previously disturbed thoughts. Raising the now warm stone to her lips, Maggie softly kissed it before tapping the door three times. Turning again, she made to return the stone to its home on the sill.

"And what are you playing at, Margaret Malone?"

Maggie swung around, stuffing the stone into the front pocket of her skirts. She scanned the murky recesses of the courtyard, frantic to locate the source of the voice. Her worst fears were confirmed when Mary Doherty, the biggest gossip this side of the River Lagan, stepped out of the shadows, a sly smile on her wrinkled features. She was no more than ten years older than Maggie, but two husbands and five children had taken their toll.

"Nothing," spluttered Maggie, desperately trying to compose herself. If Mary Doherty got a sniff of what she had been up to, then the whole of Carson's Court would know within the hour. She had a mouth the size of the Black Mountain itself. The secret needed to remain just that; Maggie's life was complicated enough without having to contend with the ire of her neighbors.

"I didn't come down in the last shower. What's that you have in your pocket?" Doherty took a step forward, her face a picture of casual innocence masking savage curiosity.

"That's none of your business. You keep your nose out of my affairs, and I'll do likewise with yours, thank you very much." Maggie hoped her air of indignation would have the desired effect. This wasn't the first time she had crossed swords with the older woman, and she knew that she had to fight her corner or be swept away by the interfering busybody.

"Sounds like the talk of a guilty woman. You wouldn't be so riled unless you had something to hide. You're nothing special. Common as muck, just like the rest of us."

"Speak for yourself," replied Maggie, warming to the task. "But I'm not the one lying on my back every night for half the men in the town." She smirked at Doherty's mortified expression. Two could play at this secrets game.

"You're a lying bitch. You dare breathe a word of that to a soul, and I'll have your eyes out." There was now less than ten feet between the two women as the drizzle intensified. Plump raindrops bounced off the cobbles, staining the already muddy attire of the sworn adversaries.

"Like I said. You keep to your side of the court, and I'll keep to mine."

Maggie raised her head and flashed a smile that she knew would infuriate her foe. She removed her hand from the pocket, reassured that the stone would protect both Jinks and her from whatever obstacles life placed in their paths. Mary Doherty was well down that list but was an added distraction she could well do without. Maggie walked past the other woman, back poker-straight, towards the entry that led onto Bank Street.

"Hark at her, little Miss High and Mighty. Just like your mother."

"What did you say? Don't you dare speak ill of the dead."

Maggie had reached the narrow entry but turned, unable to resist the venomous bait the other woman had dangled in front of her. She struggled to contain her anger, knowing where it might lead, but the red rag had been waved before her eyes.

"I'll say what I want outside my own front door. Kate Malone thought she was God's gift as well, too good for the rest of us. Well, what did that get her? A drunk of a husband and a pauper's grave. Not so special now, is she? You think that..."

The surrounding atmosphere crackled as every hair on the arms of Mary Doherty stood on end. The air in her lungs was viciously sucked from her body, as she watched the entry light up, illuminated by six large, red handprints adorning its mossy walls. They were randomly arranged as if a passing giant had thrust his hand in a pail of paint and marked the entry as he had lumbered through it. The largest handprints any man, woman, or child had ever seen.

"Bloody Hands," groaned Doherty, falling to her knees, barely able to mouth the words. She began to genuflect and mumble a hurried prayer.

"Aye, Bloody Hands. And you'll keep your distance from me and my brother if you don't want to be his fourth."

The words were out of Maggie's mouth before she knew it, followed by a guilty stream of bile that she struggled to swallow back down. She battled to subdue the energy coursing through her body, the glowing hands providing a hellish backdrop as she stood over the trembling form before her.

"You've the devil in ye, Maggie Malone, just like your mother. I caught you practicing your dark magic, and now the Evil One himself has come to take me. Oh, Jesus, Mary, and Saint Joseph, protect me." She flung herself to the ground, hands covering her head, no longer the brazen bully who had threatened Maggie less than a minute ago.

"Be quiet. You'll wake the whole court," hissed Maggie, but it was too late. Candles were being lit as the residents were awakened abruptly for the second time that morning. Maggie heard the creak of a window being unlatched as a sudden gust of wind swept through the entry into the courtyard, almost taking the cap off her head. She abandoned all hope of calming the now hysterical Doherty and turned on her heel. Before her, the handprints on the entry wall were already fading to their original state, the unnatural light no longer emanating from them.

They had been there for as long as anyone could remember. Some said it was a tribute to the butchers who plied their trade on nearby Hercules Street. The story went that a number of them lived in Carson's Court and wiped their hands on the walls every evening on their way home. Others talked of Bloody Hands, an unseen monster who had murdered six young women in one accursed year, now lost in the mists of Belfast legend. The old folk still referred to the entry as Dead Girls Alley. Now, two hundred years later, either he was back or some other lunatic had taken to the streets to slay the innocent.

Whatever the origins of the grisly marks, the superstitious residents were loath to remove them. Some sneered it was little more than some trickster with a pail of paint, but nobody dared put their theory to the test. So, the handprints remained, and now they glowed, evidencing the power within Maggie that had reduced Mary Doherty to a quivering wreck. Maggie wrapped her shawl tighter around her trembling body as she fled through the entry. She wanted nothing more than to be as far away as possible from the courtyard and the primal forces within her that had raised their head yet again.

The Black Lady had answered her prayer, and she now had no idea what had been unleashed.

A Gentleman's Agreement

❧

The Samhara had limped into Belfast, its battered hull and sails in urgent need of attention. A small army of workmen now crawled over its deck and masts, grateful for a day's labor. Even the once invincible Belfast shipyards were feeling the financial strain of the famine. The only ships to sail out of the lough now were laden with grain for England. A few rubbed their hands and counted the profits, while the majority begged on the streets for a crust of bread. The failure of the potato harvest had hit hard, leaving thousands hungry, and the winter months were biting harder than ever. A simmering tension hung over the town, exacerbated by the growing number of young women being found slaughtered in the town's alleys and courtyards. There was talk of protest marches and rallies. At the moment, it was only talk, but it would not take much to light the powder keg.

It was a different story on the passenger deck. There, the people of Connemara suffered in silence. They cared not if they sailed or remained docked, for most had given up any hope of seeing the bright lights of Philadelphia. A handful of candle stubs cast a weak light on hollow, sunken cheekbones. Sickness hung in the air, the hold reeking of illness and excrement. They lay everywhere, those that could vainly calling for water. Shivering one minute, ablaze the next, the fever ripped through their ranks like the blight had ravaged their potato fields.

One of them was Patrick Rogan.

He had been a proud landowner once, little more than five acres, but enough to grow grain for sale and potatoes to fill the bellies of his wife and three little ones, who now lay beside him in the ship's hold, barely alive. He had even managed to keep the odd pig or cow. The rent had been paid on time, and the children fed and clothed. It was a hard life, but at night they would gather round their hearth and sing the old songs in their mother tongue. They were simple times, but good times.

All that changed the morning he had awakened to the smell. It had hung over the fields like a premonition, foretelling of what was to come. White spots on a few leaves soon turned brown and gangrenous as invisible spores spread on the autumnal winds from field to field. Patrick and his eldest son had dug up the crops to find black, withered stalks, and their livelihood reduced to rotting pustules. The potatoes were inedible, reducing him to scouring the ravaged fields for grass and nettles for his wife to prepare soups that did little to ward off the hunger pangs. With grass-stained mouths and dirt-clogged nails, they had pawned their clothes and survived in rags while the landowners evicted their neighbors one by one when the rent payments fell behind. Eventually, driven out of their village by boots and batons, they roamed the countryside until they could walk no more. Friends of his, too weak to work on the road schemes, had lay down to die by the roadside. The ditches had filled with the dead, infants cast aside by dazed mothers, children gnawing on dead pets. All they knew was starvation and ruin. The harrowing memories would haunt him to his dying day, a day he knew was coming soon.

They had somehow made it to Cork and used what little savings they had to secure passage to Liverpool. From there, they had huddled in damp, putrid cellars for three tortuous weeks, the middlemen fleecing them for what little they had left before staggering onto ships like the Samhara. Patrick and his wife had fallen to their knees in thankful prayer, thinking the nightmare was at an end. Little did they know that the Promised Land was further away than ever, many merely exchanging death in their homeland for a watery grave when tossed from the deck of a coffin ship.

Patrick leaned back and smiled weakly at the pale woman as she passed his family, little more than a wispy shadow. She walked amongst them, for they were her children now. The sweep of her black skirts lifted the heads of those strong enough to still do so. Patrick saw her and believed. It was a visitation from the Holy Mother herself, in the form of the most beautiful Irish *colleen* he had ever set eyes on. Red ringlets fell to the waist of her elegant dress, high cheekbones beneath sapphire eyes that blazed into his very soul. She was their salvation, their comforter, as he watched her stop and speak to others in the sweltering hold, soothing feverish brows and whispering words of succor.

Patrick closed his eyes and heard her as clear as the church bell back home on a crisp Sunday morning.

She spoke to him of better times, both past and yet to come. She told him that he need not worry about the wild Atlantic crossing, for she had found him and his family a new home where grief and hunger would no longer torment his every waking thought. His children would play and sing again, their stomachs never empty. All Patrick and the others needed to do was believe in her, for she would save them from the squalor of the Samhara and heal them of this fever. She would do all this now that their angry God had turned his back on them, their sacred saints nowhere to be seen. She was the answer to their desperate prayers, she had heard them, and now she walked amongst them. They would rise from their sick beds and walk by her side.

For there was much for them to do.

Jeremiah Morgan paced the deck of his ship, kicking out at a coil of rope by his feet; next time, it would be a crew mate's backside. The sooner he was out of this bloody port, the better, he thought. Eventually, a holler from the bustling docks announced the imminent arrival of the long-awaited boarding party.

He leaned over the side and groaned at the two men gingerly edging up the gangway. A tall, gaunt man with lavish whiskers and a prominent hawkish nose edged ahead of a smaller, stocky man carrying a leather bag with some difficulty. The good townsfolk of Belfast had arrived. He composed himself and crossed the deck to greet them, a broad smile pasted across his face, a thin veneer of kindness that couldn't quite conceal the contempt behind his eyes.

"Welcome aboard the Samhara, gentlemen. Thank you for taking the time to come to our aid."

He extended a meaty hand which the taller man reluctantly accepted, his face aghast at being asked to shake hands with a common sailor. His stout companion peered meekly over a pair of reading glasses, which perched precariously on a ruddy, bulbous nose.

"You've asked us to inspect your hold, Captain. What cargo do you carry, and why the sudden need for our presence on this...vessel?"

Morgan's smile froze. This was going to be more difficult than he had initially anticipated.

"I'm afraid it's rather a delicate matter, Mr. Blake," he whispered, ushering the taller man away from a deckhand, who feigned mending a section of canvas mast as he eavesdropped on their conversation. The smaller man shuffled behind them, an obedient puppy following its masters.

"Delicate? What on earth are you on about, man? Come on, spit it out. Myself and Dr. Crothers are busy men. We haven't got all day to listen to your riddles."

"Of course, Mr. Blake," snarled Morgan. "And I'm very grateful for yourself and the good doctor taking the time to come down here. I'll be frank then. My cargo is human. emigrants bound for Philadelphia, originally from Connemara."

Blake frowned at the mention of the latter word, and Crothers pulled a face as if he had stepped in something unseemly.

Morgan continued. "Only Providence saved us from the storm and allowed us to find safe haven in your fine town, for which I will always be grateful to our good Lord. I'm afraid, however, that I now find myself in somewhat of a dilemma."

Blake gave nothing away, regaining his composure after the initial shock of Morgan's proclamation had washed over him. He drew himself up to his full height and fixed the squat captain with his most officious stare.

"Myself and the other town guardians pride ourselves that Belfast turns no stricken vessel away. However, I struggle to see how the contents of your hold concern myself or my colleague." He cleared his throat, a cue for Crothers to nod vigorously in agreement.

Morgan sighed. This was testing every strand of his already frayed patience.

"We are already three days behind schedule, Mr. Blake. For every day I'm late docking in Philadelphia, I'm liable to a fine from the port authorities. Even if we were to sail tonight, I'd be sorely pushed to make up for the lost time. However, if I were to lessen the weight of the ship considerably..."

Crothers started to choke while Blake's already deathly pallor took on an even more ghostly sheen.

"If you're suggesting that you abandon your cargo of filthy peasants here, Captain, then I'm afraid you're sorely mistaken. We already have our streets clogged with paupers from every county in Ulster. Every day I expect bread riots. The people are starving as it is, without you further adding to the burdens faced by our hospitals and soup kitchens. Now I bid you good day. I have much more urgent matters to attend to."

Morgan sighed inwardly as Blake turned to retrace his steps to the gangway, followed by a mightily relieved Crothers. What a pair of pompous, arrogant fools. Well, he had dealt with the likes of Blake many times before, from the Caribbean to the South Asia Sea. And, when you cut to the chase, they all spoke the same language, whatever their nationality.

Cold, hard cash.

"I wouldn't for a second insult your intelligence, Mr. Blake, and I'm well aware of the situation you and your colleagues face. However, if I were to make Philadelphia on time with a lighter cargo and then deliver the grain to Cork ahead of schedule, I would be due a handsome bonus. Which I'd only be too happy to share with you and the doctor as a mark of my gratitude for your assistance.

"Well, I. This is the most improper proposal..." Blake spluttered and blushed, his face a picture of discomfort.

"I believe you're planning to run for mayor later in the year, and I'm sure the additional funds would help you with the little law and order problem you're having at present. How many has he killed now? Three? Four?"

Morgan waited as Blake halted, one foot raised to mount the gangway, before turning, narrowly avoiding a collision with the rotund physician. The two exchanged a series of whispered exchanges, Blake bending down to gauge Crothers' views on the proposition that had been set before them. Eventually, he afforded Morgan a wan smile before stepping warily back towards him. He spoke softly, as if concerned the town's population was listening in on their conversation.

"Having discussed it with my colleague, it would be remiss of us to turn our backs on the needs of a ship in need. After all, this town was built around our maritime trade, and we have a proud tradition of providing comfort and solace to those brave enough to sail the cruel seas. Now, how much would you anticipate..." He allowed the sentence to hang, licking his thin lips, the greed seeping from his pores.

Morgan smiled back. He had him. "Ten pounds per passenger. Were you to take a hundred of them, I predict we would make double-quick time to Philly. One thousand pounds which I'm sure you two gentlemen would put to good use."

Blake stifled a cough before composing himself, holding out a hand to the crafty captain. "Indeed, Captain Morgan. Law and order, education, housing. I'm quite the philanthropist, and there are many good causes concerning the needy of this town that the money could go towards." He tentatively extended a hand, Crothers looking on like a starved hyena, anticipating his share of their unexpected windfall.

"I imagine there are," replied Morgan, accepting the offered hand and winking slyly at Blake. "Let's hope the money goes to those honorable causes, rather than being squandered away in the brothels and bars of this fine town."

Blake withdrew his hand, a look of utter repulsion crossing his features. "Have your cargo ready tomorrow morning. I will send transport. Those we can't fit in the workhouse, I'll find alternative accommodation for. I'm a reputable businessman and property owner, I'll have you know."

"Of course, of course," sneered Morgan.

It took all his willpower not to tug his cap in feigned respect. "And the paperwork?"

"I'll see that it is all processed promptly. Dr. Crothers will examine the new arrivals before they leave the ship. I'm sure they are all healthy specimens. We wouldn't want sickness entering the town on top of all our other woes."

"Most certainly, Mr. Blake. I can assure you, they are all in fine fettle." He smiled warmly at the portly medic, certain that his share of the bonus would ensure that the necessary medical documents would not reveal a sniff of illness amongst the passengers below deck. A fat cheque always helped to oil the bureaucratic wheels.

Crothers turned a peculiar shade of crimson but said nothing. The deal was done.

Jeremiah Morgan offered a final salute as Belfast's finest took their leave of his pride and joy. The Samhara would sail and all would be well. To hell with the scum below decks. The hundred that stayed in Belfast would be the fortunate ones. Any who perished on the crossing would be tipped over the side and good riddance to them. Yes, thought Morgan, Lady Luck was with him, and Philadelphia beckoned. He strode towards his cabin, a cheery whistle sounding from his lips. Belfast. What a splendid town it was.

Maggie hurried along Hercules Street, oblivious to the garish sounds and smells emanating from the butchers' shops that occupied either side of the rain-sodden thoroughfare. She dodged the sizable puddles as nimbly as she did the catcalls that greeted her the second she set foot on the street. Wolf whistles and unsavory comments filled the air, drowning out the steady metallic clang of cleaver cutting through meat and bone. Her stomach churned, a combination of hunger and the stench of offal and blood. The town's elders had congregated all the meat merchants in this part of the town so that the more well-to-do would not have to endure the unseemly aromas. Always thinking of themselves, she thought glumly as she turned right into the district they called the Madhouse. Smithfield, home of some of the seediest bars and *shebeens* in the country, the place where she hoped she would find her father.

She jumped as a team of miserable-looking draught horses plodded past, their driver chewing on a wad of tobacco as he steered his wagon along the heaving street. Belfast stretched its limbs, as the bleak sky did its best to announce the arrival of a new day. In an hour's time, those who had the money, and they were becoming fewer every day, would be pawing over the finest cuts of lamb and beef.

"Spare a penny, miss? Help an old soldier out?"

Maggie hadn't noticed the bundle of bone and rags crouched in the doorway. Huge eyes and hollowed cheeks stared up at her in hope. He could have been fifty or one hundred years old; it was difficult to tell now.

Hunger was a great leveler. It broke spirits and dragged even the hardiest soul deep down into its snarling embrace.

"I'm sorry. I haven't a penny to spare. The soup kitchen on Howard Street opens later this morning. You could try your luck there. Hot broth and bread. Good day."

She scuttled on, uncertain if the beggar had even heard her embarrassed reply. Since the last potato crop failed, Belfast had been flooded with country dwellers, driven by desperation into the town in search of sustenance. Those with a few pound notes were only passing through, bound for Liverpool, Glasgow, and further afield. New York, Philadelphia, Montreal. They were but names to Maggie. She and Jinks were going nowhere, and her only focus at present was getting Billy Thompson off their backs, no matter what the dangers of the streets posed.

Another hunger pang almost stopped her dead in her tracks. She gathered herself, grasping the two coupons in the front pocket of her skirts. Coupons to the Howard Street soup kitchen for Jinks and herself. She had waited half of yesterday to get them, but it had been worth it. The thought of a warm meal in a few blessed hours propelled her forward, past the final shop in the row, and right onto a narrow side street. The waft of stale ale and staler vomit assailed Maggie's nostrils, but she forced herself to forge deeper into the squalor of Smithfield.

She stepped gingerly over a few prostrate forms strewn on the cobbles in front of her, not waiting to ascertain if they were dead or merely the worse for drink. Increasing the pace, her eyes scanned ahead and to the sides, wary of unseen threats. Three young women had been found lifeless, their throats sliced and bellies cut open, along the sprawling maze of alleys and dead ends that constituted Belfast's most dangerous quarter.

His hunting ground.

"Left, left, then second right. That's where he'll be." Maggie muttered the mantra over and over, already regretting leaving Jinks on his own. He knew every inch of the town and was the craftiest street urchin this side of the Lagan, but she was still wracked with guilt every time she left him to fend for himself.

Callaghan's. The most squalid drinking den in the town, a place even the rats thought twice about entering. That's where she would find him. Slumped over a table, no doubt, sleeping off the excesses of the previous night. Callaghan's never really closed, its clientele always assured a strong ale or stronger spirit whatever the hour. It was where her father had retreated the day his beloved wife passed to lick old wounds and drown fresh sorrows. He had never resurfaced, bar the occasional visit to Carson's Court when funds were low to await his next pension payment. Then it would be back to the *shebeen*, where exaggerated tales of valor were exchanged with fellow veterans. Wellington had once described his army as the scum of the earth. A visitor to Callaghan's would be hard-pushed to disagree.

Maggie weaved along the twisting, narrow alley as she plunged deeper into the black heart of Smithfield. It was eerily quiet, the calm before the next alcohol-fueled storm. A dim lamp up ahead hung from a sconce above a nondescript door. You would walk past it if you didn't know any better. Emmet Callaghan liked to keep a low profile and was loath to waste money advertising his trade. His customers knew where he was and what he offered. He didn't need fancy signs and banners to lure them to his lair.

Maggie inhaled deeply, closed her eyes, and rapped the door. She hated being here, hated having to do this, to be the adult, when all she wanted to do was curl into a ball on her father's knee and sob until there were no more tears. He had been her hero, her rock, but those days were now long gone. The man she called her father was now a stumbling shadow of his former self, adrift at the bottom of a bottle.

A dog barked from inside, and Maggie took a step back as a window above opened with a shuddering squeak. A familiar head popped out and groaned, as he set eyes on the young woman who had dared to rouse him from his slumber.

"In God's name, what do you want? It's the middle of the bloody night."

"You know what I want, and it's past eight in the morning. Some of us go to our beds at a reasonable hour."

Maggie stared resolutely up into the bloodshot eyes of her father.

"Don't talk to me like that. Show some respect for your old man." John Malone rubbed the sleep from his eyes as another hangover reared its head and prepared to lay siege to his body.

"I'll show you respect when you start behaving like my father. Have you no shame? Drinking yourself into an early grave when you have an eight-year-old son barely surviving from day to day." Her pale blue eyes blazed, frustration and exasperation fueling words she never imagined saying to the man she used to idolize.

"Ah, to hell with you, I'm away back to bed." He fumbled with the latch, intent on shutting out another tiresome responsibility that had become too much for him to bear.

"Aye, do what you do best. Run away from me and the wee man. Mammy would be ashamed of you. Do you hear me? Ashamed." Tears started to flow unannounced down Maggie's cheeks, and she angrily wiped her face, furious with herself for allowing him to see how much she cared.

"Don't you dare bring your mother into it. She...she..." His heavily stubbled cheeks flushed with anger.

He used to shave every morning without fail, thought Maggie. A habit he had picked up in the army, all the way across Spain and up through France to Napoleon's last stand at Waterloo. Oh, the tales he had used to tell Jinks and her before tucking them into bed. Back when things were different. Better.

"I will so. I'll say what I have to say, to get through that thick skull of yours. Billy Thompson has been round. Says we have two days to cough up what he's owed or there will be hell to pay."

"John. Come back to bed." A woman's voice drifted lazily from the room, causing Malone to jerk around.

"Quiet, woman. I'll be in when I'm ready."

Maggie felt the blood drain from her head and thought for a second she would be overwhelmed by a wave of nausea. She watched as her father reached into a trouser pocket and hurled a handful of coins down onto the muddy street.

"Take that, it's all I have. And if Thompson wants any more, tell him I haven't got it."

"Daddy, please..." Maggie had not ventured into Smithfield to beg but suddenly wanted nothing more than to have her father home, whatever it took.

He paused, his hand still on the latch, a man torn between what was left of his family and a flea-ridden room above the roughest *shebeen* in the town. She knew all he had to do was admit he was broken, say the word, and he could be back with them. He could start again; it would be hard, but she would help him kick the grog and find work. Even if it meant breaking stones for a shilling a day, he could do it. She knew that he wasn't afraid of hard graft.

"John, come back to bed. I've a bottle of wine here I need help to drink."

Maggie watched his face crumple, the woman's voice snapping what little resolve had threatened to surface. Maggie realized, in that moment, that the call of a warm bed and a soothing drink meant more to him than his own daughter and son. This was what happened every time she set this choice before him. Too much pain, endless pain that began the day they had placed her mother in the cold, wet earth. A pain her father had been running from ever since.

"Just go, Maggie. Go. And don't come back."

The window slammed shut, and she was on her own again. She fell to her knees and scooped the pennies from a greasy puddle. One, two, three, four. Nowhere near enough to satisfy their debtors, but it was all she had to show for her troubles. It would have to do and she'd have to come up with another solution. Kneeling in the muck of the churned-up street, Maggie leaned into the faintest of hopes, a hope that had failed her mother all those months ago.

"Blessed Lady. Hear my prayer..."

I Will Have My Six

She moved through the darkened streets quietly and efficiently, well-accustomed to nocturnal visits where discretion was required. The girl had caught her eye earlier that day at the weekly market in the town square, following Fionnuala from stall to stall with a lack of subtlety that forced the older woman to bite her lip for fear of laughing out loud at the girl's nervous circling. Eventually, she dragged up the courage to speak as Fionnuala inspected a basket of apples at Old Tom's fruit stall.

"Mistress O'Kane, might I have a word with you...in private."

Fionnuala smiled before turning to face the girl. One of the Rafferty brood, if she was not mistaken. There were seven, no eight, of them, but this one was the oldest, seventeen, and thought she knew everything the way she normally paraded around the town, turning every young man's head as she and her friends giggled and flirted with them at every opportunity.

She wasn't giggling now.

Fionnuala had nodded towards an adjacent entry, off the main square, before purchasing an apple from the stall and crossing the muddy expanse,

45

lifting her skirts with one pale hand while balancing her purchases in a basket in the crook of her other arm. The crowded square parted before her, the occasional nod and smile outweighed by mistrustful glances and whispered asides as the townsfolk took in Fionnuala, who ignored them all, a distant smile proving a formidable barrier between her and the local gossips.

They all came to her, sooner or later.

Potions, cures, pick-me-ups, charms, and trinkets; she discreetly provided them all to the steady stream of customers who required her services. In the case of the Rafferty girl, it was an amorous young woman keen to win the eye of the handsome laborer recently hired to toil in the fields of her father's farm. Furtive glances across the yard had progressed to clandestine meetings and stolen kisses under the crisp winter moon. But he was poor and led a transitory lifestyle, while her parents owned more acres than the next three largest farms combined. Winning her father's approval on this delicate matter had been doomed from the start, unless...

"Can you help me, Mistress? Give me something to slip in Father's ale, something that might convince him that Joe is a good man worthy of my hand in marriage?"

There was barely room for the two of them to stand face to face in the entry, far enough back that they could not be easily spied from the square. The look of lovestruck desperation on the girl's fair complexion thawed the ice that tended to gather there when Fionnuala was left to her own devices. She preferred to keep to herself, content with her humble shack near the edge of the woods, less than a five-minute walk from the bustling town that sat huddled between the mountain and the lough shore. Cultivating her herbs, close to nature and the whispering of the woods. Some called her a witch, a *cailleach*, but never to her face. Despite the passing of the years, the old ways were still tightly entwined through local life, ensuring that the local cunning woman was afforded a blind eye by the local authorities. This allowed Fionnuala to quietly serve her community the same way that her mother and grandmother had before her, may the ancient ones bless their departed souls.

The path to her door was a well-worn one, a door that was meant to have knocked an hour last.

"Aye, I can help you. Come to me tonight, at midnight, you know where I reside. Tell nobody where you are going, and I will be waiting. I will have what you require to attain your heart's desire."

The girl had grinned, barely able to contain her soaring hopes, before melting back into the square, a fresh spring in her step. Fionnuala watched her depart before sighing and slipping out of the entry, keeping close to the edges of the square before darting down another laneway that opened out onto the fields that led to her house.

The path to her door was a well-trodden one.

Midnight came and went. And still no sign of the Rafferty girl.

Fionnuala scanned the fields nervously from her front door, hoping the sound of hurried steps approaching would allay the growing concern gnawing incessantly at her own stomach. The night was deathly quiet, not a peek from the forest behind her that normally reverberated with the sounds of the animal kingdom going about its nightly routines. Even her friends, the crows, were quiet, their reassuring caws and swooping trajectories notably absent.

Something was amiss.

Girls had been disappearing and before she was even aware she was doing it, Fionnuala had donned her cape and was hurrying across the fields toward the dim lights of the town. The air seemed to thicken with every step she took, a quickening unease that had Fionnuala curse herself for having agreed to help the girl. She should have said no but was loathe to turn away the coin and had thought such a short journey. What could possibly...

That's when she saw them.

In the shadows of the laneway that led towards the market square, a squat figure stood hunched over a bundle of cloaks and skirts huddled into a protective ball. As Fionnuala neared, her pace more frantic with every step, the figure spun around, revealing a pudgy face, its only noteworthy feature a set of dark, beady eyes that twinkled with a malevolent intelligence. His face broke into a slow snarl, and he raised a hand to his mouth, wiping it across lips that she now realized were coated in a thick layer of red.

The blood. So much of it everywhere.

The silence hung between them like a cloying shroud, the Rafferty girl's whimpers barely registering with Fionnuala as the creature cocked its head to one side and considered her with a wicked intensity.

It. For this was no man that stood before her.

"Be on your way, wench, this is none of your concern." The snarl widened into a sly smile as he took a slight step toward her, a statement of intent that sent a chill jolting down her spine.

"I'm afraid that it is now. Leave the girl, and I will make sure she gets the attention she requires. There will be no killing this night."

He nodded and studied the wretched bundle at his feet as if giving her statement serious consideration before throwing back his head and bellowing at the heavens. Fionnuala stood firm, determined not to be intimidated by his manic howl. Finally, he dabbed at imaginary tears on his cheeks and deigned her with his attention again.

"Fair enough, have it your way. I do like the feisty ones, much more sport in it for me and twice the fun. Have your bitch." He unloaded a vicious kick to the Rafferty girl's crumpled form and turned away, back towards the square. A weak shaft of moonlight penetrated the gloom, throwing a tentative light over them.

Fionnuala fell to her knees beside the girl, a quick visual examination satisfying her that, while the girl had been cut, her wounds were superficial, and she would survive the night.

"But I will have my six."

Fionnuala froze before looking sharply toward the grating voice, but the beast was nowhere to be seen. Instead, she was greeted by a flickering torch that grew in strength as it neared, accompanied by the sound of stout boots splashing through the patchwork of puddles that adorned the uneven laneway.

"Over there. Look." A man's voice cut through the gloom, and the direction of the flame veered toward Fionnuala, capturing her within its fragile light.

"Thank the Gods. I need help. The Rafferty girl, she's been..."

"Jesus, have mercy. What abomination has affronted us this night." The same voice as before, only an octave higher, shock now mixed with a growing anger.

"It's the Rafferty girl, Father. And...and..."

"It's O'Kane. The Cailleach. Good Lord. The blood."

"We have our killer. But a woman. She must have been spawned from Satan himself."

Fionnuala held her bloodied hands out, desperate to explain, but before she could utter a word, the staff came down on her head, a glancing blow that stunned her. She fell back over the Rafferty girl as further blows rained down, again and again, until the blissful darkness took her in its comforting arms, up and away from the unrelenting pain.

He had his sixth, and they had their killer. For this, she would hang.

BELFAST, 1847

"Slow down, Jinks. You'll be making yourself sick." Maggie placed a hand on the young boy's forearm as he attempted to cram another lump of soup-sodden bread into his already full mouth. He merely grinned, revealing a mush of masticated food, a thick rivulet of broth trickling down his chin.

"You've the manners of a goat." Maggie sighed, struggling to suppress a smile. They had waited for over an hour in a steady downpour outside the disused cotton mill that housed the town's largest soup kitchen. Established by the relief committee the previous autumn in anticipation of a grim winter, it was capable of feeding up to a thousand people a day. Several finely-attired ladies labored over a huge vat at one end of the building as hundreds of hungry folk patiently awaited their turn. Once they received their bowls of broth, they shuffled to another table where bread was supplied, along with a religious tract proclaiming the error of their ways. For the good ladies of Rosemary Street Presbyterian Church were intent on offering more than granary bread to the desperate, largely Catholic poor of Belfast. They also offered the bread of life, urging needy souls to turn their backs on the Vatican and accept the one true faith into their hearts and minds.

Maggie's tract lay in a crumpled ball on the floor by her feet. Her Catholic faith had died the day she lost her mother. No amount of praying had saved her, no worrying of rosary beads or lighting of candles. God had been nowhere to be seen as she had slowly wasted away in that stinking room. Whispered words from Kate Malone had revealed a new way to her daughter, a fresh faith. She prayed to a different deity now, in secret and on her own.

"Are you taking that bread, Mags?" enquired Jinks, nodding at her plate. She smiled at the hint of color that had returned to his cheeks. It was amazing what a warm meal could do to breathe fresh life and hope into their beleaguered bodies. Along their bench, dozens of famished men, women, and children were shoveling broth and bread into their mouths. For many of them, it would be the only meal they would have that day. The price of a stone of potatoes had doubled in price over the harsh winter months, not that much of the crop had survived the blight sweeping across Ireland.

Maggie smiled and ruffled her brother's mop of black, curly hair. She was still famished, despite the broth, but pushed the bread towards his plate. Every time she glanced at him, she swore he had gained another inch in height. He needed it more than her, even if it meant the few remaining items of clothing she possessed hung more loosely on her skinny frame.

"Thanks, Maggie." His smile warmed her heart and temporarily forced the ever-lurking hunger to the back of her mind. For now. John Malone's pennies jangled in Maggie's skirt pocket, taunting her. With them, there was enough to buy some oats and buttermilk. Not much, but she could mix it with water and prepare a pot of flummery, a bland paste that did little for the palate but filled the stomach.

"You'll wait your turn like everyone else." Maggie's attention was drawn to a raised female voice by the serving table. A bulky man with a shaved head was thrusting his bowl toward a young blonde-haired woman who stared defiantly back at him.

"I've been waiting an hour already. An hour listening to your religious nonsense. It's enough for any man. Now give me my food, and I'll be on my way."

He towered over her, obviously used to intimidating others with his height and build. Behind him, anxious voices murmured in discontent along the snaking queue. Maggie could sense the atmosphere in the room souring as empty bellies grated taut nerves and rising tempers. Hunger reduced humans to their basest forms; she learned that cruel lesson with each passing day.

"Eat up, Jinks. Think it might be time for us to take our leave."

"Awwwh, have a heart. Let me finish this in peace, and then..."

A piercing scream filled the room, and all heads turned to the serving table, where the young woman was now wrestling furiously with the hulking brute over a loaf of bread. It was a contest that could only end in one outcome. The young woman lost her grip on the loaf and her balance, staggering sideways into the huge vat of broth on the serving table. Hundreds of straining eyes watched in suspended horror as its life-sustaining contents spilled across the floor of the mill, a tidal wave of carrots, onions, and chunks of beef. The building erupted into chaos as a disgruntled man swung a fist at the bald hulk who had initiated the clamor now gripping the Howard Street Soup Kitchen.

The big man swayed back, his opponent's fist barely grazing his grizzled chin before leaning forward again and delivering a meaty blow that sent the smaller man crumbling to the floor, his nose bursting open like a ripe tomato. Another man ran at the giant, jumping on his back, but was tossed aside like a tumbling leaf. Screams resonated around the hall as scuffles broke out everywhere. The more resourceful fell to their knees and scrambled through tangled legs for anything they could salvage from the spilled soup. Combatants succumbed to the slippery surface and landed on top of those scavenging beneath them.

Grabbing a reluctant Jinks by the scruff of his collar, Maggie switched into survival mode. In the distance, a high-pitched whistle sounded, ringing above the cries and roars that filled the hall. The local constabulary were on their way, no doubt relishing the opportunity of cracking a few heads open with their truncheons.

"Hurry, Jinks. We need to get away from here." A few years ago, she would have whisked him into her arms, but those days were long gone. She let go of his collar and grabbed a wrist, almost yanking the young boy off his feet in her eagerness to escape the mayhem. The last thing she needed was a night in a cell and an appointment with the local magistrate the following morning.

"Wait. Let her go, you big lump of *shite*."

Maggie found herself holding onto thin air as Jinks wriggled free and sprinted toward the serving table, weaving his way through the fracas. She looked beyond her little brother in horror, as the bully who had initiated the disorder clutched a handful of the young woman's blonde hair and began hauling her toward a door at the back of the hall. He looked over his shoulder at the sound of Jinks's voice, just in time for the young boy's head to connect with the man's sizable belly. He gasped, the wind knocked from his sails, and dropped to the floor with an elongated groan, letting go of the young woman in the process.

"You wee bastard. I'm going to..."

"Come on, Miss. I'll see you come to no harm." Jinks held out a grubby hand to the young woman, who hesitantly smiled, revealing gleaming teeth the like of which Maggie had never seen before. This one had never slept on a bed of straw, her teeth chattering like a horse and carriage careening over the cobbles. The young woman reached out to accept the offered hand but was roughly jerked back as the fallen giant stretched off the ground, a huge paw wrapped around her slim ankle.

"Do something, Maggie," cried Jinks, now engaged in a human tug-of-war he was rapidly losing. Without thinking of the consequences of her actions, Maggie hitched her skirts and planted the full weight of her foot on the bully's knuckles with a vicious stamp. The man let go of the young woman's ankle with a pitiful yelp and curled into a ball, the fight finally knocked out of him. With a gleeful flourish, Jinks picked an abandoned bowl of broth from the serving table and tipped its contents over the yob's head.

A deafening series of roars announced the arrival of half a dozen green-uniformed Constables, who waded into the morass with little concern for establishing innocent parties from offenders. Maggie caught a glimpse of a raised wooden truncheon before it descended across the shoulders of some unfortunate creature, who minutes before had been relishing a hot meal and somewhere warm to sit for an hour.

"This way," urged the young woman. She led them past the serving table to another small door set in a shady alcove Maggie had not noticed before. Going through it, they found themselves in a grubby entry at the rear of the building that ran along the side of the mill before emerging onto Howard Street. Closing the door behind them, the chaos of the soup kitchen was reduced to a dull rumble.

"I want to thank you, young man. That was very brave of you." The blonde-haired woman held out her hand to a clearly smitten Jinks who, for probably the first time in his life, was speechless. He bowed awkwardly before accepting it like an awestruck courtier meeting royalty for the first time.

"My name is Annabelle Elgar. My father runs this kitchen. He's the minister of Rosemary Street Presbyterian. The Reverend Archibald Elgar. Do you know him?"

"Margaret Malone. And this is my brother Jinks...I mean John Joseph. We're not really big churchgoers."

Annabelle nodded, a serious expression crossing her face. "No, I imagine you aren't. His preaching style is...an acquired taste and not for everyone." She blew her fringe away from hazel-colored eyes and proceeded to pat down the front of a matching fitted dress. Simple, yet exquisitely made from material that most likely cost more than the residents of Carson's Court brought home in a month.

It was the most beautiful dress Maggie had ever seen, and she caught herself staring. The clergyman's daughter was no more than a couple of years older than her but she felt inferior in her plain clothing, an ordinary little girl standing at the front of the class before an exquisite head-mistress, who stood half a head taller than her. It took a nudge from Jinks to bring her to her senses, and she forced her gaze elsewhere.

"Well, we must be on our way. Thank you for the meal." Maggie turned on her heel and started to stride down the narrow entry towards the bustle of Howard Street. Jinks reluctantly fell into step behind her, casting a final forlorn look toward the new love of his life.

"Wait." Annabelle broke into a trot after them. "I can't let you leave without first offering some expression of my gratitude. It would be most uncouth of me."

"No, it's quite alright, really," stammered Maggie, much to the disgust of her brother, who looked like a man who had been offered a pardon on his final walk to the gallows.

"Good gracious, I insist," said the clergyman's daughter, beaming down at Jinks. "It's not every day I'm rescued by a handsome stranger."

His cheeks blushed furiously as he looked imploringly up at his sister. She realized her protests were futile and nodded timidly at Annabelle.

"Excellent. That's settled, then. Do you know where the church is?"

"Yes, of course," bleated Jinks. Maggie knew he hadn't a clue where the church was, but also recognized that wild horses weren't going to hold him back from this latest adventure, an opportunity to break the monotonous cycle of deprivation and need.

"Well, I will see you there at eight o'clock tomorrow evening. And do not worry. I can assure you of a supper much more sumptuous than mere soup and bread."

"Nothing wrong with soup and bread," Maggie replied sourly, her pride pricked by the casual dismissal of a meal they relied on to survive from one day to the next.

"We'll be there, Miss Annabelle." Jinks nodded so vigorously that Maggie feared his head would drop off. She eyed the taller girl awkwardly, before acquiescing to her request with a curt nod.

"Eight o'clock. But don't be trying to convert us with your Bible verses and fancy hymns. We have no interest in your ways." If Maggie had learnt nothing else since her mother's death, it was how to play the devout Catholic girl. If only they knew what really filled her soul with hope, the faith dragging her through this darkest of valleys.

"We may come from different faiths, Margaret, but Jesus loves us just the same. I respect your ways just as I'm sure you respect mine."

Annabelle's eyes twinkled with unspoken humor, leaving Maggie to wonder if she was mocking or applauding her. There was certainly more to this prim young woman than met the eye. Without another word, she turned, opened the alcove door, and disappeared back into the furor of the soup kitchen.

Maggie also turned, her mind full of unanswered questions, oblivious to the excited chattering of Jinks by her side. This was turning out to be quite the day. She produced a crust of bread from the pocket of her skirts, purloined during the chaos, and thrust it into his babbling mouth.

"Quiet, Jinks. I'm trying to think."

The Black Lady

S he led the human dregs off the Samhara and down the gangplank, watched by the astonished crew. She smiled, playing with their fragile, malleable minds like a harpist casually plucking a string. She ensured that, if anyone asked them later who the flame-haired woman was, they would stare at the inquirer as if they were stark, raving mad. She was there, and yet she was not, her aura a fleeting, cool caress across the fevered brows of the half-dead souls who dragged themselves from one hell into another. She watched as they huddled together, their wide, white eyes adjusting to the dull light after days holed up in a black abyss, with barely a candle wick to distinguish the living from the dead.

They were her children, her flock, and she ushered them past the contemptuous stares and muttered expletives. They were scum, Connemara filth, not fit to walk the streets of the finest town in Ireland. These Belfast folk were as vain and arrogant as the day they had hung her from that barren tree on the mountain. Her mountain now, and they dared not walk its paths too late, for she would pluck the eyeballs from their heads and feed them to her crows. Such tasty, succulent morsels. They would find the bodies the next morning, hanging just as she had swung two hundred years ago. Damn them and their Twelve Apostles. She recognized only one; they would end their days hanging from the Judas Tree, eye sockets empty and bellies sliced open.

She thought of his smug, squashed face as he had watched her step into the void, the last face she saw before darkness had claimed her body and soul. Only temporarily though for now she was back, fueled by a ravenous desire to avenge his betrayal two centuries before. For it was he who had pointed the accusatory finger, he who had informed the authorities that she was responsible for the trail of bodies he had left in his wake. They called him Bloody Hands but it was her blood on his hands the day he had watched her swing from the town gallows.

The Samhara's passengers shuffled onto the carts awaiting them on the docks, where there was no grand welcome or decorous parade for Belfast's newest inhabitants. Mothers held their newborns to their breasts, sucked dry of milk and the will to live, their husbands left behind in canvas shrouds on deck, the open, cavernous seas to be their final resting place. The drivers shook the reins, and she was with them as they clattered through the unwelcome streets. Fine ladies held perfumed handkerchiefs to their pretty noses as they passed, aghast that such vermin should be allowed to pollute their magnificent town. There would be words with the mayor, letters to the newspapers; this was outrageous, unacceptable.

They saw her, yet they would not remember, as she caught every eye, read every mind. She savored their fear and repulsion, watching as the lough air caught the sickness, spreading it indiscriminately. They breathed it in, oblivious to the microscopic particles that nestled within their new, fleshy abodes. Soon the coughing and sweating would start, and they would empty their bowels and stomachs on their knees in their own filth where they belonged.

Well, let them perish; she did not care. This was her moment, her time, when the ancestors of her persecutors would pay for the sins of their fathers. She threw back the hood of her fur-lined cape, to reveal pale skin and cruel, cutting eyes. Eyes that would haunt their feverish dreams and whisper of their imminent demise as they wakened screaming, their bodies on fire. Eyes as green as the lush fields the peasants farmed before the blight reduced their hopes of betterment to row after row of stinking, inedible mush.

Just as Bloody Hands would pay, so would the town whose streets he now roamed again. He had returned, but she was waiting for him. Waiting to strike him down and reduce his town to ruins. Two birds with two stones.

Fever and famine.

She rose and floated high above the cavalcade, as it wound its way to the workhouse. Several of the carts were unloaded, and she watched as its grim doors opened to admit the new arrivals. Stern-faced doctors and porters offered no welcome. She smiled, for they would be dead within the month, their limbs and staring eyes intertwined with the poor and pestilent in makeshift mounds at the rear of the fever ward. The doors closed, and she swooped higher still, the remaining carts plodding deeper into the maze of cramped streets.   She knew their final home, for she had whispered in the ear of Mr. Andrew Blake just as she had murmured in the ear of Captain Jeremiah Morgan. Weak, impressionable minds that folded like a deck of cards when enough coin was thrown in their direction.

Carson's Court. The drivers leaned back, straining to halt their anxious mounts. The beasts could sense its malevolent past, hear the screams of the girls as he cut them, smearing their blood on the entry wall. An evil man, a monster, and yet they had dragged *her* through the streets, kicked to her feet every time she had stumbled and fallen. The trial had been a travesty, her testimony ignored and vilified. Yes, she practiced a different faith from them, but she meant them no harm. People came to her for help, and she healed and offered sound counsel. Special teas and poultices that had been handed down through generations of wise women. They were the guardians of the old ways, the *bean feasa*, at one with the Earth and its many secrets.

They had called her a daughter of Satan, accused her of cavorting with the Evil One on the Black Mountain. None of it was true. She had harmlessly walked the mountain paths for peace and solitude, to gather herbs and listen to the whisperings of the Ancient Ones, the *Tuatha*. She wanted nothing of King James and his Holy Book; angels and demons held no sway over her. Her reasoned pleas had fallen on deaf, uncaring ears. For her sinful ways she would hang, framed by his sly and twisted trickery. Every misfortune that had befallen their town was laid at her feet. Butchered girls, stillborn babes, failed crops, every ache and ailment had led to her door and an alliance with the Devil and his hordes. And for that, she had to die.

She returned to the present, watching over a huddled family as they climbed from the back of the cart and were led down the entry. She mouthed a silent ward that would protect their new lodgings from residents, who no doubt were already plotting and conniving a sudden, violent end to their unwelcome tenancy. Blake owned half the properties in the town, and those that couldn't be crammed into the workhouse would be sheltered within his various abodes. She would watch over them, waiting for when the time was right.

She frowned at the bloody handprints as the family shuffled through the entry. Those hands had been the final straw, five dead girls and a beast amok. They never caught him of course, Old Bloody Hands, instead blaming a poor, innocent girl who wouldn't hurt a fly. She had supposedly summoned Lucifer himself, who feasted on the flesh of the virtuous, tearing all five innocents limb from limb, allowing his evil acolytes to celebrate the Black Mass with fresh, virginal blood. Those handprints had sealed her fate, ensured a shameful end, swinging from a rope as her bladder emptied and the good people of Belfast hollered at her demise.

And he had watched, relishing every last second of it.

Deamhan. Son of Balor. Descendant of the Fomoire.

Now they would pay. The cart lurched forward, and she focused on the next sickly family, the human vessels who would bring this town to its knees. Only those who practiced the old ways would survive, and they were but a handful. She counted them on her elongated, bony fingers, sharp nails painted black and curved to cut and slash. One shone above them all, and their paths would cross soon enough, for she recognized something of herself in this faithful soul. She had known the girl's great-grandmother and had followed future generations from afar, only intervening when required and, even then, in ways that would never arouse suspicion.

She pulled the hood over her head, concealing the tell-tale red curls that cascaded down her back. Those eyes again, blazing an emerald path through the dark, cold hearts of the proud ladies and gentlemen who crowded the streets, tutting and crowing at the unfortunate brood of the Samhara. Beneath their satin finery and perfumed veneers, she saw the sordid truth. The debt and addiction, the jealousy and petty hate. Their god was a cruel god, they knew only of fire and brimstone, a lake of fire where their enemies would scream eternally. Screams that they would echo soon enough; she would see to that.

They knew her as the Black Lady, a *cailleach*, whose tale was told to frighten bold children who strayed too far from their hearth and home on the dark, wild nights that swept in off the lough. She was a myth, a legend, spoken in the same breath as the leprechauns and faeries. They were nothing more than that, but she was real, so very real, and craved the recognition she so richly deserved. She would rise from her shadowy home and sweep off the mountain to scatter their ashes to the four corners of the island. This pompous town would be no more, and she would reign as it had been foretold, ages before their Holy Book was writ-ten. For her kind had been present when the first man and woman fled from Eden, had watched from afar in times of flood and fire. They had watched as kingdoms rose and empires fell, petty kings and queens, no more than an irksome distraction as their tiresome wars flickered and faded from view.

The carts rolled on to their next destination. Soon, the suffering of their occupants would mercifully end, but as for the others? It was but the opening chapter in a tale that knew no happy ending. She was death and she was ravenous.

They called him Bloody Hands but she knew his true name.
Abhartach. The Undead One.

He chose them with care, for it had to be right. If it wasn't right, then it didn't count and he would have to start again. And he didn't want to do that, for he was a being of many responsibilities and there were only so many hours in the day. He was up early every morning, long before dawn cast its furtive fingers over his domain. Domain. He liked that word. It made him feel important, valued. He deserved no less, and that was why he did what he did. They needed to open their eyes and prick their ears. His time was now, and they were his witnesses.

Every two hundred years he harvested six. It had always been that way. It would always be that way.

He had watched this one for weeks and she would be his fourth. She wasn't the most beautiful of girls but there was something about her. A spring in her step, a twinkle of the eye as she swanned through the streets every morning. He had watched her many times but avoided eye contact for he feared if his met hers, then he would be lost forever in the depths of her innocence. His mother had always warned him that a pretty face would be the ruin of him. He chuckled. How wrong the old crone had been.

The pretty ones were the making of him.

Tonight was the night and everything had to be perfect. He had a reputation to maintain, after all. Time was a vague distraction, an unnecessary concept that he paid scant attention to for he came and went as he pleased, be it this century or the next. What was a year but an abstract collection of numbers. Humans were humans, however they dressed or wherever they resided.

Blood would always be blood.

He paused, nostrils twitching as his breath clouded, uncertain why he had suddenly started to shiver. He was impervious to cold or heat; such mortal concerns did not bother him. Yet, here he was, festooned in the gloomy shadows, trembling like a newborn calf. He held out an arm bursting with corded muscle. Beneath the thick coating of wiry hair that adorned the limb, an army of goosebumps had emerged, signaling all was not as it should be. A sudden noise reduced him to a feral crouch, fists clenched, his beady eyes scanning the alley for signs of threat or harm. His quarry was now out of sight, blissfully unaware that she had escaped death by the narrowest of margins.

"Are you there, *cailleach*?" He hissed the words under his breath, dark eyes blazing with fury that the kill had eluded him. No matter, there were plenty more and he would dine at a different table when all this was over, one where a finer cut of meat was on the menu.

His question went unanswered, but he sensed her, the one who refused to leave him be, always skirmishing at the edges of his consciousness, refusing to let the past go. It was her only discernible flaw, a festering anger that kept her chained to this stinking town and its vermin population. Threatening to get in the way, meddling with his work, honest work that needed to be done. The streets needed to be kept clean, and he was the man for the job. Clinical, efficient, a no-fuss approach to his trade. For it was a trade, an art that he had fine-tuned down the millennia, and one he wasn't minded to give up now because of some petty grudge.

"I know you are. I can smell ye. Show yourself and let us have a civilized conversation like two old friends."

He inhaled deeply, the heady aroma filling his nostrils, the air crackling with old wards and spells. Yes, she was close, very close.

"Wasn't my fault they strung you up. If you'd kept your nose out of my business, then nothing would have been said. Only yourself to blame, haven't ye? Still, you made a delightful sixth."

He detected her response in the slightest ripple that ran through a puddle by his feet. He looked at it, his reflection a mixture of contempt and frustration, framed by a startling moon overhead. He lifted his head again, rotating both shoulders until his fat neck emitted a satisfying crack. He wouldn't let her tricks get under his skin; he was beyond her tiresome ways, a god in all but name.

"You might act all high and mighty but you know the old ways must continue. This is my town and you are not welcome. You cannot vanquish me; we both know that. So, show yourself and we shall settle this once and for all." He spat in the puddle, shattering the snarling reflection, as he stepped out into the middle of the alley, arms extended as he performed a slow circle. He so wanted her to reveal herself, hoping his goading would pierce her normally impenetrable resolve.

A wind whipped down the alley out of nowhere, an unnatural gust from a cloudless, starlit sky. He smirked and rubbed at his ragged, patchy dark beard. He was starting to enjoy this. Maybe it would be a worthwhile evening after all. He had walked these streets for centuries and not every night could end the way he had initially planned it.

"You need to learn to respect my boundaries," he snarled, his words reverberating around the deserted alley. "This is how it has always been. Now, show yourself or move on. Either way, I will have my six. I always have my six, you should know that better than anyone."

The wind intensified, and he threw back his head, laughing into the starlit void. My, she was rattled.

"You do not frighten me. Show yourself and let us dance." He produced a wicked knife from a concealed pocket in the sleeve of his jacket.

"They may have killed ye once, but I know you still bleed. Come dance with me and let my blade caress your throat. They snapped it on the Judas Tree. Let me slice it open again just to make sure, my pretty *colleen*."

The wind stopped as abruptly as it had started and he knew she had declined the offer, leaving him alone in the alley. A moral victory, but it did little to satisfy the hunger that the stalking of the wench had triggered within him. He ground his teeth in irritation, scanning the alley for something, anything that would curtail the carnal urge roaring behind his ears.

The stray mongrel stood no chance as he plucked it from where it cowered in a doorway, its canine instincts warning of impending danger. It cowered, growling in a futile attempt to ward off its hunter, before sharp teeth severed its carotid artery, ending its miserable existence living off scraps on the back streets of a town that would know a blood-letting like no other this time around. Two hundred years ago he had prowled these streets. Five dead women had been only the beginning, until the good citizens of the town had hanged an innocent girl for his orgy of sin.

An innocent girl who was now his deadliest foe.

She had paid the price and his reign of terror had filtered away, diluted, and diminished with each passing generation. "Old Bloody Hands" they had called him, a crude name he did not care for, even though it captured his signature trademark. He threw the dead animal onto the damp cobbles, its throat ruined, an empty husk. Its blood had been dirty and bitter, barely scratching tonight's itch thanks to the *cailleach's* unwelcome intervention. He wiped a hand across his mouth, thick globules of saliva mixing with the dog's essence. Staring at his palm he grinned, a bloody leer that would have chilled to the bone anyone unfortunate enough to have stumbled into the alley at that very moment. Licking the tip of a stained digit, he planted his palm against the alley wall, fingers splayed to leave a grotesque mark that was the stuff of whispered legend on the streets of Belfast. He stood back to admire his handiwork before adjusting his jacket and striding off in search of fresh prey, his hunger barely quenched.

For the night was young and four was nowhere near enough for the one they called Bloody Hands. He could bide his time but eventually she would have to show her face. And when she did, he would be ready. He was always ready.

Love Thy Neighbor

"**M**ags?"

"Wha..."

"Maggie. Quick, get up. There's a commotion out in the courtyard."

Maggie grunted and reluctantly lifted her head above the blankets. After their eventful afternoon at the soup kitchen, they had returned to their room. Exhausted, but her stomach thankfully full, she had huddled down to rest her eyes and drifted off into a blissful, dreamless sleep, a welcome reprieve from the daily trials that plagued her every waking moment. Being rudely awakened by the restless bundle of energy that was her younger brother was far from appreciated.

"There's always some drama going on out there. Can't it wait for five..."

She was glad to be lying down, otherwise her head might have been removed as Jinks hurdled over her, dashing out of their room into the hallway. Maggie forced herself into a sitting position and watched as several other occupants of their seedy tenement scurried past the open door, down the hallway, and out into the courtyard. A babble of voices indicated that an argument was coming to a head. Maggie sighed, threw back the blankets, and struggled to her feet. If there was trouble to be found, Jinks would be sure to locate it. All she could do was chase after him and hope the damage was kept to a minimum.

Chaos greeted her as she stepped outside. A throng of bodies ebbed and flowed around a tall, well-dressed man struggling to make himself heard above the furor. Beside him, a man and woman cast furtive glances in all directions, a young boy wedged between them. They looked haggard and exhausted, utterly overwhelmed by the noise and clamor. Eventually, the piercing shriek of a police whistle filled the air and all turned to watch two green-coated Constables wade through the crowd towards its center.

"The next one to holler will be getting my truncheon over their head and a visit to the magistrate. Am I making myself clear?"

Maggie recognized the thick brogue of Sergeant Joseph Quinn, the senior officer in the district. The crowd fell silent, knowing that he was a man of his word when it came to dispensing harsh, arbitrary justice. Many a local man had been on the receiving end of the Constabulary's boots and batons down the years. Catholic, Protestant—it didn't matter who you were. One foot out of line and the no-nonsense local police force came down on its good citizens like a ton of bricks.

"That's better. Now if you would all be so kind as to let the gentleman speak, then perhaps he can explain the situation and address any concerns that you might have. Please proceed, sir." He smiled benevolently at the well-dressed man who cleared his throat and nodded.

Maggie rolled her eyes. No doubt a few shillings had been slipped to Quinn, who was never one to turn down a discreet bribe. She vaguely recognized the tall man but, having reassured herself that Jinks was on the edge of the crowd and in no obvious trouble, folded her arms and waited for him to speak.

"Thank you, Sergeant. Now many of you know me. Many of you have voted for me. Therefore, you know that I have a proven record as a fair and charitable man." The tall man cleared his throat and scanned the wall of faces before him, daring any of them to question his opening statement. When he was satisfied there would be no argument, he proceeded, his pale, pinched features standing out in marked contrast to the funereal business attire he wore. The crowd thinned slightly and Maggie noticed a smaller, rotund figure next to the speaker. Crothers, the local physician.

Maggie had only heard bad things about the man. A quack and a charlatan of the highest order, who was in the back pocket of the man now addressing them. The penny dropped for her and what a bad penny it was.

Andrew Blake no less—town guardian, businessman, landlord, and one of the most sanctimonious hypocrites to grace God's earth.

"You may have heard of the plight of the poor souls aboard the Samhara, which docked in Belfast earlier this week."

"Heard it's full of Connacht scroungers," a voice piped up from the back of the assembled gathering. Blake peered into the throng before him but the dissenter declined to reveal himself to the guardian or his police escort.

"As men of God, my fellow guardians and I pride ourselves on calling our great town a place where the homeless and destitute can lay their weary heads and find solace." He paused, daring anyone to challenge his sincerity, but this time the crowd greeted him with silence. He smiled, seemingly satisfied that his authority had been re-established, before forging on with his worthy soliloquy.

"Never let it be said that the people of Ulster turned their backs on their southern brethren in their greatest hour of need. For while they might lack our natural work ethic and creativity, we are all children of Christ under God's eye."

A few exasperated coughs and shuffling feet echoed through the court-yard but nothing else under Sergeant Quinn's watchful eye.

Blake turned towards the bewildered couple at his side with a theatrical flourish. The young boy struggled to be free of his mother's grip, already bored with events and keen to explore this strange, new home.

"Providence has brought these wretched souls to the gates of this great town. Who are we to abandon them, whatever their heathen ways?"

He glared at the residents of Carson's Court, but few of them dared meet his eye. He was landlord to many a family and Maggie knew that to fall foul of him was an unwise move if you wanted a roof over your head that night. She watched as he savored the moment, the silence and sheepish expressions a testament to the power he held over the crowd. She was no expert on local politics but the talk was that a guardian's post was a mere stepping stone; the local gossip was that, one day, he hoped to slip the mayoral chains over his neck. And after that? Well, the world was his oyster, they reckoned. A seat in the Lords, a knighthood?

"How do we know they ain't sick?"

All heads turned in the direction of the anonymous voice. For one horrific moment, Maggie thought it was Jinks who had raised the question that sat unspoken on all their lips. Her heartbeat rose, but then steadied as she identified the lone critic—Tom Boyd.

Blake narrowed his eyes and peered through the crowd, which parted to reveal a muscular figure sporting a bloodied apron. Boyd owned a butcher's shop on Hercules Street and was renowned as a hard man who backed down to nobody, be it dissatisfied customers or the future mayor of Belfast. His massive forearms sported a swathe of green India-ink tattoos, earned during a naval career where he had acquired enough coin to set up in business following his nautical retirement.

"I beg your pardon?" Blake's lip curled in disdain, while Crothers looked as if he wanted the Earth to open up and swallow him whole. Difficult questions were not part of the plan, but now every resident in Carson's Court was staring at them in anticipation of a reply.

"I...well...," spluttered Crothers, his podgy face growing more puce by the second. A thin sheen of sweat had broken out on his upper lip.

"What my learned friend is trying to say is that he carried out a full examination of all the Samhara's passengers before they disembarked and ensures me that all are hale and hearty. Isn't that correct, Dr. Crothers?"

Crothers nodded weakly, raising his battered bag as if to vouch for his medical qualifications.

"Why can't he say that himself then?" growled Boyd, removing his flat cap to reveal a bald head with enough lumps and scars to suggest that this was not the first argument he had initiated.

Sergeant Quinn eyed him warily, one hand creeping slowly towards his trusty truncheon. "You don't want to be asking too many questions, Tom. Remember the last time you did that how it ended. Three weeks in *gaol*. Won't do your business much good if you're locked up and the shutters are down. Plenty more places people can go to buy their meat." The police officer's dark eyes glinted, spoiling for a fight, as the Constables under his charge also stepped forward, albeit somewhat less enthusiastically.

Boyd grunted, weighing up his options, as the remainder of the residents took in a collective breath. Maggie desperately tried to catch the attention of Jinks who had now burrowed his way to the front of the crowd, eager not to miss the entertainment at hand. She sighed. Wherever there was trouble, you would be sure to find that boy. She watched as the uneasy standoff developed, hoping a full-scale riot was not about to ensue.

It appeared that Dr. Crothers shared her fears as he edged behind the migrant family, towards the entry which led to the freedom of Bank Street.

Time seemed to stand suspended inside the tiny square until Boyd slowly placed his cap back on his head, deciding that, on this occasion, the odds were not in his favor.

"Just don't bring them near my door. Filthy beggars." He scowled at the assembled police presence before barging a few hapless bystanders aside and storming down the entry.

A murmur rippled through the remaining residents, part relief, part disappointment that the drama appeared to be at an end.

"That's that, then," said Blake, rubbing his hands together and turning to Sergeant Quinn. "If you would escort this family to their room, my good man, Dr. Crothers and I will be on our way. We have other urgent matters to attend to."

He nodded curtly and marched down the entry, his long legs eating up the ground as a stumbling Crothers waddled behind. All eyes turned to Sergeant Quinn and the new family. The streetwise police officer tucked the truncheon back in his pocket and patted his considerable stomach, mulling over his next words.

"Well," he rumbled. "You heard Mr. Blake. You can all be on your way and I'm sure you will make Mr...Mr..." He turned to the father by his side, who now had a protective arm around his wife and son.

"O'Hara," he replied softly. "Michael O'Hara."

"Indeed. I'm sure you will make Mr. O'Hara and his family welcome. And if I were to hear otherwise, I would be most disappointed." He allowed the barely veiled threat to linger on the damp, chill air, the residents of Carson's Court left in no doubt as to what the implications were if they were to ignore his warning.

"Now, go on, be about your business." Quinn held out his arms like a farmer herding stray sheep. The crowd began to disperse, Jinks reluctantly creeping over to Maggie, frustrated by the lack of fisticuffs. She grabbed him by his jacket collar, causing the young boy to howl in protest.

"Ow, what's that for then? I was only looking." He glared rebelliously up at her, straightening the collar.

She released her grip. "That's for bolting outside without my permission. You're going to get yourself killed gallivanting round this town the way you do. And then what am I supposed to do?"

"Sorry, Mags."

"Sorry, nothing. Now get inside before you catch your death of cold out here."

Maggie breathed out hard, gathering her composure, as her brother slammed the front door behind him. She closed her eyes and inwardly counted to ten. Jinks had a heart of gold and wouldn't hurt a fly, but if she didn't try and curb his wilder instincts then who would? With his mother in the grave and father in the gutter, she was his only hope of surviving childhood and having a chance of a decent life. She would fight tooth and nail to preserve that bond.

She watched as Mr. O'Hara ushered his wife and son into the murky depths of the house across the street under the watchful eye of Sergeant Quinn and his men. Before he disappeared into the hallway, the young boy glanced over his shoulder and smiled shyly, melting Maggie's heart. The poor wee lad, a year or two younger than Jinks, dumped in a strange and hostile town, hundreds of miles from his own home and friends.

Maggie smiled back and lifted a hand in a tenuous greeting. The boy's dark eyes sparkled as if he sucked in the kindly reciprocation, oxygen for his parched soul. Then he was gone, ushered in by his mother, who cast Maggie a suspicious parting glance.

Maggie sighed and reached for the stone in her skirts.

"Blessed lady, protect their home and hearts..."

Little did she know, her prayer had already been answered.

Annabelle scrubbed the floor as if her life depended on it, but it was to no avail. The stubborn soup stain refused to budge, despite her best efforts. Eventually, recognizing defeat, she leaned back and stretched her back, easing the nagging ache developing along her spine. She stared at the stain before lobbing the scrubbing brush she had been using into a bucket of soapy water. It could wait for another day.

The kitchen has been ruthlessly cleared by the Constabulary, leaving more than a few with cracked heads to nurse on their way home. The ladies of the parish had immediately taken to the clean-up operation with considerable gusto, all keen to catch the eye of her father. Although he stated his life was devoted to God and spreading the Gospel, that had not stopped several of the more ambitious women in the congregation doing everything within their powers to catch his eye and earn his favor. He was a vibrant and powerful character in the prime of his life at the head of one of the most prosperous churches in the town. To become the next Mrs. Archibald Edgar was a feather in the cap that was worthy of the most diligent endeavors on their part.

Her mother had died in childbirth and, raised within the church, Annabelle had been fussed over by all manner of surrogate maternal figures. She had seen little of her father in those formative years, as he had forged a career as a clerical firebrand, traveling the length and breadth of the country with an evangelical fervor, battered Bible, and hell-raising sermons always to the fore.

Intent on sweeping the evil of Roman Catholicism from the island of Ireland, just like his predecessor Saint Patrick had ousted the snakes, the Reverend Edgar had little time for soiled nappies and teething toddlers.

Truth be told, he had prayed for a boy but the Lord worked in mysterious ways and having lost his wife, he viewed the arrival of a daughter as adequate compensation from the Heavenly Father. It had all worked out in the end and great grace had been bestowed upon his Rosemary Street flock, which contained some of the most wealthy and influential families in the town. If he could win their hearts and souls, then their wallets and connections were bound to follow.

Annabelle yawned; it was barely mid-afternoon, yet she was already dreaming of retiring to her bedroom with Regina Maria Roche's *The Children of the Abbey*. Her father would have frowned if he had known she was reading such a book. For him there was only one book, the Good Book, that contained instruction for everything a man or woman would require in life. Annabelle ensured that a copy sat open on her bedside dresser, for when he knocked the door each evening to bid her goodnight. A lifetime of playing the dutiful clergyman's daughter had taught her enough tricks to usually stay one step ahead of his prying eyes.

She did read her Bible but was drawn to the softer passages, the ministry of Jesus as opposed to the more inflammatory sections of the Old Testament her father would bellow from the pulpit every Sunday morning. She was more interested in love and forgiveness than the eternal suffering that awaited all those who failed to turn their backs on Rome and follow the one true Protestant faith. It was the reason why she had thrown all her energies into the soup kitchen, preferring to roll her sleeves up and dish out broth and bread to the needy, whatever their faith, as opposed to her father's embarrassing efforts to find her a suitable husband from amongst his thriving congregation.

Yes, Annabelle had been blessed with fair looks but she often regarded them as more of a curse. The young gentlemen of the parish were regular callers to the doors of the splendid manse she shared with her father, and she had endured endless afternoon teas filled with stilted conversation and awkward glances. She had little interest in their gratuitous wealth and forced social etiquette, preferring to walk the parish and do what she could to help the desperate and destitute instead.

Every day, more and more homeless families flooded into Belfast from the outlying counties, having been driven off their land by merciless land-lords who demanded their rent, irrespective of the hunger sweeping the land. The streets were overflowing with a pain and desperation she could no longer ignore. Utilizing the little influence she held as an Edgar, she had harassed her father and other notable dignitaries until, after much grumbling, they had opened their coffers and supplied her with sufficient funds to set up the kitchen. Combined with an army of ladies with too much time on their hands and a willingness to do anything for their poten-tial future daughter-in-law, she had launched her dream project.

"Annabelle, what on Earth are you still doing here?"

The bracing baritone voice of Archibald Edgar reverberated around the cavernous mill, as he strode through the front doors with all the pomp of a man who loved a grand entrance. He frowned at the sight of his only child on her hands and knees like a common servant girl, deep furrows forming on his brow atop a set of dark, foreboding eyebrows.

"Father," stammered Annabelle, caught unawares by his unexpected arrival. Her father had reluctantly allowed her to become involved in the kitchen venture, with the strict caveat that she was not to indulge in menial tasks unbecoming of a young lady who aspired to a much higher station in life. She rubbed furiously at a stain on her sleeve, before accepting defeat and humbly bowing her head, prepared to be chastised for her subterfuge.

The Reverend Edgar scanned the hall with a disapproving look, his piercing eyes surveying the overturned chairs and tables yet to be restored to their original positions. He was a tall, stick-thin man, protruding cheek-bones and a widow's peak hairline giving him the appearance of the Grim Reaper. A pallid complexion and thinly pursed lips belied the blood and thunder persona that burned inside. He prided himself on being a godly warrior, modeling himself on his scriptural hero David who rose from humble beginnings to slay Goliath and the many other enemies of Israel.

"I see the heathens have shown their true colors to you. I knew this frivolous venture would end in calamity. A leopard never changes its spots, especially a Roman Catholic leopard." He frowned at a grimy patch on Annabelle's sleeve, a frown she knew well. He had lectured her often; how was she ever going to find a reputable young man if she continued to indulge in these adolescent whims with the lower classes?

"I'm sorry, Father, but the people are so hungry and that makes them desperate. They..."

"Silence." Edgar stepped forward and placed a hand on his daughter's cheek, inspecting a flowering bruise that was darkening by the moment. "What is the nature of this mark?"

"It's nothing, Father. Just a scratch. One of the men..."

Edgar dropped his hand and wheeled away in disgust, theatrically flinging his arms into the air, a silent plea to his Lord and Savior to intervene and resolve his daughter's feckless nature.

"A scratch," he boomed, his words echoing around the spacious building. "We have evening service in a matter of hours. How am I supposed to preach when I look down from the pulpit to see my daughter battered and bruised before me?"

"Oh, Father. Save the performance for the congregation, not me." Annabelle was shocked by the rebellious nature of her tone. She had never addressed her father in such a disrespectful manner before and regretted the outburst the second the words left her lips. There would be hell to pay for her insubordination.

"Honor thy mother and father, child," roared the cleric, spittle flying from his lips. He took a step towards his kneeling daughter, hand raised, but wrestled back control of his emotions and lowered it again.

"You will finish what you are doing and then return to the manse and reflect on your behavior. Perhaps some solitary time with the Lord and his Word will assist in revealing the error of your ways."

"Yes, Father," said Annabelle meekly. She had overstepped an invisible line that had been drawn between them the day her mother had passed away. She rose to her feet and stood before the clergyman, whose features lightened slightly.

"That's better, girl. You need to be spiritually prepared for our service tomorrow. A number of our finest young bachelors are attending. I have been telling them all about my fine, virtuous daughter and they are very keen to meet you. From some of the most influential families in Belfast."

He smiled a greasy leer that chilled Annabelle, turning her blood to a turgid slush. She was nothing more than a bargaining chip, a piece of meat to this godly, principled man. His hypocrisy sickened her, shameless social ambition more important to him than the well-being of his only child.

"Yes, Father." It took every sliver of resolve to retain a neutral tone and play the docile daughter, as every fiber of her being wanted to scream in his face and tell him her true feelings.

"Excellent. I will see you then at dinner."

He straightened his clerical collar, turned, and strode back across the factory floor toward the entrance. This was an important day in the life of Archibald Edgar and he would not allow a silly, deluded girl to disrupt his plans. He had granted some leeway in recent months, allowing her various schemes to reach out to the working classes and aid the papist poor. But enough was enough. Spare the rod and spoil the child, the Bible instructed. Perhaps it was time to set aside his lenient ways and adopt a firmer approach. He was too soft and times were hard. Perhaps he too needed to be harder.

"And don't be bringing any of your waifs and strays along to the service," he sniped over a shoulder. "I will not be embarrassed in front of these gentlemen." He pushed open the doors and was gone, leaving Annabelle alone on her knees.

She bowed her head and allowed the tears to flow. Tears for her dead mother, tears for the poor of the town, tears for the father she no longer recognized.

A Slight Problem

A butcher found the fourth woman, stumbling across her viscera as he cut through Smithfield on his way to work. He had initially thought it was a sleeping drunk until closer inspection revealed the cobbles slick with blood and gore. The Constabulary and a local physician were summoned to the scene, closely followed by the coroner. Inquisitive residents were kept at bay by burly officers, as the grisly discovery was examined.

"Never seen anything like it, sir," whispered the young Constable as he stepped aside to allow Quinn to inspect the remains. The young lad was less than a year in the force and, by the looks of the vomit-splattered wall, had lost his breakfast on his arrival at the entry. A veteran of over twenty years, Quinn had seen a lot of dead bodies but even he struggled to process the abominable sight before him. He gagged involuntarily and looked away, producing a handkerchief which he held over his mouth and nostrils before he could look again.

He knew the young woman. A street girl by the name of Rafferty. Barely eighteen years old, if that. Her throat had been sliced open from ear to ear with such ferocity that her head lolled at an obscene angle, barely attached to her body by a tendril of glistening muscle. What was left of her shredded internal organs were strewn across the entry like visceral confetti. Her dark eyes stared into his, an almost quizzical expression adorning her otherwise unblemished face. She had been a pretty girl but the ravages of drink and street life had taken their toll. The grizzled veteran turned away and mumbled a prayer into his handkerchief.

"What was that, sir?"

"Get Father Brady down here now. The least we can do is ensure the poor girl is afforded her last rights."

"Right you are, sir," replied the young Constable, relieved to be offered the opportunity to leave the entry. He scuttled off, leaving Quinn alone with his thoughts. At the other end of the entry, the coroner and that useless physician, Crothers, were deep in conversation. What they were discussing, God only knew, for it was as clear as the nose on your head how the young woman had met her end. A blind man on a galloping horse could have deduced that.

"Good morning, Sergeant. It appears we have a slight problem on our hands."

Quinn jolted to attention. Andrew Blake had the unnerving habit of seemingly appearing from nowhere, forever perched on his shoulder when he least expected it. This morning had proven to be no exception.

"Morning sir; yes, you could say that," he replied, regaining his composure. He was a Sergeant in the Royal Irish Constabulary, afraid of no man, least of all a stuffy pen-pusher from the town hall. But there was something about Blake, something amiss in the way his calculated words and knowing looks always suggested that he was three steps ahead of you with his plots and machinations.

Blake stared at the body of the young woman, splayed like a broken doll. Her limbs were arranged at unnatural angles, the puppet master's strings snipped for the final time. His nose wrinkled.

"Problem, indeed. Thankfully, however, you're going to deliver me a solution, aren't you? We have a mayoral election coming later in the year and, as you well know, I intend to mount a strong challenge for office. My benefactors have significant business interests in this town and demand a strong economy underpinned by an even stronger police force. Do you understand?" He arched an eyebrow to emphasize his point as a flustered Quinn formulated a response.

"I do indeed, Mr. Blake. Very much so." Quinn hated to hear himself groveling in such an obsequious manner, but his distinguished police career had taught him to pick his battles and know when to toe the line. Now was one of those moments.

"So what do you and your fine body of men propose to do? Three dead already on your patch and now a fourth. The people are hysterical with all this Bloody Hands nonsense. We can't have some madman stalking the streets and causing this...this..." Blake's voice trailed off, and he gestured towards the body with the flick of a wrist.

"I'll double patrols, have a man on every street corner, sir. You have my word, we will catch this fiend." Quinn wanted the conversation to end as soon as possible and the sight of the returning Constable was a welcome reprieve. The haunted expression on the young man's face was less so.

"Sergeant, I think you need to see this." He turned without waiting for an answer and Quinn took the opportunity to follow suit, leaving Blake standing awkwardly, the young woman's body now his solitary companion. He caught up with Quinn as the young Constable led them down an alley off the main entry. It was barely broad enough to accommodate them in a single file, the stale odor of urine assailing their nostrils as they delved deeper along its snaking path. Blake squirmed as something brushed past his ankle, the accompanying squeak setting his nerves on end.

Eventually, the Constable stopped and Quinn almost collided with him, earning a foul look from the older officer.

"Well, what is it, Connors? Spit it out. There's a murderer loose and I haven't the time to..."

The words stalled in his throat as the dull, throbbing red glow from the handprint on the wall rendered him silent. They had heard the legend; every man, woman, and child in Belfast knew the tale, passed down from generation to generation, an unwanted baton that they had reluctantly inherited. Bloody Hands. The deranged lunatic who had once stalked the town, butchering with abandon before leaving a gruesome signature at the scene of each atrocity.

"Is that what I think..." Connors could not find the strength to finish the question as what little remaining color drained from his cheeks.

Quinn removed his cap and watched, mesmerized, as a steady trickle of fresh blood wound its way down the wall from the pulsating handprint to the cobbles where it gathered in a sticky, viscous puddle.

"Aye lad, it is. He's back."

She had watched him at his work, her presence curling through the alley like fingers of fog across a dew-doused meadow. It had been swift and brutal, a flash of steel and the girl was no more, a sickening end to a life that had promised so much, yet yielded so little. She had watched him kill and drink his fill, desperate to intervene and make him suffer like he rejoiced in the suffering of others. But she could not, would not, for that was what he wanted, that was why he was back. Killing in plain sight, daring her to challenge his new reign of terror on streets that knew nothing but death and misery.

She now watched from the mountain, the slightest of frowns creasing her features. Dawn had broken, yet a thick covering of cloud and drizzle meant the town remained shrouded in darkness that showed no sign of lifting in the foreseeable future. He was at his work, and by that, a threat to *her* work. He was goading her, tempting her to come out and reveal herself to him. If he were allowed to slay without censure, then history would repeat itself. One more and his hold on the town would be secured for another two hundred years. She wanted nothing more than to confront him, to rip the entrails from his sagging, pasty flesh just as he did to his victims. And yet, she could not.

For she had been the sixth last time.

Her green eyes flared with frustration at the memory, as she raised them to the sullen skies. This was her time, yet there he was, a thorn still nestled deep in her side. He needed to be prised out and thrown into the fires, never to darken this island again. Yet, she was powerless to intervene, hamstrung by a curse older than the land itself. Yes, her rage at the injustice of her passing had allowed her to return and prepare for this time, to plot the downfall of the town that had betrayed her. But the jewel in the crown, the one she wanted more than anything else, the *abhartach*, lay tantalizingly beyond her reach.

But not the girl's.

She smiled and turned, retracing her steps up the old, well-worn path that led to the mountain's barren summit. A first ominous rumble of thunder followed the abrupt flash of lightning that illuminated her domain. Sheep scattered in terror, and a resting crow took flight from a stone wall that enclosed the terrified livestock. The isolated wilderness was captured for a fleeting second, its rugged features a stark contrast to the pampered lifestyles of those below in the town that had watched her swing from a rope. Choking, twitching while he had watched with gleeful relish.

Well, no more. She leaned into the squall, red hair plastered to her forehead as the elements dared to batter her: the Black Lady, Mistress of the Mountain. Ahead of her, the Judas Tree stood bare and defiant, the celestial light of another lightning strike highlighting its dead, black branches. Others would hang from it before this was at an end, of that she was certain. She trailed a long, spindly finger along its trunk as she passed, a ghastly vision amidst the desolate setting.

The creature they called Bloody Hands would pay. Not at her hands, rather at those of one who had been groomed for this very moment, one who held a dormant power that even she could not surpass.

Her smile widened. "Yes, I think it's time that you and I finally met, Maggie Malone. But first, the trap must be set."

The first cough did not emanate from a filthy hovel or rat-ridden tenement building. Rather, it was heard in the more sumptuous setting of the Mulholland residence, a townhouse on a leafy avenue dripping with status and prosperity. Catherine Mulholland, the lady of the house, kept a clean and orderly household, aided by a cook, several maids, and a house porter who was an heirloom from her father's estate. She had married James Mulholland, a prominent shipping tycoon, who ran all manner of cargoes between Belfast and the major English ports. She rarely saw him, but, that aside, they had forged a successful relationship. He worked outrageous hours while she maintained the home and raised the boys. Three now, stepping stones spanning their eight-year marriage. The town of Belfast had been good to them.

The Mulholland family was founded on a strong cornerstone of faith and, come rain or shine, attended Rosemary Street Presbyterian Church every Sunday to worship and hear the inspirational preaching of the Reverend Edgar. He filled his flock with a fiery virtue, preaching the

Gospel plain and simple. They placed their hopes and fears at the foot of the cross. Catherine prided herself on a strong attachment to the church and utilized what little spare time she had to give back to it. After all, without God's bounteous Providence would she be where she was in life? She had it all and was grateful and content.

But now she was coughing.

It had started the previous day, after she had finished her shift at the soup kitchen managed by Annabelle Edgar, the delightful daughter of her pastor. Following that, she had instructed her carriage driver to take her to her husband's offices at the docks to deliver some documents he had forgotten that morning. Honestly, the man was one of the most prosperous businessmen in the town, shipping grain, mutton, and spirits across the Irish Sea at a prodigious rate. But there were days she thought he would forget his head, were it not screwed onto his shoulders.

The dockside had been bustling with activity, the Samhara, one of her husband's ships, undocking. It had caused quite a stir due to its unusual cargo, the most wretched collection of human beings she had ever set eyes upon. Pale, emaciated creatures, barely covered in filthy rags, over a hundred of them had hobbled down the gangway, to be herded into carts like pigs on their way to the slaughterhouse. She had whispered a quiet prayer for the salvation of their souls as, without doubt, Judgment Day awaited many of them in the not-too-distant future. At the same time, she produced a perfumed handkerchief to protect her delicate nostrils from the ungodly stench seeping from the crowded carts. She saw no reason to meddle in the affairs of her husband, for that was not her place, but perhaps a quiet word at dinner would be required regarding the nature of this aspect of his business.

Having deposited the relevant documentation with one of her husband's army of clerks, she returned to their tasteful townhouse, its striking architecture nestling beneath one of the many elm trees that stood watch over their avenue. The remainder of the day was the usual bustle of running a sizable residence, ensuring all was in order so dinner was ready to be served the instant Mr. Mulholland crossed the threshold. He was not a man who liked to wait on an empty stomach; she had learned that lesson the hard way.

Dinner itself had been the usual polite exchange of conversation between husband and wife, albeit largely of a one-way nature. James

Mulholland had regaled his wife with the many trials and tribulations of being a successful shipping magnate. He spoke of incompetent employees and disreputable clients, while his wife nodded and sighed at the appropriate junctures. It was not her place to tell him about her day for, frankly, he had little interest in her affairs, other than she perched prettily on his arm at the various functions they were required to attend on the hectic Belfast social circuit.

Given her husband's irascible frame of mind that evening, she had thought better of raising the prickly matter of the contents of the Samhara's hold. There was a time and a place when it came to influencing his often stubborn mind and tonight was not the time. In any event, she felt slightly faint as the main course was being served, no doubt because of her own industrious day. She declined her usual glass of white wine and instead opted for water, discreetly wiping her brow with a napkin while her husband rambled on about profits and margins, oblivious to her growing discomfort. When she announced that she intended to retire earlier than normal, he merely grunted before heading to his study with the day's broadsheet and a generous glass of brandy.

The coughing started later that night, toward midnight. Catherine attempted to stifle the fit but it was to no avail and, eventually, her husband rose and stormed off to one of their guest rooms, muttering darkly under his breath about the inconsiderate nature of others. By morning, when her personal maid entered to rouse the lady of the house, she found her mistress in a lamentable condition, sweating profusely, yet complaining of being chilled to the bone. Catherine attempted to rise, as she had her morning sewing circle to attend with the church ladies, but was forced to admit defeat and remain in her chambers. The serving staff did their utmost to make her comfortable but eventually, their formidable housekeeper, Mrs. Brown, intervened and called for a doctor, much to the chagrin of Catherine, who insisted it was nothing more than a winter cold.

Their physician, one of the finest in town, immediately concluded that Catherine was of too delicate a nature to resume her busy schedule. He recommended a week of bed rest and strictly no visitors during that period. Mr. Mulholland peered around the matrimonial door on the first evening to dutifully enquire about his wife's welfare, before promptly forgetting about her for the remainder of the week.

Catherine Mulholland was buried nine days later.

The fever spread quickly through the household. Mrs. Brown passed away by the end of the month, as did old Kincaid, the Mulholland's carriage driver. Several of the scullery maids fell foul to the affliction but their youth and stout constitution allowed them to survive the bout. The same, unfortunately, could not be said for several of their elderly relatives and, most tragically of all, the three-year-old daughter of Sadie Magee, the personal maid to Mrs. Mulholland. The widower Mulholland retired swiftly to his country residence where he grieved his wife briefly before setting about the important business of keeping his empire afloat and deflecting scurrilous rumors that his greed was to blame for the sickness establishing a foothold in the town. Several threatening letters from his solicitor were promptly dispatched to business rivals and a local news-paper intent on sullying the name of James Edward Mulholland.

The sad events at the Mulholland residence, however, were only the tip of the iceberg as pockets of typhus fever sprouted up throughout the town, linked to individuals who had either disembarked from the Samhara or had some form of interaction with them. An already hungry population made rich pickings for the sickness, as it rampaged unchecked through cramped tenement housing where families lived on top of one another with little, if any, hygiene. The already under-resourced General Hospital began to rapidly fill, and both the workhouse and asylum had to open fever wards to deal with the overflow. The town's municipal authorities declared the cemetery at Friar's Bush full, and a new plot of land had to be hastily purchased to account for the unprecedented demand for graves.

The fever cared not who it claimed; it respected neither wealth nor status, for all were fair game when it came calling. Try as he might, James Mulholland was never able to restore his tarnished reputation, as the busi-ness he had spent two decades building crumbled within a matter of months. He took to hard liquor as his debts mounted, refusing to respond to increasingly insistent correspondence that he meet with numerous creditors at his earliest convenience. Correspondence escalated to personal calls to his rural address, where a grotesque aroma greeted the burly bailiffs who eventually broke down the front door of the residence.

They found him slumped over a desk in his study, pistol still in hand. A half-empty decanter of brandy and hastily scribbled note were the only other items of importance. A note where he maintained his innocence and blamed an assortment of individuals for his misfortune. A misfortune that had led to him ending his life on a bleak, forlorn evening. He was buried with his wife the following week, with what little money remained of their once considerable fortune. The funeral was sparsely attended, indicative of how far his fortune had fallen within Belfast society.

The fever was unrelenting in its fury.

A Godly Man

"**H**ave you washed that filthy face of yours?"

Maggie knelt on the floor of their room, vainly attempting to tame her tangled mane. She winced, as the teeth of the comb encountered another knot of Gordian proportions. Accepting defeat, she swept a hand through her dark hair, sighed, and tossed the comb to the side. The good folk of Rosemary Street Presbyterian Church would have to take her as they found her. A wave of worry seized her, temporarily dispelling the usual nagging hunger that was the constant backdrop to her waking life. It was only the promise of another hot meal that was luring them to an establishment she would normally never dream of entering. That, and the prospect of meeting Annabelle Edgar again. Maggie had yearned for friendship since the day her mother passed away. She needed to remain strong for her brother, but aching loneliness dueled daily with the hunger pangs, both reminding her of the sad reality of her current plight.

"Yes, your Majesty," groaned Jinks, his high voice carrying from the courtyard outside where she had dispatched him to the communal water barrel.

Maggie smiled. The little man was usually allergic to soap and water, but even he was making an effort this evening. Almost as crushing as the hunger was the daily monotony of their lives, the tedious routine they undertook just to stay one step ahead of it. Maggie rose to her feet and peered through the grubby windowpane. True to his word, her brother was applying himself to a pretense of cleanliness. Miss Edgar had truly made an impression if the scruffiest boy in Belfast was willing to stand and scrub the dirt from his neck.

"And don't forget your hands. There's enough dirt under those nails to..."

Maggie stopped herself and smiled sadly. She was becoming more like her mother with each passing day, inheriting Kate Malone's sayings and mannerisms. Her father, in a rare moment of sobriety, had once tearfully announced that she was the double of her mother, a mirror image of his lost love. She was proud of his gentle words that day, a rare glimpse of the strong, proud man she had once known before grief and liquor had stolen him away.

She looked down at the row of stones outside on the windowsill; twenty-six in all. She knew their various weights and textures intimately, her fingers often gently grazing each of them in turn. Passed down by her dying mother and, before then, generations of women who had guarded the stones with a feverish loyalty. They looked so insignificant but were at the core of everything that Maggie now believed. She wandered outside and lifted one of them, pressing it against her chapped lips.

"Blessed Lady, protect this house, and all who dwell within its walls. Blessed be your name."

She replaced the stone, reassured that her prayer would ensure that what little possessions they owned would remain safe from pilfering hands. Sneaking up on her brother, she tickled his ribcage, the resulting peal of laughter like manna from heaven to her jaded ears. They used to have so much fun, the two of them.

"Come on, we'll be late," she said, taking his hand. The two of them strode across the courtyard towards the entry. A smattering of bored neighbors sat outside their doors, making the most of a rare shaft of early evening sunshine that basked the square in a pleasant glow. Maggie glanced towards the door that held the newly arrived O'Hara family but it was shut tight, their window shrouded in darkness. Best keeping a low profile until all this fuss over the migrant ship had died down. Maggie had been raised to treat people as she found them, irrespective of their faith or status. She had no time for the religious and political squabbling that occupied so many in this town. The Orangemen with their flutes and drums, or the firebrand Young Irishmen who handed out pamphlets in the streets and muttered of uniting the people against the English oppressors. All her time and energy was taken up with staying alive, the Black Lady her sole beacon of hope. She was all that Maggie Malone needed.

"Bloody Hands, Bloody Hands, where can he be..."

"John Joseph Malone, you'll quit that nonsense now." She quickened her step as they passed through the narrow entry that separated Carson's Court from the rest of the town, taking pains not to look at the six hand-prints that decorated its murky interior. She had enough on her plate without Jinks filling his head with ghost stories that would keep him up half the night. She had heard talk that another woman's body had been found in Smithfield the previous night. Details were scant, but there were enough bad men on the streets without singing songs about lunatics from years gone by.

They emerged from the entry and turned left onto Bank Street, which remained busy despite the working day having drawn to a close. A pocket of children dashed from cover across the cobbles, narrowly avoiding a cart loaded with barrels. The driver roared at them as he pulled hard on the reins of his startled horse, its ears pricked and nostrils flaring as it swerved to avoid trampling the children under its hooves. Maggie placed a protective arm around the shoulder of her brother, steering him past the cart. The driver raised a fist at the children and unleashed a barrage of exple-tives as they continued their journey, giggling with nervous energy at their close shave with death.

"That's why I don't like you running off without telling me where you're going. If you ended up under a cart like that, I'd never forgive myself."

Jinks grunted, shrugging off his sister's arm while warily scanning the street in case one of his friends had witnessed the embarrassing show of affection. Once released from her smothering grip, he itched at his neck, unaccustomed to the restrictive starched shirt he had been forced to wear.

"I don't know why I have to wear these fancy clothes. It's not as if we're meeting the Queen." He shot Maggie a withering look as they turned off the main thoroughfare onto Rosemary Street.

"You'll wear what I tell you to wear. You were the one desperate to come here. I'd be quite content staying in the house. Just mind your language, only speak when spoken to, and don't be gulping your food down."

Jinks rolled his eyes, narrowly avoiding a playful cuff around the ear from his watchful sibling. Up ahead, they observed a line of carriages depositing parishioners at the steps to the imposing church, its foreboding oak doors flanked by a pair of grandiose marble columns. The Reverend Edgar, attired from head to toe in ominous black, stood patiently, shaking the hands of his flock as they arrived. Maggie gulped, the hairs on the back of her neck quivering with anxiety. Annabelle was nowhere to be seen and the thought of scaling the steps where the dour clergyman was standing filled her with dread. These were not her people and she felt hopelessly adrift and out of her depth. Would he see through her, sensing immediately that she was raised a Catholic? Worse still, what if his dark eyes drilled deeper into her soul and discovered her true spiritual allegiance? Maggie may have turned her back on the church but still retained a healthy fear and respect for those who donned clerical robes, whatever their denomination.

"Margaret..."

Maggie turned to look in all directions for the source of the voice, but the street contained nobody but well-dressed gentlemen and ladies, descending from all directions towards the elegant building that housed the Reverend Edgar's congregation.

"Over here. Quickly," the voice hissed again. Maggie felt Jinks tugging at her sleeve and pointing towards the side of the church building, where Annabelle crouched, frantically signaling for them to join her. Despite the now bleak skies, she sparkled in a pale beige gown, as simple in design as it was captivating. Maggie immediately felt self-conscious, regarding her own modest garb, but was almost pulled off her feet by Jinks in his desire to cross the gap between them. Giving the Reverend Edgar a final cautionary glance, she crossed the street towards his daughter who seemed intent on remaining concealed from her father, back flat against the granite wall of the building.

"I'm afraid there has been a change of plan," she whispered, indicating for them to follow her down the entry that ran along the side of the church.

"Change of plan?" queried Maggie. "If there's no supper, then Jinks and I will be on our way. We only came for..."

"Shut up, Mags," said Jinks, his face reddening at the thought of being humiliated by his clumsy sister. He glared at her, his eyes daring her to finish the sentence.

Maggie took a deep breath and turned to face a clearly flustered Annabelle. "What seems to be the problem, Miss Edgar?" She offered her most polite smile, inwardly grinding her teeth at the prospect of another hungry evening.

"Unfortunately, I will not be able to accommodate you in the main body of the church due to...unforeseen circumstances." Annabelle squirmed before her guests. Maggie sensed that she was not being entirely truthful, but was choosing her words carefully to avoid causing even greater offence to her guests.

Maggie nodded, not an unkind gesture, before pushing a crestfallen Jinks before her back down the entry.

Annabelle scuttled after them, lifting the hems of her dress to keep apace. "I'm sorry I cannot provide the supper I promised but rest assured, I will not allow you to leave hungry, given your valiant actions yesterday. Please, come with me, before we are seen."

Maggie opened her mouth to protest, but a firm hand on the small of the back persuaded her otherwise. She felt akin to a ewe being herded into a sheep pen, as she and Jinks were bustled back along the entry by an anxious Annabelle, who frequently checked over her shoulder to ensure they were not being watched from the street.

"In here," she whispered, stopping before a small door set in the side of the building. The muted sound of organ music reached their ears as she fiddled at the lock with a cumbersome brass key before the door clicked. "This way," Annabelle announced, cheerier than previously, as she flung open the door before disappearing inside.

Jinks looked up towards his sister for guidance, his eyes twinkling at the thought of more adventures ahead.

Maggie could only sigh and shrug her shoulders in defeat, a sign for her brother to scamper inside and up a steep flight of stairs towards a dull light above. She gave the entry a cursory sweep to ensure their presence was still undetected before following, closing the door behind her. While she would never admit it, she was also warming to the evening's events. The prospect of a full belly, courtesy of the mysterious Annabelle Edgar, was preferable to another wretched evening in their smelly tenement hovel.

Arriving at the top of the stairs, Maggie found herself looking down on the main body of the church from a tiny gallery that, given the thick layer of dust running along its single line of varnished wooden pews, showed little sign of recent use. Below, the church was beginning to fill, the great and the good of Belfast society being entertained, if that was the word, by a stern-faced octogenarian earnestly playing a suitably grim dirge on an impressive organ, its shining steel pipes rising into the alcoves of the building.

"Behold, a feast for my friends."

Maggie turned round, as a beaming Annabelle produced a basket from underneath the nearest pew. Whipping off the linen covering, Maggie's jaw dropped in tandem with that of her little brother at the collection of bread, meats, and cheeses.

Setting it on the pew, Annabelle returned to rummaging before emerging with a jug of iced lemonade.

"Freshly made this afternoon by my own fair hand." She giggled. It was obvious to Maggie that the clergyman's daughter was enjoying this just as much as she and Jinks were. The three of them settled on the floor in a conspiratorial circle and soon the only sound was the massed ranks of Rosemary Street Presbyterian Church launching into an earnest rendition of 'The Old Rugged Cross,' as the three worked their way through the contents of the basket.

While Annabelle ate sparingly, nibbling on a slice of buttered bran, Maggie and Jinks gorged themselves until, finally sated, they fell back against the side of the pew, stomachs fit to burst.

"Thank you, Miss Annabelle," groaned Jinks, after a final huge gulp from the lemonade jug. "I don't think I'll need to eat again for the rest of my life."

"Don't lie," said Maggie. "You'll be starving again this time tomorrow. The boy's stomach is a bottomless pit." She caught herself smiling at Annabelle, who returned the gesture, unspoken gratitude offered and accepted.

Below, the first notes of 'Amazing Grace' roared from the organ, as the congregation rose as one to offer a second offering of melodic worship to the heavens.

"So, if I were to suggest sneaking downstairs to the parlor for a wedge of freshly baked apple tart, I imagine you would have no interest?" Annabelle left the question hanging and smirked at Maggie, as Jinks's eyes widened with delight.

"I suppose I could manage a small slice," he replied, a sly grin creasing his youthful features.

"Then right this way, kind sir," said Annabelle. "But keep your head down and be as quiet as a mouse. Father is about to start his sermon."

"Squeak, Squeak," replied the curly-headed boy, following his new best friend towards the stairs. "Will I bring you up a slice?" he asked Maggie, suddenly mindful of his manners.

"No, thank you. I've eaten enough to feed the five thousand." Maggie smiled, as her brother scurried down the stairs after Annabelle. Perhaps this evening had not been such a bad idea after all. She settled back against the side of the pew and, within minutes, the stuffy atmosphere in the church combined with the hearty supper saw her eyelids grow heavy. She felt herself drifting into a satisfied doze, as the last notes of the hymn carried her off to better times, dreaming of her mother washing and combing her hair, every meticulous stroke a testimony of the love between them. Of her father returning home from work to pick her up and twirl her round and round, as she screamed with dizzy delight. Better times, simpler times, times that would never come to pass again.

"OUR GOD IS A JEALOUS GOD, A VENGEFUL GOD!"

Maggie awoke with a start and, for a second, thought the entire congregation had ascended to rip her limb from limb. She scrambled across the dusty gallery floor, desperate to escape, before her heartbeat steadied and she realized she was alone. There was no sign of Annabelle or Jinks, only the booming baritone voice below.

Maggie crawled to the waist-high ledge and peered over it, down into the packed church. Directly opposite her, the Reverend Edgar stood behind a raised pulpit, a huge Bible in his right hand, as he gesticulated wildly with the other, spittle spraying from his lips to baptize the front pews of his devout onlookers.

"Just as the ten mighty plagues befell the Egyptians, so our land is now plagued with famine and pestilence. Our Lord is capable of multitudinous grace, but he is equally capable of taking from those who turn their backs on his loving countenance." He paused for effect, a master orator, as a murmur of consent rippled through the full pews.

At the rear of the church, others stood, hanging on the pastor's every word. They waited, cupped in the palm of his raised hand, as he prepared to unleash his next ecclesiastical salvo.

Maggie found herself similarly enthralled, eyes peeking above the ledge. It was as though he had hypnotized her with his mellifluous tones. She was frozen to the spot, all thoughts of Jinks and apple tarts dispatched to the farthest reaches of her mind.

"We are being tested, my brethren. Tested, just as our Lord and Savior was tested in the wilderness by Lucifer, the Great Deceiver. Our fair isle has succumbed to the wicked ways of Rome, the poor and the desolate now suffer for neglecting Jesus Christ and the ultimate sacrifice he made for all on that old rugged cross. Am I wrong? Am I?"

A loud roar of consensus erupted from Edgar's followers and several stood to applaud his words, before being hauled back into their seats by less volatile spouses and siblings.

"Those who abandon the straight and narrow path and take the wanton highway to Rome will perish."

"Yes!" bellowed the congregation.

"Those who choose an idle life, relying on the potato, with no other income or desire to socially advance, will wither on the vine."

"Yes!" Louder, a growing fervor possessing the ladies and gentlemen of the clerk, peppered with a healthy sprinkling of "Amens" and "Hallelujahs." Maggie could sense the tension rising, the skilled cleric artfully bringing the pot to the boil.

"They flee their rotten crops and where do they come? Begging and spreading their disease and pagan ways? Why, to our fine town, of course, an economic giant, a jewel in the crown of our most glorious Empire. The papist hordes fully intend to bring the decent, honest, hard-working Protestant people of Ulster to their knees. We are entering the end of days; the time of great revelation is upon us." He slammed his Bible onto the pulpit, the thundering impact causing an elderly lady in the fourth pew to slump to the ground with a theatrical flourish.

As several members of the congregation rushed to revive her, Edgar plowed on, his sermon nearing its final crescendo. Maggie, much as she wanted to, could not tear her eyes away from his piercing dark eyes and severe widow's peak. Thin as a rake, he was suddenly a giant of a man, filling the auditorium with his magnetic presence. Sensing he had his audience exactly where he wanted them, he dropped his voice by several decibels, so that those at the rear of the church had to strain their ears to catch his next words.

"These heathens have brought nothing but misery and death to our doors. We have lost many good, honest folk to their filthy pox. And who is to say you won't be next, or you, or you?" He pointed at a few mortified parishioners as a nervous silence descended, punctuated only by the occasional clearing of a throat.

"Death walks these streets again. Famine, fever, and even last night a young woman brutally slain not half a mile from where we sit today, a cruel imitation of murders from years gone by. Vile, ungodly acts that can only lead me to one sorrowful conclusion."

Archibald Edgar raised his arms aloft and closed his eyes, reveling in the dramatics. It was as if this was his defining moment; he had been chosen to lead his people from the arms of evil, just as his Biblical heroes Moses and David had done in the past. He lifted his head, eyes still closed in rapturous contemplation, as if savoring the exquisite power racing through his veins.

Maggie's world froze as the cleric suddenly opened his eyes, locking on hers across the gaping expanse of the church. His lips twitched, the suggestion of a smirk convincing her that he saw deep inside her, ripping away the layers to see the truth of who she really was. No more secrets, no more lies, for he knew.

"My brethren. It pains me to say this but I know it to be true...there are witches among us."

The Craft

Maggie took the stairs two at a time, Edgar's words ringing in her ears. He knew, but how? She launched herself from the final flight and burst out into the entry, her only thought finding her brother and getting as far as possible from this horrid place as swiftly as they could. She cursed herself for having allowed Jinks to talk her into—

"Maggie! What's wrong?"

She spun around and wrapped Jinks in a hug so tight, it caused him to expel a mouthful of apple tart across the entry. Annabelle watched on, bemused by the disheveled young woman who had exploded from the alcove door.

"We have to go, Jinks, right now. Thank you for your kind hospitality, Miss Edgar, but we really must be leaving."

"Mags," whined Jinks as his sister grabbed the sleeve of his jacket and began to drag him down the entry towards the street. "Annabelle was going to show me the basement. They have all sorts of treasure down there." He looked pleadingly up at her, digging his heels into the ground to halt their progress.

"Well, hardly treasure," replied Annabelle sheepishly. "Just a load of old church artifacts, really." She looked quizzically at Maggie who realized that, not half an hour earlier, the clergyman's daughter had left her, seemingly happy and content, alone in the gallery. Suddenly Annabelle's face creased in concern, as it all became painfully clear.

"What has my father done?"

Maggie grasped for a reply, struggling at the same time to restrain a wriggling Jinks who had no intention of complying with her. She was a cornered animal and knew there was only one place she could go now, the place her mother had told her of in her final moments.

There will come a time, Maggie, when you will need her...

"It's just...we have to go. I don't feel safe here. Your father. He..."

"ANNABELLE!"

Maggie jumped, the stern voice akin to a thousand boots trampling over her grave. She spun around, still clutching a now placid Jinks, to be greeted by the sight of the Reverend Edgar pacing down the entry, a wide-brimmed cleric's hat concealing the upper half of his face. Several steps behind him, a smartly dressed young man struggled to keep pace.

"Father. Mr. Jones. I mean...Aubrey." Annabelle shot her new friends an apologetic look as her father closed the gap between them, ending any fleeting hopes of escape. He looked from his daughter to Maggie, his dark eyes penetrating her feeble defenses.

He knows. He knows.

"And what do we have here? Did I not tell you that guests were not permitted this evening? We were holding a closed meeting."

He frowned, as Aubrey Jones offered Annabelle the weakest of conciliatory smiles. Maggie already despised the young man before he had uttered a word.

"I know Father, and I fully intended to honor your instructions. But I lost track of time and these poor people... They are desperate. As a follower of Christ, I could not in good conscience walk away from them. I..."

"Silence. I will deal with you later. For now, I have more pressing matters to attend to." Edgar raised a hand, clearly tired of his daughter's continued insubordination. He afforded Jinks the most perfunctory of examinations, before moving on to Maggie. She flinched, deeply uncomfortable at being the center of his attention.

"Did you enjoy my sermon, young lady? I observed you watching from the gallery." Maggie blushed and could only nod in response, silently berating herself. Why had she insisted on looking? Her mother had drummed being inconspicuous into her from an early age.

Don't be putting your head above the parapet, Maggie. Our kind must remain in the shadows.

"The Lord does indeed work in mysterious ways. I thank Him that He brings sinners to my very door. Just as he instructed his disciples to cast their nets to the side of the boat, I too have returned a full haul this evening. Praise be indeed."

"Father. I..."

"You may go now, Annabelle. Mr. Jones will escort you back to our carriage. I will join you shortly, after I have spoken with these two lost souls."

"But I..."

"You will obey me, girl." The mask slipped, and Maggie caught a glimpse of the anger that simmered beneath the slick veneer. The minister sensed he had been exposed and adjusted his clerical collar, which his uncharacteristic outburst had nudged out of place.

Annabelle nodded and, giving Maggie a crestfallen look, turned and trudged back down the entry, while a flustered Mr. Jones attempted to engage her in stilted pleasantries.

Edgar watched them turn the corner before, satisfied they were out of earshot, rounding on his cornered prey.

"Are you of the Catholic faith?" He raised an eyebrow, a disingenuous smile placing Maggie on instant alert. There was something of the snake in this man. She knew little of the Protestant clergy, but an aura of sly insincerity leaked from every pore of his papery skin.

"We used to go to St. Mary's but haven't since Mother..."

"Quiet, John Joseph. Let me answer the man," hissed Maggie, squeezing her brother's hand so hard he winced in pain and shot his sister an accusatory glare. The cleric smirked, obviously toying with their emotions. Maggie realized they were puppets dangling before him and only he would decide when the string was cut.

"What's your name, girl?" His presence seemed to fill the entry and an unnatural still had fallen, the hubbub from the main street now a distant murmur.

"What business is that of yours, sir? Why should I offer up my name when you would not allow me to partake in your service."

Edgar smiled but it was a humorless gesture, a thin slit across his granite features. His eyes flared imperceptibly and Maggie cursed herself for having dared to poke the lion.

"I take an interest in all God's children," murmured the pastor, retaining his composure, his words like honeyed barbs. "It is my life's mission to rescue as many souls as possible from a life of sinful despair." He paused. "Souls such as those of you and your brother."

"We are just fine sir; now, if you would only let us pass, we will be on our way." Maggie fought to remain firm but was unable to stop the quaver in her voice as she grabbed Jinks by the wrist and made to walk past the minister.

He stepped smartly to his left, however, blocking their path and holding out a hand. "Please, you misunderstand me. Can I at least offer you my carriage to get you safely home? The streets are not safe these days. There is a lunatic running amok, a young woman was butchered nearby last night. The disciples of the Evil One are rising again, worshipping their dark master by performing such heinous acts."

Maggie met his eyes, but his steely gaze eroded what little resilience she had left. She could feel Jinks shaking by her side, terrified by the words of the man of God. "Thank you for the kind offer, but we know these streets well. Now if you would please..."

"Oh, I see. Perhaps you have nothing to fear from such deviants. Perhaps...you are familiar with their ways?" He allowed the question to hang in the air, as a persistent rain started to fall.

Maggie frantically scrambled for a response, unable to take her eyes off the all-seeing Edgar, the steady pulse of raindrops dripping from the brim of his hat.

"I know nothing of such behavior, sir. We are decent, law-abiding folk."

"Indeed, indeed," he replied. "But even the purest of hearts can be polluted by Satan. He beguiles, he misleads. That is why God sent men like me to correct and, if necessary, chastise."

He knows.

"The Lord has entrusted me to do his work amongst the squalor and filth of this town. He has beseeched me to root out the evil that threatens to smother the good work of his people. His Protestant people. The Roman way is the path to hell and eternal damnation. It is the way of sorcery and...witchcraft."

"Please sir," stammered Jinks, tears now flowing down his cheeks. "We just want to go home."

"And I am determined to destroy the dark forces that have brought famine, murder, and disease upon the good people of Belfast. We have been cursed before by such decadent perversion, but my ancestors hunted them down with righteous anger and watched them hang by their necks until dead. I fully intend to do the same. There is devilry within your papist slums and I intend to crush it with a fiery sword." He was shouting now, his elongated index finger jabbing inches from Maggie's face to enunciate each hateful point spewing from his lips.

"Stop it," screamed Maggie, finally cracking under the withering barrage. She barged past the ranting cleric, shielding Jinks protectively with her free arm.

Edgar raised his palms in faux alarm, his face filling with a pretense of concern.

Maggie launched into a run, dragging her terrified brother behind.

"God bless you, my children. I shall be praying for your souls until we meet again."

The braying laughter of the clergyman sent them on their way, as they sprinted from the entry and turned right onto Rosemary Street. Maggie did not afford the church a glance, she needed to be as far away from it as possible. All she wanted now was to burrow deep beneath the blankets in their room, her brother safe in her arms. There was comfort there, protection. Her Lady would ensure that.

"Maggie. Jinks. Wait..." Annabelle watched from the carriage window as her father emerged from the entry and joined her, seated opposite a bewildered Mr. Jones. He studiously ignored her, a certain sign that she had crossed the unspoken line that formed and solidified whenever she dared test his patience. A patience far from that of another of his biblical heroes, Job, at the best of times.

"Drive on, Michael. There's a good man."

The driver nodded and jolted the reins. The two chestnut bays in harness took off at a brisk trot away from the church, where a handful of parishioners still mingled around the steps, desperate to catch a final wave from their departing minister. To be acknowledged by the Reverend Edgar, no matter how fleeting, was a tale worth telling over breakfast the following morning.

"Father. I..."

"Silence, Annabelle. I have some business to discuss with young Mr. Jones."

"But I..."

"Matters that should not concern you with your delicate sensibilities. If we are to find you a suitable husband, then I must know he is able to keep you in the manner to which you are accustomed. God rest your mother's soul; she would turn in her grave if I acted otherwise."

"Yes, Father."

Annabelle stared forlornly out of the carriage window as it clattered out of the town and toward the more salubrious outskirts where the Edgar residence was situated. At times such as these, it was better to draw up one's drawbridge and wait until the passing storm had abated. Living with such an unpredictable man, she had learned how to negotiate his regular squalls and ride out the storm until brighter skies arrived, allowing her to converse with him again in a reasonably civilized manner.

"Dreadful weather we're having, don't you think?" Jones winced shortly after he uttered the words, his woeful attempt at thawing the icy atmosphere earning a steely glance from Edgar.

Annabelle snorted and quickly averted her attention from the hapless young suitor to the passing countryside. The young man's meteorological observation could not have come at a worse juncture, clashing with her own inner monologue regarding her father's less-than-sunny disposition. She said a silent prayer that he had not noticed this latest act of disobedience.

"Would you care to share your thoughts with us, girl? As to why you find the words of our guest so amusing?" Edgar glared across the carriage, and she sensed the waves of undiluted anger rolling off him until she was forced to return her attention to the carriage's occupants.

"I do apologize, Father. And to you, Mr. Jones. That was very impolite of me. I was just thinking back to a silly comment Sarah McCann made during Sunday School last week. She thought that Jonah had swallowed the whale and not the other way round." It was a feeble explanation, but the best she could concoct at such short notice.

Jones nodded, a vague, confused smile forming on his features.

Annabelle smiled back in as conciliatory a manner as she could muster. He was a harmless soul, she thought, and probably as uncomfortable at their enforced courtship as she was.

Her father eyed her for what seemed an eternity, prompting another unspoken missive to Heaven that her words had calmed his simmering fury.

"Hmm, I may need to have a word with her parents, if her knowledge of the Good Book is so flawed." He settled back in his seat across from her, and Annabelle breathed easy again, although slightly annoyed with herself for having cast Sarah as the unwitting sacrificial lamb in this latest battle of wits with her father.

Her relief, however, was short-lived.

"And worry not about your latest stray kittens. That Catholic girl is not the sort of company you should be keeping. I sense an unclean spirit about her that I want no daughter of mine near. I do not want you meeting with her again. The Lord will take care of that one and her ilk."

"Her name is Maggie and..."

"Maggie, Kathy, whatever her name is, you will not be fraternizing with her again. Do you hear me?"

"Yes, Father."

Annabelle kept her face an emotionless mask, even as her stomach churned and her mind raced with worried thoughts. She was aware of the two men opposite poring over her features as she contemplated the passing scenery through the now rain-streaked window. She would not give them the satisfaction of knowing her stomach was a nauseous knot, worried sick at what unhinged plan her father was preparing to unleash upon those two poor unfortunates.

Maggie and Jinks were being ripped from her grasp before she even had a chance to further explore their tentative friendship.

God have mercy on them.

It was Jinks who saved them. Life on the streets had taught him to always scan ahead for dangers that lurked on every corner. He and his mates had formed a network of lookouts and signals that had served them well in various run-ins with competing groups of urchins in the area. They had crossed Bank Street and were headed towards the entry that led onto Carson's Court when a shrill whistle caused them to spin around. There, positioned on the other side of the street, stood Tommy Reilly, his principal partner in crime. The other boy's hands became a blur before he ducked down an adjacent entry.

"What was that? What's he saying?"

Without replying, Jinks grabbed Maggie's sleeve and pulled her down the entry after Tommy, just as one of Billy Thompson's heavies swaggered out of the courtyard entry, hands on hips. Thompson scanned the street for signs of his quarry. A second earlier and he would have been staring them straight in the face. Maggie was almost lifted off her feet, as Jinks careered along the twisting, narrowing entry. Thankfully nobody was coming in the opposite direction, otherwise, there would have been a calamitous collision. Eventually, her brother slowed his pace and let go of Maggie as they emerged into a shadowy square, reminiscent of Carson's Court. Maggie managed to find her bearings and realized they were at the rear of Kelly's Cellars, one of the premier drinking establishments in the town. Perched atop a barrel of ale, his heels swinging, was the lad who had gestured manically at Jinks moments earlier.

"Thanks, Tom. I owe ye a favor." Jinks mock-saluted the other boy, who smiled in return, his grin brightening a gaunt, filthy face. He started to drum a beat on the barrel with his heels as a couple of drunks stumbled out of the rear of Kelly's, bellowing loudly at a ribald joke one had just shared with the other.

"What was that all about?" gasped Maggie, bending over to regain her breath. It had been many a year since she had been required to run so fast at such short notice.

"It's Thompson. He was at our house. Turning it upside down, according to Tommy." He glanced over at the little lad, who was now harassing the two drunks for a penny to bring their drinks to and from the bar.

"Wait, he told you all that? By just waving his hands in the air?" Maggie straightened, content she was no longer going to vomit. She brushed a hand through her hair, once more a tangle of knots.

"It's how we talk on the streets, Mags," replied her brother, rolling his eyes at his sister's lack of knowledge. "Keeps us one step ahead of the Constabulary. And the likes of Thompson and his mates."

Maggie slumped against the wall of the yard, welcoming the cool stonework against her back, the sweat of their exertions having soaked through her blouse. Her world had been turned upside down in the space of an hour. First, the unwanted attention of the Reverend Edgar, and now this. Their safe place, their bolthole no longer an option, her precious stones out of reach. Her mother had warned that this day would come and she had been preparing for it. But never in her wildest dreams had she reckoned it would arrive so soon, her attempts at rebuilding their lives falling apart in the space of a solitary evening. She suddenly felt dizzy with fear, overcome with the dread of what she must tell her brother.

"What is it, Mags? Are you alright?" Jinks kneeled by her side, as she slid down the wall onto her haunches. She struggled to catch a breath, clammy sweat now coating every inch of her skin.

"Maggie, you're scaring me. Will I get a doctor?" He half-turned to make off, but Maggie held his wrist, shaking her head and swallowing hard to clear the dryness in the back of her throat.

"I'm grand. Just give me a minute. But we can't go back."

"What do you mean we can't go back? Thompson can't stand at our front door forever. And it's not as if there's anything worth taking from our place. We haven't two pennies to rub together. We can lie low for a few hours, then head home. We can borrow the money, there must be something we can pawn." He eyed Maggie's shawl, which she protectively pulled over her shoulders, shaking her head vigorously.

"I mean we can't go back. The room, Carson's Court, Belfast. We have to leave. Before he finds us."

"What do you mean, Belfast? This is our home. It might be a dirty hole but I'm not afraid of that big hellion." Barely reaching her shoulder, and Maggie was no giant, the little boy stood on the tips of his toes and stuck out his chin as if determined to show her he wasn't afraid.

Maggie smiled sadly and placed a hand against his grubby cheek. "John Joseph Malone, you've got the heart of a lion but this is one battle we can't fight on our own. Come on, there's something I want to show you."

She led him across the yard; Tommy had trailed into the bar behind the two men, still sniping for a penny. Maggie smiled ruefully. If he was anything like her brother, the boy would have their pockets picked for six times as much before the night was over. Jinks joined Maggie in the farthest corner of the yard, the fading light providing them with a degree of privacy. Any patron exiting the tavern would have been oblivious to their presence, less than twenty yards away.

Maggie turned and fixed her brother with her most severe stare. "Do you remember when Mammy used to tell you her stories? To get you to go to sleep at night?"

"Of course, I do. My favorite was the one about the good leprechaun who fought the bad faeries that were stealing the babies from their cots."

"Aye, that was a good one," smiled Maggie, reminiscing fondly at those cozy evenings when the hearth was stacked high with peat and sticks, their bellies full of wholesome stew. Back when they were a family, when they had little but enough to get by as they had each other.

"Do you remember the story about the Black Lady?"

"I do. The bad men hanged her and, since then, she has looked over the city, making sure nothing like that would ever happen again. That's why they named the mountain after her, to make sure she's never forgotten. It scared me a bit, that one, but Mammy said she was a good woman who was hard done by."

"And Mammy was right. She would never lie to us, would she?"

Jinks nodded his head gravely.

"Well, what if I were to tell you that the Black Lady is watching over us, you and me, right this very minute?"

Jinks looked at Maggie and screwed his face, uncertain if she was serious or pulling his leg. A low mist was beginning to creep into the yard, its fingers curling around their ankles like playful kittens.

"And the leprechauns as well?" His grave tone forced a sliver of a smile from Maggie, despite the dire scenario they found themselves in.

"We will talk of them another time, brother. For now, just watch and say nothing more until I show you something."

Maggie knelt on the cobbles behind a stack of barrels and reached deep into the pocket of her skirts, as Jinks watched on. She opened a clenched fist to reveal a small stone. She smiled at her brother, before lowering her head and gently blowing on it, as if trying to rekindle a dying fire.

Jinks gasped as the previously dull, gray stone started to glow with a golden light, illuminating his incredulous face to Maggie's delight.

"What? How?"

"Hush. No words, remember? Just watch." Maggie gradually lowered her cupped hands, the glow from the stone intensifying as it floated towards the ground as a single, piercing light rose from it, bathing the corner of the yard in a vermilion glow.

Jinks opened his mouth to speak again but thought better off it, as tiny shards of flame began to erupt from the stone, cobalt blue jolts that resonated in sharp contrast to the eerie light.

"There are 26 stones, one for each who has perfected the craft. There were 27..." She paused, uncertain how to frame the words for her still grieving brother. She need not have worried as realization dawned on his receptive young face.

"The Black Lady is real? Mother was a witch?"

Maggie nodded. "Maybe witch is not the word, but she followed the ways of the Black Lady and practiced her craft. Her story has been tainted, corrupted by the wicked tongues of men who carry nothing but rage in their hearts. A rage born of fear."

"Fear? What are they afraid of? Mammy would never harm a soul. All she wanted to do was help folk."

"Exactly," said Maggie, her eyes never leaving the stone, her sole focus feeding and nurturing the flames. "Mammy used the craft for good purposes. Some call her kind cunning women, others *cailleach*. She healed and prayed, and performed small mercies that aided our friends and neighbors. Often, they were not even aware of it. Curing ailments, unexpected windfalls, and dividends. She could not be too open, too obvious. She did not want to swing from the end of a rope as our Lady did."

"*Our* Lady?"

He was only a wee boy, but as sharp as the keenest blade, thought Maggie. He did not miss a trick.

"Yes, Jinks. When Mammy passed away, she spent her last days teaching me all she knew of the craft. I lapped it all up. And I'm afraid now is the time I will have to reveal what I was taught, for we are in desperate peril and in need of her aid."

"From Billy Thompson. We can handle him, Mags. I told you..."

"No, he is the least of our concerns. There is a greater threat to us, and I saw it with my own eyes earlier this evening. The preacher man. He knows, do not ask me how or why, but he knows and is coming for us."

"Miss Annabelle's father? He was a strange man, alright."

"Yes. I fear the mistrust and hysteria that led to our Lady's death is about to rise again in this town. There is a new persecution coming, masked beneath the cross and holy book he holds so precious to his black heart."

Jinks watched, his gaunt face paling by the second, as the stone rose into the air until it twinkled before Maggie's nose.

The cobalt flames pulsing from its core suddenly congregated and engulfed Maggie. She convulsed on her knees, powerless to do anything but yield to its force. Her head shot back and she began to mumble, an incoherent deluge of noises that meant nothing to her. She was aware of Jinks crouched by her twitching form, his young face a mask of concern. As suddenly as it had started, the glittering stone dropped out of the air, falling into her hand. The fantastic colors dulled and faded until they were no more, the courtyard returning to its normal murky light. Maggie turned to face her sibling, her eyes clear and focused, a reassuring smile greeting his anxious stare.

"It's alright, I know what we must do now, I know where we have to go. There are others like Mammy, like me, women who can help us."

Jinks nodded. She needed no more words, as he trusted his sister like no other. He would follow her blindly, his love for her shining through in every word he spoke and deed he performed. Maggie knew that if she told him that this Black Lady was real and could help them, then that was good enough for him. No questions were required, no explanations needed.

The thud of heavy leather boots echoing along the damp entry behind them brought Maggie to her feet. For a few fleeting seconds, the unnatural glow of the stone flickered deep within her eyes again. It faded as soon as it had appeared, only to be replaced by a stern resolve.

"Come on, little man. It's time we left this place." She held out a hand and he took it without question, their eyes locking in unspoken solidarity before the nearing footfall forced them to reluctantly forgo the temporary sanctuary of the yard and take flight again, the stone safely ensconced in the folds of Maggie's skirts.

Crossing the open space, they darted through the back entrance of Kelly's so quickly Maggie just missed Billy Thompson and his thuggish companions explode into the yard, his eyes blazing with fury.

The Glowing

She knew that it had been decades since the stones last glowed. Of the remaining twenty-six, only three resided within the town's boundaries, the others scattered across Ireland and further afield. The old woman had watched the others flee starvation and ruin, emigrating to England, Scotland, and the New World. Of the three left, one was in the asylum, her mind no longer capable of understanding the ramifications of what was to pass, while another lay on her sick bed, delirious with a fever that no number of wet cloths and poultices could abate. She was the only one left, the only one capable of responding to the plea for help from one of her own kind.

She was known as Nell; nobody had ever cared enough to ask her full name. Likewise, nobody knew much of anything about her. She had always been there, in the end cottage of the little whitewashed row in Ballymacarrett. It fell within the town limits but only just, more akin to a sleepy rural village than the economic giant that spewed its smoke into the skies not two miles away. The cottages had stood long before any factory was raised from the ground, small plots of land providing a meager existence, yet one that kept their occupants fed and clothed all year round. The men tended their crops while the women gathered the eggs, milked the goats, did the darning and sewing—anything to bring a few extra coins into the home. By night, they would gather and sing the old songs, their mugs as full as their hearts, safe and warm within their close-knit community.

That was before the hunger came.

Nell had been asleep when the itching started, an itch she had not felt since a young girl almost half a century before. One of their own had drowned that distant day, a poor wretch of a girl down on her luck who had been reduced to scraping a living catering for the lascivious needs of sailors docked in Belfast. One such beast had left her for dead, dazed and bleeding as he had swaggered back to his ship, whistling a merry tune to himself.

Disorientated and alone, she had stumbled and fallen into the lough, where she had clung by bloody nails to the slick harbor wall, screaming for help. She had prayed to their Lady, and the stones had glowed in homes across the land. Nell had been too young to understand, but her aunt had risen from bed to run to the aid of the girl. The stones had glowed, just as they did now, just as Nell hobbled along the dirt track that joined the main road meandering along the dozing Lagan until it stretched its wings and opened out, flowing through built-up areas of ramshackle housing on its way to the bustling hub of the town.

The stones, arranged in a semi-circle around her tiny hearth, had sparked and glowed, a sure sign that one of their own was in need. Her bones ached, and pains shot along her inflamed and swollen joints. It mattered not, as she limped along the rutted dirt track, navigating a host of muddy puddles, the ground churned up by the daily rumble of carts and livestock. There was one of her own in need; she knew not who they were or their circumstances. All she knew was that the stones had spoken and she must answer. She mumbled a prayer through gritted teeth, a mantra to the one who had guided her all these years, who had never forsaken her when others had turned their backs on the strange old woman at the bottom of the lane.

The lights of the town inched closer, as she reached the end of the lane and joined the main road that led towards the beacon drawing her ever closer. A carriage rumbled past, narrowly avoiding her, its driver roaring curses at her hunched back as he struggled with the reins to take evasive action. Nell ignored him; the taunts and abuse of those who deemed themselves better than her had been a common thread throughout her life. She had quietly endured them, erecting a stoic barrier, safe in the knowledge that she was protected, so long as she clung to her faith in the one who had endured more than any of them.

The Black Lady.

He sensed it as well; one of the *cailleach's* was in grave danger, but he would not be running to their aid. As opposed to the quiet determination of Nell, he gleefully relished the waves of anxiety and desperation washing over him. It suited his plans to see her coven weakened, to watch them fall one by one. This was his land, long before her kind had set foot on it, with their foul enchantments that stifled his wanton, bloody reign. She was old, yet he was older and the equilibrium was waiting to be restored.

He had walked this land long before the English had arrived and built their settlements. Back when this now sprawling port had been nothing more than a smattering of hovels, huddled together against the biting winds that raced up the lough toward their pitiful shacks. He had been their Lord and Master then, his tower perched on the mountain that she now called home. They even had the audacity to name it after her—Black Mountain. But it had been his long before she had set foot on it.

He had protected the villagers from marauders and the word soon spread; woe betide any brigand or chieftain who sought to cross swords with him. He was of insignificant appearance, short and stout. They called him *abhartach* behind his back, meaning dwarf. But those words were never uttered to his face for even the mightiest warriors feared him.

He stirred, a shaft of moonlight seeping through the blanket that covered the sole window set high in the basement wall. It was a weak light but still, it irritated his ancient, weathered skin to be exposed to any at all, be it from sun or moon. A whimper to his right irritated him more, and he kicked out savagely at the inert form huddled in the corner.

"Quiet! Or I'll suck you dry the next time. You see if I won't."

The whimpering stopped and the small figure huddled into a tight ball, pale fingers wrapped around bloody knees. She was young, no more than sixteen, and he had kept her alive because her blood had tasted sweeter than the usual rotten fare he had recently been forced to exist on. This one was pure, her virtue unsullied like the others he had preyed upon during this, his most recent visitation.

She would be the fifth.

Visitation. He grunted in disgust at the word. This time would be no visit, a fleeting glimpse of the town that he once ruled. This time he was here to finish the witch once and for all, and there was nothing that she and her vile brood could do to stand in his way. For as he grew stronger on the blood of the living, she had become distracted, such was her manic obsession with avenging her own death. Her coven grew weaker, a mere handful of followers, and her need to destroy the town and its inhabitants had lowered her defenses. These humans would be her downfall, her reluctance to sever the bond that existed between them and the woman she used to be. Emotions clouded her judgement. Hate of the town, love of her coven. She was juggling too many balls, and all he had to do was sit back and wait for one to fall. Just the one, and then he would feast on the blood of a witch, a delectable nectar that left his extended canines throbbing with anticipation.

Her blood was his by right, just as the blood of the villagers had been his all those years ago. Every month, each householder was required to leave a bowl of blood outside their abode as payment for his protection. He would come in the dead of night and sup his fill. Those days were long gone, no more bowls left in his honor. The old ways had been neglected, eroded away by a modern world that he feared and despised in equal measure. Yet, he remained and still took what was rightfully his to take. Once there had been bowls but now there were six throats to slash, six bellies to gouge open, so that he could feed.

He stretched out a muscled arm and pulled the girl into his arms, her pathetic pleas ignored as he sunk his fangs into the exposed flesh of her throat. It was good, so good, but nowhere near as succulent as the vein he craved more than any other.

She was the fifth, a pitiful mortal, but the sixth would be so much more. He would drink the blood of a witch, one of her coven, and make the Black Lady watch. Make her watch before dispatching her too into the darkness, never to return. She had finally acquiesced to meeting him. It was time.

"Another drink, Mr. Blake?"

The Reverend Edgar smiled as he raised the decanter and gestured towards his guest's near-empty glass. Blake nodded, savoring the fine brandy the clergyman had produced after their hearty dinner. He raised the fat cigar that had been cut and lit for him, sucking greedily and inhaling the heady fumes deep into his lungs.

"The collection plates must be full every Sunday to afford such treats as these, Edgar. Vintage brandy, hand-rolled cigars, whatever happened to a man of God living a humble, basic life."

Edgar chuckled, settling back into the comfortable recesses of his leather upholstered armchair. Only the roaring hearth separated him from one of the most powerful men in Belfast. A man he had been courting for some time, softening him up for the day when he would call home the favor he had been nurturing.

"What can I say, Andrew," he smirked, extending his arms to take in the luxurious settings of his personal study. "The Lord looks after his own. I have worked hard for God, and he has blessed me most bounteously."

Blake erupted into a booming laugh, quite unbefitting of his skeletal frame.

Edgar watched uneasily, uncertain as to whether the man was laughing at or with him. Eventually, the bellowing subsided to a gentler chuckle, Blake producing an exquisite, monogrammed handkerchief to mop his glistening brow. The flames from the fire reflected off his forehead as Edgar waited patiently for negotiations to begin. He had the man exactly where he wanted him, there would be no wriggling off the hook this time.

"Now, we both know that you didn't invite me here tonight for a prayer meeting. You've always treated me well, and I much appreciated your impassioned plea from the pulpit for my campaign when I ran for office last spring. I know how the game is played, and I feel it may be time that I scratch your back as you once scratched mine. You're not one to hold your tongue, so come, come. Out with it."

Edgar nodded sagely and placed his glass on the nest of tables by his side. Blake hadn't slithered up the greasy pole of local politics without learning how to read a man. It was time to lay his cards on the table. He said a silent prayer for God to open another door on his righteous quest to purge Belfast of the heathen underbelly that sickened him to the core.

"You are a good man, Andrew. A godly man whose faith is at the forefront of the very difficult decisions one in such high office is required to make."

"Indeed, Archibald. I will admit this vocation is not for everyone. I have made many enemies down the years, but I stand firm. I know that the Lord is by my side, and I pray that he remains there as I continue his work."

Edgar straightened in his chair, uncertain if Blake was genuine or merely playing along. He was a canny operator and gave nothing away in his dour countenance. He decided to forge ahead, for to hesitate now would see his only opportunity slip through sweating palms. It was now or never.

"We are living in a time of crisis, Andrew. The town is on its knees. Businesses are failing everywhere, and the people are ravaged by sickness and hunger. The papist hordes are flooding our streets, bringing with them their idle, dirty ways. Young women can no longer walk the streets in safety. And now, this ship from Connemara. They say it has brought the plague fever."

Edgar realized his voice was at a higher pitch than he had intended. He was on the edge of his seat, his hands clenched tightly to its armrests. He was momentarily concerned that his overly zealous outburst had been too severe but felt relieved to see the guardian nodding fervently, a light sheen of sweat coating his upper lip.

"Yes," he stammered. "The Samhara. A most damnable business. Heads will roll when I find out what crooked harbor official allowed it to disembark its diseased cargo." He tugged at the collar of his starched collar, suddenly looking decidedly pale.

"Are you alright, Andrew? Shall I have a window opened? Perhaps the cigar smoke does not agree with you." Edgar rose to summon a maid, but Blake motioned for him to sit down.

"Nonsense, man, I'm perfectly fine. Now carry on, what were you saying?" He dabbed at his brow with a handkerchief, blinking furiously to clear his vision.

Edgar settled and cleared his throat, which was suddenly very dry. He inhaled deeply. Satan would not claim his tongue now, not when he had worked so hard to curry favor with the likes of Andrew Blake. Onwards, equipped with the armor of God.

"Do you believe in evil, Andrew? Actual evil?"

Blake eyed him warily, as if sensing a trap, before answering. "Why, of course, I do. The Devil is everywhere, watching us, waiting to pounce like a roaring lion. First Peter, Chapter Five..."

"How I love to hear a man quoting the word of God. Truly, you are a soldier of Christ, Andrew. Which is why this town needs you more than ever. I have brought you here to enlighten you as to why this great town is now suffering so grievously. For we are under spiritual attack, the likes of which I have never experienced in all my days. We stand on the cusp of the end times. The final battle is almost upon us."

He fixed Blake with his most judicious stare before continuing. It was working; the lanky frame opposite him seemed to be visibly shrinking into the armchair.

"End times? What do you mean?" He could offer nothing more and merely nodded weakly for Edgar to continue.

"Witchcraft, Andrew. Pure and simple. Dark magic and sorcery from the bowels of Rome itself."

"Witchcraft?" Blake appeared on the verge of slithering off his leather plinth to form an oily puddle on the plush, carpeted floor. He peered around the well-lit study, as if expecting to be dragged down into the bowels of the underworld at any moment. Edgar allowed his guard to relax a little. The man was falling apart before his very eyes; perhaps he was a God-fearing soul after all.

"Yes, my friend. Witchcraft. Two hundred years ago, this month, our forefathers were plagued by a spate of abominable murders. Six innocent, virtuous young women were slain by one of Lucifer's emissaries. Their mortal remains were left as a testimony to the cruel sacrifices that took place on these very streets."

"I've heard the tales. But surely, they are nothing more than that." Blake, who did not possess a healthy pallor at the best of times, now resembled a wraith as a grayish tint crept across his features.

"Don't treat me like a fool, Andrew. I know there have been more killings. For all your coin and attempts to still the rumor mill, tongues have still wagged. Girls killed in the same heinous manner; disgusting hand marks smeared on the walls. If this gets out and the people believe that Bloody Hands is back, on top of everything else that has befallen the town, there will be chaos. The ignorant lower classes will riot, for sure. Empty bellies and fearful minds are a certain recipe for disaster. A disaster that will result in less votes for you, a man intending to run for mayor on a platform of law and order."

"I know, I know," blurted Blake, springing from his chair like a startled deer. He began pacing the study much to the disdain of the cleric. "Curse that Sergeant. I knew I couldn't trust him to keep his mouth shut."

He stopped his lap of the study and knelt before Edgar, his fingers digging into the minister's forearm.

"What are we to do, Archibald? There's an election to be won. If this gets out and the people panic, all will be lost, years of hard work undone. We both know that these are the acts of some lunatic, yet the townsfolk believe that this demon, this spirit, has returned. The town is already teetering on the brink."

Edgar smiled benevolently down at his startled guest. He had played him like a fiddle, leading him like a veritable lamb to slaughter.

"I'm so glad you asked, Andrew. So very glad you asked."

The stair she crouched on creaked. Annabelle's heart skipped several beats, convinced that her eavesdropping would be discovered. She held her breath, eyes squeezed shut, expecting the thunderous disapproval of her outraged father to rain down upon her. The seconds passed painfully, and she eventually allowed herself to open an eyelid. Below her, the hallway remained silent, bar the dull murmur of conversation from the study. An imposing grandfather clock sat guardian at its door, and she squinted to make out the time. Just gone ten.

She had caught snippets of the conversation, enough to know that there was trouble afoot, but her eyes widened further as her father's voice rose in growing excitement. He had always been a deeply devout man, but since the death of her mother, he had reached a new level of ecclesiastical fervor. His sermons had grown more inflammatory as his church had grown, far removed from the loving, pious man who used to tuck her into bed every night and read her bedtime stories, no matter how tired he was or how much work awaited in his study. The story of Daniel and the Lions'

Den had been her favorite, and she used to squeal with delight and duck beneath the bed sheets as he mimicked the bloodthirsty beasts who Daniel subdued through faith and prayer.

He preached division and mistrust now, as opposed to love and charity. Social advancement and overflowing collection plates were his primary focus, as he fed on the fears of his congregation, stoking dormant sectarian fires that were never far from the surface of Belfast society. Be it the Orangemen marching or the Young Irishmen protesting, there was always an uneasy tension on the streets. Famine, and now disease, had been great levelers but Archibald Edgar sensed the despair and knew the people wanted a scapegoat, a visible target who they could direct their ire towards.

The second she heard Maggie Malone's name, she knew who it would be.

Annabelle listened with increasing incredulity as her father, growing more unhinged with every passing sentence, detailed a vision God had revealed to him in the pulpit. He had been praying and fasting fervently all week, pleading with the Almighty to show him a solution to the town's ills. There had been nothing for days, but the Lord had taught him to be patient and persevere just like Moses and the Israelites had in the wilderness for forty barren years. Finally, when even his iron-clad faith was failing him, he had looked up, and there she was, brazenly staring down at him from a lofty vantage point in the gallery.

"There are witches in our midst, Mr. Blake. One materialized before my very eyes in God's house, hovering above the faithful, blaspheming us with her wicked presence."

"Are you sure? Could you have been mistaken?"

"I will swear as to what I saw on the Holy Bible itself. Just as our town was plagued with them before, so we are again. They are the reason why our people are starving."

Annabelle was already running down the remaining stairs, no longer caring if she was heard above her father's cresting rage.

"They are the reason we are afflicted with the disease."

She scrambled at the latch to the front door, barely able to open it due to trembling hands and tearful eyes. Was this really the man who had bounced her on his knee all those years ago, who had doted on her with a fierce, unbridled love?

"They are the reason why our townspeople are being ritually slain again and offered as sacrifices to the Evil One. And they must pay, starting with the Malone girl. She must be made an example of; she must hang as a warning of the dangers of sorcery. She is marked by Satan, a creature of the night."

Annabelle was no longer listening, finally flinging open the door and bounding down the stone steps of the townhouse three at a time until her feet found the pavement. She turned left, narrowly avoiding a passing couple on their evening stroll along the tranquil boulevard. All she cared about was finding and warning her new friend. She had only the vaguest recollection of where Jinks and Maggie lived, something about a court near the butchers' quarter, but if it meant knocking on every door in the town, she would find them. For if her insane father had his way, Maggie was doomed.

Annabelle ran blindly into the night as the rain continued to fall. A storm was brewing.

She stood on the headland, surveying the town, inhaling the sights and emotions of those most deeply affected by the glowing of the stones. The rain intensified, a steady patter of heavy drops that danced around her ankles like sprouting tulips. The wind lashed across her angular face, the clouds above dark and ominous.

The glowing stones had brought her to this place as she looked down along the winding path. They called it the Twelve Apostles; in ancient times, the faithful had climbed it barefoot, a painful pilgrimage they performed once a year in honor of their absent God. Hermit priests had lived atop the mountain then, eking an existence off the land, determined to be as close as possible to their Heavenly Father. She scoffed at the thought of it, how gullible these mortal wretches were.

She rose and levitated effortlessly along the path, her only witness a startled crow unaccustomed to sharing its aerial domain. Alighting by a whitewashed stone marker, she brushed her hand against its weathered surface, the numbers barely legible after decades exposed to the elements. One marker for each mile, each a tribute to the men who had sat at the feet of Christ when he walked this earth. Eleven good men, she was led to believe. But every barrel contained a rotten apple.

The Judas Tree.

Mile Twelve, just below the mountain's summit, was marked differently. A solitary birch tree that never flowered, its naked branches reaching haphazardly into the heavens, a silent tribute to the one who had betrayed their Lord and Savior for a bag of silver. This was the boundary to her domain, and no man nor beast ever passed beneath its mournful gaze to crest the summit and look down upon the town and lough. They knew better. The last mortal who dared had been found the following morning, hanging from a stout rope, his distended stomach slit open, entrails spattered on the ground by the base of the trunk.

This was her mountain now.

And yet he continued to claim it as his, this fiend known as the *abhartach*. She hurled her presence across the town far below her and sensed his presence, holed up in a filthy lair, feeding from the throat of some poor unfortunate wench, his fifth of 1847. After that he needed only one more to satisfy his craving and pay the blood penance that he claimed was his right.

He wanted Kate Malone's girl as his sixth, just as she had been his sixth two centuries before. Then he thought he would crush her as well. Well, two could play at that game. She would let him think she was falling for his tricks, before producing her trump card. This Bloody Hands knew a lot but what he did not know was that the Malone girl possessed a power that would end him once and for all, allowing her to have her final vengeance on the town and the fiend that had watched her hang.

All around, the final pieces were falling into place. She had foreseen it all and her meticulous plans were finally coming to fruition. He taunted her from where he skulked in his lair, calling her out to confront him face-to-face. She had rejected his first offer, the time had not been right, but now was the moment to pounce. She would play the unsuspecting prey, thinking he had her exactly where he wanted, before crushing his fat neck beneath her foot.

Yes, she would meet the one they called Bloody Hands and let him think he had the upper hand; first him and then the preacher.

She had been watching Edgar for some time, his black heart masquerading beneath a cloak of godly virtue. He was the one who dared challenge her children, hunting down the one she needed to realize her final vengeance. He pursued Maggie Malone now, would chase her onto this very mountain. Well, let him come, fueled by a naive belief that his God would protect him and his followers from her brutal wrath. They would come, and they would die.

Kelly's Cellars

The stench of stale ale, mixed with staler sweat, hit Maggie like an anvil as she charged into the murky midst of Kelly's Cellars, closely followed by Jinks. A dozen or so surly males sat around a collection of tables, hands clasped around their tankards. Several glowered at the new arrivals, annoyed that their evening's inebriation had been so rudely interrupted. They came to Kelly's to forget and to be forgotten. Its clientele had nowhere better to go, and that was exactly what they wanted. Life had given up on them, so they had decided to return the favor. 1847 was no longer a concern to them, all that mattered was finding a few coins to purchase their next pint.

Maggie was momentarily distracted by the overbearing silence before remembering their predicament and diving under an unoccupied table next to the bar, closely followed by her brother. The bar was little more than a plank set across two sturdy barrels, but it served its purpose. From there, the establishment's fiery proprietor, all five foot four inches of him, ran his business with a steel fist. Maggie knew of the man through tales passed down by her father. Many a burly docker had erred the wrath of Jack Kelly after fancying their chances against the diminutive publican. He was small in stature but constructed of hard muscle and a right hook that few could handle. Of traveling stock, he had been the best pound-for-pound fighter on the circuit until settling down and investing his winnings in one of the most popular taverns in Belfast.

She looked up from underneath the table into his eyes, silently pleading that he did not give them away. Kelly responded with a quizzical look. She had no doubt he was accustomed to all sorts of shenanigans in his line of business, but where would his allegiances lie regarding a young woman and her little brother bursting onto his premises unannounced?

Their attention was diverted to the rear door as Thompson barreled through it, his two accomplices almost knocking him over in a desire to catch their quarry. Thompson shot them a foul look before recovering his balance and scanning the dimly lit tavern. He stepped towards the bar, ducking to avoid smacking his head on the low rafters. Jack Kelly did not apparently like tall men and had constructed his liquor empire accordingly.

"Mr. Thompson," he snarled through gritted teeth. "It's a rare pleasure to see you come through my doors. What can I get you and your two friends?"

Maggie knew that there was no love lost between the two men. Her father had regaled her with tales of a nasty turf war when Thompson's employer had attempted to put Kelly out of business so that his own licensing interests in the town could flourish. Jack, however, was not one to be cowed by bullies and had taught Thompson a hard lesson that resulted in the loss of two front teeth.

"Jack," sneered Thompson, his scowl causing the regulars to keep their eyes firmly fixed on their drinks. Making eye contact with a fellow like that never ended well, and their lives were miserable enough without crossing his path. His heavies scanned the bar for any sign of their prey, causing Maggie and Jinks to scuttle back into the furthest recess of the room, thankful that the poor glow from the dust-caked oil lamps did not extend as far as their corner of the pub. She winced as Jinks dug his nails into her forearm but dared not make a noise for fear of giving away their whereabouts.

"Did a girl and a wee fella come through here?" Thompson never took his eyes off Kelly, scanning his features for the slightest giveaway that he might be lying. He was dueling with the wrong man, Maggie knew, for Jack Kelly backed down to nobody, especially a bully boy like Thompson with ideas above his station.

"Can't say I have," he replied, wiping his hands on a grubby apron that he permanently wore around his waist. "I don't let young ones in here. My customers come here to get away from screaming *wains*. Now, if there's nothing else, I'll bid you good day. I've a pub to run, and I don't have..."

Thompson's clenched fist crashed down onto the plank separating them, causing several patrons to jump. Maggie wrapped her arm around Jinks, who buried his face into her shoulder to stifle a scream. Kelly leaned forward, both hands clenched on his side of the plank, knuckles whitening as each second of silence dragged, neither man willing to be the first to drop their gaze. What little background noise there had been in the inn vanished as everyone else looked on, afraid to blink lest they miss the climax of this developing drama.

"If I find out you're lying to me, Kelly, me and my boys will come back here and burn your bloody bar to the ground. With you in it, if need be."

He paused, accustomed to men falling apart before his taunts and threats. His heavies looked on, eyes glistening at the prospect of a brawl where they could display their pugilistic skills. Maggie squeezed her eyes shut, Jinks pinned against her chest, and whispered a silent prayer to the Black Lady, begging her to send aid swiftly before they were discovered and beaten black and blue.

"I look forward to you trying that, Mr. Thompson. I most sincerely do." Kelly's voice was little more than a grated whisper, and the regulars furthest from the bar had to lean forward and strain their ears to catch his words. The intent, however, was loud and clear. Here was a man who could not be intimidated and was willing to go toe-to-toe with any bullying upstart who tried such a trick on him.

Thompson's eye twitched the slightest tremor, but enough for Kelly to seize the initiative provided by this minuscule gesture of weakness. The publican leaned back and folded his arms, revealing an impressive set of biceps threatening to burst from his shirt.

"I'll bid you and your associates a good evening, Mr. Thompson. Now, if you'll excuse me, I have an establishment to run here and thirsty customers to serve." He turned and, with a flick of the grimy towel he was holding, dismissed a furious Thompson.

Thompson swiveled round, glowering at the sea of faces studying him from the assorted tables.

"What are you dogs looking at?" Rather than endure further humiliation, he stormed out of the bar, kicking over a vacant chair in a last, futile effort to restore his credibility. His heavies sheepishly exited in his wake, looking disappointed that the situation had not deteriorated further. Maggie knew, however, that Jack Kelly's fighting prowess was legendary, and even Thompson and his thugs would have struggled had it come to a free-for-all. The hinges of the door squealed in protest as it closed, and a collective calm fell over the bar.

"You can come out now," said Kelly, folding the towel and sighing. He watched with a bemused expression on his weathered face as first Maggie and then Jinks extricated themselves from beneath the table and stood awkwardly before him. The majority of his customers had already lost interest, returning to their slurred conversations and jaded thoughts.

"Sorry, Mr. Kelly," mumbled Maggie, peeking out from beneath her disturbed fringe. Jinks loitered behind her, suddenly lost for words in the presence of the infamous Jack Kelly.

"You do know children are not permitted on these premises. If word got out, I could lose my license."

The nervous siblings exchanged guilty glances, uncertain how to reply. Maggie knew they owed Kelly a favor, but his stern gaze left her in no doubt that he had been distinctly unimpressed by their dramatic entrance. She was also deeply conscious that the longer they remained, the more likely it would be that Thompson or the Reverend Edgar would discover their whereabouts. She began to slowly inch backward towards the main entrance, stretching out a hand to guide Jinks in the same direction.

"Leaving so soon?" Kelly moved around the far barrel with surprising ease, and Maggie and Jinks found themselves cut off from their intended escape route. He was a small man but compact and lean, with not an ounce of fat on him. He looked closer, and his features lightened as recognition dawned.

"You're John Malone's *wains*, aren't youse? I thought I recognized you, girl. Your Da owes me two pounds, the scoundrel."

"I'm sorry, Mr. Kelly sir, but we haven't a penny to our name. Please don't call the Constabulary. Thompson has half of them in his back pocket, and if he gets his hands on us, then..."

"Och, hold your tongue, wee girl. I'm not going to tell nobody. The less dealings I have with the Constabulary, the better. And as for that runt,

Thompson, the next time he darkens my door, he'll find himself being carried out."

"Oh," replied Maggie, not sure how to respond. Thankfully, her younger brother had regained his voice.

"We'll do whatever you need done around here, Mr. Kelly, to pay what our father owes. Maggie can cook and clean, and I'll run errands anywhere in the town for you. I'm as quick as a flash I am." He stood proudly, attempting to add an inch to his diminutive frame. Maggie could not help but grin at his efforts to protect her, and even Kelly's granite features showed signs of softening.

"Will you now, lad? And how long do you think it will take for your swift feet to clear your father's debt?" He knelt and placed his hands on his knees so that his eyes met those of Jinks.

"Er...a week?"

Kelly sprung back to his full height with a fulsome laugh, earning a few bemused looks from his regulars. This was a side of the publican they were unaccustomed to, and they were not sure if they appreciated it.

"Never worry yourself, wee man," replied Kelly, still chortling much to the bemusement of Maggie and Jinks. "I appreciate the offer, but I've more than enough people in my employment without hiring you two. But thank you. It takes guts to face up to your responsibilities at such a young age."

Jinks paused, uncertain if Kelly was being sincere or merely playing with him before shrugging and going with the flow.

"My mother always taught us to settle our debts. Reckon we owe you... for my Da."

"I knew your mother."

Maggie tensed, uncertain where the conversation was headed. Her mother had been a pillar of the community, she had never tasted alcohol in her life. What would this rough and ready publican know about her? Their world had been rocked enough these past few days, and she was unsure as to how many more startling revelations Jinks and she could take. Seeming to sense their discomfort, Kelly did his best to smile reassuringly. Maggie was uncertain whether it had the desired effect. He was a man accustomed to banging heads together, not winning hearts and minds with kind words and soothing looks.

"She used to come here to collect your father when he was the worse for wear. Many a night, I helped her haul him out of here. She always offered to settle his debts, just like you did, but I refused her as well. I have all the money I need and then some. She was a good woman. I was sorry to hear of your loss." He shuffled awkwardly, toying with the edge of his apron.

Jinks nodded in return, an unspoken acknowledgment of the gesture and the heart-breaking memories it conjured up. He looked to Maggie, again lost for words. She patted his shoulder and faced the landlord, oblivious to the drunken murmuring and rattling of tankards. A bearded customer stumbled erratically towards the bar, on the brink of tumbling headfirst onto the sawdust-strewn floor.

"Thank you, sir. We appreciate your words and your recent protection. But we must be on our way. We have...have...an urgent appointment to attend." The lie sat uncomfortably on her tongue, like a mouthful of ash. It was not in her nature to veer away from the truth, but unnatural behavior was increasingly becoming her normality. She began to edge toward the main entrance, Jinks obediently following her cue.

"An urgent appointment, you say," replied Kelly, an amused twinkle in his eye. "Well, who am I to stand in the way of a young lady and gentleman with such an arduous schedule? But, if I were you, I'd give the front entrance a miss. If you don't want to run into your friends again, that is. This way, if you please." Without another word, he turned and marched behind the bar, ignoring the bearded drunk who vainly waved a coin in the air, attempting to place an order.

"What do you think, Mags, is it a trap?" Jinks eyed the retreating Kelly suspiciously, uncertain if they should follow. She knew that his trust in adults had never been particularly high, and it was eroding by the day. Maggie sighed and shrugged her shoulders, temporarily at a loss. She was so tired, and hopelessness threatened to overwhelm her, like a dark wave sucking her further out from the sanctity of a moonlit shore.

"I do not know, brother, but what choice do we have? If Thompson or that cleric get their hands on us, we're finished."

She looked towards Kelly, now standing at a door that she had not noticed before, off to the side of the shadowy establishment. He jerked his head, mild impatience etched across his furrowed brow. He was not a man to offend or keep waiting. Groaning inwardly, she hitched her skirts and wove through the tables, ignoring the mumbled greetings and half-hearted attempts at conversation from an assortment of men who could not remember the last time they had seen a woman, let alone a young woman, on the premises. Jinks followed at a half-jog, keen to remain at arm's length in case one of them sought to grapple him.

Kelly held the door open with an outstretched arm, guiding them inside before leading them down a narrow flight of creaking stairs toward another door. He shouldered it open, and they found themselves in a cobbled alley, a row of wooden barrels opposite them against the far wall. A fat rat with a tail the length of her forearm scurried past Maggie, causing her to hop backward, barely holding back a strangled scream.

"Don't be such a *ginny-anne*," said Jinks, rolling his eyes towards Kelly in a gesture of manly camaraderie.

The publican winked at him, his sullen eyes brightening slightly. "You've got spirit, wee lad, I'll give you that. Now get yourselves onto those barrels and over that wall. It will take you to Squeeze Gut Entry. Turn right and then right again at the gate on its hinges. Over that patch of rough ground and left at the manure heap. Right and then left. It will bring you to the far side of Hercules Street. That's Wallace territory. Thompson and his goons won't dare set foot there. After that, I wish you well, for you're on your own. If anyone asks me or my customers, we ain't see youse."

He turned to head back into the bar, his good deed done for another day. Maggie knew that his past had been far from sparkling, and he was no saint in the here and now either, but beneath the gruff exterior, she believed that Jack Kelly was a man who knew right from wrong. He fought hard, but he fought fair, and Thompson's mob against a young woman and her wee brother was anything but fair.

"Mr. Kelly?"

"Aye, lass," said Kelly, peering over his shoulder.

"Thank you again."

"You're welcome. Now get out of here." He shut the door behind him.

Maggie heard him yell, "Quit that carry-on, Seamy, or I'll throw you in the Lagan myself." And Jack Kelly, publican, pugilist, and protector of waifs and strays, returned to his work.

Old Nell

The stone burned against Maggie's hip, nestled in the deepest pocket of her skirts. She winced, but it was a reassuring pain, the dying promise of a mother who had never let her down in life. A mother who was now, from beyond the abyss, casting a protective web around Jinks and her. Maggie hauled one leg, then the other, over the wall before letting go, hoping for a soft landing. Her knees bent and braced as they connected with the hard, unforgiving cobbles. Then she was running again, Jinks by her side, desperately trying to remember the directions that Jack Kelly had barked at them less than a minute before.

They moved through the broken gate, across the waste ground, and past the brutal but reassuring stench of one of the town's many manure heaps. Maggie pulled her shawl across her mouth and nostrils as she stumbled past, to stymie the stench. They neared the end of Hercules Street, where she and her people rarely strayed, the Protestant end where the Wallace family ruled with ruthless efficiency. Even the ever-wandering Jinks and his mates never ventured this far into enemy territory, where the Orangemen marched, and any stray Catholic was guaranteed a good kicking before being dumped by the roadside.

"What do we do now?" gasped Jinks, their feet finding cobbles again as they darted down another narrow alley.

"I don't know, Jinks. Just run. I'll think of something when we..."

The comforting warmth of the stone intensified to a searing heat that sent her tumbling to the ground, and she skinned both palms as she reached out to break her fall. Her body jerked as a foreign power surged through her body, forcing her limbs to respond to its urgings.

"What's wrong, Mags?" Jinks yelped, skidding to a halt and dropping to his sister's side as she curled into a protective ball on the uneven ground.

Maggie could only grimace in response, riding the wave of pain that wracked her body. It felt as if her every nerve end had been set alight, sizzling touch papers racing inwards until she felt her heart would explode. She was vaguely aware of her brother's panicked words as she opened her eyes and looked into the night sky. Amazement filled her as she saw the town's perpetual blanket of smog had cleared, laying the heavens bare in their starry majesty. She watched as a bright light raced across her field of vision, its fiery tail cutting a swathe through the indigo depths of space.

"Woah. What the hell was that?"

Maggie watched the star explode in a ball of dazzling white, illuminating Jinks's awestruck expression. What the two did not know was that a collective gasp simultaneously rolled across Belfast. Children watched open-mouthed as devout mothers made the sign of the cross and fidgeted with their rosary beads. It was an omen, but a sign of what, they did not know. 1847 would be a year like no other, a year that none of them would forget. Those of them that lived to tell the tale.

"Hand me the stone, child."

Maggie realized the pain was no more. Where the fireball had streaked through the skies a second ago, a deeply wrinkled face now looked down at her. The woman was of indeterminate age, but her back was straight, and her blue eyes twinkled beneath a head of graying curls. She wore a plain dress and shawl but carried herself with an air of distinction and strength. Maggie immediately sensed that she was in the presence of goodness.

"Did...did she send you?" she whispered, accepting the hand offered by the old woman, hauling Maggie to her feet with alarming ease.

"If you mean our Lady, then yes, in a manner of speaking. She holds the power that sets the stones alight. Now, hand it to me. Its work is done for the night."

Maggie nodded, digging into her pocket and removing the stone, which was now cold to the touch.

The woman smiled and held out her cupped hands, receiving the stone with almost reverential respect. Before another word could be spoken, she flung her hands into the air, launching the stone skyward.

Maggie and Jinks covered their heads with their hands, fully expecting to be peppered with a shower of tiny meteorites. After several seconds, they looked up in astonishment. The stone had vanished as if it had sprouted wings and fluttered off into the ether.

"Now, come with me," said the woman, turning sharply and setting off at a brisk pace. She followed the route that Jack Kelly had told them to take along a series of narrow, weed-riddled alleys until they emerged onto the lower end of Hercules Street. Gas lamps cast an eerie glow over a marble building across the street; the sound of drums could be heard, their staccato beat accompanied by a rising melody of flutes.

"Bloody Orangemen. Always making a racket that would wake the dead themselves." The old woman grimaced at the building before striding past it toward the bottom of the street.

"Is this safe?" Maggie sought to remain calm but was acutely aware that every step took them deeper into Wallace territory. Their situation was perilous enough without being yanked into a dark doorway and pummeled with fists and hob-nailed boots.

"Worry not, child," replied the woman. "They see us not. We are under our Lady's protection from this point onwards." As if to illustrate her point, two rough-looking men staggered around the corner and passed them without a second glance, immersed in a heated conversation about a game of cards that had ended badly for one of them.

"Can they not see us?" croaked Jinks.

"They see what our Lady allows them to see. No more and no less." She stopped and turned to face them before pointing back the way they had come.

"She has sent me to bring you to her, for these are dark days, and they come for us."

"They?" Jinks swallowed hard. "Who's they?"

"The money lender. The man of God. The *abhartach*. They all come. For it is time, and she is ready. It has been released, and they will pay a heavy price."

"A what-atach? Jesus, missus. I haven't a notion what you're on about."

"Hold your tongue, you cheeky wee *shite*," hissed Maggie, aiming a swipe in the direction of her brother's head, who ducked, easily evading the blow. "I apologize for my brother, madam. We are grateful for any help you can provide." She offered the old woman a weak smile who, in turn, considered Maggie, her features softening.

"I knew your mother. She was a good woman with a strong faith. Our Lady will honor her memory by saving you and your brother from what is coming."

"Coming? I don't understand. The town is already in turmoil. There are no jobs, no food. They say the fever is upon us now. Are you telling me that our Lady is responsible? I thought she was a force of good, of kindness. That's what my mother taught me before she..." Maggie struggled to finish the sentence.

The woman nodded, acknowledging her pain. "You may call me Nell, for that is what everyone else calls me. Now, quickly, we must waste no more time with idle chatter. She awaits us."

Annabelle had no recollection of how she reached Carson's Court, but somehow, she arrived, edging into the moonlit courtyard. It was empty, with the exception of a middle-aged woman who was struggling to peg a petticoat to a sagging clothesline. She finally succeeded, but her exertions took their toll, and she doubled over, a rasping cough consuming her frail figure. She turned away, unleashing a mouthful of sticky phlegm onto the cobbles, before straightening and leaning back against a door that Annabelle presumed was the entrance to her home.

"Excuse me. Madam? Do you require assistance?" She inched toward the woman, who looked up, unaware she had an audience.

"Who are you?" she asked aggressively, sizing Annabelle up and down. "We don't see many fancy frocks like yours 'round here."

"I'm a friend of a neighbor of yours, I believe. Margaret Malone?"

The woman eyed her suspiciously, and Annabelle noticed for the first time the thin sheen of sweat that coated her forehead. Annabelle was no physician, but this woman was unwell, even her untrained eye could tell. The woman considered the name, mulling it over before realization dawned, and she scowled at Annabelle.

"You mean that little madam, Maggie Malone. And her nuisance of a brother. Has ideas above her station, that one. Thinks she's a proper lady, but she's no better than the rest of us." She paused as another coughing fit overcame her, reaching into her skirt pocket for a handkerchief that was once white but had seen much better days. She held it over her mouth until the coughing subsided. Annabelle could not help but notice bloody flecks before the woman stuffed it back into her pocket.

"Yes, that's her. Do you know where she might be?"

"Probably halfway to Dublin by now if she knows what's good for her. Billy Thompson and his men were snooping 'round here earlier looking for her. Reckon her deadbeat father owes money, and they're wanting her to settle up. By the sounds of it, they wrecked their room and turned it upside down. If I was Miss Fancy Drawers, I wouldn't be coming back here in a hurry."

Annabelle opened her mouth to reply, determined to elicit whatever information she could from the haggard woman, but before she could utter another word, the courtyard was lit up by a brilliant light as if the sun had risen prematurely to breach the nocturnal gloom. Annabelle raised an arm to shield her eyes and looked toward the source of the light as a silvery streak raced overhead, a distant rumble marking its path.

"Mother Mary, have mercy on our souls, for it's surely the end," wailed the woman as she dropped to her knees, cheeks wet with tears. All around her, the courtyard burst into life as men, women, and children streamed from every door to witness the surreal sight arcing overhead.

"It's a demon, come to take us all."

"Sweet Jesus. Forgive us. Rescue us from our troubles."

"Ma, is that the Black Lady? She can take flight; she has the faerie magic in her."

Annabelle spun and twisted to avoid the swirl of bodies around her but was tossed to the ground, curling into a ball to avoid being trampled to death. A boy fell in front of her and screamed as several boots clattered across his exposed back. Annabelle readjusted her position and crouched beside him, forming a protective shield as bodies passed either side of her, attempting to flee the fireball or obtain a better vantage point. It was all the boy needed to regain his feet and scuttle under a cart missing a wheel nestled in the corner of the yard. Not knowing what else to do, Annabelle followed suit, the boy shuffling across to allow her to join him.

"This is all my fault," he moaned, his chin resting on knees barely covered by threadbare trousers. He stifled a cough that Annabelle was becoming all too familiar with, one that had swept across the town, claiming poor and rich alike with its ominous rattle. She knew she was putting herself at risk of falling ill but was beyond caring now, such was her fear for Maggie and Jinks's safety.

"Don't be silly." She hoped it was a reassuring smile, but the boy merely stared glumly ahead at the wall of legs crossing in all directions beyond the sanctuary of the cart.

"Where are your parents?"

"In there," he replied, pointing toward a house to their left. "But they're both dead. I'm on my own." He spluttered again before wiping the sleeve of his shirt across his snotty face.

"Dead? Had they been unwell? Surely not. Let me go find a doctor, I can get help."

"Wasting your time, Miss. I've seen enough death to know they ain't coming back. Half the boat was coughing before we got off. It'll get us all in the end." Annabelle wished she could summon up the words to make it better, to ease his pain and loneliness. But she could offer no soothing platitudes. The next time she looked, the boy had melted away from under the cart into the surrounding forest of legs.

Perhaps, this time, it was the end after all.

"Do you see it, Andrew? Do you? The Lord is guiding us, he has looked down upon his people and heard our cry. Hallelujah. Praise be." The Reverend Edgar punched the cover of his Bible with delight as his long legs devoured the ground.

Andrew Blake and a gaggle of church elders and town officials struggled to keep abreast of him as the preacher forced his way through the crowds gazing at the mesmerizing sight flaring across the sky.

Blake could only nod miserably, a broken man. He realized now that his greed had precipitated the runaway train that was the clergyman's fanatical zeal. If word were to get out that Jeremiah Morgan had greased his palm to oil the creaking administrative wheels and bypass harbor regulations, his political career was finished. The fever that had disembarked from the Samhara was now spreading through the town like wildfire, and Edgar was seizing on the growing panic and hysteria like a deranged fiend.

After their hurried brandy, the preacher had called an emergency meeting of the church elders, which comprised half the town council. Edgar declared it a call for spiritual guidance, which largely involved him roaring at and badgering his terrified audience until they conceded there must be a spiritual reason for the recent misfortunes that had befallen their once great town. Blake hadn't uttered a word during the gathering, aware that his deal with Morgan was now imploding before his eyes, and his political career now hung by the finest of threads.

He had sheepishly followed, as Edgar swept around the corner onto Bank Street, his black overcoat billowing outwards like the leathery wings of an avenging demon, his face the color of hellfire. Ahead of them, the crowds parted like a hot knife through butter, for here was a man possessed by a righteous anger that would not be satisfied until justice had been served and the root of this recent devilry was ripped from the heart of the town once and for all. "Get out of my way, you heathens."

They reached the narrow entry that led onto Carson's Court. The spindly arm of the Reverend Edgar shoved a brace of curious onlookers aside before plunging into the courtyard, followed by Blake and the remainder of his hesitant entourage. Edgar took one look at the bedlam on all sides before asserting his authority and grabbing the thistle by its thorns.

"Silence!" he boomed. The command reverberated through the courtyard as the residents stopped what they were doing and turned as one to study the new arrival. Edgar's eyes narrowed and he scanned the crowd before him, before launching into another round of thunderous rhetoric.

"And the Lord sayeth, 'Thou shalt not suffer a witch to live!'"

His words fell on a stunned audience as the sick and the starving battled to process the sight of the tall, gaunt figure, his pale face bathed in the fading light of the starry light passing overhead. The preacher surveyed his new congregation, the Good Book held above his widow's peak. Behind him, Sergeant Quinn and a dozen of his men fanned out behind the elders and officials. It was their second visit to Carson's Court in as many days, but this time, their wooden batons were drawn from the outset. They had been told to expect trouble and God help any fool who tried to obstruct the Queen's business this night. Heads would be cracked, and blood would flow. Protestant, Catholic; it didn't matter. They had been promised a shilling a man if they turned out tonight and did the cleric's bidding. Edgar turned and gave Quinn a sickly smile, the gruff Sergeant nodding in response.

"There is one amongst you who has brought great misfortune upon us all. One who thrives in the darkness that is shrouding this town."

The residents of Carson's Court fidgeted before the wall of men facing them. Children huddled at their mother's sides, the women fearfully gripping their shoulders. Several of the older men exchanged glances, silently weighing up their chances if a brawl did break out. Most of them were handy with their fists if called upon, but taking on Quinn and his bully boys was a whole different proposition.

Sensing the latent tension, Edgar relaxed his shoulders and lowered the Bible, his next words tempered with uncharacteristic softness.

Blake cringed at the saccharine tone, which he knew only too well. Here was a man used to getting his way, a master of oily manipulation and deceit.

"My children, I know you are of a different faith to me. But we all worship the same God, do we not?"

His question was largely greeted by indifference, but a smattering of the residents nodded hesitantly, one woman making the sign of the cross as she did so. Cracks were already beginning to form along the united front offered by the Carson's Court residents. A few stifled coughs from the rear of the throng only focused less willing minds on the preacher's words. He smiled, clasped his hands, and waited. Blake, a fine orator himself, knew that silence could be just as effective a weapon if wielded in the proper manner.

The seconds dragged, but he knew they would talk. They always talked in the end.

"You ain't our priest, but it's the Malone girl, isn't it? I'm sick of sitting around watching our kids die. She's to blame for all this. Doesn't go to Mass anymore. She's a wicked one, just like her mother."

"I've seen her doing strange stuff at her front door. Mumbling weird words. They weren't no Christian prayers, that's for sure. About the same time as they started finding the dead girls up in Smithfield."

"I heard her talking to that dog the night it dug up the McDowell child. Reckon she cast a spell on it, reckon she's cast a spell on the whole bloody lot of us."

Edgar held his hands aloft again to quell the clamor of agitated, fearful voices. The dam had burst as a flood of evidence spewed forth from desperate lips. That was the beauty of the eternal battle between good and evil—one never had to look too far for a suitable villain.

Sergeant Quinn took a step forward, his face an emotionless mask. He was a man of the law, and Blake knew that he had little time for these people and their superstitious babbling. Quinn had a job to do, one he had been well-paid to carry out.

"You all know me, and you all know what will happen if the truth doesn't come out. Grave robbing is a very serious matter in the eyes of the law. If that's what is found to have happened, then the girl is in a lot of trouble. Who here is willing to stand before the magistrate and testify to this?" Quinn was met with a wall of silence, punctuated with only more coughs and spluttering.

It was one thing to make such accusations at your front door, quite another to stand up in front of the entire town and swear on the Holy Bible that their long-standing neighbor was marked by the Devil.

"I'll stand up in your court."

All eyes turned, and more than one mouth fell open as the woman pushed her way to the front of the crowd. She had aged years in less than a week, her mousy-brown hair now shot through with strands of gray. A slim woman to begin with, what little flesh she had left now hung from bones that jutted through at painful angles. Her eyes, once bright and vivacious, were muddy puddles of sludge.

"Eileen, you don't want to be saying that. The girl might not be right, but she's still one of our—"

Eileen McDowell turned and snarled, her actions daring any one of them to dissuade her. Her child was dead, and though she had other little ones who needed to be clothed and fed, she seemed to care no more. The loss of the wee man, her baby blue eyes, had sucked what little fight she had left out of her failing body.

"I'll say what I want when I want. To hell with Maggie Malone, to hell with you all."

"Step forward, madam," encouraged Edgar.

Blake was slightly surprised at how easy it had been. He attempted a courteous nod but stalled as the woman stared through him as if he were an illusion, before Edgar resorted to a more direct approach.

"What will you say of this Margaret Malone?"

"I will say that she is a daughter of Satan, as her mother was. I will say that I heard them cavorting in the dead of night, saw them copulating with a cloven-hoofed beast, and watched as they promised my unborn child to their dark Lord. The hunger may have taken the mother, but the bitch she spawned persevered until my child was born and snatched from me again. My baby boy, burning in hell now." Her rising voice cracked, and she fell to her knees, shoulders heaving as guttural sobs consumed her.

Nobody went to her aid. An excruciating silence fell over the crowd as personal tragedies were silently processed. Was Eileen speaking the truth, or was it merely the crazed grief of a woman pushed to the end, and beyond, by life and its twisted paths?

Blake scanned the crowd, watching for the next crack in the ice to appear. He did not have long to wait, and when it came, the waters burst forth in a torrent of repressed anger and sorrow.

"Yes. I saw them as well. The Malone girl. She's the cause of all this."

"I had words with her one morning, and by evening, my whole body had broken out in hives."

"I saw her talking to that Rafferty girl the night she was murdered. Reckon she lured her into Smithfield so Bloody Hands could have her."

"She did. It's true. And I heard her brother was with her. Maybe he's in on it as well."

Edgar turned in triumph, his overcoat cutting a dark arc through the babble of confessions, leaving the recording of details to Sergeant Quinn and his colleagues. His work was done. He had his scapegoat, his sacrificial lamb.

Blake nipped at his heels as they raced back through the entry. "Can this be true, Archibald? Witchcraft? It's 1847. Surely those dark times are behind us."

"You heard the people, Mr. Blake. They are falling over each other to testify."

They emerged onto Bank Street, Blake glad to be rid of the chaos raging in the courtyard. The night had reclaimed its grip on the town, the fiery intrusion above no more now than a vivid image seared into the memories of all who had witnessed it. Edgar increased his pace, for there was still much work ahead. He was in the hands of the Lord now, guiding him along a path that few were asked to tread and even fewer accepted.

"But that woman was deranged. She did not know what she was saying…"

Edgar stopped, turning so violently that Blake stumbled backward; he raised a hand, convincing the town guardian that the holy man was about to strike him. The hand hung in the air before dropping slowly and gently stroking the cheek of the terrified Blake. The preacher smiled, savoring the trembling flesh beneath his touch.

"She will say whatever we want her to say, Andrew. They all will. They are papist scum, but the Lord is using them just as he is using us. This will be a great victory and the deaf shall hear the truth, the scales will fall from their eyes, the shackles from their wrists. Belfast will rise again, stronger in faith and industry. I will build a new church, and all will flock to it, whatever their denomination. Can you not hear the death knell of the Roman faith that has cursed you and me for so many years?"

"I don't know. I think so. But I…"

"Or would you rather the truth of your transaction with Captain Jeremiah Morgan be known to all?"

He knew.

Blake dropped his head, the shame of his greedy ambition leaving him nowhere to go, the last argument withering on his defeated lips. "Of course not."

"Excellent," said Edgar, dropping his hand to the other man's shoulder. "Then, let us proceed. We have our witnesses. Now all we must do is find the girl."

Blake nodded meekly. And so, the fate of Maggie Malone was signed, sealed, and delivered. Before a gavel had been struck, a holy oath had been sworn. Edgar had his witch, and Belfast had the answer to all its woes. The rest was immaterial. She would hang, and Edgar would have his new church, its pews packed and collection plates overflowing.

The Lord truly did work in mysterious ways.

A Deal Is Struck

This time, he knew she would answer his call.

The wind whipped across the courtyard, picking up debris and sending it scuttling over the cobbles in a chaotic dance. He smirked, recalling the night they had first met two hundred years ago. On that occasion, he had secured the upper hand, an advantage that had swept her to the gallows and secured him the sixth succulent kill he cherished more than anything, a death that had allowed him to retain his stranglehold over this land. The town had grown since then, its rooftops now extending in all directions from the lough. Industry was thriving, or it had been until the toxic twins of famine and disease had bitten down hard on Belfast's wealth and success. A misfortune that the witch was now callously attempting to use her own devices to destroy his people. Well, he would not stand idly by and let her have her way with those whose blood his very existence relied upon.

"Well, come on. I haven't all night to be playing your tiresome games. There's killing to be done." He scratched at the graying stubble on his chin, in stark contrast to a bald head that reflected the sole gas lamp illuminating this rarely used thoroughfare on the edge of the butcher's district. He smiled to himself. Yes, he was at home here, where the coppery tang of blood hung ever present in the air, thick with glorious memories of strangled cries and the thrill of that first, delicious arterial spurt across the slick, wet walls where he prowled and took what was his.

"Patience never was your strong card, was it?"

He swiveled where he lurched in the center of the courtyard, searching for the mellifluous voice that filled the vacant space, dripping with sarcasm and barely veiled contempt at his presence. How dare she challenge his authority. This was his town, and he'd be damned if some bitch would come off that miserable mountain and snatch it from him.

"You weren't so cocky the last time we met," he spat, a grain of uncertainty underpinning his gruff tone. "A snapped neck tends to kill conversation even in the most talkative of souls, wouldn't you agree?"

She nibbled at that tasty snack, stepping out of the shifting shadows and throwing back the hood of a dowdy, nondescript cape to reveal a head of tumbling locks that would have turned every head in the town had she been to parade through its parks in the afternoons, with all the fine ladies and gentlemen who normally promenaded at that time of day.

Those that weren't lying sweating and shaking on their deathbeds.

"I stepped into the afterlife, and yet here I am, back to rain on your obscene parade. You didn't think I'd turn my back on your treachery that easily, did you? I am a woman who is prepared to wait for what she wants. And here you are. A dish served cold for me to feast upon at my leisure."

"You're a dirty, filthy witch, and I'd have your guts smeared on the walls of this courtyard if I didn't need you alive right now." He took a step toward her, corded veins straining on his thick neck. The bitch had it coming and then some, but he managed to rein in his spite and hold back from ripping that pretty neck from her shoulders.

"Temper, temper. No need for such a foul-mouthed tirade. I'm here now. Speak your terms." She took another step toward him, and he hesitated slightly before speaking again, the power flowing off her in languorous waves, taunting him that this reincarnation of Fionnuala O'Kane was a much more daunting opponent than the frightened young woman he had previously bested. He licked his lips, his tongue darting from his mouth like an agitated viper, before responding.

"I hear you've got a little helper now. Fresh as a daisy. Unlike her mother..." He paused, studying her intently for a reaction, a crack in her impassive mask, but there was nothing, no frown or twitch to indicate that he had wormed beneath her devices.

"That was...unfortunate, but yes, the girl shows great promise." She lifted her chin defiantly, emerald eyes twinkling with curiosity, he thought. She's interested, a deal can be struck here. Oh yes, a most tasty deal.

"Bet she tastes good. Sweet like strawberries, straight off the bush." He wiped a grubby hand across his twisted mouth, salivating at the thought of lowering his aching incisors to that pale, vulnerable throat. It was all he could do to shake the delightfully intrusive thought from his addled mind and focus on more immediate matters.

"If you so desire her, then I'm sure we can come to some form of amicable arrangement." She smiled again, a smile devoid of a shred of humanity.

"What? You'd give up your darling protégé? To me? Do you think I came down with the last shower?" He was right, she was obviously up to something, plotting his demise via some nefarious, underhand method. Yet, still, a tempting offer. He considered her as she stood before him, skin as translucent as the moon's surface, the only color that shock of red hair as vivid as the sanguinary handprints he left for all to see at the scenes of his crimes.

"Take it or leave it." Her expression edged towards indifference, and he shuffled uncomfortably, sensing he had overplayed the offer. "I will make the offer only once." She pulled the hood back up over her head and made to turn away from him, to melt back into the inky night, no doubt returning to that desolate mountain she haunted. He tensed, weighing up the options before him. A decision had to be made, their negotiations now teetering on the cusp of dissolution.

"Let's say I were to take it. What do you ask of me?" The hint of a smile left him in no doubt that she was interested again. Back and forth like a spider weaving its web. Yet, who was the spider and who was the fly, he wondered, who hunted who on this night where the future of tens of thousands hung in the balance?

She shrugged as if the question was so trifling that she could barely find the enthusiasm to reply to it. "Well, there's the beauty of it for you. Nothing. Absolutely nothing. Take the girl, make her your sixth, then leave me be, and allow me to do what I must do. I will make this town mine. Its descendants shall pay the price for allowing me to hang. And I will overlook your part in my demise."

"I will be back, you know. I always return. But what will I return to in two hundred years' time? Will I have a town to return to, for I shall have my penance, by hook or by crook." He began to circle her, and she instinctively reacted, matching him step for step, a quiet, malevolent dance. One slip, one word that showed her intentions were anything but genuine, and he would be supping from her gaping throat tonight.

"That's the beauty of it. You will return to a city. I will give you a thousand fresh throats, a million, though you say you need only six. These streets will run red until the end of time, I will make sure of that. They will kill their enemies and each other in such numbers that the sweet blood you so desire in the girl will run through all their veins the next time you deign us with your presence. Imagine the feast you will have."

He nodded, continuing to circle her as he imagined the succulent sensation of dining on the blood of the *cailleach* forever more.

"Seems an offer too good to be true. What's the catch?"

She laughed, a melodious tinkle that enamored as much as it infuriated him. "Oh, believe me, I am too good to be true, and that is why you will say yes."

"Oh, will I now?"

"You will."

Silence again as he considered the various permutations. He had called her, yet it was she who was calling him out, bringing their little dialogue to such an intriguing conclusion. The silence stretched between them, a flicker of mirth dancing across her lips the longer he mulled over her offer. Eventually, he leaned back, decision made.

"Very well. But if this is a double cross..."

"I can assure you it isn't. I've grown tired of our feud. I want what is mine, and if that means accommodating your unedifying needs, then so be it."

"I will have my blood penance. I'll sup from my bowl, or I swear I'll cut you open."

She sighed, and he relented. The six were everything, and the lure of the blood of a *cailleach* was already starting to niggle at the outer edges of his being. It was a great, all-consuming need that tore away the last nagging doubts and firmed his resolve.

"Bring her to me then. After the fifth. To the entry. Where I marked the wall the last time."

She stirred, a fragment of a frown taking hold. And what else? Was that irritation?

"I'll do no such thing. I will have need for her on my mountain soon and after that, she is yours. How you get her to the courtyard is not my concern. Just do it and do it quickly before I change my mind."

The shriek of fighting cats nearby breached their bubble. He would watch her, study the girl, and identify her weaknesses, the chink in her armor that would bring her to the place they called Carson's Court, where his powers were at their greatest. To the heart of the town, his town, where the blood flowed thick and fast.

He opened his mouth to launch one final barb in the witch's direction, but she was gone, vanished into the thick darkness from whence she had come. Back to that damnable mountain, no doubt, to plot and sulk the remainder of the night. That was the difference between them. Vision. Ambition. Her blinkered hunger for vengeance was understandable, but then what? She had no plan beyond crushing the town. Whereas he played the long game, saw the bigger picture: a city teeming with the blood of the *cailleach's* descendants, a delectable well that would never run dry.

That was the difference between them. For she was but a common witch, and he was a god. He turned and made his own way from the court-yard as the first fingers of dawn began to edge across the cobbles. There was work to be done and now that he had removed the final hurdle in his path, the clock was ticking. The girl was his, and his legacy was secured.

He would have his sixth. He would have his blood penance. And if he did not, then he would walk the slopes of that mountain himself and watch her swing again. This time from her precious tree. He'd mark its bark with his hands. Feed it the blood of its vile mistress.

Of that, there would be no doubt.

I Am But A Goddess

They followed Nell, winding through the maze of alleys and courtyards in the heart of Wallace territory like ghosts through a graveyard. More than once, Maggie's breath caught in her throat, heart thumping against her ribcage as they encountered members of the gang patrolling their territory with clubs and sticks in hand. Barely a handspan separated them as they passed, yet the men trudged on, unaware of their presence. The Black Lady cloaked their movements, the air around them filled with ancient wards and spells.

Eventually, their journey progressed from cramped streets onto open ground. They left the town behind as they traversed a series of water-logged fields, the moonlight glistening off temporary lakes of lying water. Their only company was the occasional cow, raising its head from nocturnal grazing to lazily watch them trudge past. Maggie stumbled several times, the soggy, uneven ground rising to meet her, but each time, Nell's strong grip restored her footing. The older woman did not speak, her eyes never straying from the brooding mass rising before them.

She was taking them onto the mountain.

Jinks squelched behind them, every step forward a chore as the sucking mud threatened to remove his boots from tired feet. The skies had cleared now, a rare sight over a town normally shrouded in the smog of industry. It was as though the shooting star had been a brush, sweeping the heavens clear of any unwanted obstructions, allowing the gods an uncluttered view of the final act to be played out beneath them.

They reached a thorny hedge, the last bastion of civilization, before they entered the Black Lady's kingdom. Maggie had heard the stories, but had long thought them nothing more than tall tales spun by storytellers to pass the long, wintry evenings. That was until her mother had educated her as to the truth. She now knew that straying onto the Black Mountain was sheer folly, and few who ventured there ever returned. Those that did, spoke little of it but were never the same again. They kept their knowledge locked deep inside, for to talk of what they had witnessed would surely mark them as mad.

A gap in the hedge revealed a muddy ditch of indeterminate depth, which led to a mossy bank rising steeply before them. Even if they could have leaped the ditch unscathed, they would surely have slipped back down the bank into its watery clutches.

"Hold my hands," said Nell, her voice filled with authority, her creased face fixed on the bank. Maggie and Jinks, standing on either side of her, did as instructed for fear of displeasing their new guide. With their fingers barely entwined, they felt their feet leaving the sodden grass and rising up and over the ditch. They exchanged baffled glances as Nell guided them over the watery barrier. Rising still, they negotiated the bank until gently returning to earth on a stony path on the other side. Ahead of them, the path snaked upwards.

"The Apostles Path."

"Aye, girl, that it is. Come along now. Time is against us."

"Are you a witch? A real witch?" The words babbled from Jinks's mouth before Maggie had an opportunity to stop him. She eyed Nell with trepidation, uncertain if his youthful inquisitiveness would offend.

The old woman turned and looked down at the young boy, who was still holding her hand. The flicker of a smile crossed her features, a distant sparkle lurking at the back of a dark, intense stare. "A witch, you say? Now, there's a question. I've been called that in my time, and a lot worse besides."

"Can you teach me how to fly?"

"Jinks. Hush," Maggie scolded. "That's enough now, no more questions."

Nell laughed, a watery, crackling sound that originated deep in her lungs.

Maggie smiled nervously, uncertain how and where the conversation was going.

"He's grand. A curious boy, but there's no harm in that. It's the only way the young ones learn." She crouched so that her nose was mere inches from the small boy, her knees cracking, although she gave no indication that the motion caused her pain. "Maybe one day, lad, for you have the old blood running through your veins, that's for sure. But it's your sister who carries on the line, passed down from your mother. Men cannot be fully trusted to protect our ways; it is the women folk who must preserve our Lady's craft."

"So that's why Maggie could make the stone lift off the ground and glow. She's a witch like you and my mammy."

"She has a mighty power within her and, in time, will be taught to fully harness it. There are only twenty-six of us left, and she has now joined our ranks. But, before any of that can pass, she must meet our Lady and be deemed worthy of such an honor and a burden. Which is why we must walk this path tonight."

Without another word, she stepped forward, leaving her two companions with no choice but to follow.

The mountain towered above them, its dark outline bordered by the star-smattered sky. Maggie and Jinks had been born and reared beneath its shadow but had never dared set foot on it. Very few had, bar a handful of religious pilgrims who had ventured onto it in the mistaken belief that scaling it would bring them closer to their God. That was before they had hung her, before pilgrims had started to disappear.

"Are we walking all the way up it? The whole twelve miles?" Jinks asked.

"Aye, lad. That is my intention."

"Can't we fly?"

"John Joseph! Enough!"

Nell stopped and turned, and for a second Maggie could have sworn a pale light coalesced around her, highlighting every nook and cranny of her ancient face. Then it was gone again, and her features withdrew into the leaden night.

"Twelve miles the pilgrims walked, and so must we, for we are also on a journey to pay homage. They had their God, and we have our Lady. Just consider yourself fortunate you have shoes on your feet, unlike them. Now, as your sister said, enough, or we will never get to where we need to be. She will make herself known to us when she sees fit. Until then, we walk."

The path snaked across the barren slopes, with neither rhyme nor reason to its route. Had they attempted a direct approach, it would have halved the journey. However, to stray off the stones would have led them into uncharted bogland where one step in error could lead to a slow, lonely death sucked beneath the peaty soil. Maggie had no intention of sharing a common grave with other reckless souls who had made the same mistake years before.

The sky began to cloud over again, and Maggie shivered as the temperature dropped the higher they climbed. A light drizzle started to fall, which, when picked up by the chilling breeze, turned to sleet. Jinks hunkered close beside her, cap pulled down over his ears so that only stray tufts of his curls were exposed to the elements. Never more than half a dozen steps ahead of them, Nell plodded on. Neither her advancing years nor the worsening conditions seemed to have any effect on her steady progress. As the gloom deepened, Maggie noted the ethereal glow around the old woman again, a beacon for them to follow, preventing them from straying off the path. She pressed on, a protective arm around Jinks, her eyes reduced to slits as the sleet developed into scathing hail that marked their already ruddy cheeks.

Each mile was marked by a small wooden cross at the side of the path, one for each of the disciples that had met in the Upper Room before their final meal. A last gathering before their ministry unraveled, and Christ began his inexorable journey to the top of another hill where the one true cross awaited him.

Shortly after the second-mile marker, when Maggie thought the wind could not whip around them any more cruelly, Jinks succumbed to its ferocity and slumped to his knees. Maggie immediately fell beside him, her back turned to the gale to buffer the worst excesses of its incessant assault. She squinted up the path, where the faint outline of Nell was barely visible.

"Stop. Please. He can't go any further." Maggie fought to quell the rising tide of panic in her voice. Was this how it was going to end, freezing to death on a lonely path? If so, she would rather they had taken their chances against Thompson and that mad preacher. Perhaps his daughter, Annabelle, could have spoken up for her and others as well. At the very least, even if she hung or spent the rest of her days in some stinking debtors' *gaol*, her brother would have had some hope of a reprieve or pardon. He was only a boy; she would take full responsibility for whatever outlandish charges they might dream up.

The ghostly figure up ahead paused, her back still turned to them as if contemplating whether they were worthy of a response. For one lingering, horrific moment, Maggie thought that this had all been a trick, a ruse to lure them onto the mountain for reasons unknown. Would they vanish just as the early pilgrims had, another frightening tale for parents to tell their children as they tucked them into bed on wild, wanton nights such as this one? Jinks began to shiver uncontrollably, his body capitulating to the bitter conditions. Maggie tilted his chin, his eyes rolling in their sockets, as he struggled to stay conscious.

"Don't you dare go to sleep, John Joseph Malone. Do you hear me?" She shook her brother, his body limp and unresponsive. Panic began to claw its way from her stomach to the back of her throat, the scream forming, a scream that might never end.

"Are you ready, child?"

The proximity of the voice made Maggie start, looking up to find the old woman standing over them. She seemed impervious to the raging storm, not a hair out of place, her voice as clear and calm as if they were picnicking in a tranquil summer's meadow. Maggie struggled to understand how she had covered the ground between them in the blink of an eye. She merely nodded, too tired and scared to do much else.

The old woman nodded back, and, in an instant, they were standing higher up the mountain. It was so much higher, the town twinkling beneath them, oblivious to the drama unfolding above it. The wind and hail had eased slightly, enough for Maggie to catch a breath and take in their new surroundings. Jinks buried his face into her shoulder. He was warmer, not much, but his steady breath against her cheek reassured her that his condition had improved slightly.

"This is where she breathed her last."

Maggie looked up. They were huddled at the base of a solitary birch tree, its naked branches reaching into the void like broken fingers, crooked and brittle. A flash of unnatural lightning from a cloudless sky illuminated the tree's backdrop, revealing the summit of the mountain, much closer than it had been previously. Maggie mouthed the words, not quite believing what she was seeing.

"The Judas Tree."

"Aye," said Nell. "Your mother taught you well then. This is where they hung our Lady. Hung for nothing more than being different and not trying to help others. Much like yourself, lass."

Another searing crack to Maggie's left, and the sky exploded with a raucous scream, revealing the body of a young woman suspended from the highest branch of the birch, arms hanging limply by her side, long, lank hair covering her face. It was an image that would never leave Maggie, but as quickly as the strike had lit up the sky, it darkened again, concealing the ghastly sight. When Maggie looked again, the tree was as it had first been, the hanging woman no longer there.

"She was but one of many hung here. For all manner of alleged crimes. This mountain is cursed with their wandering souls, begging to be laid to rest. Only she rose again, seeking vengeance. She walked this path, past eleven saintly markers, to a tree where they hung a traitor for thirty pieces of silver."

Maggie could only nod again, hair plastered across her forehead. Part of her, detached and hovering beyond their circumstances, considered whether she was hallucinating or, worse, had frozen to death on the mountain, and this was the beginning of their endless journey through the afterlife. Was this purgatory? Were they consigned to roam the bleak mountainous terrain, waiting for judgment, the faint flicker of paradise forever just beyond their fumbling grasp?

A harrowing shriek cut across Maggie's thoughts and returned her to the present as a fat, sleek crow launched itself from the same branch where, seconds before, the young woman had hung. Its wings flapped noiselessly as it rose into the air and soared toward the summit, moving effortlessly through the tumult. Maggie caught a flash of visceral red, stringy flesh hanging from its beak. She shuddered, not wishing to know from where the gruesome treat had originated.

Nell followed the bird's trajectory as it shrank to an ebony fleck before disappearing into the unflinching dark. She returned her gaze to Maggie and the fetal form of Jinks, a kinder look on her craggy features.

"She knows we are here. Her messenger precedes us. It is time for us to cross over."

"Cross over. Don't you mean..."

Another furious crack of lightning hammered into the earth. Maggie fell forward, Jinks beneath her; she was determined to protect him, even if it meant sacrificing her own body to the strike's impact. She buried her forehead into the spongy soil, whispering prayers her mother had taught her, old words from another time when women ruled the land rather than the besuited men who now held sway. She counted, anticipating another strike, a strike that would likely end them once and for all.

"Why do you quiver, child? You need not fear. This is a safe place."

The voice was warm and mellifluous with a slight echo to it like honey poured over a spoon at a sun-drenched afternoon picnic. Maggie became aware that the wintry gale had ceased. The air about her was still and warm. She creaked open an eyelid and risked a look at her immediate surroundings, now swathed in bright sunshine, turning her head slightly to the side so that her cheek rested on the grass—soft, dry grass, as opposed to the boggy soil she thought she was resting on.

Raising her head slightly, she was met with the sight of lush, clipped lawns as far as the eye could see. Dotted randomly throughout were well-weeded flower beds housing flowers of every imaginable color and species. Dazzling white giant lilies stood proudly over luscious blood-red roses, interspersed with drooping mauve tulips, exquisite lilac pansies, and an army of daffodils, every shade of yellow.

"Are we in heaven, Maggie?"

"I don't know, Jinks. I'm not sure I know anything anymore."

"Heaven? That place is vastly overrated." The sumptuous voice again, this time followed by a peal of laughter that was accompanied by a flurry of multi-colored butterflies fluttering across Maggie's line of vision, all the colors of the rainbow, and more. The sky was a flawless blue, without a wisp of cloud, as the welcoming sun warmed their previously chilled bones.

Maggie rose to her knees and found herself facing the most remarkable creature she had ever set eyes on in her nineteen years on the planet.

Seated in a high-backed wicker chair, the woman could not have been ten years older than Maggie, yet she carried the air of one who had seen so much more, her vivid emerald-green eyes awash with wisdom and knowledge. The dress she wore matched her eyes, fine satin sweeping to her ankles, the hems and necklines embroidered with a hue of colors reminiscent of the butterflies who had now vanished from sight. Red curls tumbled over her exposed shoulders, sweeping down her back. She was pale, with a smattering of freckles that brightened her nose and pronounced cheekbones. There was a sad dignity about her, but she possessed an underlying savagery that sent an involuntary shiver through Maggie.

"What's wrong, child? You look as though you've seen a ghost."

Her tinkling laughter seemed to engulf Maggie from all sides. She was unable to form a response as the woman rose from the chair and floated towards them. Maggie couldn't see her feet or shoes beneath the flowing dress, giving the impression that she was levitating over the lawn, just as they had traversed the ditch earlier. She crossed the ground between them in the blink of an eye. As she approached, Nell performed an awkward curtsey before respectfully stepping aside.

"Thank you, loyal and faithful servant. You will be rewarded for this in due course." The melodic tones did not quite mask a Belfast accent that somehow did not sit right with Maggie. It was as if she came from a different time altogether, her lilt and tone different than any she had experienced before.

"It was nothing, my Lady." Nell beamed with pride, suddenly a blushing teenage girl again, giddy at a compliment handed down by a besotted suitor.

"You may return now. You know what is required. Leave with my blessing, I commend the boy to you now."

"What? No. Wait." Maggie turned to face Jinks to find both Nell and him had vanished. She was alone with the mysterious woman who held a hand out to her, an amused smile adorning her features. Maggie slapped it aside and jumped to her feet, spinning round to take in the grassy expanse, her beloved sibling nowhere to be seen.

"Where is he? I swear to God above if you've hurt a hair on his head." She was half a foot smaller than the woman but squared up to her anyway, ready to fight tooth and nail to protect her brother.

"You will do what, exactly? Hurt me? Kill me? You cannot kill what is already dead. And before you attempt anything foolish, you might wish to know that your brother is safe and well. No harm will come to him while he is under my care." Her eyes bored into Maggie, daring her to take the argument any further.

Maggie swallowed hard and took a step back, thinking of her mother's words.

"Our blessed Lady of the Mountain will always protect us, Maggie. We can place our trust in her."

"Where is he?"

"In a safe place. Where he will remain until our work is done." She raised an eyebrow, inviting Maggie to ask another question. It was clear that the conversation would be on her terms.

"Our work? What do you mean?"

The woman laughed again, this time with a harder edge to the sound. She pointed beyond Maggie to the town that glittered below, clothed in frosty darkness despite their bright and balmy surroundings. It was as though they were in a temperate bubble atop the mountain, basking in glorious sunshine, while beneath them, the squall laid siege to a shivering Belfast.

"You *do* know who I am?" That icy stare again failed to curtail a hint of impatience in her voice.

"You're her. The Lady of the Mountain. I know that much. I've prayed to you every day; my mother taught me about you, but I never believed we would meet."

"Well, at least we have established that then. I, therefore, take it that your mother will have told you of my demise."

Maggie tensed, aware that she was being tested. She had to choose her words carefully; there was too much at stake for glib, vacuous answers.

"I know they hung you. Said you were a witch. But mother told me you were an innocent, preyed upon by vile, bitter men. Fuelled by fear and paranoia. You vowed vengeance, and since then, the mountain has been your home. Your kingdom until the day you return to avenge the great injustice done to you."

The woman nodded and bent to breathe in the fragrance from a nearby flowerbed, savoring the subtle scents that Maggie found almost overpowering. It had been many years since the smell of fresh flowers had caressed her nostrils.

"Your mother taught you well. I was sorry to hear of her death. It was beyond my powers to stop her passing."

"She loved you. Turned her back on the church for you." Maggie blurted the words out before realizing the potential consequences.

The woman's jaw tightened marginally, the only visible sign that the words had struck home. She cupped the petals of a pale pink rose in her hand, long, bony fingers caressing its petals.

"This I know. Which is why I have chosen you for when the time comes."

"What time? Will you stop talking in riddles? Why have you brought me here? What is this place?"

"This place?" She looked around as if aware of her surroundings for the first time. "Why, this is your new home, Maggie Malone. This is where I will teach you so that you are ready when I come down from this mountain and reclaim this land. For when they killed me, I was naught but a mortal woman. Now I am more, so much more. I am a goddess, and you will carry my sword before me."

"Me? I'm nothing. What can I possibly offer to one like you?"

The woman rose from the flowerbed and placed a hand on Maggie's shoulder, a soft warmth resonating from it, sending waves of calm and comfort through her.

"You offer more than you can possibly begin to understand. For you have been chosen, Maggie Malone. I am but a goddess, but you will be so much more. For you will slay the *abhartach*."

The Turnip Thief

T he Reverend Edgar's words had fallen on fertile minds, feeding their fears until accusations and allegations flowered. The residents of Carson's Court fell over each other to condemn their absent neighbor, eager to expunge their own demons and find a reason for the fresh dread that had befallen their already miserable lives. They were not of Edgar's faith, but they worshiped the same God and feared the same Devil. The cleric spoke in a language they had never heard when attending the drab, monotone Latin mass that none of them understood.

The priests were cold, inaccessible figures whom they saw from a distance once a week. None of them displayed the fiery passion of Archibald Edgar, who had stood before them waving the Bible that the priests so rarely put on display. Here was a man of God who brought them answers as opposed to further questions, a man not afraid to look them in the eye and get his hands dirty. Here was a man of action, one who was prepared to lead from the front. He gave them something, someone, to blame, and the more he talked that wondrous evening, the more it made sense to them. Within an hour, he had turned a surly, rebellious mob into his own private army.

Annabelle had hunkered beneath the cart, her dismay growing by the second. She wanted to scream, cry, emerge from her hiding place, and tell the poor, deluded fools they were being spun a web of artful lies. The more he spoke, the more reluctant murmurs turned to full-hearted agreement, sealing Maggie's fate. They fell for it all, this mishmash of religious trickery mixed with older, deeper fears passed down through the generations. Talk of a banshee who stalked the mountain that overlooked Belfast, a faerie witch in concert with Satan and his demonic legions. It was *her* followers who had brought famine and fever to Belfast, who had blazed through the streets at night butchering innocent young women for their dark lord.

She had listened as he buttered them up with promises of porridge and biscuits in the morning, washed down with sweet tea and roaring fires. All they needed to do was attend Rosemary Street, where an impromptu open-air service would be held, a great revival aimed at uniting the God-fearing folk of Belfast, be they Protestant or Catholic. Afterward, their bellies full and hearts emboldened, they would walk to the mountain as one, tackle the Apostles Trail, and find the girl witch and her crafty brother. He was young and had been led astray; the workhouse would straighten him out and if that failed, he would be thrown on the next boat to Australia.

As for the girl, he knew there would be a trial; justice had to be administered. She would be given the opportunity to argue her case and prove her innocence; however, Annabelle sensed that, in the minds of most, the sentence had already been passed. There were too many loose ends, too much evidence stacked against her to sway their minds. She was guilty, Edgar was certain of that, and an example had to be set to dissuade other young, impressionable minds who might be led astray. In addition, where there was one, there would be others, a lair of rats he needed to smoke out into the open. Once the girl swung from the gallows, they would panic and break for cover, where he and his followers would be waiting for them. He would strike quick and hard with a fiery sword of righteousness. Annabelle took it all in, her disbelief growing that this monster spouting such vile hatred was her father.

Eventually, after what seemed an interminable age, he concluded the sermon, and the residents dispersed back to their crowded, infested homes. He assured them that the end was in sight, an end to soaring temperatures and empty bellies. Just one more night, and they would be on the mountain with him hunting for the witch. And when they found her...

Annabelle watched as her father and his suited entourage of town guardians and church elders left the court, flanked by the green-tunic-clad Constabulary. She waited, certain that if she emerged too early, she would be pounced on by an eagle-eyed officer of the law. The lamps dimmed about the court until the only light cast on the cobbles was the moon's mellow glow. Her imagination toyed with her resolve, like a contented cat playing with its prey, until she could take no more and crawled out from under the cart. Her Sunday best was coated in grime and detritus, and she frowned at the muddy streaks on her dress as she clambered to her feet. Silence greeted her, the din from the crowd replaced by an ominous calm. And yet she had to try, for she knew right from wrong and could not idly stand by and watch an innocent young woman being persecuted by a man she no longer recognized as her father.

She clung to the shadows of a wall, creeping along the side of the courtyard, until she could duck into the entry that led to the equally still Bank Street. She spilled out onto the street, unaware of the handprints on the entry wall glowing a garish red as she passed. So focused was she on what she must do, what she had to do, that she did not catch the hunched figure watching from the shadows. She looked both ways before dashing across the street and down an alley. An alley that she knew would take her in the general direction of a mountain that she dreaded but knew she must climb.

The figure entered the same alley not ten seconds later.

Nell was one of the oldest women Jinks had ever set eyes on, yet she moved deceptively fast, forcing him to gulp down great mouthfuls of air to keep in step with her. One minute he had been in his sister's arms on the haunted mountain, the next, they were separated, and he was on the old road to Ballymacarrett, an area he knew well. In recent months, when the famine had started to wrap its skeletal fingers around the throat of the starving town, he and Tommy had raided cottagers' back gardens for turnips and any other vegetables they could find. It was thieving, and he wasn't proud of it, but his mother had been on her deathbed, wasting away before his eyes. He had felt useless as, for all his bravado, he was a silly, little boy full of big words that amounted to nothing. So he had set out in the dead of night and returned with a sack full of vegetables. Maggie had rolled her eyes and sighed but said nothing, instead concocting a tasty soup that had revived their mother for a couple of days. She had even been able to sit up a little, smiling and listening to Jinks regale her with his tales of mischief.

But that was then. Now, he was trudging along the uneven dirt road, hopping over waterlogged cart tracks gouged from the soft earth by the daily traffic that clattered in and out of town. Nell glided ahead of him, refusing to answer the myriad of questions he had bombarded her with following their unexpected arrival on the outskirts. At one point, he had planted his backside on a grassy verge by the roadside, proclaiming he was not moving until she told him the whereabouts of his sister. It had been a futile gesture as, with unnerving strength and speed, she had hauled him to his feet and shoved him ahead of her.

"There will be time for questions when we get back to my cottage. Until then, walk, don't talk."

So he had. For what seemed forever, the dark and bitter wind was their only companion until they reached a fork in the road where a dirt track broke off and fell away into a hollow of shacks and cottages. Ballymacarrett. The turnip thief had returned to the scene of his most notorious crime.

"You'll not be marauding through Patrick Sweeney's vegetable patch tonight, lad."

Jinks stared up into the hooded eyes of the old woman, uncertain whether she was chastising or mocking him.

"Wait. How did you..."

"I know everything that goes on in these parts," she replied. "Now, come on, let's get you inside and a fire going. You're as pale as a whitewashed wall, and when did you last eat? Can you even remember?"

Without another word, she led him down the dirt track and into the hollow, which protected them from the worst ravages of the incessant wind. They passed rows of simple yet well-maintained cottages on either side, wisps of smoke swirling from chimneys bringing the comforting scent of burning peat into the pre-dawn air. Jinks shivered, wishing he was in front of a roaring hearth and out of the frozen night.

She stopped by the end cottage on the left, slightly separate from the others but no less well-tended. Jinks swallowed a shard of guilt. These were poor folk, but they obviously took pride in what little they had, making ends meet and reluctant to rely on the charity of others. He vowed never to steal again so long as he lived, be that another night on this earth or if he died a contented old man surrounded by a brood of doting grandchildren.

Reaching the door, Nell looked around furtively before sharply clapping her hands. The stout wooden frame swung noiselessly inwards, and, with a jerk of the head to Jinks, she ducked inside.

"I've no time for keys at my age. Keep setting them aside and forgetting where I've left them."

Jinks followed, finding himself in a low-ceilinged single room. A small, cracked window to his left offered the only natural light as the old woman busied herself at the dusty hearth in the far corner, festooned with an array of silvery cobwebs. A faltering light momentarily glowed before a stronger light rose, brightening the interior of the cottage. Jinks blinked, a wall of warm air forcing him to take a step back. Nell stood back to admire her handiwork as a well-stacked pile of turf and sticks crackled merrily. He had no idea how she had manufactured the blaze but was quickly learning not to question anything on this most peculiar of nights.

She gestured for Jinks to take a seat on a narrow cot wedged in a corner of the room. He hurried to its far end, nearest the fire, grateful for its joyous warmth. The old woman leaned against the opposite wall, little more than a dozen feet separating them.

"Well, if you have questions, lad, you had better ask them now, for who knows what daylight will bring for us two."

Jinks eyed her warily, weighing up what he considered was an acceptable opening salvo. He was not used to interrogating adults besides Maggie and his mother, may God rest her soul. The last time he had dared question his father about his nocturnal whereabouts, he had been rewarded with a fat lip and a string of curse words.

"Was that the Black Lady we met? On the mountain?"

"She has many names, but aye, that is one of them"

"So, she's real then? I thought it was just a faerie tale."

Nell leaned off the wall and took a step toward the hearth. The flames soared even higher, as if responding to some unspoken command she had uttered. She looked deep into its molten heart, her eyes igniting like tiny suns as the fire reflected off her pupils.

"The faerie folk are as real as you and me, lad, but they choose when we see them and when we don't. She is not one of them, but she knows their ways. She respects their circles as they respect her mountain."

"Did the townspeople really hang her?"

"Aye, they did. Said she was a witch when she was nothing of the sort. Just a young woman with a bit of knowledge, helping other young women to bear their children and ease their pains."

"Then why did they kill her?"

Nell laughed, a hard, humorless snort, before turning to face the young boy. Her face softened and for a second, he thought she would shed a tear before she gathered her composure and smiled sadly.

"Men don't need a reason to kill women. It's what they do. Has been for centuries, and I don't see that changing any time soon." She laughed again, with more sincerity this time, at the confused boy facing her.

"You're a tough little cub, that's for sure, but you still have a lot to learn about the ways of the world."

"I know enough." Jinks puffed out his chest, causing Nell to guffaw again before continuing.

"They hung our Lady because they could, but the light in her shone too bright to be snuffed out by a bloody rope. So, she remained on the mountain, waiting for the day when she could return and have her vengeance on the town that turned its back on her. Tomorrow will be that day."

Jinks started, as an icy blast of wind rattled the window, threatening to breach their cozy setting. His mind was a flurry of questions, but one rose above all others. "Why does she want to kill them all? They weren't the ones that hung her."

He regretted the question the second it left his lips, for the woman's face momentarily darkened, her furrowed brow a sea of deep crevasses. Jinks could have sworn her eyes flashed an angry red.

She turned towards a lopsided shelf on the wall, taking down a battered iron kettle. "Some wounds are too deep to heal, lad. And it is not for us to question one of her kind. I took an oath to serve her, as did your mother, and that is what we have done. Now, no more questions. Will you take some tea and bread?"

"Aye. Thank you. I meant no harm."

"I know, lad, I know. I'm away to the pump for water. I'll be only a minute."

With that, the door flung open, again of its own accord, and she was gone into the night, leaving Jinks alone with even more questions than before. He eyed the open door and, for a fleeting instant, considered following her into the storm and attempting to make his own way back to Maggie. The thought vanished as quickly as it had formed, like the clogging smoke rising from the fire through a hole in the thatched cottage roof.

Something tethered him to the bed. He felt safe in this strange little place with this even stranger woman acting as his guardian. Being separated from Maggie would normally have driven him insane with worry, but it was as if a calming hand now rested on his shoulder, reassuring him that he was safe where he was and should stay put. He leaned back onto the lumpy cot and stared out of the door, willing the woman to return soon. She was his connection to Maggie, and he needed her close.

Outside, the kettle lay discarded as Nell hauled her tired body back along the dirt track toward the main road. There she stood, leaning into the gale that threatened to lift her brittle frame and toss it into the skies. Her lips moved, and a tried and tested ward soundlessly spun across the track to mask their presence in the hollow. She reached deep into the pocket of her skirts and cast a handful of salt across the path, another barrier against those who sought to do her and the boy harm. It would have been hard work half a lifetime ago, but now it sapped her essence dry of what little remaining power dwelt within her aging form.

She swayed on her feet, reeling from each incantation as they drained her further. It mattered not. She had lived a long and largely happy life, protected by the Black Lady at every step of her journey. She knew that this would be her last day on the planet and was grateful that it would be spent serving the one who had guided her all these years. Ahead, she heard the rumbling of hooves above the growing storm. With a final grimace, she raised her hands in the air, illuminated as a streak of lightning ripped through the suddenly-formed cloud cover and unleashed its fearsome kinetic energy on the fork in the road before her.

The approaching horses reared up onto their hind legs, nostrils flaring with fear at the inferno before them. The hedgerows bordering the roar ignited like bone-dry kindling despite the rains that now battered them from all angles. A tree overhanging the fork also exploded into flames, shedding flaming branches down upon the riders below. One man toppled from his mount, landing with a sickening thud on the road. The horse bolted, leaping a section of the hedgerow that had not caught ablaze before galloping off into the darkness. The other riders struggled to control their steeds, frantic to escape the wall of flames.

"Pull back, damn it, before we are burnt to a crisp. We will have to find another way down there."

"That was no act of nature. It's witchcraft, I tell ye. The Black Lady, she's coming for us."

"Don't talk nonsense, man. The guardians are paying you a week's wages to catch an *auld* woman and a wee boy. Show a bit of backbone."

"I don't care if the Reverend Edgar calls all the angels in Heaven to strike me down, I'm not risking my neck. They can keep their money, it's cursed."

The second rider pulled on his horse's reins. It wheeled away from the flames and trotted smartly in the opposite direction, back towards the town. Several of his companions followed suit, leaving the first rider frustrated but powerless to convince them otherwise. He glared at the furnace, as if willing it to subside, but eventually realized the futility of his plight and reluctantly took off after the other men.

Silence fell on the fork again as the receding hooves and curses of the men were consumed once more by the darkness. Dawn showed little interest in penetrating the heavy gloom. The flames began to falter as the heavens emptied, weighty raindrops reducing the inferno to a smoldering mess. Just beyond the smoke-stained ground, the old woman lay on her side as a young boy watched on, disturbed from his hiding place by the noise of the lightning bolt.

Jinks knelt by the huddled form, little more than a bundle of skin and bones, her eyes staring toward the skies, a contented smile on her face. She looked decades younger, at peace with her fate. Jinks knelt forward and gently stroked the side of her face, still pink and warm. As soon as his fingers caressed her cheek, a blinding light forced him to fall back onto his haunches, forearm raised to shield his eyes from the dazzling glow. It faded as soon as it had arrived, and when he looked back, there was no sign of his elderly guide.

He was a boy alone, on a windswept night, in the depths of winter. No parents, no sister, utterly alone, and reliant on his wits now to stay alive. Jinks smiled ruefully as his stomach grumbled. Perhaps it was time to return to the Ballymacarrett vegetable patches after all.

Black Mountain, Black Hearts

ithin seconds, Annabelle knew she was being followed. Ahead, the alley twisted and turned with no end in sight, no door or courtyard to juke into in the hope that her pursuer would pass her by. She initially thought it was her imagination. It had started to rain again, and she thought she might be mistaking the raindrops tapping the cobbles for the echo of footsteps behind her. She stopped and turned, but there was nothing except the empty alley.

She quickened her step, determined to evade whatever thugs her father had sent to track her down. Well, no more would she play the contrite preacher's daughter. The scales had fallen from Annabelle's eyes, and she had witnessed the real Archibald Edgar, just as Paul had encountered the Lord on the road to Damascus. Although one professed an undying love for the other, Annabelle now saw the two as polar opposites—her father's swirling darkness threatening to eclipse the light of the Gospel that she had attempted to display in the chaotic soup kitchen, saving both lives and souls.

Annabelle pushed a lock of damp hair from her face, her feet aching as she hurried beneath a gas lamp. Would this alley never end? She was now certain there was someone behind her, the heavy footsteps unmistakable above the steady downpour. She broke into a run, hitching her dress and hoping her sturdy boots would keep her from slipping on the slick cobbles. The shadows shot past in a blur as she lengthened her stride, praying that the next kink in the alley would emerge onto a well-lit street, hopefully with a Constable patrolling its length. Her breath rattled like a rake across gravel. The footsteps behind her quickened in tandem with her own, competing with her pounding heartbeat as she struggled to suck enough air into her lungs. A light ahead suggested she was nearing the end of the alley, the swirling drizzle falling beneath a lamp beckoning her to safety.

Suddenly, she was flying, all thoughts of escape or rescue banished from her mind. It was a curiously peaceful sensation before she landed heavily on her shoulder, winded and shaken. The pain barely had time to register before she was hauled off the hard ground and flung against a wall, her teeth grinding together on impact. She blinked, attempting to fight down the rising tide of nausea and retain consciousness. Bile rose in her throat, stars flickering before her dazed eyes. She vaguely registered that she was upright, yet her feet were now barely scraping the ground.

His face was painfully thin, cheeks corrupted with cratered pockmarks. A hooked nose dominated dark, weasel eyes and bushy brows that joined in an impenetrable line. He was balding, his ears protruding like prize cauliflower from graying tufts on either side of his head. One of them was horribly mangled, as if it had been chewed up and spat out. Annabelle struggled to turn her face away when he spoke, his breath reminding her of a stagnant pond. Her assailant leered, enjoying the power as his hand gradually squeezed around her throat.

"I wouldn't make a sound, pretty lady, for if you do, I will gut you right here and now. Leave you for the rats to nibble on." He scrunched his nose and mimicked a feasting rodent, his lips smacking noisily. He loosened his grip slightly and nodded at Annabelle, an invitation for her to respond. The man was in no hurry and appeared unworried that they would be disturbed.

"Let me go. I have no money. Let me go now and be on your way. I will never speak of this to another soul."

The man cocked his head as if seriously considering the offer before lowering her to the ground, the palm of his hand pinning her shoulder against the wall. She realized he was at least a foot taller than her, lean but powerfully built. He was quite possibly the most unseemly man she had ever set eyes on, possessing an aura of desperate malevolence that chilled her to the bone.

"Much as I would like to accommodate your request, I'm afraid I cannot, for I haven't had a drink all day, and I'm shaking like a baby. Now give me what coin you have and be quick about it.'

"I have no money. Now, unhand me before I scream. The Constabulary are nearby, I've just seen them in Carson's Court." Annabelle attempted to wriggle free, but his hand was like a vice burrowing into her clavicle. Another inch of pressure, and she feared it might snap like a dry twig.

"I ain't afraid of Quinn and his boys. You hand it over, or I'll squeeze that pretty throat 'til your eyes pop. And no point you praying, miss. Your Lord Jesus can't help you here."

"How did you... Why..." Annabelle's face contorted into a mask of fear. She vaguely recognized that she was crying, an act that seemed to send her captor into even better spirits.

"Oh, the tears, the tears, they all cry in the end, even the bravest of girls." He darted forward and slid a rough tongue along the length of Annabelle's cheek, causing her to squirm and cry out in horror.

"So sorry, Miss, so sorry, but old Mikey can't resist. I knows who you are. The preacher's daughter. I've been watching you. Young ladies like yourself should take more care and not be out and about at night. Pretty little thing like..."

Annabelle struck at speed, the letter opener she had earlier secreted from her father's desk puncturing the man's liver several times in quick succession before he could finish the sentence. He looked at her quizzically before releasing his grip and slumping to the ground, a reedy gargling his only attempt at further communication as he clutched at the blade buried in his side.

She glanced down at his squirming form before straightening her dress and stepping over the man. He clawed at her leg, but a well-aimed kick ended any further interest he might have had in her. Her days of playing the victim were no more; Maggie Malone had taught her to stand tall and fight her corner. No man would have the better of her again. She walked on, every step bringing her closer to the mountain.

The cottage was like nothing Maggie had seen before, nestled in a hollow of rolling grass by the side of a burbling brook. A small copse of willow trees bowed deferentially over the stream as they made their way down the hill, Maggie half a stride behind the elegant woman who seemed to glide over the surface, her gown trailing lazily behind her. Maggie tried several times to glimpse her feet, but they were lost within the folds of the dress, its exquisite sequins sparkling as the sun from a cloudless sky warmed their backs.

By Maggie's reckoning, it was still the dead of night, and a thunderstorm should have been raging above them. The filth and squalor of the town seemed worlds away as she breathed deeply, gratefully inhaling the crisp, pure air devoid of the smog and soot of Belfast's mills and docks.

"Where are we? This ain't the mountain."

"We are where we are. Now, come along and join me for some tea." They reached the bottom of the slope and set foot on a winding gravel path that led to the front door of the cottage, flanked by patches of lavender bluebells on either side. An industrious bee flitted from one flower to the next, oblivious to their arrival.

"Is this your home?"

"For now, yes, this meets my needs. I have unfinished business to attend to before I can contemplate my next abode."

They entered the cottage through an open door, the single room dominated by a sturdy wooden table, upon which sat a steaming kettle. The woman indicated for Maggie to take one of the chairs while she busied herself, slipping a variety of herbs into the still bubbling water. She stirred and inspected its contents to ensure the brew had steeped sufficiently before tipping the kettle over two earthen mugs and filling them, the scent of peppermint and sage filling the air. Maggie smiled. She hastily accepted the mug offered to her and sipped. It was piping hot and delicious; a satisfying warmth spread from her core to the tips of her fingers and toes.

"Thank you. I've never tasted tea so good."

"You are most welcome," said the woman, holding her own mug between clasped hands. "I do not have many visitors, so when I do, I like to ensure they are well looked after."

Maggie set the mug down and met the woman's penetrating stare. Her eyes were the purest green, mesmerizing and frightening in equal measure;

they spoke of unspoken terrors yet to be revealed to Maggie. The woman appeared mildly amused at the curiosity of her guest, finally raising her mug to thin lips.

"What am I to call you?"

"By the name I was given, of course. Fionnuala. It did me well enough in my nearly thirty years of life, so it can do me just as well now that I have crossed over. They have called me many names since, but I see no reason to burden you with them."

"The Black Lady. The Banshee of the Mountain. The Winter Queen."

Fionnuala threw back her head and laughed, her russet curls falling over one shoulder. "My, the good citizens of Belfast have active imaginations. As creative as the false charges they concocted that led me to that damnable tree." She wrinkled her nose and stared out of the door beyond Maggie's shoulder. The room darkened slightly as if a sizeable cloud had passed over before the sun broke through again.

"Are you behind all this misfortune? The hunger, the sickness? Killing thousands of innocent folk who had nothing to do with what happened centuries ago." The fire in Maggie's voice surprised her, and she swallowed hard, suddenly mindful of how vulnerable her present circumstances were. The woman facing her across the table only smiled quizzically, more amused than angered by the outburst.

"You certainly have your mother's fiery spirit. That could be very useful."

"What do you know of my mother?" Maggie stiffened. She had lost her mother to hunger, her father to drink, and had no idea where her brother was. Part of her wanted to scream and scramble over the table, digging her dirty fingernails into the smug features facing her.

"I know she raised you well and taught you some of my ways. Now, you can master the stones, but that is only scratching the surface of the power within you, Maggie Malone. You have been chosen, nurtured, and are now ready to ascend to your true calling. Your destiny."

"If you think I am going to help you lay waste to my hometown, then you are sorely mistaken. I am grateful for your assistance, but I will take no part in such madness."

Fionnuala toyed with her mug, swirling the tea as if seeking a suitable response to the determined young woman daring to challenge her plans.

"Whilst I do admire your humanity, I am afraid that mine deserted me at the end of a rope. I care not for these people now; they are no longer my kin. I will protect those who have kept my name alive, yourself and your brother included. But no others."

"Care for my brother? Cast out at the mercy of religious zealots with only an old woman to protect him? You care for nothing but your own selfish pursuits. I am sorry about what happened to you, but I will not participate in the death of innocent people."

"As I said before, the boy is safe so long as he is with Nell. Just as you are safe, so long as you remain here. Or perhaps you would care to return to the town and take your chances with these zealots you speak of?"

Maggie fought hard to keep herself from flinging the remainder of her tea at the heartless creature chastising her. She had her mother's countenance and powers, but a streak of her father's temper also surged through her veins. She chewed hard on the inside of her cheek until the metallic tang of blood filled her mouth. It hurt, but it worked, and her fury subsided.

"That's better," murmured Fionnuala in a placatory tone far removed from her earlier disdain. She rose from her chair and negotiated the table until she stood beside Maggie, placing long, almost skeletal fingers on her guest's shoulders. She wore no rings, and a speckle of freckles adorned her knuckles, in stark contrast to her otherwise lily-white skin.

She was without a wrinkle or flaw, but Maggie resisted looking up into those beguiling eyes. To look would result in her losing all control of her senses and succumbing to the will of the witch. As if reading her thoughts, Fionnuala snorted and removed the hand.

"Oh, worry not; if I had wanted to enchant you, I would have done so by now. What I have in mind for you must be of your own volition, otherwise, it will not work."

Maggie glowered straight ahead at the far wall, her face a grim mask of resistance.

"And as I said, I will not help you destroy my own town."

"Destroy? Don't be ridiculous, girl. What do you take me for, the heartless villain? Quite the contrary, I require your dormant powers for an entirely different purpose. Not to destroy, but to save a life. The life of one you hold dear to your heart."

Fionnuala kept talking after that, and Maggie did not interrupt. Not once.

It took Edgar longer than he expected to convince the men to join him. Blatant cowardice, rooted in superstitious nonsense, meant that his words initially fell on reluctant ears. They were sold on his belief that their recent misfortune must have a supernatural origin, and few had any sympathy for the Malone girl. Not after the steady flow of witnesses from Carson's Court and further afield, testifying to her strange ways and outlandish behavior. She had been branded a witch and the cause of all their troubles well before the service had commenced that morning. The steps outside Rosemary Street Presbyterian Church were now packed with Protestants and Catholics alike, united against a common enemy.

There was no issue with the problem, but the solution was a more delicate manner. A boy had been produced who, after some cajoling and a shilling being placed in his grimy hand, told the gathering that he had seen the girl and her brother heading towards the mountain with an elderly woman. Edgar had been ecstatic, certain that the devil was at work. For why else would an innocent young woman flee her hometown, bound for the wicked slopes of the witch's realm? And who could their companion be but one of their coven? When pressed, the boy had testified to seeing them fly as well. The crowd had erupted, baying for blood and an end to the curse that had hung over their families these last two years.

All that changed when Reverend Edgar asked for volunteers to accompany him onto the mountain's bleak slopes. Strident voices quieted and eyes averted as the minister glared down at them from the top of the church steps. He had to resort to thinly veiled threats and premonitions of eternal damnation before an acceptable number of men gathered at the front of the church building.

"Not since David's Mighty Men slayed the Philistines has our Lord called upon his faithful to battle such an evil. I bless you, my brothers, and anoint your heads with God's almighty grace and provenance. We march protected by the blood of Christ, assured of eternal life whatever might befall us at this darkest of times. Amen, and Praise be to our Lord and Savior."

His rousing words aggrieved as many as they roused, and many tears were shed by wives and children as the men of the parish gathered outside the church beneath the town's slated rooftops. At their head stood Edgar, resplendent in his black-brimmed hat, his Bible in hand. It had all the answers he had ever needed in life. Rejuvenated by the Holy Spirit surging through his mortal body, he gave little thought to the whereabouts of his only child. Flanked by a less enthusiastic Blake and a sullen Dr. Crothers, he turned to the boy who had betrayed Jinks for a shiny coin and promises of an apprenticeship with one of Edgar's wealthier patrons.

"Now, Tommy lad. Lead on."

Tommy Reilly led them through a maze of alleys, drunks, and other undesirables skulking in the shadows as the body of men passed. They marched beyond the town limits and across the fields, sodden and damp. Their boots sank into the earth, a procession of stumbles and muttered oaths. Ahead of them, the mountain loomed, its mass gradually revealed to them as the daylight grappled the gloom for control of the heavens. A lone crow rose from a crumbling stone wall, its wings extending in isolated glory. It swooped low over the snaking line of men, cawing indignantly before soaring upward.

"The witch sends her familiars to frighten us, but we will not stray from the one true path." Edgar cast a dark look after the departing bird, ignoring the grumbling from behind him as the less stout-hearted members of the party voiced their fears and concerns. Blake chose to ignore the dissension whilst Crothers looked utterly miserable, his stout frame unsuited for the challenging terrain. Sergeant Quinn and his grim-faced Constabulary brought up the rear, on hand to deter those who decided they'd had enough and sought to return to the safer confines of the town.

They reached the end of the farthest field, where a ditch barred them from the lower slopes of the mountain. Edgar bent down and engaged in a hurried conversation with Tommy, who, at its conclusion, broke into a jog back in the direction they had come, his monetary reward already burning a hole in his waistcoat pocket.

"This is where they flew, a true sign that they are in league with Satan." Edgar flung his arms out, his followers fanned before him in a loose semi-circle.

"We will use more conventional means, my brothers, for the boy has informed me of a crossing plank further along the ditch. From there, we can connect with the path."

"You mean us to walk the Twelve Apostles?"

Edgar swung towards the protesting voice, his dark eyes boring a hole in the forehead of the man who now wished more than anything that he had kept his mouth firmly shut. "I do indeed, for that is the swiftest means of climbing this accursed mountain and rooting out the evil that has afflicted the town. And I fear it not, for the angels will be above, before, and around us. What man among you is too cowardly to join me?"

The man bowed his head in defeat as all around him, whatever support he may have hoped for melted away. The slow slap of Quinn's truncheon against his palm accompanied Edgar's words, a choreographed action to dissuade those thinking of abandoning the pastor's mission.

"Very well," continued Edgar, a smug smile doing nothing to improve his normally sour features. "Let us continue and worry not, my brothers. We shall burn this coven out of these hills just like our Lord burned the deviant and the diseased from Sodom and Gomorrah. With the fire of righteousness." He turned, another performance complete, and stalked along the bank of the ditch, followed in varying degrees of enthusiasm by his retinue.

High on the mountain, Fionnuala watched. In another dimension, she entertained the young woman who would allow her to bring the deluded preacher and his followers to their knees. For they would die on this mountain, and one would hang from the same tree that had ended her mortal existence. The mountain would no longer be black but would turn red with their blood, soaking the ancient turf with new memories and ghosts.

When they were slain, she would descend with Maggie and destroy what remained of the town that hadn't yet been cleansed by plague and famine. She would rise, and they would fall, just as the *abartach* would fall at the feet of the girl. He stood as the last barrier in her path. He would take a hostage, as they had agreed, and she would bring him his final victim—the sixth. He always was a theatrical creature, thriving on the drama of their brutal tussle. Little did he know, however, that the sixth would be his downfall, clearing the way for Fionnuala to rule this land for all eternity.

She smiled. Today would be a good day.

The Worry Stone

Jinks watched as Tommy Reilly made straight for the bakery, his mouth no doubt already salivating at the thought of cramming fresh buttered bread into his mouth. Tommy walked briskly, no doubt afraid that breaking into a run might draw unwanted attention. A thread of guilt pulled irritably at the back of Jink's mind, but the overpowering thought of gaining revenge quickly dispelled any lingering thoughts of what he had to do next. If he had learned nothing else in his eight short years, it was that you did not have friends on the street. Acquaintances, yes, but friendship was a sign of weakness, and Maggie was the only person he was loyal to now.

So lost in his thoughts was Tommy, that he was completely unprepared for the forceful blow that threw him against the wall of the alley, his stomach taking the impact. He slumped to the ground and barely had time to cover his face as a flurry of punches rained down on his head and upper body. His attacker sat astride him, pinning him down with their knees on either side of his flailing body. Try as he might, he could not wriggle free as the first blow penetrated his waning defenses, drawing blood as a fist connected with his exposed nose.

"Rat me out, would ye Tommy Reilly? Rat me and my sister!"

"Gerroff, I'm no rat. Get your dirty hands off me."

A final hook connected with the side of the boy's head, ending what little resistance remained. He squirmed onto his side, spitting a tooth from his bloody mouth.

"Alright. You win, Jinks. I give up."

Jinks swung a leg over his prostate victim's chest and bounced to his feet, adopting a wary boxing stance that had served him well in previous street altercations. He had won a few and lost a few, but earned the respect of his peers in both victory and defeat. Tommy knew only too well that he had met his match.

"Get up, you coward. Get up, or I'll give you a shiner to go with that busted nose."

Tommy reluctantly crawled onto all fours, bloody droplets dripping from his tender mouth. He rose uncertainly to his feet, anchoring his back against the alley wall as he struggled to regain his bearings.

"Now tell me what you told that preacher. I know it was you. Jack Kelly wouldn't have ratted on us, and none of his regulars would have dared go against him. You were the only other one who saw us leave that bar. You followed us, didn't ye?"

"I never done anything. You're talking out of your hole."

Another slap to the face, administered before he had any opportunity to deflect it, doubled Tommy over, hands raised over his head as he cowered before his inquisitor.

"Alright, alright, I told the preacher. I was starving, and my wee brother wasn't well. I was desperate." He started to cry, a pathetic sniveling that caused Jinks to refrain from another blow. Nobody was getting it easy. Didn't make what Reilly had done any more palatable, but what was the point knocking him about anymore?

"Well, I hope he paid you well, for you've lost a mate and probably landed me and my sister in a load of bother."

"I'm sorry," sobbed Tommy, head bowed, unable to look his former friend in the eye.

"The least you can do now is tell me what you told them. Maggie was always good to you. Hid you that time old Sergeant Quinn chased you for stealing them apples."

"I can't. They'll batter me if..."

Another slap, this time catching the tip of Tommy's nose. "I'll batter ye. Now, talk. It's the only way you're going to get out of this alley with your head still attached to your shoulders."

Tommy nodded in final, abject defeat. "That preacher, Edgar. He's a madman. All this mumbo jumbo about your Maggie being a witch and bringing a curse down on the town. Blames her for the sickness."

"So, what did you tell him?"

"What he wanted to hear. That I saw youse leaving Kelly's and meeting some *auld* woman. Then youse headed over the fields and onto the mountain. I stopped following after that and went back. Them hills are bad. I don't want no banshee wailing outside my door."

"And?"

Jinks folded his arms and waited, convinced that he wasn't being told the full story. Tommy tried to stare him out but eventually folded like a deck of cards, such was his fear of another clout.

"I might have mentioned something about flying. It was dark, and I was half a field away, but I could have sworn you rose over that ditch like the Virgin Mother herself. The preacher went mad at that and said Maggie was gonna hang. Gathered up a load of men and took off up the mountain after her. I swear to God, Jinks, I never meant no trouble. I..."

He was unable to complete the sentence as he was hauled to his feet, the leather of a hobnailed boot connecting with his backside, sending Tommy stumbling down the alley. He regained his balance and, with a final, fearful look over his shoulder, sprinted off, leaving Jinks alone, mulling over his options. He could lie low and wait for Maggie to return; he knew a thousand hiding places about the town and normally trusted his sister to fight her own battles. But this was something else, and he knew in his heart that he would never forgive himself if he allowed her to be dragged back down the mountain to face the hangman's noose.

John Joseph Malone, all four foot eleven of him, six stone heavy when soaking wet, turned on his heel and headed toward the edge of town, to the saturated fields, and beyond them, the mountain where his sister was being hunted like an animal. She might have the Black Lady herself on her side and all the witches and banshees on the island, but he wasn't going to stand idly by and leave her fate to chance. He was the man of the Malone household now, more than willing to fill the void that his good-for-nothing lush of a father had vacated.

"Hang on, Mags. Your wee brother is coming to get ye."

He did not see the punch coming and was unconscious before he hit the wet earth.

"Are you listening to me?"

Maggie sat back in her chair, suspiciously eyeing the creature opposite her, who stared into the distance, a glazed, faraway expression suggesting that she was somewhere else entirely.

"They are coming."

"Who's coming? What are you talking about?"

Fionnuala rose and crossed the distance to the door in a single, floating movement. As she stepped outside, Maggie turned and followed her gaze. A distant fleck in the cloudless sky grew until it took the form of a large crow, its powerful wings beating soundlessly as it approached. When it seemed destined to fly past, it swooped low, landing elegantly a few feet in front of Fionnuala. She spoke to it in a tongue unknown to Maggie, a series of guttural clicking noises that the bird responded to, cawing and hopping irritably from foot to foot. The bizarre exchange continued until the crow pecked at the lawn, unearthing a fat earthworm, and ascended again out of sight. Fionnuala turned and, without a word, gestured for Maggie to follow her.

They crossed the perfectly manicured lawn that seemed to stretch in all directions for as far as the eye could see. Maggie wondered who maintained the gardens but then dismissed the thought with a shake of her head. In this outlandish environment, it was perhaps best not to think too hard for fear of irretrievably losing your mind. They ascended a slight gradient where a solitary granite stone sat, utterly out of place in the otherwise exquisite setting.

"This is the Worry Stone," announced Fionnuala, unable to mask the hint of pride in her soft, whimsical voice. "It is where we cast off our worldly concerns, allowing us to open channels to what lies beyond." She fondly stroked the rough, pitted surface of the stone, her fingers tracing a line along it. It stood no higher than Maggie's forehead, yet she sensed a hidden, latent aura that convinced her that this was a special place.

"See for yourself," said Fionnuala, nodding to her companion. "This is where you will be transformed, Maggie Malone, fully awakened to the powers that lie within you. Your mother had only a fraction of what you possess. Cast your anxieties aside and discover your true calling." She smiled again, but it was a distant expression that did little to assuage Maggie's growing concerns.

"And what if I don't want to? What if I want to get out of wherever the hell this is and go back to living as normal a life as I can with my brother? What are you going to do? Enchant me? Kill me?"

Fionnuala laughed again, infuriating the younger woman.

"What, do you think this is funny? Sitting up here in your world of make-believe while ordinary, decent folk are starving to death, coughing up blood, filling the graveyards to bursting. How's that fair? How's that vengeance?"

A flash of fury crossed Fionnuala's face, her emerald eyes blazing, as a dark scowl sullied her normally impassive features. The sky reverberated with thunder but when Maggie glanced up, she was again met with a cloudless expanse.

"Do you know what is coming, child? This very minute, there are men entering my domain with one intention on their minds. To see you hang for what has befallen this town. And when they are finished with you, they will find your beloved brother and throw him in the workhouse. Or worse, on to the first ship to Australia. Do you want that, or do you want to follow me and practice the ways of your mother? Choose now, but choose quickly, for time is no longer our friend."

Maggie stiffened, the image of a shackled Jinks in the hold of a cramped ship filling her mind. She knew the likelihood of a young boy on his own surviving such a crossing was slim. And, even if he did survive, what hope had he in such a harsh new world? Her heart filled with regret, but left with little choice, she stepped forward and placed her hand against the moss-stained stone. Fionnuala smiled and nodded, laying a hand on Maggie's shoulder.

"You choose wisely, child. This is a fresh beginning, not the end. Now open your mind and embrace what was always meant for you."

Maggie jolted as a sensation like nothing she had ever experienced before surged up her arms and through her core. It was neither painful nor unpleasant, a forceful tingling like standing ankle-deep in seawater, the incoming waves caressing your skin. She shuddered, a sudden icy feeling replacing the tingling, no longer aware of Fionnuala's hand on her. Although her eyes remained open, the fringes of her vision began to blacken while the stone and lawn blurred to such an extent that she thought she might faint. She stumbled backward but then regained her strength and planted both hands on the cool surface of the stone.

"Margaret."

Maggie spun around, incredulous at the voice. Fionnuala was no longer there, replaced by a face she had dreamed about every night since the funeral.

"Mammy. I—but..."

"Relax, girl. Now don't be getting yourself all *het* up. Deep breaths. Your woman is right about one thing, we don't have long."

Kate Malone stood before her daughter, no sign of the sickness that had ravaged her body before she was mercifully taken from its grasp. She was the healthy woman that Maggie recalled before she took ill, able to carry Jinks on one hip and a sack of vegetables on the other. Her cheeks were full and pink, no longer collapsed by hunger and illness. She had Maggie's dark curls without the gray streaks that had appeared toward the end. Her dark brown eyes sparkled with a mischievous glint, gone were the sunken sockets and deathly pallor. Here was a woman bursting with life, a woman whom Maggie had watched lowered into a pauper's grave three months ago.

"Tell me you've come back for us, tell me you're real." Maggie took a hesitant step toward her mother, not knowing whether to laugh or cry. Kate stepped back, and Maggie noticed a hazy aura around her as if she were a mirage on a desert plain.

"I've no time for your sentimental nonsense, Margaret Jane Malone. Now listen to me. Do not trust our Lady, for she has been corrupted by a terrible anger and will not rest until our town is in ruins. The power within her has been tarnished by a rage that will not cease until this land is scourged. She is not the Lady who I swore to serve back when I was a young girl."

"You've been a witch all your life?"

Her mother laughed, a blissful noise that filled Maggie's heart with both joy at what was and pain at what had been taken away.

"A witch, you say? Well, I suppose I am. It's not the word I would use, but if it helps you understand, then I see no reason not to use it. Just remember this: the powers I have handed down to you are for good, not evil. I no more cavorted with the devil than old Mrs. Crilly cavorted with Father Byrne."

Despite the intensity of the moment, Maggie could not refrain from laughing at the image of their octogenarian neighbor romancing the equally decrepit parish priest. Her mother joined in her mirth, and for a precious second, all was as before. A normal exchange between a mother and daughter. Eventually, the giggles subsided, and a comfortable silence descended between them. Maggie wished that it would last forever, but knew it was nothing more than a fleeting respite from the gathering storm.

"Can she hear us?"

"No, Maggie, which is why I must make this brief."

"What can I do? I know nothing of her ways, bar the bits and pieces you taught me."

"Oh, Maggie, you have no idea of the power inside you. She has waited generations for you, and I cherished that I had been deemed worthy enough to deliver you into this world. You were always destined for greatness to prepare her return to the world. But the years have taken their toll. Now, instead of a benevolent force, she has set course on a path of ruin and destruction. And she means to use you to that end."

"I will not assist her; she can kill me for all I care." The color rose in Maggie's cheeks, and she could feel hot tears welling behind her eyelids. She dug her nails into the palms of her hands, determined to quell their arrival.

"No, you must not, or many will perish. But you must play a careful game, and this will be my only chance to guide you. Only one stands in the way of Fionnuala, a darker force than even her, hellbent on taking the lives of many innocents himself. A creature known to the people of Belfast as Bloody Hands."

"Bloody Hands. Surely that's nothing more than a story to scare naughty children." Maggie shook her head in disbelief, struggling to process the influx of outrageous information.

"People thought the Black Lady was a faerie tale, but now you know her to be as real as you and I. Bloody Hands is very real, an *abhartach*."

"An *abhartach*?"

"He once was a local landowner, but something happened, something very bad, and he developed a taste for blood, human blood. He terrorized his tenants for decades until they rose up against him and hired a great warrior, *Fionn Mac Cumhail*, to slay him. They buried him beneath a mound of stones on the mountain, hoping that would entrap him, but he somehow escaped and haunts this town now, returning every two hundred years to claim what he believes is his birthright."

Maggie's face grew pale. "That's why he's killing the girls."

"Six every time. He calls it his blood penance. He intends to drown this land in the blood of the innocent again.

"But what has this got to do with our Lady...I mean, Fionnuala?"

Now, it was time for Kate Malone's face to blanch.

"She interrupted his killing the last time he tormented Belfast. But he had his revenge, convincing the authorities that she was a witch and to blame for the deaths. Those stupid, shallow men believed him and sent her to the gallows. Before she hung, she vowed vengeance on him and the town that gathered to watch her die. That's why she has returned, warped by hatred and spite."

Maggie looked around, at any moment expecting Fionnuala to appear and catch them in the act of revealing her true nature. "She was his sixth, then? The last time."

"She was. And that's why she needs you. Needs you more than anything."

"Me? But why?"

She paused, and Maggie thought her heart would stop, such was the stricken expression on her mother's face.

"What is it, Mammy? Tell me, please."

"Oh, child, only you have the power. He has a hold over her as she was one of his six. He is immune to her powers. But not yours. Fionnuala intends to use you to defeat this creature, then cast you aside as surplus to her requirements. You must kill them both, for while they engage in this infernal struggle as enemies, they are forged from the same dark source. Neither of them can be allowed to succeed, and only you can ensure that."

The tears fell freely now, Maggie no longer able to curtail their flow as they dampened her cheeks. Finally, Kate stepped forward, stroking her daughter's face with a hand that felt as soft as duck down. Maggie leaned into the caress, savoring a touch she had yearned for every day since her mother's passing.

"You must kill them both, Maggie. Then save yourself and Jinks. Get away from this damnable town and never look back."

"Jinks? I don't even know where he..."

"She's done a deal with him. Given up Jinks to the fiend. Nell knew nothing about it. She's a good woman, and Fionnuala has tricked her just like she's tried to trick the rest of us. Bloody Hands knows you will come to his aid and plans to take you as his sixth. The ultimate triumph. Slaying the protege of his nemesis."

Maggie opened her eyes to speak, but the dormant words fell away helplessly, her anguish only matched mounting incomprehension.

"She knows that only you possess the power to kill him. Only you can remove him and allow her evil to reign over this town. She's pitching you against him, and when you defeat him, Jinks and you will be expendable."

"But where do I even begin? I'm just an ordinary girl. How do I kill these devils?"

"Only you can answer those questions, child. Play the long game and follow the signs. I will be with you."

Maggie stepped forward to smother her mother in an embrace but was greeted only by thin air. She opened her eyes to find Fionnuala standing where Kate had been, a mildly bored expression on her face. She straightened and smiled, eager for the confirmation she so badly needed.

"Well, is it done? Have you made your choice?"

Play the long game, Margaret.

"Speak up, girl. I have no time for your mulish antics."

Follow the signs. I will be with you.

"Aye. It is done, and I have chosen. Use me as you see fit. I'll not swing from a hangman's noose for no man. And God help the first one of them who seeks to separate me from my brother."

Fionnuala smirked, cruel satisfaction creasing the freckles that adorned the bridge of her nose.

"Excellent, my dear. And believe me, when our work is done, God will be the least of their worries."

She beckoned Maggie to join her, and the two women walked back down the slope. They no longer crossed an idyllic lawn, for the mountain had reverted to its natural origins, wild and windswept for as far as the eye could see. There was no sun, but the clouds to the east carried a lighter hue, silhouetting the distant Mourne Mountains as they sloped down to the Irish Sea. Maggie walked surely, never looking back or to the side as her feet found the dirt path that meandered down the side of the haunted peak. She was blanketed in an unnatural serenity, safe in the knowledge that her mother was close. Fionnuala's web would not entangle her; she did not know how yet, but she would find a way. Death may have claimed her mother, but it would not take Jinks.

Above them, a lone crow was joined by another and then another again until the sky above the two women was a roiling mass of avian flesh. Fionnuala stopped and raised her head to the surging mass, a gleeful smile revealing teeth as white as the purest snow. She closed her eyes, inhaled deeply, and began to softly incant words foreign to Maggie, ancient words as old as the mountain itself. When she re-opened them, her eyes were black and glassy, devoid of humanity. Maggie gasped as crows began to swoop low over their heads, descending the mountain as a dense fog materialized around them. She looked at Fionnuala, whose eyes had reverted to their original emerald green, a sly smile adorning her pale features.

"Come, my child. It has begun."

The Judas Tree

They lost the first man within minutes of the fog descending, reducing vision to a handful of yards. Several of them lit oil-soaked bundles of wood they had been carrying, but these did little to penetrate the gloom. Edgar turned and looked back down the path at the shadowy figures snaking down the side of the barren slopes. The lights of Belfast were gone, buried behind a bleak wall of gray.

A gust of wind swept across his face, and he ducked low, as a screeching noise from above pierced the morning gloom. A shot sounded, the flare from a musket barrel temporarily lightening the sky. It was followed, seconds later, by a scream that every man on the mountain would never forget. Those that survived.

More muskets sounded, and a chilling squeal caused Edgar to fall to his knees behind a sizable rock at the edge of the path.

Blake joined him as panic spilled down the slope, men shouting and scrambling for cover from their unseen assailants. "What in God's name is happening, Edgar? What madness have you dragged us into?" Gone was the cool, calculated demeanor that had served him so well as he had effortlessly risen through the ranks of local government. The mask had slipped to reveal a terrified man trying to make sense of the unfolding horror.

"Demons. From the air. She knows we draw close, so she has unlocked the gates of Hell. This proves I was correct all along."

Edgar peered around the rock as a man stumbled past, clinging to a torch. He turned and, looking skyward, desperately waved the fiery projectile about his head. The concealed pastor, frozen by fear, watched as a flurry of feathers and claws enveloped the man before he was plucked into the sky, his face contorted in terror. His screams faded, and Edgar watched the flaming torch rise into the air like a hot air balloon, gradually growing smaller until it disappeared, extinguished like the life that had clung to it. A thud to their right caused both men to start and clutch each other; a dismembered arm lay on the ground where, seconds earlier, a member of Edgar's congregation had stood. Blake recoiled before emptying the contents of his stomach onto the bloodstained ground.

Edgar turned and sat, his back to the rock, mumbling prayers of protection, begging the sickening screams to end. When he opened his eyes again, the fog had lifted. He rose shakily to his feet to be greeted by Sergeant Quinn ascending the path, pistol in hand. His face was deathly pale, and Edgar watched his hand tremble as he struggled to return the firearm to its holster.

"What happened, Sergeant?" Edgar demanded. "Where are your men? Assemble them immediately."

Quinn grunted, finally succeeding in securing the pistol. "I'll assemble those who are left, sir. Half of them are probably at the bottom of the mountain by now, jumping that ditch, along with your parishioners. They won't stop, either, until they are back home hiding under their bedsheets."

"This venture is utter folly," Crothers gasped, joining the two men on the path. He looked as if his legs might give way at any moment.

"Nonsense, man. If anything, it proves my point. We may have entered the Valley of Death, but the Lord is by our side and will guide us to victory. We owe it to those we have lost, martyrs who will now live on in eternal glory. Sergeant, how many men have you left?"

Quinn frowned, less than impressed with the pastor's religious fervor. "Of an initial complement of twenty, eight are unaccounted for, although I saw young O'Donnell being plucked into the skies by whatever those creatures were. I doubt we will see him again."

"In one piece, anyway," added Crothers unnecessarily, dabbing at his mouth with a handkerchief.

"Most of your congregation have departed," added Sergeant Quinn, the dismissive tone of his voice conveying what he thought of their resolve. "But all the town guardians remain with the exception of Mr. Blake, who I saw being taken by one of those damned beasts."

"What? He was with me only a moment ago." Edgar wheeled about, searching in vain for his political ally, who was nowhere to be seen.

The loss of Blake was the final straw for Crothers, who crumpled to the ground as if he had been pounded by a prizefighter.

Edgar stepped over him, wholly unimpressed, and strode past a small cross, the third marker they had passed on the ascent.

"What about the garrison, sir? I could send word back to Major Sanderson and have a platoon of dragoons sent up to us."

"No," snapped Edgar. "This is an Irish matter. I have God on my side and, therefore, no need for the English as well. Besides, there are bread riots in the town every day now. They are run ragged as it is."

Quinn fidgeted nervously. Edgar had always known him to be a man of few words, so was unprepared for the impassioned monologue that followed.

"What would you have me do then, sir? In all my thirty years in the Constabulary, I've never experienced anything quite like this. I stood in a square at Waterloo, watching my friends being torn to shreds by French cannon. That day, I swore to God if I survived, that I would never touch another drop of alcohol again. I've kept true to my word but, at this very moment, want nothing more than a bottle of Jack Kelly's finest whiskey."

"We go on, Sergeant. Onward and upward. Did our Lord flinch in the face of his Roman tormentors? No, he did not. And neither will we in this damned and forsaken place."

"Very well, sir," replied Quinn, less enthusiastically than Edgar would have expected. "And what should I tell the men? I'm afraid quoting scripture to them might not have the effect you desire."

"Tell them there's an extra shilling for every one of them that follows me to the top and a guinea to the man who brings me the witch. And I don't care if the abomination is breathing or not."

"I'll do that, sir." Quinn smiled ruefully. Money always talked.

Edgar drew back a boot but resisted kicking the prostate Crothers, who cowered at his feet. He had a reputation to maintain as a man of God and could not be seen resorting to his baser instincts. Not in front of

Sergeant Quinn, anyway. He turned and surveyed the gravel path that twisted up the mountain past the marker. Eleven in total until they reached the Judas Tree, where all this had begun. That was where they would find the Malone girl. She would hang from that tree before the day was done.

Blake groaned, his head throbbing in time to the beat of his heart, eyes groggy and unfocused. He made to raise a hand to his aching temples but found his limbs restrained. His vision gradually clearing, he looked down to discover that his chest and legs were bound by rope. No matter how much he struggled, he could not move an inch. His breathing quickened, and he started to panic as he realized he was some distance off the ground, Belfast and the lough stretched out far below him.

He was tied to a tree, but not any tree; as realization dawned, Andrew Blake started to scream. For a very long time.

His wretched cries carried over the desolate terrain, but nobody came to his aid. As the Reverend Edgar and his company toiled on the lower slopes of the mountain, Blake found himself near the top with no recollection as to how he had arrived there. He had heard all about this tree but had never set eyes on it before as he was a gentleman of some importance with no inclination to frequent such obscene locations. The tree had gained a reputation in local folklore, but he did not share the superstitious nonsense of the lower classes.

Yet here he was, unable to budge a muscle. Trussed up like a prize turkey, at the mercy of the elements and God knows what else.

The winged beast.

Blake began to struggle again, suddenly recalling the abomination that had plucked him from the ground and carried him, as effortlessly as a feather, over bog and bracken. Outlandish as the creature may have been, surely it could not have been responsible for his current predicament.

"Are you quite comfortable up there? I could loosen the ropes a little if you wished."

He jerked his head in both directions, trying to focus on the female voice. It was soft and beguiling but carried a sinister undercurrent.

Andrew Blake was a proud man but barely noticed the trickle of urine that meandered down his inner thigh, soiling already muddied breeches.

"Oh dear. Now, there's no need for such theatrics, Mr. Blake. Although I must admit, there will be quite the mess before we are finished here today."

"Who are you? Show yourself to me!" His demand was a reedy, pitiful whine that only earned mocking laughter from the voice.

"Why, you need only look down, good sir, for we are standing right before you."

Blake craned his neck forward, beyond his trapped legs, to the foot of the tree where a woman stood. Quite possibly the most beautiful woman he had ever set eyes upon. She was slim and pale, with flaming red curls cascading over her shoulders, reaching to her hips. Strong, pronounced cheekbones and dazzling green eyes matched a sequined emerald gown more befitting of a society ball than a windswept hillside.

"Let me down from here this instance, woman. Have you any idea who I am?" He was a man used to getting what he wanted, but his words were hollow as it dawned on him who she was and why he had been taken.

"Oh, I know exactly who you are. It would be rude to have company and not be aware of their esteemed status. Mr. Andrew Blake, successful businessman and youngest ever town guardian. A man on an upward spiral. I hear talk of the mayor's office in time."

Blake spluttered but could formulate no response, his eyes locked on the witch whom he had always dismissed as a ridiculous myth.

"The same Andrew Blake who struck a most surreptitious deal with one Jeremiah Morgan, the captain of the good ship Samhara, to allow a rather dubious cargo to be disembarked in Belfast. Now, what was it again?" She tapped her chin with a long finger, teasing and taunting her helpless audience.

"Please. I'm begging you. Let me go. I have money. Whatever you want. Just cut me down, and I'll never speak of this again to anyone. I swear."

That laughter again. Mocking. He felt powerless, a sensation he was entirely unaccustomed to as a town guardian.

"Oh, I know you have money, Mr. Blake. I believe Captain Morgan rewarded you very handsomely for turning a blind eye to his little problem. Unfortunately, his little problem is now spreading through the slums like wildfire. The hospitals are overflowing with the sick and dying. The cemetery has to be extended to hold all the bodies. A small price to you, no doubt, for greasing the wheels of business."

"How can you say that, given you were the one who all but signed the deal? Were it not for your sorcery, the Samhara would have sailed by on a fair wind and never darkened these shores."

Blake's head turned instinctively towards the other voice. Equally soft, but with a hint of humanity and opposition to the witch who prowled by his feet. A second woman appeared to his left, younger and more modestly dressed than the first. Tangled hair and sad, sullen eyes. It was her—the girl that Edgar had insisted was at the heart of their current misfortune.

"Margaret. Thank God. We were so worried about you that this...this... thing had abducted you for her despicable deeds. There are men coming, many men. To rescue you. Now help me down. In the name of God, please."

"That name holds no sway on this mountain. I am the only authority here. I was killed as a woman but reborn as a higher power. Your God and his little black book mean nothing to me. Now, come, Mr. Blake. I tire of our conversation. It is time for you to be held accountable for your sins and those of your forefathers."

"Let the man go; he has done nothing worthy of this fate. My mother would have nothing to do with this. This is not revenge—it is murder, plain and simple." Maggie took a step towards the witch but found she could not take a second, her feet rooted to the sticky ground as Fionnuala turned her glacial stare away from Blake.

"You will say no more, child; otherwise, your tongue will be frozen to the roof of your mouth as your feet are to the earth. Do not dare question my intentions. Were it not for me, you and your brat of a brother would be rotting in the town *gaol* by now."

Maggie opened her mouth to remonstrate but, true to Fionnuala's threat, found no words were forthcoming. She swayed helplessly on legs that would not respond as the red-haired woman returned her attention to the helpless town guardian.

"Let you be a lesson, Andrew Blake, to all those who would dare follow you onto my mountain. I was going to hang you but believe that to be too good a death for a wretched man like you. Too quick and far too painless."

"Please. I beg of you."

"Silence."

She flicked a pale hand, and his pleas turned to ineligible mumbles as if an invisible gag had been placed over his mouth. Maggie watched as the ropes binding Blake's chest slowly constricted. He initially struggled, floundering like a netted haul of mackerel in the hold of a fishing vessel. His pleas became gargled oaths, then stifled screams, as his contorted face turned first red, then an ugly purple, what little air left squeezed from his stricken lungs. Maggie watched the unveiling horror, helpless to intervene, unable even to jolt as the first sickening cracked rib was swiftly followed by others.

"You see, my dear, this is what happens to those who cross our path. Not my path, ours. For I want you to be part of my coming glory; you have been groomed to serve me and share in the spoils. You and your brother can have whatever you so desire when I claim this land as mine. Oppose me, however, and little Jinks will be the next one to face the Judas Tree. And who knows what delights I will have in store for him."

She stepped forward, head raised and cocked at an angle, savoring every last second of Blake's demise. His tongue lolled uselessly from his mouth, black and swollen, as multiple capillaries burst in his eyeballs, turning his irises a demonic red. She smirked as the last bubbles emerged from his mouth and flecked his chin. A final, shuddering gurgle heralded the end as Maggie was released from invisible bonds. She fell to the damp earth, gasping with shock at what she had witnessed. She swayed unsteadily, her nails digging into the soft, pliant mud. Above, she heard the crows cawing, already anticipating the visceral feast that awaited them.

"I regret that you had to see that, but it was a necessary part of your education. We must rid you of this irritating compassion that you humans possess. It clouds the judgment and muddies one's thoughts. I must admit that I was restrained by it in my youth as well, but we cannot dally with your development. There is much to do and little time within which to accomplish it. Now, up on your feet, your dress is a muddy mess. I will have to find you some fresh clothes, something more befitting of your new position."

She bent down and hooked a hand under Maggie's arm, lifting her from the ground with effortless ease. Maggie refrained from looking up, for to gaze again at the body of Blake may have unraveled the last tenuous strands of her sanity. All she clung to was the fragile hope that her brother was still alive and she could somehow manipulate events so that she could reach him in time. If that meant acquiescing to the demands of the beautiful demon by her side for now, then so be it. She timidly accepted the offer of help and followed Fionnuala as they made their way down the trail. By the time the winding path had taken them out of sight of the Judas Tree, the first crow had already started to feast on the late Andrew Blake's eyeballs.

Annabelle heard the muffled screams as she scrambled up the path, the fog so thick she was forced to almost crawl on all fours to ensure she did not stray off the narrow track. She could taste the dampness in the air and something else, a rusty essence like sucking on a copper coin. Every shout was distorted by the cloying fog, one minute far in the distance, the next seemingly by her shoulder. She lost her footing several times, her satin shoes wholly inadequate for the rugged terrain. She persevered, however, a grim determination belying her slight frame.

Another roar caused her to stop and straighten. Was that her father's voice, strong and clear above the babble? It was answered by a sickening squeal, a sound unlike any Annabelle had heard before. Then silence. She doubled her pace, gripped by icy terror but determined to help Maggie and any other soul floundering on the slopes above. A shadow barrelled out of the gloom, colliding with her shoulder and sending Annabelle spinning to the wet ground. The gravel dug through the flimsy fabric of her dress, scouring her already bloody knees. She turned to watch a shadowy figure bounding down the path before another scream rang out, and the figure rose sharply into the air. It hung suspended, flailing helplessly before falling again, dropped like a discarded pebble lobbed into a stream. The body landed on the path with a dull crunch, splintering bone and splitting skin. It did not move, and Annabelle had no intention of retracing her steps to inspect the grisly remains.

A whimpering noise caught her attention, shifting it to the path above as a short, rotund figure emerged from the grayness. She vaguely recognized the man as a local physician who always seemed to lurk near the town guardian, Blake, whenever he graced them with his presence. The physician staggered to a halt, resting both hands on his knees to allow his labored breathing to revert to something resembling normality. Annabelle allowed the man to compose himself while warily scanning the mist in all directions. Eventually, her patience deserted her, the man showing no signs of having recovered from his exertions.

"Have you seen my father?"

The stout figure eventually raised his head, eyeing Annabelle with a mixture of fear and disbelief.

"Good Lord, child. What are you doing up here? You must come with me if you are to have any hope. To continue will take you to the very gates of Hell."

He reached for Annabelle's forearm to guide her back down the path, but she twisted from his grip, damned if another stupid old man was going to tell her what to do when it resulted in nothing but ruin.

"Get your dirty hands off me. I'm going nowhere until I find my father. Now, are you going to tell me where he is, you useless lump?"

Crothers winced at the words, looking as though it was not the first time they had been spoken to him. He cowered slightly from the stern young woman before sighing in defeat, he raised a trembling arm, pointing back up the path.

"Those that remain are nearing the fourth marker. But don't say I didn't warn you. On your head, be it. You're as mad as they are."

The doctor rose unsteadily, his flabby stomach threatening to burst from the confines of his protesting waistcoat. He nodded curtly at Annabelle before stumbling off down the path, making as much progress as his portly build would allow. She turned and grimly stepped forward. She would find Maggie and her father and bring them off this damned mountain if it was the last act she ever performed on earth.

Frozen once more, Maggie watched helplessly as Fionnuala made short work of the remaining members of Edgar's ill-fated party. Those with truncheons did not get within striking range of the pale sorceress as she tossed them into the air with a dismissive flick of her wrist. None of them returned to earth, instead plucked from the foggy skies by her shadowy flock of corvid beasts. Maggie shuddered to think how the poor, deluded men would spend their final seconds before their bellies were scooped open, exposed by cruel beaks and scything claws.

Finally, only Edgar himself knelt before them, Sergeant Quinn's pistol having rang out pitifully before he was hurled skywards. The preacher had fallen to his knees, Bible in hand, mumbling incoherently to a God who no longer seemed interested in his acolyte's future. Fionnuala smiled an insufferable smirk that infuriated Maggie the more she spent in the woman's company. She wondered if any shred of humanity remained within the beautiful creature gliding along the path toward where the wretched Edgar trembled. Or had it all been snuffed out the moment the hangman's noose was tightened around her neck? She gasped, realizing she had been released from the invisible bonds that the witch had, once again, used to restrain her during the slaughter.

"At least you know your place, on your knees before me," purred Fionnuala, the wind picking up, red hair billowing around her face as the fog began to clear. Maggie was relieved to see that there were no bodies littering the mountainside. She had been exposed to quite enough gore for a lifetime, thanks to the unfortunate demise of Mr Blake. The Edgar party was no more, scattered effortlessly to the four winds by the powerful witch now towering above the stricken preacher.

"Love does not delight with evil but rejoices with the truth." Edgar's eyes were closed, lost in prayer as he clung to scripture, unable to accept what had befallen his followers.

"Love," spat Fionnuala, her features contorted in disdain. "What do you know of love? You are a selfish, vain man who gives no consideration to the needs of others. You care not for the sick and starving so long as your collection plates are full every Sunday morning."

She placed a hand on Edgar's shoulder, before flicking his broad-brimmed hat from his head. The wind caught it, and it danced down the path like a stricken sailor tossed overboard. The preacher shivered, but his eyes remained closed, beads of sweat trickling down his exposed forehead as what little color was left drained from his haunted face.

"I will not submit to the authority of a witch. This will be my final resting place, I now know that, but I have stayed the course and fought the good fight. I only thank God that my daughter is at home, safe from this horror." A single tear tracked a lonely path down his pallid cheek.

"It is too late to shed tears, preacher. Your brethren shed none the day they watched me die."

"You don't need to do this," protested Maggie, making her way toward where the flame-haired woman stood over Edgar. "You have all the power you need. There's been enough bloodshed on this mountain. Just let him go."

"Your interruptions grow tiresome, Margaret. You will do as I have instructed. To suggest that you have some leverage in our arrangement is naïve in the extreme."

"Do what you must do." Edgar raised his head, at last, opening dark, vanquished eyes to face the witch. "I die with a clear conscience and am prepared to meet my God. I will sit by his feet while you rot in eternal damnation, you despicable..."

Fionnuala's face contorted, the bones shifting beneath her porcelain skin, revealing for a second what really lay beneath her earthly beauty. It was only a flicker, but Maggie saw it and, at last, understood what she was facing. This was no benevolent creature but a twisted soul polluted beyond repair by an unbridled hatred that would never be satisfied. Her mother had been initially fooled, and Nell had been fooled. There was no love or kindness to be found on this mountain.

She stepped forward instinctively, as Fionnuala raised a hand to bring it down on Edgar's exposed face. Surges of silver crackled between her fingers as the gray skies above erupted in reciprocation, the stark hillside illuminated with multiple lightning strikes. As Fionnuala's raised hand reached its zenith and began its descent toward the stricken preacher, Maggie raised her own, blocking the blow. As they touched, a noise like nails on a chalkboard, but magnified many times, scraped the air. Maggie fell to her knees, hands over her ears to dull the nauseating aural assault. Fionnuala turned away, as if slapped on the cheek, staggering a few steps before regaining her balance. She threw back her head to reveal a sliver of blood trickling from her nostril. She wiped a sleeve across her face as Maggie knelt by the man who had sought to entrap her like a hunted deer. Edgar buried his face in her shoulder and wailed, finally broken. All she could do was wrap a comforting arm around his bowed shoulders and glare at the being she had dared challenge.

"Perhaps even I have underestimated your potential," leered Fionnuala, spitting out a mouthful of blood. She smiled, gums and chin coated with a ruby smear.

"Perhaps you have. I'll do your bidding. But only until I can find my brother. After that, you may no longer count on my loyalty. I will not support one who seeks to murder the innocent."

The witch nodded, ruefully tugging at a loosened tooth. "So be it. Kill Bloody Hands and the boy, the preacher, the whole damned town is yours. For now. But hurry, hurry, for I fear Nell has failed me, and your beloved Jinks is now in the hands of our ravenous friend."

"You evil wench..."

Fionnuala tossed her head back, her shrill laughter splicing the damp air. "Oh, Maggie, your flattery knows no bounds. Thank you. But know this. I am coming. And when I do, I will show no mercy to you or your kin, no matter who your mother was. I will destroy all who dare oppose me, yourself included. Do not fail me. Kill the *abhartach* or say goodbye to your darling sibling."

Maggie nodded; no more words were required. She had crossed one line, and another had been instantly drawn. The two women stared at each other for seconds that stretched for what seemed like eons. It appeared neither would succumb and drop the other's gaze until a heartfelt cry shattered the ominous silence.

"Father!"

Maggie turned as Annabelle rounded a bend in the path, her fine dress in tatters, the palms of her once dainty hands caked in gravel and drying blood. Her hair hung loose over a shoulder, a far cry from the sophisticated young lady Maggie and Jinks had first encountered. Upon seeing his daughter, the Reverend Edgar emitted a howl that caused Maggie to let go of him. The man seemed to have aged decades in minutes as he clambered to his feet and staggered unsteadily down the path into the open arms of his weeping daughter.

"My girl, my darling girl. I thought I had lost you forever."

"Oh, Father, I will never leave you, you silly man. You know that."

Maggie smiled sadly as the two embraced, yearning for nothing more than to be reunited with her own brother. Who knew where he was and what horrors he was experiencing at the hands of that monster? Turning to question Fionnuala further, she was greeted with an empty hillside, no sign of the witch or her winged familiars. The supernatural fog had also cleared, a few remaining wisps the only reminder that it had ever been there. Maggie sighed, looking down on a teeming town, oblivious to the battle that had raged above its rooftops. She shivered and hunched her shoulders, suddenly aware of the heavy responsibility that now sat upon them.

She had to find him.

"Maggie, are you alright?" She turned to see Annabelle walking towards her, a protective arm around the waist of her exhausted father.

"I will be. Just as long as I get my brother back."

"I'm so sorry, my child. I have wronged you greatly. I knew there was a shroud of evil over this town, but had no idea of the danger that threatened us. You saved my life. I owe you my undying thanks. Please forgive an idiotic, reckless man." He smiled weakly at Maggie, all the anger and hatred drained from his body.

At least some good had come from this hellish morning. Maggie bit her lip, part of her wanting to rant and scream at the vain, sanctimonious cretin now mumbling worthless apologies at her. Newfound power crackled within her, and she knew she could crush his vacuous skull with a raised eyebrow or flick of her wrist. But that made her no better than the beautiful monster that had stood before them less than a minute ago. If she were to kill the pastor, then she was no better than Fionnuala, no better than a common murderer. The pleading look in Annabelle's sad blue eyes confirmed the decision she had already made.

"What does the Bible say, Mr. Edgar? 'Let they who have not sinned cast the first stone.' Well, look. You will see no stones in my hand." She opened her palms and smiled as Annabelle mouthed silent thanks. Edgar merely dropped his head and nodded, a relieved man. The wind whistled across the exposed hillside, the somber day gradually revealing the mountain in all its brutal glory.

Maggie reached out a hand, and a grateful Edgar accepted it, his gaunt, tear-streaked face a far cry from the arrogant, hateful visage that had glowered at her from the pulpit not long ago. With Maggie and Annabelle on either side of him, they gingerly began to descend the slope back towards the town that sat unaware of the events that had irrevocably changed both it and the three sad figures who called it home.

Towards Jinks.

Maggie stared impassively ahead. This mountain had changed her, and she was no longer the naive, desperate young woman who had set foot on its lower slopes a few hours ago. Hours that now felt like decades, centuries, huge chunks of time that were seared into her soul, making her unrecognizable from the girl who had scrambled from one day to the next, struggling to keep her brother alive. Now she had focus and a purpose— Jinks was somewhere out there. She would find and save him and woe betide any unfortunate creature who came between them. Fionnuala, Bloody Hands; all the demons in Hell could come and try.

They could come. But they would fail.

Ugly Gods

Fionnuala watched as death knocked on many a door that bland, grotesque day, its vile grip on the town tightening. The early morning wind fell away to a growling whisper, as the first mournful cries filled her ears, heralding a day like no other. The blackest day of Black '47, a year that would irrevocably scar Belfast. The dead and the dying were everywhere. No street, no courtyard was untouched. Hunger and fever plucked the victims from their homes with frightening ease. Rich or poor, fine ladies or stinking peasants, it mattered not, for neither money nor influence found favor with her unrelenting rage. Fionnuala saw it all and smiled.

The girl had irked her, but no more than that. A trifling inconvenience to be dealt with later; she refused to allow it to distract her from the day she had waited so long for. When she had served her purpose, Maggie's body would be just one more to throw on the funeral pyre that would light up this land, casting a cleansing light across the island for all to see and know that she was coming. For this was only the beginning—when the girl removed Bloody Hands, Fionnuala would reveal her true identity. No more skulking on the mountain, nothing more than a whispered tale passed down through the ages. She would rise and reign, a new deity for them to fall on their knees and worship.

They piled the carts high that dreadful morning, bodies tossed like broken dolls on top of each other, a teetering tower of decay. Limbs sat at unnatural angles, glassy eyes staring blankly at the dour skies. She breathed deeply, walking amongst them, oblivious to all. The gravediggers wore scarves across their faces, doused in vinegar, to ward off the obscene stench. They dragged the carts directly to the cemetery, no church service or wake afforded. There was no dignity in death for them or their families, who shuffled behind the carts, a pitiful cortège that stretched and grew as it snaked through the narrow streets of the town.

She led them, the hem of her dress casually dragging along the mucky, churned-up track. The numbers increased after every heart-breaking stop, each one signifying another devastated household, another family changed forever. She smirked, the suffocating grief filling her with a giddy joy unlike any she had experienced before. She greedily inhaled it, sucking in their sorrow, relishing every last wail and sob. Every last wheezing breath inspired her to channel every ounce of her remaining energy into the disintegration of Belfast. It consumed her, a stagnant obsession, and pushed her onward to new depths. Soon, the town would crumble, Bloody Hands would be no more, and she would reveal herself to the few who remained. They would worship her, their savior and goddess.

The door was ajar; one final push was all that was required. Though she had disappointed Fionnuala with her histrionics on the mountain, she knew Maggie would accede to her demands when the time came. The boy would make sure of that. Fionnuala did not have the power to challenge Bloody Hands *and* take the town, but the girl did. The girl would kill him. And when she did, when his blood was on her hands, her fate would also be sealed.

Fionnuala smiled as another body was thrown onto the cart behind her. Another coal on the fire, a fire that would burn like no other before she was finished.

Today would be a good day.

Today was not a good day.

Maggie wiped a grimy hand across her sweating brow as Annabelle edged across the ditch that marked the base of the mountain and their return to civilization. Across the fields lay Belfast, a blanket of smoggy clouds concealing a weak morning sun that battled to breach the gloomy barrier with its soothing rays. Edgar crouched by her feet, sucking in great lungfuls of air. Fionnuala and her murderous flock may not have killed him, but their breathless descent down the mountain had been an entirely different matter. He had fallen on several occasions and pleaded with Annabelle to leave him be and die alone as he deserved. His daughter had refused, however, impressing Maggie with her dogged loyalty despite the atrocious recent behavior of her father. If only she had a similar resolve. She raised an anguished face to the murky skies, anxiety threatening to overwhelm her.

"You're not on your own."

Maggie turned to face the preacher's daughter, who had negotiated the treacherous ditch and now stood before her on the other side, the narrow plank separating them. A bell tolled in the distance, its lugubrious tone befitting the unfolding events. Maggie smiled weakly before replying.

"I feel as if I am. I renounced the church when my mother died, and now the Lady of the Mountain has revealed her true colors to me. Colors that I am not much minded to like. Who can I turn to now?" She cast a look at Edgar, who turned his head away in shame. It was his daughter who again spoke, offering comforting words that her disgraced father was no longer capable of uttering.

"You turn within, Maggie Malone. I recognized it the first time I set eyes on you in the soup kitchen. Look what you have achieved so far. Surviving the death of your mother and raising a fine young man like John Joseph. A finer gentleman in this town I have yet to meet. You should be proud of him and of yourself."

Maggie smiled shyly, unused to compliments, and awkwardly twisted the hem of her shawl. The shawl her mother had worn around her shoulders, in service of an angel, now unveiled as a venomous foe. Reassured by the gesture, Annabelle persisted with her gentle interrogation of a young woman she liked more and more with each moment she spent in her company.

"I was born into a Christian family, a home where love and gracious acts were taught to us as second nature. You may practice a different faith, but I see the same values in you. For that, I respect your ways, alien though they may seem to me." She looked down at her father, who seemed a million miles away, entranced by a clump of daffodils that stood resplendent amidst the mucky field.

"We were taught to be different, to stand out from the crowd, a bit like those daffodils. We were to turn the other cheek, to rise above our basic urges, and resist sinful behavior. Well, look where that got us." She flapped her hands by her side in exasperation, her dress billowing in a wind that had tempered now to a stiff breeze and no more.

"You mustn't think that. Your father is not well, that is the only explanation I can find for his behavior. You are a good person. Look how you fed and clothed the poor with little thought as to your own safety."

Now, it was Annabelle's turn to look sheepishly aside. She had never viewed her work at the soup kitchen as anything worthy of praise but rather as a necessary act in response to the horrendous conditions she witnessed on the streets every day. It was nothing extraordinary, but rather the most ordinary of reactions to a situation that was spiraling out of control.

"I am nothing special, Maggie, but you are."

She stepped forward and took the hands of her friend, for that was how she now regarded the disheveled, confused young woman standing before her. A lone ray of sunlight penetrated the clouds, bathing them in a warm glow that eased their aching bones.

"You may regard it as a curse, but I view it as rather a blessing. I have seen what this witch is capable of, and she is intent on destroying us all. As did my father, although he has approached the matter in entirely the wrong way and consequently learned a very hard lesson."

"It is not for me to judge," replied Maggie, who smiled sadly at the slumped form of Edgar, still struggling to regain his breath after their descent.

"Yet *you* have the power to judge Fionnuala and stop her from destroying our town, our country. Who knows, maybe the entire world. I have seen what you are capable of, and she fears you for that. Yes, kill this demon, Bloody Hands, I will do everything in my power to help you save Jinks. But afterward, you must kill her as well."

"I don't know if..."

Annabelle frowned and raised a hand, stopping Maggie in mid-sentence. The prim clergyman's daughter had a steely edge that Maggie was fast becoming familiar with. She smiled in defeat and allowed her newfound friend to continue. "Stop right this instance and answer me this. Can you sense him? Tell me where he is. Concentrate."

Maggie looked helplessly at Annabelle. All this power, but not the first inkling of how to utilize it. She stared across the fields and over the smoking rooftops in exasperation, desperate for some clue as to where her brother might be held. It was then that she saw it.

A solitary beam of sunlight had somehow penetrated the ever-present cloud cover, casting its warm rays over an area of the town that Maggie knew all too well, a squalid courtyard that attracted the lowest of clientele. She had spent many a freezing day there, struggling to make ends meet, abandoned by a father who had downed tools and neglected his parental duties the day his wife was buried, instead seeking solace in whatever alcoholic beverage he could afford.

"What is it, Maggie? What do you see?"

Annabelle followed her friend's gaze and could only watch in amazement as the beacon illuminated the path ahead. Had he not been already on his knees, Edgar would have fallen to them. Tears streaked his gaunt cheeks.

"It's a sign from the Lord. His gracious light shines on his people. He, and only he, can save us."

"Oh, do be quiet, you foolish old man," snapped Maggie, already striding out across the field towards the town. "Come along, Annabelle. We will ensure your father is returned safely home, and then I know exactly where we will find Jinks."

"What? Where?" Annabelle scurried to raise her father to his feet, fearful that Maggie would be out of sight before the pastor was ready to resume their journey.

"Carson's Court. The filthiest quarter of this filthy town. That's where he will be. And that's where I will finish this."

He saw the shaft of light as well, frowning as it cast a glittering swathe across the only window of his cellar lair. He retreated into its dimmest corner, snarling indignantly at the creeping light as it inched towards him.

Opposite him in the far corner, the boy flinched before the darkness claimed him again. He had hit him hard, but not so hard that he would not open his eyes again. He would feed from him later but held back for now, wanting to leave it to the last possible moment, for he would need every drop of the youth's sweet essence when she came for him. In time, the boy's sister would be the sixth, but before then, he would have his fun.

He snorted in disgust, for he now knew the *cailleach* did not possess the power to challenge him. Their meeting had proven that. No, she would send one of her stinking coven to placate him while she occupied her time with this ridiculous vendetta against the mortal scum who fouled the land. He had little time for their pathetic lives; they were nothing more than a food source to him, a means to an end. He needed six, and if the witch was willing to serve the girl up on a plate to him, then who was he to look a gift horse in the mouth? The *cailleach* thought that would be the end of it then, he would then leave her for another two hundred years to rule the land unchallenged.

The stupid bitch.

When he had killed the girl, he would kill the boy, and anyone else who stood in his way; kill and kill again until he eventually sank his teeth into the *cailleach's* sweet, sweet throat. She thought she could appease him with this girl, Maggie, but it was nowhere near enough. This time, he was hungrier, famished, but focused; everything was in place and just as it should be, whereas the *cailleach* was a wounded animal, fragile and distracted.

The light caught the first bone in the protective circle he had formed. It sparked a tibia if he was not mistaken. From the first or the third, he frowned as his memory was not as it had once been. Time did that, even to a being like him who had watched kingdoms rise and fall with detached boredom, satisfied only by the scarlet stream that ran freely through the ages whenever he chose to roam. He knew the circle would contain the light, the bones of those he had already killed and claimed as trophies, protecting him from her tiresome spells.

He stretched and turned awkwardly, the damp chill of the cellar doing little for the aches and pains that bothered him more with each passing decade. When all this was over, he might travel further south and holiday in warmer climes. Cork, perhaps. He had visited Skibbereen in the past, and its deathly odor had filled his nostrils with an enticing aroma. So much death down there, so many destitute and displaced. He would be in his element, hiding in plain sight, for who would miss a homeless laborer or orphaned child amidst the horrors of the hunger? Yes, that would suit him very well.

He lay back against a sack of sodden grain and rested both hands behind his bald, scarred head. Beyond his feet, the bones crackled and flared, warding off the last of the passing shaft of light. So what if they knew where he was? That was part of the plan. The girl would come, she would fail, and then he would have Fionnuala exactly where he wanted her. Alone and exposed, he would feast on the sixth and rise from this dark hole to end her once and for all.

"Bloody Hands, Bloody Hands. Where can he be?
Bloody Hands, Bloody Hands, he's coming for ye
Bloody Hands, Bloody Hands one, two, three
Bloody Hands, Bloody Hands, where can he be?"

He chuckled to himself. He was a legend, a myth, a song that children sang as they hopped and skipped through the puddles of the streets above. Well, who was he to disappoint his army of admirers? It was time to put on a show, the likes of which this wretched town had never witnessed before.

"That's him sleeping," sighed Annabelle, slumping into her father's favorite armchair. Maggie sat facing her, a steaming cup of sugary tea warming her cupped hands. It was only upon arriving at the Edgar town-house and sitting down that the exhaustion struck her, harder than the most ravaging hunger pang. She had found herself nodding off on more than one occasion while Annabelle tended to her muddled father, who had babbled most of the way back, raving about winged demons and Jezebels sent from the fiery furnace to test his faith. Several passers-by had shot them bemused looks, but thankfully, they had not encountered any of his congregation, where awkward questions would have been difficult to answer. Those of his congregation still alive, that was.

"Good," replied Maggie. She had been nibbling on a slice of bread slathered in thick raspberry jam but now set the plate aside, her normally constant hunger stilled by the thought of her brother's continued incarceration. She stared across the study at nothing in particular as another cart rumbled by outside, the hooves of horses and whistling drivers belying a town on the brink of collapse. Life went on, normality continued, even when people held dear slipped from their grasp. Rather embrace the mundane than turn and stare into the abyss.

"John Joseph? Is he..." Annabelle floundered for the appropriate words but was reduced to silence and a pained expression that touched Maggie's heart. Amidst all the upheaval and chaos, she truly believed that she had, at last, found the friend to fill the gaping hole left by the loss of her mother.

"Alive? Yes, he is alive and unharmed for now, but do not ask me how I know that. I feel like a rusty tap that has finally been loosened. These powers. I can sense them swirling within me, surfacing to answer my needs. And yet, I have little knowledge of how to control them." She smiled helplessly and took another sip of her tea, savoring its warmth.

"Should we not be setting out to find him? I'm as tired as you, but we need to act soon, surely?"

"Bloody Hands, whatever that creature is, will wait until darkness. His kind cannot abide the light. He intends me to be his sixth but must return to Carson's Court to complete his sick ritual. Dead Girl's Alley, that's what the locals call it. That's where he must finish it. Jinks will be safe until then, as he's the bait Bloody Hands is using to lure me into his net."

"How do you know all this?" Annabelle furrowed her brow, intrigued by this slip of a girl who now resonated with a wisdom and knowledge well beyond her tender years.

Maggie shrugged, not wanting to reveal her mother's warning. That had been a private, precious moment that she did not yet want to share with another soul, irrespective of how much she trusted the preacher's daughter. "I don't really know. It's like the light we saw earlier. It's as if I'm being nudged along. Thoughts and information are being planted in my mind that I know to be true."

"I wish I shared your confidence." Annabelle glanced at the sturdy oak grandfather clock that hung on the wall above them. It was late afternoon, although it felt much later to her exhausted body.

"I do not know about confidence, but that is where Jinks will be, so that is where I must go to find him."

"Where *we* will go to find him," corrected Annabelle. The determined set of her normally carefree features caused Maggie to laugh despite the gravity of their circumstances.

"Oh, Annabelle Edgar, I am so glad I made your acquaintance. But you need not accompany me. You have already done so much. You owe us nothing. Besides, I will not be alone."

"Won't be alone? Whatever do you mean?" Annabelle's eyes widened, and she glanced around the study nervously. This day was getting stranger by the hour.

"Oh, you need not worry," giggled Maggie, leaning forward and taking her friend's hand. It felt warm and comforting, a welcome connection after the horrors of the day. They were alive, they were together, and there was shared hope between them, a hope that they would emerge from the other side of this nightmare.

Annabelle smiled weakly and squeezed Maggie's hand. Tears did not look far from her eyes, and she blinked rapidly to hold them at bay.

"I trust you, Maggie. But I will also not allow you to face this monster alone, and that is the end of the matter."

Maggie laughed, and it felt good. She had initially dismissed the preacher's daughter as just another well-meaning but naive young woman out of her depth and cosseted from the struggles that Jinks and she battled on a daily basis. Yet, she had layers beneath her prim collars and polished accent. Layers of strength and compassion that perfectly suited her to the trials that lay ahead. Realizing that the young woman facing her was in no mood to back down, Maggie nodded and acquiesced to the ultimatum.

"Very well then, as you are so insistent. We will wait until dark and then make our way to Carson's Court. Although I have no great desire to meet most of my neighbors again."

"Good. I am glad that it is decided. I will check on Father and be back with you presently." She rose and hesitated before turning and bending to engulf Maggie in a warm embrace. Maggie tensed, unaccustomed to such shows of affection, before relaxing her shoulders and enjoying the moment. She closed her eyes and savored every second of human contact, not knowing when, if ever, she would hold her brother again. A secondary wave of regret nipped at her heart when Annabelle eventually broke the clutch. With a fleeting smile, she turned and hurried from the study, eager to check on her ailing father. Maggie watched her leave, her mind a flurry of conflicting thoughts and emotions.

"She is a lovely young woman."

"Oh, Mother. You must stop this habit of sneaking up on me unannounced or I'll be joining you in the afterlife." Maggie turned and smiled at the hazy figure standing by the window, surveying the street outside. Kate Malone glowed, the edges of her outline shimmering like a hazy mirage drifting across a desert plain.

"You need a friend, Maggie, now that I am gone. Now that your father..." She paused, their shared pain not requiring further words. Maggie looked away. They may as well have buried John Malone the day they sealed his wife's cheap coffin. Eventually, Maggie groped for words to fill the yawning silence.

"What's done is done. And what will be will be. And as for Annabelle? Well, yes, I do believe she and I will become firm friends." She smiled, and the tension between them evaporated, her mother stepping forward into the room, her form taking greater substance as she did.

"Indeed. But now you must proceed, my girl. You have much to do, and time is not our friend. That beast has my wee boy and as much as I love Jinks, I do not want him by my side before this day is over. He has a life to lead, as do you when all this is done. It ends today."

"I know where he is, Mammy. I know so much now. Have you been guiding me all this time?"

"I have, love. Me and many others who have passed before me. We are many and all so different, but we are agreed on one thing. This ends today. Do you understand?"

Maggie understood.

"It ends today."

Billy Thompson wiped the sweat from his grubby brow before rubbing his hand on even grubbier trousers. He looked down and frowned, his sturdy leather boots caked in mud. Shrugging, he pushed open the door and entered the murky interior of the pub. Callaghan's, his second home. Not the most salubrious ale house in Belfast, but certainly one of the cheapest. The beer was foul, but he didn't care at the end of a busy day of chasing up rent arrears. He just wanted to forget the day and retreat into a comforting, intoxicated haze.

"Usual, Billy?" smiled the barmaid, revealing a set of yellowing teeth. The smile did not extend to her eyes. She was tired—every soul who entered this rundown establishment was tired and at the end of their tether. The sad reality was that they all had nowhere else to go. So, they congregated in Callaghan's to drown their various sorrows and keep their heads somehow above the turbulent, unpredictable waters of life.

"Aye, bring it over to me. And a bowl of stew if there's any going."

He dug deep into a pocket and tossed a handful of coins in her direction. It was more than the grub and ale cost, but he knew the barmaid would keep the drink coming as long as he remained in the bar, and not bother him with idle chatter. Billy spent most of his working day talking when he was not busting lips and blackening eyes, so solitude was a precious asset in the little recreational time that he had. He surveyed the bar, where a handful of downbeat patrons studiously avoided eye contact and focused on their own inner demons. A lifetime of brawling had honed broad shoulders and provided him with a wiry physique that meant few bothered to annoy him. He could handle himself, and many a man had regretted exchanging drunken words with him in the past. He'd even got in a few good digs the one time that bastard, Jack Kelly, had squared up to him.

Two hours later, the bowl of now cold stew lay untouched in front of him as he drained the contents of another tankard. He belched and rose unsteadily to his feet, nodding at the barmaid who eyed him curiously. He staggered unsteadily towards a side entrance that led out onto an alley that functioned as a bathroom for the almost exclusively male clientele. Billy allowed the door to close behind him and stumbled down the alley, narrowly avoiding a mewling cat in the process. It was later than he thought, and the scant light of the day had almost departed. Further along, a giggling couple could be heard, but Billy had no interest in their sordid antics. He fumbled with his trousers and placed a palm against the alley wall before closing his eyes and groaning in pleasure as the contents of his full bladder spattered down the brickwork before trickling lazily along the alley.

He turned to admire his handiwork, the urine splashing over the cobbles, disturbing a rat scuttling across the alley. That's when he saw the boy.

Thinking back, he was certain that he and the girl had been hiding in Kelly's, and the publican had pulled the wool over his eyes. He had kicked himself for backing down to the man, but the gap in his front teeth had been enough to make him err on the side of caution. He would cross Kelly again when the odds were more in his favor. Long runs the fox, Jack, long runs the fox.

"C'mere, you wee runt," he snarled, hastily fixing his trousers, before lurching towards the Malone boy, who stood facing him with an odd, detached look on his face. Why wasn't he running? Something wasn't right here if...

He didn't even hear the sound of his own neck being jerked at an obscene angle and the sickening crack before his limp body was hurled against the wall. Nobody disturbed the *abhartach*, for a glamor had been cast over the surrounding area, ensuring that an uneasy fear settled on any passing drunk who considered a shortcut through the alley, instead giving it a wide berth.

The glamor extended to the small boy who stood motionless behind the grisly scene, his blank eyes and slack jaw instead focused on the urine-stained wall. He would have no memory of the carnage not six feet from him, enthralled by the one who now cast the body of Billy Thompson aside, one of the dozens he would casually slaughter for crossing his path between his lair and the place where he would find the sixth. He was merely warming up, an aperitif before the main course that had him licking his lips in devilish anticipation. Billy would be just another casualty of Smithfield, to be picked up by the Constabulary and thrown onto a cart bound for the cemetery where he had previously dispatched so many others. One of the gravediggers might even recognize him, tossed into a shallow grave with the hundreds of others delivered daily, ravaged by hunger or riddled with the fever.

"Come on, boy. Thirsty work this killing. But, worry not, I'll take care of your darling sister soon enough."

"Yes, sir." The words were monotone, devoid of the bubbling emotions that normally spewed from his effervescent lips. Jinks shuffled after his new master, his normally curious mind devoid of a shred of independent thought.

"That's the boy. Won't be long before it's all over. Your lovely sister will make six, and then all will be well again with this stinking city. Old Bloody Hands will make certain of that." To emphasize the point, he bent down, fondly patting the still-warm neck of his broken victim.

Bloody Hands smiled. It was not his real name, but it had grown on him. The smile did nothing to improve his features. He did not care, for when this night was over, he would be a god, worshipped by all. Ugly gods were still gods.

Say The Words

⚜

T he streets were unnaturally quiet, as though the town had been plunged into a period of mourning in their absence. They avoided the main thoroughfares and kept to the back streets but even then, the normal hustle and bustle was missing. Maggie strode purposefully, eyes fixed firmly ahead, while a less resolute Annabelle struggled to keep up, unaccustomed to walking at such an accelerated pace. There had been no conversation between them since they had left the Edgar townhouse. Maggie had insisted that Annabelle sleep for a few hours once her father had settled. Reluctantly, and after much haranguing, the blonde-haired young woman had agreed, although insisting that she would be unable to rest. However, her head had barely touched her soft and familiar pillow, and she had fallen into a deep and restful slumber.

She awakened once, convinced she heard voices in the study below. Initially, she thought it was Maggie conversing with an unwanted caller, but Annabelle had dozed off again, persuading herself that it was the overflow of a comforting dream she had been having about her own late mother. When she later asked Maggie about it, the other girl had shrugged and dismissed the inquiry, a furtive expression crossing her features. Annabelle had not asked again, instead channeling her energy on keeping pace with her companion, who marched through the empty streets at a frightening speed, half a step off a full-blown dash.

"And what are we expected to do when we reach Carson's Court? Do you simply expect this beast to hand over your brother with a cheery smile and a wave?"

Maggie slowed to a halt as they reached a deserted junction. At this time of the day, it should have been a bustling thoroughfare. Opposite them, a young man sat slumped in a doorway, the silence breached by watery coughs that wracked his emaciated frame. Annabelle mouthed a silent prayer for his soul as he did not look much longer for this earth.

"All we need do is be there. The rest will take care of itself."

"What does that even mean, Margaret? Why must you persist with these riddles?" She rolled her eyes in exasperation, her patience clearly wearing thin.

"I've been chosen of her followers to slay this creature. Bloody Hands rises every two hundred years to prey on those foolish enough to walk these streets at night. I am intended as his sixth. Other than that, I don't really know what will happen. These powers within me, I'm still coming to terms with what I can and cannot do." Maggie gave her friend a sheepish glance and shrugged her shoulders, once more the shy, young woman Annabelle had first met in the soup kitchen at Howard Street. Only a handful of days had passed since then, but it felt like a lifetime.

Annabelle laughed, partly to conceal her growing nerves, before her face dropped, gazing into the distance. "Bloody Hands. Every child in Belfast is told that story to ensure they stay in their beds at night. Who would have thought that it's..."

Now, it was Maggie's turn to laugh.

"True? Oh, I'm afraid it is. It's all true. Every last damned ghost story and faerie tale our parents fed us as children. Bloody Hands is as real as you and I. Which is why I say again, Miss Edgar, that you do not have to accompany me into this horror. Go home and spend time with your father, none of us may have much of it left."

"I understand all that, but I'm going nowhere." It was all Annabelle could muster in response, but it was enough for Maggie.

"Thank you." She reached out and squeezed Annabelle's hand with her own, a small but sufficient gesture.

"So, you kill him. What then?"

Maggie smiled a grim smile that contained no trace of humor.

"When I kill Bloody Hands?"

"Yes. What will become of the witch?"
"Why, then I will kill her as well."

The gravediggers had long departed, their somber work done for another day. Darkness was descending, claiming the cemetery as its own once more. Fionnuala wandered through the swathe of freshly dug, unmarked graves, an elegant shadow savoring the sweet stench of decay and disease that clung to this hallowed ground. Occasionally, she would drop to her knees and bury her face in the soil, inhaling the ruin of their broken dreams. The dead lay in their thousands all about her, and she sucked every last ounce of poisoned energy from the lingering essence of their mortal existences. This was her succor, the honeyed nectar she required to bring her powers to an ecstatic peak that would allow her to descend upon the remnants of this wretched town with unrivaled fury.

Listening, her ear cupped to the recently disturbed soil, she could hear their murmured yearnings, a distant desire to return to the realm of the living and resume their nondescript existences. She smiled, a red slash across her otherwise luminescent complexion. They would not pass, and nothing awaited them but the company of worms and decay. She flung her head back and laughed, a guttural shriek that caused the town to fold in on itself, cowering at the prospect of a new night of terror.

Gas lamps flickered, their feeble flames stuttering in defiance of her call. Families huddled around their meager fires, ravaged by gnawing hunger and cloying sickness. Not a house was untouched, from the grandest townhouse to the slums of the penniless. They all heard her call, the cry of the Banshee, the Black Lady come to take them in their beds. All dreaded the morning, knowing they would awaken to the screams of the newly bereaved. She would walk amongst them this night and take lives with the ease of fat grapes being plucked from the vine.

Maggie and Annabelle froze as a piercing cry cut across the night sky, the lamps flickering like crazed moths. They were nearing Bank Street, the streets still deserted.

"What was that?"

Annabelle turned in all directions, but the sound was all around and within them, rising to a chilling crescendo before ceasing as abruptly as it had begun.

"I fear the Black Lady has come down off the mountain to witness the final act. I only pray that this will bring an end to it all. Now hurry, it's not far."

Annabelle nodded, and they quickened their pace again, weaving across the cluttered maze of alleys and courtyards until finally emerging onto the wider thoroughfare of Bank Street. Facing them was the unlit, narrow entry that led into Carson's Court. There was an eerie stillness, a million miles from the normal noises that should have greeted them. Belfast was devoid of life, as if the rapture had taken every last soul from their homes and transported them to glorious eternity. Maggie sniffed the air; it crackled with magical energy. He was close, and if he was close, then Jinks was surely with him.

"Come on."

She gripped Annabelle's sleeve and hauled her across the cobbles, the yawning mouth of the entry seeming to widen before them, daring the two young women to brave its depths. They continued, consumed by the impenetrable blackness, unable to see their own hands as they fumbled along the damp brickwork. Seconds became a minute and then two as a growing, unspoken panic threatened to overwhelm them. The entry was not this long, surely they should have emerged from the other side by now, into the courtyard?

"What's happening, Maggie? What is this place?" Annabelle clutched blindly at her friend's shoulder, stumbling and almost falling, as the entry showed no signs of an end.

Maggie opened her mouth to reply, although uncertain as to what solace she could provide, but a spectral figure ahead stymied her words. As they neared, a young woman came into view, not more than a few years older than her. An unnatural red glow surrounded her as she clutched at her stomach, unable to contain its gory contents from spilling onto the ground with a sickening slap. She looked down in mild consternation before raising her face to stare at Maggie, an unhinged grin on her gray, clammy face.

"I was his first, and you will be his last. Six of the best for Bloody Hands. Hurry, hurry, you don't want to miss the show."

Annabelle screamed as Maggie flung her arm outwards, reciting words in a language she did not understand. They rolled off her tongue, ancient and powerful, relishing the opportunity to be uttered again after centuries of lying dormant. The figure before them erupted into a fireball and began to flail about the entry like a broken marionette doll before dropping away in a cloud of ash and smoke. Maggie forged ahead, bowing her head, as Annabelle desperately struggled behind her.

"What did you say?" Annabelle coughed, the sulfurous fumes threatening to choke her as the scent of charred flesh polluted her nostrils.

"I have no idea, but it seemed to work. Look. Up ahead. I see a light. We're almost there."

Maggie broke into a run, and Annabelle gave up all hope of maintaining a hold on her. Hitching her skirts, she emerged from the grotesque cloud and cried with delight at the sight of an archway not far ahead of them. Maggie accelerated, pulling away and finally out of the entry, before coming to a shuddering halt. Unable to curtail her own momentum, Annabelle barreled into the back of her friend, grappling to maintain some semblance of balance. She looked up and was greeted by a hellish assembly of gaunt, vacant faces.

"Jesus, have mercy..."

Before them, the remaining inhabitants of Carson's Court were gathered, spaced across the slick cobbles. Their arms lay limply by their sides as they hung suspended, their feet somehow several feet off the ground. Maggie stared into the faces of men, women, and children that she had been reared with, entire families now oblivious to her presence. They occupied every inch of the courtyard, ensnared by a dastardly presence that now emerged from behind the first row of levitating bodies.

He was utterly unremarkable, his only outstanding feature being his ugliness. His head was bald and pitted with dents and scars, his shoulders hunched and sloping. His face was paunchy, rolls of fat surrounding a squashed nose and cloudy, nondescript eyes. A sneer dominated his features, drawing their eyes away from his squat, short body. A sneer that encapsulated his essence, his unfiltered disgust at the living, at the two pure souls who stood before him, daring to challenge his unholy right to complete the ritual and retain his stranglehold on the town.

"What's the matter? Cat got your tongue, girls?" His words dripped with unbridled sarcasm as he turned to either side, admiring his grotesque handiwork. They hung lifeless and unseeing, dead eyes silently mocking the audacity of the two young women who dared to interfere with what he most desired.

"Where is my brother? Tell me where he is or, so help me God, I'll..."

"You'll do what exactly?" He took a step forward, causing Annabelle to unconsciously recoil, much to his demented glee.

Maggie stood her ground, determined not to yield an inch in the quest to find Jinks. The evil rolled off the creature facing her in putrid waves, but something else was there, lingering just beneath his callous surface, something that provided her with a sliver of hope. He was uncertain, wary of the forces that bubbled inside her, swirling and surging with each passing second.

"Give me back my brother, and be on your way. You are not welcome. The Black Lady has sent me; this is her realm, and you have no place here." The words stuck in her throat, but she spoke them anyway, swallowing her disgust and continuing with the charade.

Play the long game, Maggie. Play it patiently and play it well.

"Ah, the magnificent Black Lady. Sending out a little girl to fight her battles." He raised his hands and laughed, an unhinged cackle that did nothing to alleviate the unease resonating from Annabelle. Maggie cast a glance in her friend's direction, hoping that the connection would reassure the terrified young woman. Annabelle was dangerously pale, but she nodded and held firm. Maggie returned the gesture, grateful that, if nothing else, she had unearthed a friend for life. She swallowed hard before turning to face her adversary again.

"I am no girl, and you will learn that in due course. And this will be a most one-sided battle. The Lady has chosen me for a reason, a reason that will become apparent to you very shortly. Now I will ask you one more time and one more time only. Where is my brother?"

She surprised herself with the words as if she was merely a vessel, and they came from a foreign source that was manipulating her lips and vocal cords. A soothing peace descended over her skin, goosebumps breaking out in regulated ranks, a subtle shift in the energy raging through the courtyard. He sensed it as well. The laughter stopped.

"Very well." He snapped his fingers and looked skywards, Maggie and

Annabelle following his eyes. What Maggie saw was a sight that chilled her to her core. There, above the rooftops of the courtyard, was Jinks, chin resting on his chest, which barely rose, comforting Maggie that at least he was alive. Alive, if little else. Slowly, the little boy's limp body descended until he hovered above his tormentor, who reverted his smug, self-satisfied attention back to Maggie.

It crushed her, and she stepped towards him, her face a mask of raw hatred. Sparks danced between her fingers, and she spoke the ancient, unknown words again.

"I wouldn't do that if I were you." A bead of sweat had formed on his expansive forehead, and Maggie seized upon it, a solitary sign that beneath the bravado and gusto, he feared who she was, what grew inside her.

She stalled as first one, then another, body dropped to the cobbles before her. They landed with sickening cracks, lying lifeless, like leaves cast from swaying trees on a windswept October morning. Neighbors and friends sucked dry and cast aside, mercilessly felled by a beast that knew no guilt or remorse. Maggie hesitated, fumbling for the connection with a dead mother who had guided her this far, but now seemed to have abdicated all remaining responsibility. Clutching, grappling, and then it was there—a sparkling thread spinning deep within her, connecting her with the woman who birthed her, the woman who would tell her what she needed to know to save her other child; a little boy who hung above them like a rag doll, while all around him, bodies rained down from a mournful sky.

Say the words, girl. Say them loud.

"*Lig muid sor deamhan.*"

The creature frowned as if processing the words, still uncertain he had heard what the girl had uttered. Annabelle also looked on in disbelief, although she shuffled nearer her friend as a dim emerald light began to form itself around Maggie.

"*Lig muid sor deamhan.*" Louder this time, crisp and clearly reverberating around the courtyard. He heard her that time and responded by clapping his hands together, causing more bodies to drop to the ground, the newly harvested dead of Carson's Court. The lone bead of sweat had progressed into a steady trickle.

He pointed a filthy digit above his head, and Jinks began to slowly descend towards his waiting arms. The young boy was oblivious of the struggle for his body and soul, and Maggie yearned for him to open those inquisitive chocolate-brown eyes that lit up his face, the double of his mother and everything their wretched father was not. She would not lose another loved one, not this day.

"*Ardaim na mairbh chun d'fheoil a eileamh.*"

"Curb your tongue, witch, before I remove it from your head." He spat the words out, laced with venom, but continued to sweat even more freely than before. His tongue shot out nervously like a cornered viper, considering his options as they narrowed one by one. He was a creature not used to being bested by magic and had expected the girl to be a trifling inconvenience, a mere appetizer to the main course. A prelude to a confrontation he had been relishing for two hundred years.

Sensing his uncertainty, Maggie took a hesitant step forward as if pushed in the back by some invisible hand. She fought to contain the billowing surge of power within her that threatened to rip through her ribcage and reduce the courtyard, the town, the entire island to a smoldering husk. A cool gust caressed her brow, and she sensed her mother nearby. A hand on her arm caused her to glance around, mild surprise coursing her features as she realized that Annabelle still stood with her, having not fled for her life.

"Do what must be done, Margaret. End this monstrosity once and for all."

Another heavy thud reverted her attention to the creature as the remaining bodies dropped out of the sky. Jinks remained above his tormentor, oblivious to the unfolding chaos as the rain began to fall, cutting them all as it lashed across the courtyard. The wind picked up, and the skies darkened within seconds, the heavens raging at the battle below for control of the blood-soaked cobbles. Maggie focused on the leering lump of pasty flesh before her, refusing to be distracted by the growing pile of corpses on all sides of them. The courtyard was beginning to resemble an abattoir.

"*Dail me tu le deatach agus cloch. Gan na sraideanna seo a shiul riomh aris.*"

The creature slumped to one knee as if struck across the shoulders. Above him, Jinks began to sway crazily, propelled by the gusting squall. He attempted to stand again and momentarily regained his footing before an unseen force brought him to his knees again. He wiped a sleeve across his pockmarked face, leaving a ruddy smear, blood flowing freely from both nostrils. He marveled at the sight of his own blood, not quite believing what was happening. The one known as Bloody Hands, who had butchered so many, was now bleeding himself.

That was when the first of them stirred. Annabelle froze, her hand on Maggie's sleeve, as one of the fallen jerked to its feet in a single, fluid motion. It had been a woman, Mrs. Moyne, whose generous laughter had often cheered Maggie as she hung her washing on the communal clothes-line strung across the courtyard. There was no laughter now, however, only twitching, sporadic movements focused on the crouching creature before her. She cared not for his reputation or power, all her heightened senses craved was the bloody rivulet trickling from his flared nostrils.

Others rose with her as rapidly as they had dropped from their suspended imprisonment. Splayed, broken limbs and crushed skulls could not curb their desire to feast on the one who had condemned them to an eternal, desperate hunger that no amount of visceral, glistening flesh could ever satisfy. Mothers, fathers, and children, all shared a common purpose, as the last body fell and, seconds later, regained its footing on the wet cobbles. They formed a ragged semi-circle around him as he struggled to cast off the magical weight pressing down on his broad shoulders.

"What? You expect me to yield? To one such as you? I think not."

They were bold words, but his normally dull, expressionless eyes held a fear that was not there moments before. Maggie could smell it, rising off his rotund body in sickly, pungent waves. She met it with her own newly discovered aura, a fresh, cleansing breeze that dispelled the foul toxicity that oozed from his every pore. He cringed as his victims edged ever nearer.

"Yield? I fear it is much too late for that. But release my brother, and I will spare you what you refused to spare so many. Look at them, they desire your blood and so much more. I need only nod, and they will rip you apart, gorge on your organs, and gnaw on your bones. The irony cannot possibly be lost on you, no?"

He raised his hands to his ears as the wind intensified, reinforcing the message that he was no longer welcome in a town he had haunted for generations. Hunter became hunted as he acknowledged their voices, the grating chorus demanding vengeance for the manner in which he had ripped their hopes and dreams to shreds.

"Enough."

The shambling wall of flesh halted mere inches from his huddled form. They swayed, silent witnesses to the end of a terrible era, a shifting of power as seismic as it was abrupt. All that held them from falling on the ancient creature was the power that raged within her. Maggie inhaled and held the air in her lungs, savoring it, the oxygen mixed with the primal fury coursing through her frame. It was exhilarating and terrifying, the knowledge that she could end centuries of untold misery with a flick of her wrist.

"You finish me, and he falls as well. They will have him, too, you hear me."

He cowered before Maggie, unable to meet her eyes, which had taken on a wild, ethereal sheen. She stepped away, partly in awe but also trepidation at the young woman who was so much more now. She was transformed, a cathartic force that teetered on the brink of a new creation. Annabelle watched, unable to do little more than offer up a quiet prayer, pleading with her God to guide them through the horrors of this night. Horrors, as she witnessed a titanic struggle inside the slight frame of Maggie Malone. A struggle that promised hope and restoration, but also threatened unspeakable pain and devastation if it deviated an inch from its pre-ordained path.

"You harm a hair on his head, and the Black Lady will be the least of your concerns. Release him now, and I will allow your sorry existence to continue. You will leave this town and swear never to return. For if you do, I will have your head."

He looked up, flinching at the aura that surrounded her, an emerald glow that bathed the courtyard. It was strong, stronger than he had ever encountered. On either side, the dead shuffled ever nearer. A nod of her head and they would be on him, tearing him asunder, like he had torn so many before him. He was cornered, trapped, and at her mercy.

"Agreed. Take the brat. You and your mistress whore are welcome to this land. I curse it and all who dwell on it for all eternity."

Maggie maintained her steely grip on the ravenous mob, her eyes never leaving the bald-headed demon as Jinks slowly lowered to the ground. When his boots touched the cobbles, his eyelids flickered, opening to reveal eyes that flared with joy at seeing his sister and Annabelle standing before him. He bounded into Maggie's arms, who enveloped him, burying her face in his mop of tangled curls.

"What happened, Mags? I was going up the mountain after you, and then...I don't remember anything."

"It doesn't matter. You're safe now. And I'm not letting you out of my sight again. Now, come on. Let's get out of this pit. It's no longer our home."

She turned, sweeping Jinks with her, and Annabelle was forced to jump smartly aside to avoid being trampled underfoot. Maggie's eyes had returned to their natural pale blue hue, but Annabelle would never forget the unsettling green flare that preceded the supernatural acts she could scarcely believe had just transpired. Maggie smiled at her, and Annabelle returned the favor, but it was a forced gesture as she fell into line behind the siblings who had shattered her hitherto mundane existence. The smile faded as they passed, for something had subtly changed, as the Maggie Malone leaving the courtyard was a different woman from the one who had entered it not five minutes before.

"What about me?" wailed the creature, his cocky snarl now replaced by a worried whine. The slavering mob around him showed no signs of backing off. Yes, he could have attempted to fight his way out, but there were too many of them. He kicked out as a filthy hand grabbed at the hem of his overcoat.

"What about you?" sneered Maggie over a shoulder as she swept into the entry, the bloody hand marks on the wall glowing brighter than ever.

"You promised. A deal is a deal. Get your stinking hands off me."

He swung a fist, his meaty hand connecting with the upper lip of an elderly man, smashing bone and tooth. The man stumbled backward, his arms flailing like an errant windmill, cannoning off several more bodies before disappearing beneath the undead maul. The flurry of activity agitated the mob further, and several of them rushed forward, too quick for the creature as they grabbed limbs and loose clothing.

"You promised."

A scream now, as the first set of drooling teeth clamped down on his wrist, piercing skin and drawing blood. He stood for a moment, a solitary island in a sea of dreary death. Then he was gone, subsumed by a hunger that, for the first time in this darkest of years, would be satiated by the flesh of a monster.

"I lied."

Maggie strode out of the entry onto Bank Street, Jinks trotting by her skirts. Annabelle gasped, the callous dismissal shocking despite the evil that they were condemning to a grisly end. A dull roar echoed along the entry, an aural wall of misery that masked the final shrieks of the creature. She broke into a run, exiting the entry as a sharp cracking sound heralded the arched roof collapsing behind her, burying the only means of accessing Carson's Court. Struggling to hold back the tears, she refused to look back for fear that one or more of the undead had escaped and were stalking her hurried steps.

The tears came quick enough, and she sobbed, for Annabelle Edgar was no fool. This was only the beginning of a day that would haunt the minds of those who survived to tell the tale. Burning bright red and never to fade, like the eerie, red glow still pulsing from the rubble of what once was Carson's Court.

No Child of God

❧❀❧

T he wind would not be tamed that day, rampaging down the lough, whipping the waters into a raging tempest that battered the docks, sturdy boats tossed like matchstick toys against their moorings. More men were lost than had perished in the decade before, thrown from their vessels as they struggled to save their livelihoods. There was talk of strange creatures sighted amidst the mayhem, rising to snatch flailing mariners between rows of serrated teeth, dragging them down to hidden depths, never to rise again.

The streets were no safer. Rumors spread of unprovoked assaults throughout the town, roaming lunatics attacking hapless citizens. No money was stolen, and the remaining Constabulary struggled to find any rhyme or reason for the disorder. There was talk that asylum inmates had escaped and were running amok, falling on those unfortunate enough to cross their paths. Others reasoned that the fever had driven its poor victims mad, causing them to attack the poor and wealthy alike. Whatever the cause, the tall tales reached new extremes when stories circulated of ghoulish acts of cannibalism and dismemberment. Those that could barricaded their properties and huddled in upper rooms, armed with loaded pistols and whatever other weapons they could lay their hands on.

The lower classes were less fortunate, the slums of the town a tinderbox of tension waiting to explode. Maggie, Jinks, and Annabelle kept to the back streets as best they could and were largely undisturbed, bar the occasional anguished scream. It never lasted for long, cut off abruptly and replaced by unspeakable sounds that chilled Annabelle's heart, sounds more akin to a pack of famished wolves than the good citizens of the place she called home.

"Where are we going, Mags?"

It was Jinks who asked the question that had been playing on Annabelle's mind since they had left the devastated courtyard. Although relieved to be free of its horror, a growing knot of unease was working its way from the pit of her stomach up into her throat, burning like acid.

"I will know when we get there. But don't you be worrying. Mammy is watching over us now. She will make sure we are safe."

Maggie did not slow her pace or look at her brother. Annabelle breathed more easily, as the kind-hearted young woman seemed to have returned, replacing the uncaring tone of the witch who had destroyed Carson's Court. Ahead of them, the alley widened, and Annabelle recognized the familiar thoroughfare of Hercules Street. Beyond that lay Smithfield, a notorious part of the town that she rarely frequented except when on missionary work as directed by her father. It was a den of sin and debauchery, no place for a young lady at any time of the day. Yet here she was, scuttling across Hercules Street, about to be plunged into its vile depths.

"I don't like this place, Maggie. The memories are coming back. It's where...he brought me." Jinks hesitated, clinging closer to Maggie's skirts. She stopped and kneeled beside him, a reassuring hand on his hip.

"He, or whatever the hell *it* was, can't hurt you now Jinks. Do you remember when Mammy used to tell us stories about the Black Lady. About how she would look over our house at night and protect us from evil."

The young boy nodded, but his pale complexion indicated he was far from reassured. Maggie frowned but continued in her efforts to ease his fears.

"Well, we didn't know this at the time, but Mammy and the Black Lady were good friends back then. We never got to meet her, but they talked a lot and made plans for the future when we needed them most."

"And that day is now?"

"You're a bright spark, my boy, that's for sure." Maggie smiled and glanced up at Annabelle. She returned the gesture, further assured that the Maggie she witnessed in the courtyard had been a temporary aberration caused by the stress and turmoil of the situation they had faced.

"Well, the Black Lady looked after Mammy and taught her some tricks, and now the tricks have been passed on to me. That's why that old monster is lying under a ton of bricks, and we are here, safe as can be.'

"Tricks? You mean, your magic, like what you did with the stone?"

"You could call it that, yes."

"Can you pull a shilling from behind my ear?"

Maggie laughed, her voice echoing along the deserted street. It may have been her imagination, but Annabelle was convinced the gloomy clouds lightened slightly at the sound of her friend's voice. Yes, this was the Maggie Malone she knew, and the further they moved from the charnel house of Carson's Court, the more she became certain of that.

"I haven't advanced to that level...yet. But give me enough time, and I'm sure I will get there. For now, though, we must go into Smithfield. I know it's a bad place, but remember, Mammy's tricks will keep us safe."

Jinks screwed his face, a sign that he was giving his sister's proposition some serious consideration. After several seconds, his trademark grin appeared, and he nodded, swayed by her argument.

"Very well, then. If Mammy and you say it's alright, then that's good enough for me. Come on, Miss Annabelle, take my hand, and I'll make sure you'll be safe. My sister knows a few tricks, you see."

Now it was Annabelle's turn to laugh, and it felt good, a weight unburdened by the simple act of expressing joy at another's words.

"Oh, I know this very well, Master John Joseph. Your sister is a most impressive and resourceful young woman." She smiled, averting her eyes from Maggie. Had she looked, she would have witnessed a beaming face, no longer troubled by the unwanted responsibilities that had been heaped on her slim shoulders.

"You are most impressive yourself, Miss Annabelle. Jinks and I will always be grateful for the way you have supported us. Shall we?"

Annabelle looked down at the extended hand before gratefully accepting it. In any other situation, the sight of two young women who were not related holding hands would have been scandalous. But today, even if there had been witnesses, it felt right. Annabelle closed her eyes and savored the warmth of Maggie's skin on her own. It felt right, and, for probably the first time in her life, so did she. Whole, complete, no longer having to play the dutiful daughter, a role that always felt awkward and unfulfilling. She was where she belonged now, whatever lay ahead of them.

They stepped forward as one into the dimly lit confines of Smithfield.

She watched them from the shadows, a wry smile on her lips. So, the little one was free, which meant that Bloody Hands was no more. She cast out invisible tendrils, probing, feeling for him. But where his malignancy had once festered, there was now nothing but a yawning emptiness. He was gone. The path was clear, her pupil had learned fast and well.

Fionnuala slipped from the darkness, the hood from the heavy cape concealing her red curls. Her face was also largely hidden, yet those emerald eyes burned as bright as ever, two shards of prasiolite quartz, hard and unyielding. She watched as her prey rounded a bend in the street, arm-in-arm—how very touching. She could have crushed them there, and then, their betrayal sickening, after all, she had sacrificed for the brats and their family.

Could have, but would not. For where was the fun in that? The girl now had the temerity to believe that she could challenge Fionnuala, a handful of cheap tricks convincing her she could overcome one who had diligently practiced the craft for centuries on end. Well, let her try, for she had served her purpose, defeating the fiend the townspeople called Bloody Hands. He had many names: *deamhan, spiorad olc, abhartach*. He had crawled from beyond the realms of human consciousness, a worthy foe, if truth be told. But now he was no more, and the town was at her mercy. Those not dead already would be by morning, through hunger, disease, or at the hands of the roaming packs of the undead who had escaped from Carson's Court. One by one, they would rise again, and, led by her, they would march across this island, laying waste to its population.

Fionnuala wrapped her cloak around her shoulders, for even she was no longer impervious to this biting, ungodly cold. She knew where Maggie was going even before the girl did herself. To the grave where they had cast her own body, an unmarked plot with no flowers or mourners to send her into the afterlife. She had lingered, though, her earthly remains rotting into the dark soil until all that was left were a bundle of bones and a few scraps of cheap clothing. They had forgotten about her, but she had not forgotten about them, rising from the earth to bide her time and strike when they were at their lowest, weakened by hunger and sickness.

That time was now.

The sick and starving lay everywhere, their ravaged bodies stacked in every doorway, against every wall. A suffocating silence lay over Smithfield, punctuated only by the occasional pained sigh or heaving cough. Men, women, and children, already weakened by two years of hunger, were ripe pickings for the fever that had swept into Belfast aboard the Samhara.

Jinks eyed them warily, never leaving Maggie's side as they edged along the narrow street, normally alive with raucous laughter and drunken bonhomie at this time of the day. The bars were empty now, their shutters closed, as those who could have staggered to their beds where they would perish alone, caked in their own sweat and vomit. They were the fortunate ones, who at least were afforded some privacy and perhaps a relative to hold their hand. The rest died where they fell, the homeless vagrants who had crammed into the port from outlying districts in the hope of a better life, an escape from relentless, unforgiving famine. How wrong they had been.

"Margaret," hissed Annabelle, anxiety weighing heavier with every step they took into the foul heart of the town. "Where are you taking us?" Her heart ached from the scenes on either side of her, but there was little she could do other than mouth a silent prayer that their agonies would not persist for much longer.

"I know," Jinks replied on behalf of his sister, his voice dull and listless. "To see him."

"He has a name, John Joseph," snapped Maggie, scowling down at her sullen brother. "Don't talk of your father like that."

"He's no father to us."

"Hush your tongue, or I'll hush it for ye."

Annabelle could not help but smile, the bickering siblings a fragment of normality in this otherwise anguished, surreal setting. Maggie veered to her right, tugging a reluctant Jinks with her, and Annabelle was forced to step back as a famished man, more dead than alive, tugged at the hem of her dress.

"Please, Miss. Water. For the love of God, water."

"I'm sorry, I..." Annabelle hurried past, guilt brightening her cheeks. She should stop, she should help these poor people in their final moments, it was what her Lord would have done. Yet, she didn't, she scurried on, leaving the living skeleton pawing at empty air, vanquished eyes set deep above cadaverous cheekbones. One of many who were paying a heavy price for the sins of their forefathers, the men who had consigned Fionnuala to the hangman's rope.

"There, up ahead, that's the inn where he sups now." Maggie pointed to the nondescript building, its whitewashed walls peeling and sorely in need of a lick of paint. A man sat hunched outside the front door, a bottle hanging limply from his hand. He looked up as they neared, and Maggie and Jinks found themselves staring into the rheumy eyes of their father. Seeing them, he grunted and raised the bottle to his chapped lips, drinking deeply before tossing it aside.

"Come to gloat at your old man, have ye?" He scratched at a stubbly cheek before raising an arm to cover his mouth as a raking cough consumed his body. Maggie and Jinks watched impassively, Annabelle several steps behind them, uncertain of her role in this unfolding family drama.

"The time for gloating is long past," replied Maggie, her head held high. Annabelle sensed that her friend would not let this man have the pleasure of knowing she cared, forcing every emotion she'd ever had for him deep inside, where it mingled with the powers that sizzled and crackled, aching to be released once more.

"You not coming any closer, lad? Come on, give your old man a cuddle." He reached out toward Jinks, who froze, uncertain if he should recoil or reciprocate the gesture. Maggie stepped between them, making the decision for her brother, her arms folded in defiance.

"We've come to say our goodbyes. It's what Mammy would have wanted."

He laughed, a bitter, humorless sound that degenerated into a phlegmy wheeze. Annabelle winced at the sweaty film coating his skin, bloody spittle fizzing between yellowed teeth.

"Your Mammy, eh? Now, how would you know that, given she's lying up the road in a dirty grave."

"Daddy. Don't." Jinks peeked out from behind his sister's skirts. His features were tinged with apprehension, but he refused to let his mother be disrespected, even by his own blood.

John Malone smirked and picked up the bottle again, taking another generous slug. "Well, listen to you. Acting the big man while hiding behind your sister's skirts. I dare ye to come out from there and say that to my face." He made to rise but fell back again, overcome by another fit of coughing. He turned his head to the side and hacked, a mouthful of bloody phlegm staining the ground at his feet.

"You're lucky I'm not a well man, or I'd tan your hide, boy, for your lip."

"You touch a hair on his head, and I'll make sure your end is more painful than your current predicament." Maggie's dark stare left the stricken man in no doubt that his daughter was deadly serious.

"You wee tramp. Don't you dare talk to your father like..."

"You lost the right to call yourself our father the day you abandoned us for the drink. And where's your fancy bit? Entertaining one of her many gentleman callers?" Maggie's lip curled, and Annabelle again saw a darker side, one that contained no warmth. She had come down from the mountain a different woman, as if a stone from its granite summit had lodged in her heart, calcifying and hardening it.

John Malone saw it as well, and suddenly, the fight was gone from him. His chest sagged, and he rested his chin on it, unable to meet his daughter's eye.

"She was called Edith. And she died during the night. She's upstairs if you don't believe me."

An uneasy silence settled over the alley, as Maggie and Jinks internally juggled a range of conflicting emotions. Annabelle recognized their dilemma, her own father generating love and loathing within her. Eventually, it was Maggie who swallowed her own pride and spoke.

"I'm sorry for your loss. Truly. Is there anything we can do before we..."

"Leave?" Malone raised his head now, his eyes glistening with tears. "No, I'm grand. Just leave me be and get the hell out of this bloody town. It's cursed. Always has been and always will."

Maggie nodded as there was nothing else to say. All she could do was place a hand on her brother's slumped shoulders, steering him away from the man who had raised them. Annabelle gave Malone a final, pitying look, but he had lifted the bottle again, draining the dregs, before hurling it against the opposite wall in a final act of despair. She turned and walked away, as his anguished roar was cut short by the raking signature cough that had become the death knell of this stricken town.

The next hour was a catalog of terror as Annabelle witnessed desperate sights, the dead and dying littering the alleys and entries of Smithfield like unwanted offal. A mother lay in a doorway, her dead baby clutched to her chest. She stared through Annabelle as if she wasn't there, eyes vacant, awaiting her own demise. Further along, a trio of feral dogs pawed at a fallen form, snarling at Annabelle as she passed, a warning that their kill was not for sharing. Ahead of her, Maggie strode impassively on, looking neither left nor right, silent except for the occasional murmured word of comfort to her brother, who was an ever-present shadow at her side.

"Where are you taking us, Margaret? Shouldn't we be trying to help some of these people? There must be something we can do?" She initially thought her plea had fallen on barren ground, for Maggie gave no indication that she had heard. Eventually, though, she replied, although it did little to lessen the weight pressing down on Annabelle's aching heart.

"They are beyond our help. The sickness is out of control. Stopping to help one will mean that thousands more will die. We have to strike at the heart of this poison. Kill the witch and end her curse. It's the only way."

Maggie cast a glance over her shoulder, daring Annabelle to challenge, but the blonde-haired young woman could offer nothing in return. While her natural instinct was to care for the sick and needy, she knew her efforts would make little difference. It was too late for that, too late for kind hearts and soothing words. Their only salvation now was to nip the evolving terror in the bud by facing Fionnuala, where they would find her. It suddenly dawned on Annabelle where that would be.

"We're going to the cemetery, aren't we? Friar's Bush?"

"Where Mammy is buried?" Jinks's voice wavered as he realized where they were headed. He had not set foot in the cemetery since the day he had followed Eileen McDowell's dog to the grave of her son. The day that...

"It's where she has been feeding."

"Feeding?"

Maggie stopped by a bakery, its front window lying shattered in a thousand fragments on the street. Hunger had overwhelmed what little law and order existed in the town, and, with the Constabulary largely absent, desperate citizens had stormed the premises, emptying the shelves. She gestured towards the ransacked shop before bending to retrieve a stray crust, which she handed to Jinks, who gratefully began to gnaw on it.

"She needs to feed as much as we do, except broth and bread do not pass her lips. She feasts on misery and despair; it makes her even stronger and more powerful. Where better than a cemetery to replenish her strength before facing me."

"Must you? Can't we not just flee this damned place? We could head to the docks see if there are any ships set to sail. My father has money; we could secure passage."

"Your father can barely lift his head from his pillow, let alone survive a sea crossing. No, Annabelle, we must end this now, for better or worse."

They pressed on past the huddled bodies and sickly stench of death that hung in the air like a corpulent shroud. Eventually, Annabelle became numb to the sights and sounds of Fionnuala's vengeance, opting to adopt Maggie's tactic of not allowing her eyes to stray. For that way lay madness.

Finally, the narrow street widened, and the buildings thinned out as they reached the edge of the town. Annabelle knew this area, for her father had presided over many funerals at Friar's Bush. She shuddered, as a bracing wind cut across their path, disturbing a wet clump of leaves that covered a winding path that climbed towards the cemetery. Annabelle had lost count of the number of times she had followed mourners up the path toward the graveyard perched at the top of the solitary, forlorn hill. It was a place of great sadness and despair. Despite the conciliatory words that the Reverend Edgar boomed at the graveside, she had never sensed the presence of a comforting higher power to offer solace and comfort.

She sensed something today, though, and it was far from comforting. As they started the weary ascent, a thick swarm of crows rose from the granite headstones above, spiralling into the low cloud, their cruel beaks cawing in fury at the approaching visitors. Jinks and Annabelle instinctively ducked as the black mass swooped low over their heads, mere inches from clawing at their scalps. Maggie stood tall, however, and was untouched as the murder parted to avoid colliding with her. It was as if they sensed her emerging power and knew that to tangle with it would bring nothing but their demise.

"She is coming. They will tell her." Maggie's voice was stern and impassive again, glancing at the crouched forms of her brother and Annabelle. "Come. We must find the place where I will make my stand."

This time, Jinks reached for Annabelle's hand as opposed to that of his sister. He looked up at Annabelle, his expression a mixture of confusion and fear. She sensed it as well. A part of Maggie Malone was missing again, replaced by a swirling void of tension. They both sensed it but had little choice but to follow her. Reaching the rusting iron gates, Maggie flung out a hand. They swung inwards, their aging hinges screaming in protest at the unwanted intrusion. They entered the graveyard, a shallow oval of headstones and open ground, surrounded by steep banks on all sides clogged with weeds and debris. Beyond the banks, the cemetery was fringed with a dense wall of hardy conifers, offering some protection to mourners from the unforgiving elements. A single crow kept watch atop one of them, its glassy eyes never leaving the trio as they picked their way through the uneven plots.

Jinks nervously looked toward the far end of the cemetery where Maggie was headed, toward the last resting place of the woman who had delivered them into this world. Maggie kneeled at the foot of the simple grave, marked only by a plain wooden cross that the parish priest had insisted be planted before allowing the burial to take place. Annabelle and Jinks hung back, uncertain and edgy as Maggie leaned forward and placed a cheek against the damp earth beneath which her mother's remains lay.

"Mammy, I have come. It is time. Prepare me, for our Lady is no longer as we knew her. Grant me the strength to challenge and overcome her. Feed me as she has fed off the bones of the dead."

"Why is she speaking so strangely?"

"Hush, Jinks. Watch and see. It is not our place to intervene." Annabelle placed a hand on the young boy's shoulder, a gentle reminder that he should edge no nearer. She watched, her mouth slowly opening in shock, as Maggie began to rise from the ground and hover over her mother's grave, the turned soil less than a foot below her. She stretched out both arms and arched her back as the wooden cross was flung from the earth into the bank behind the grave. The ground began to tremble, barely noticeable at first, as small stones and clods of earth started to dance a jig atop the grave.

Annabelle took a step back, pulling Jinks with her, as the conifers began to crazily sway, bending so far inwards that she feared they would break. A sharp crack to the left caused her to spin around to an adjacent headstone, which had cleaved in half. Maggie looked skywards, but the drab, charcoal canopy was as before, with no rumble of thunder or accompanying lightning strike.

She jumped and wrapped Jinks in her arms as the first beam of light broke through the consecrated ground, immersing Maggie in a shimmering glow that sparkled as if she was encased within a cloud of diamonds.

"My sister is an angel," mouthed Jinks, his words little more than a stunned whisper.

"I pray to God she is," replied Annabelle.

A second shard pierced the grave, followed by several others until it was a ball of light, continuing to lift Maggie until she was level with the tallest headstone, an ancient, weather-worn Celtic cross. She lay atop a shimmering tower, transformed from a dowdy slum dweller to an ethereal being, her features flawless, all blemishes removed. Her hair had grown at least six inches, and her eyes, although still pale blue, sparkled with a new intensity. Suddenly, she began to descend as the wind gradually diminished, the conifers reverting to their upright poses. Slowly, the light dimmed as it deposited its precious cargo back on the ground, where she stood before her dumbstruck brother and friend. It was Maggie, but a new creation, effervescent and refreshed. She smiled at them, and it was a heartfelt, jubilant smile. Gone was the foreboding worry that had dogged her on every step of this transformative journey.

"Maggie, is that really you?" Jinks did not know whether to bow or run to his sister. He chose neither, instead dithering on his heels.

"It is, indeed, John Joseph. Now come on, mister. Are you not going to give your sister a big hug?"

The boy needed no second invitation, bounding into Maggie's arms like an exuberant puppy. She held him tight, inhaling his mop of unruly hair like it was the most fragrant floral bouquet, before looking up and meeting Annabel's moistened eyes.

"No need for tears, Miss Annabelle. For now, we finish it. Once and for all."

Edgar stirred in his bed, what little light there was outside struggling to penetrate the heavy drapes across the solitary window. His eyes creaked open, and he instantly regretted the action, a dull headache starting to metronomically throb. He closed them again, and gradually, the events of the preceding hours began to filter through his mind, each one more horrific than the last. All those men, good men, lost to that evil creature on the mountain. She had shaken the foundations of his faith, laughed in the face of his God, and reduced him to a pathetic wreck.

"I must say, you are being rather unfair on yourself, Reverend Edgar. Nobody forced those men to follow you, you merely...what is the word I'm looking for, ah yes, *encouraged* them."

Edgar wriggled to untangle himself from crumpled sheets at the sound of the soft, melodious voice. Melodious but dripping with undisguised venom. It was her; she was in his chambers. He struggled to a sitting position and peered across the room where a shaded figure reclined in a cushioned armchair by his writing desk. He squinted and then gasped as the candle on the desk roared to life, revealing the chair's occupant.

Fionnuala was draped over the chair in a most unladylike manner, one leg draped over its arm. Edgar blushed and averted his gaze at the sight of the exposed calf and hint of thigh. In normal times, this would have been scandalous behavior, a man of the cloth visited by such a harlot in his private chambers. These were not normal times, however.

"Oh, don't worry, I have no intention of seducing you, you vain, deluded man."

"Then what are your intentions?" replied Edgar, mustering what little indignation he could manage, heart beating like a docker's mallet.

"Why, to kill you, of course."

Edgar blinked rapidly, as his brain processed the outrageous words the creature facing him had so blandly delivered. It took all his willpower not to sag back onto his pillows, and the edges of his vision began to blur, a clammy sweat erupting from every pore of his body.

Fionnuala smiled. Her beauty was only exceeded by her chilling cruelty. She lowered her leg and sat forward in the armchair, hands cupped under her chin, a look of fake concern on her face.

"Come now, Pastor, I thought you might be pleased. No more having to stand up in the pulpit every Sunday and deliver the same sanctimonious message to your little sheep. Now you can be with your Lord and Maker?"

"I...It..." Edgar struggled and failed abjectly to find words to combat the sarcasm that dripped from the creature's vile tongue. For this was no woman, no child of God. The evil facing him was spawned in the deepest vaults of Hell.

Fionnuala smirked, her long, pale fingers playing with a loose curl, clearly enjoying the clergyman's anguish. She watched as it flowed off him in languid waves, inhaling his torment and doubt. She had been well fed at the graveyard, but a little more human sustenance was always welcome, especially with her final battle looming large.

"What? No prayers of protection, no passages of scripture to dispatch me from whence I came? Well, I must say I am a little disappointed. I expected more of a challenge from such a worthy man of God."

"You have no authority here, witch. My forefathers were entirely justified in hanging you for your devilry. My only regret is that I was not there to watch you choke on the end of the rope."

Fionnuala raised a hand to her chest in mock terror before dismissing the spluttering clergyman with a flick of the wrist.

Edgar watched, frozen with horror, as the crumpled sheets covering him snaked along his bed of their own volition, twisting into a linen knot that wrapped around his protesting throat at dizzying speed.

"May I then offer you the next best alternative, Pastor? Instead of watching me choke, I'll return the favor and watch you breathe your last."

Edgar clutched forlornly at the knot of sheets, but despite his best efforts, they budged not an inch, instead racing up the wall behind the bed, trailing the reluctant clergyman in their wake. His feet flailed to find purchase on the bed, but to no avail as the cord of bed linen wrapped itself around the upper frame of the bed, leaving Edgar suspended, his legs dangling helplessly.

Fionnuala stood and lifted the hem of her gown, drifting effortlessly across the carpeted floor until she was standing beneath the floundering clergyman. Edgar kicked out, his hands clutching at the noose, his face darkening like a bruised piece of fruit. His eyeballs bulged, huge and terrified, as the breath was squeezed from his writhing body. She watched impassively, cocking her head to one side, savoring every last second of his torment as she drained every last drop of misery from his soon-to-be corpse.

Eventually, the thrashing subsided, then ceased, as a fine stream of urine emerged from the hem of Edgar's nightshirt, trickling down his leg before dribbling onto the mattress below. Fionnuala watched his lifeless form hang limply from the bed frame, his head bowed as if in silent prayer, before turning and walking away from the undignified sight. She opened the bedroom door, and no sooner had the trail of her gown slithered beyond it, the sheets erupted into flames. The wooden frame of the bed was soon ablaze as the fire licked at the feet of the Reverend Archibald Edgar, recently deceased. It was a fitting end for the man who had established his reputation as a preacher who often roared from the pulpit about the fiery furnace that awaited those who turned their backs on the Lord.

A day like no other continued in the town of Belfast. A day of hellfire.

Pity the Witch

❧

They watched as the smoke rose into the already gray sky, mingling with the low cloud cover, thickening the blanket that lay across the town, as immovable as it was intimidating.

"Look over there, Maggie. Fire." Jinks had the sharpest eyes of them and pointed excitedly from their lofty vantage point in the cemetery. He turned and urged his sister to see what he was seeing, the first flames creeping above the rooftops to announce the next phase of Belfast's demise.

"I see it," murmured Maggie, although she seemed adrift, her mind elsewhere, as the acrid scent began to drift across the graveyard. Annabelle coughed and raised the sleeve of her dress to her mouth, causing Maggie to place a hand on the small of her back.

"I am sorry for your loss, Annabelle."

Annabelle frowned, confused by the words. She opened her mouth to reply but was halted by a piercing shriek that filled the air. They stood on the weed-riddled slope and watched as the rusted cemetery gates were propelled upwards by an invisible force, ripped from their hinges, and tossed into the sky. A headstone to their left cracked, an ever-widening fissure dancing along its length until it shattered as if smote by a mighty Arthurian broadsword.

"What's happening, Maggie?" Gone was the tough, streetwise boy, replaced by a frightened child who clutched at his sister, fighting to maintain his balance as the earth shook, more headstones splintering and toppling over. Annabelle swayed unsteadily, while frantically looking around for the source of the growing maelstrom.

"It's her. She comes. Now, I must make my stand."

Maggie took several steps forward, gently prising Jinks away and ushering him toward Annabelle. The boy watched helplessly, as his last remaining family member raised her arms and screamed at the skies, a defiant roar that was all but lost in the surrounding bedlam.

Annabelle fell to a knee, crouching in terror, with Jinks clutched close to her body. Graves began to collapse inwards, dropping into the earth while spewing partially decomposed bodies upward, regurgitated corpses that rained down on the holy ground in a torrent of rotting limbs encased in filthy rags. Annabelle raised her head, struggling to find Maggie in the morbid downpour, but then saw her, edging down the slope, seemingly impervious to the hellish scenes all about her. She reached the gap where the gates had previously stood and raised her voice again, words lost amidst the deafening cacophony.

Just when Annabelle thought her eardrums would explode, a shadow crossed overhead. She raised her head and watched, aghast, as a granite cross soared above before plummeting towards them. For one horrific instance, Annabelle thought Maggie was in danger of being crushed beneath it, but the cross narrowly missed her friend before planting itself in the soft ground just beyond the entrance to the cemetery, where it perched at a perilous angle. Its impact coincided with an end to the uproar, and an unseemly silence fell over them.

"An inverted cross. How very original of you, Fionnuala."

Maggie's dry voice resonated with sarcasm as she eyed its new resting place before turning briefly to survey the devastated graveyard. She smiled at Annabelle and mouthed soothing words to Jinks, another glimpse of the working-class girl who had laughed and joked with them less than two days ago. Two days that now seemed like several lifetimes. Annabelle fought back a thickening lump in her throat, a mixture of grief and pride that threatened to overwhelm her. She clung to Jinks for fear that what little courage she had left would evaporate were she to let go and fully consider the unfolding events.

Her town. Her friends.

Her father.

"I am nothing if not consistent, child."

Fionnuala's voice resonated with derision, her outline forming as Annabelle squinted beyond Maggie and the recently deposited cross. She blinked hard, and when her eyes adjusted, the witch was there, her vivid red hair and sweeping emerald gown in stark contrast to the drab hillside they occupied. Beyond that, the town glowed red as a ravenous fire ripped through the narrow streets, devouring the cramped housing and all who lay stricken in its path.

"I have come for what is mine, for what could be ours. A new kingdom with you by my side. I had always wanted a daughter, an heiress to all this." She swung a skeletal hand out before withdrawing it, eyeing Maggie with eyes that gleamed with unspoken malice.

Maggie met and matched her stare, refusing to succumb to the witch's barbed tongue. Less than twenty feet separated the two of them, and the air sizzled with latent magic that threatened to rip open the hillside and swallow them both, never to be seen again. They were poles apart, yet hewn from the same ancient force, destined to meet on the high land overlooking the lough to settle the future of the lands below once and for all.

"Liar. You have no intention of making me your kin. I'm just another pawn in your insane game. And even if your offer was genuine, I want no part of your wicked schemes. This is not the honorable craft that my mother learned from you. You have been corrupted and polluted; you have allowed hate and rage to twist the goodness inside you. It is foul now, withered and dead."

Fionnuala nodded slowly, contemplating the words of her adversary before speaking again. The cemetery was now shrouded in silence, their faces bathed in the crimson glow of Belfast ablaze. "I see you have inherited your mother's stubborn nature, so I will not attempt to change your mind. She and I also had a difference of opinion regarding my methods toward the end. Her end, that is." She allowed her carefully crafted words to seep home under Maggie's defenses. The young woman showed no sign of emotion as the doubt that had been nagging at her finally unfurled its dark petals and flowered into concrete reality.

"You let her die. You could have saved her, couldn't you?" Her voice was imperiously aloof, her chin raised, refusing to show a glimmer of weakness to the beautiful horror facing her.

"Could is such a subjective word, all wrapped up in emotions and conscience. I do not dabble with such mortal foibles. The simple truth is that she chose a different path from the one I asked her to follow, just as you have. And for that, there must be consequences."

"So, you killed her..."

"I allowed her to die," corrected the nightmarish vision before Maggie.

"You killed her, and now you propose to kill me, my brother, my friend, this entire town. All because of the sins of men who lived over two hundred years ago." Maggie's voice trembled slightly, but she still stood tall, arms fixed by her sides, controlling her rising fury.

"Well, if you put it like that, I suppose I am. Reluctantly, and not by choice. For it is you who have set these wheels in motion. I once had plans for you, great plans. We could have ruled this land together. Why, I would even have allowed your sniveling brat of a brother to live, although I am less certain of the preacher's daughter. She may have had to go the way of her sanctimonious hypocrite of a father."

Jinks surged forward, a tiny ball of rage, and it took all of Annabelle's flagging strength to restrain him from bounding down the slope toward the witch beyond the gates. Fionnuala grinned, enjoying the impact of her words and the hateful web she spun, snaring another broken heart. Annabelle sobbed into the small boy's shoulder, tears for a father she had loved despite his many imperfections.

An explosion cut through the gloom, illuminating the graveyard, as a fireball erupted below, rising over the town in an unheralded fireworks display, green and red tendrils of fire fizzing outward in a kaleidoscope of destructive color.

"There goes the police barracks, by the sounds of it. The last bastion of law and order is no more. I rule this town now, and it will be the first of many, until all this land is mine."

Maggie screamed and ran forward, hands outstretched, as strands of blinding light surged from her raised palms, snaking towards Fionnuala, a deadly wave of unearthly power. The witch did not flinch, creasing her nose in mild amusement as the deadly fireballs exploded against the space where the cemetery gates had stood. Maggie howled in frustration as Fionnuala stepped towards the graveyard's perimeter, unharmed. Her gown trailed behind her, its sparkling jade sequins in sharp contrast to the muddy terrain it traversed.

"Your powers impress me, child. They are developing at an unprecedented rate. Such a shame I won't be able to see them reach their full potential. Your mother would have been very proud of you."

Maggie launched herself forward again, her only thought removing the smug look from her adversary's features. She reached the spot where the fireballs had dissolved into thin air and was flung back by an invisible force, landing near the top of the slope with a sickening impact. Annabelle and Jinks slipped and slid to where she lay, writhing in pain on the sodden turf.

"Powerful and pretty, but not the most observant," remarked Fionnuala from below them, pale face in stark contrast to her emerald eyes, which sparkled with devilish satisfaction. The aroma of burning wood and flesh had reached them, creeping up the hillside until it filled their nostrils. The fire had reached the outskirts of the town, and its greedy fingers were now laying claim to the lower slopes, its unnatural heat undeterred by the damp habitat.

"You chose well when you concluded that you would find me here. Unfortunately for you, that was because I planted the idea in that adorably vacuous head of yours. Your final stand, as you so sweetly called it, will now be your final resting place. As I said, such a shame, but at least you can be together with your dear mother again."

Maggie struggled to sit up but gasped and shuddered, prevented from rising. Something was wrong, broken beyond repair. She gritted her teeth to speak through the pain.

"You trapped us, you bitch. I fought your war, killed Bloody Hands. But in the end, I was just used by you, expendable like every other sorry soul in this town. All so you could have your petty moment of vengeance. I hope you rot..."

"Maggie, please. You're hurt. Don't be upsetting yourself." Jinks kneeled by his sister's side, powerless to help or heal. He winced at the spreading pool of dark red staining the ground beneath her. They exchanged a look, transferring knowledge forged by an intangible sibling bond no sorcery could breach. Annabelle looked on, helpless, as her injured friend grew paler by the second. She smiled at Annabelle, seemingly at peace with her predicament, and reached out to take her hand. It was ice-cold as her essence shriveled ever inwards.

"We tried, dear Annabelle. We tried."

"Don't you dare leave us, Margaret Malone. I will not allow it, do you hear me." Annabelle scowled, but only because, otherwise, the tears would flow, and she would dissolve at a moment when her friend most needed her to be strong.

"I'm sorry to interrupt this most poignant moment, but I'm afraid I must be moving on soon. So much to do."

Fionnuala held out her hands, her feigned apology dripping with insincerity. Wisps of choking smoke began to curl around her feet as the flames raced up the hillside, eager to be reunited with their vile creator. Annabelle looked beyond, where a wall of flame now obscured what was left of the town. Her home, as she had known it, was no more.

She looked frantically to either side and behind, desperate for some avenue of escape. It was obvious that Maggie could not be moved, her shattered body lying listless on the mossy bank. She felt her hand being squeezed and met the calm, clear eyes of the young woman who had changed her life forever.

"It's alright, my friend. Save my brother. Go, live your life."

"I will do no such thing. We can get you out of here. If only..."

A lounging willow tree to their right caught alight at the edge of the cemetery, its spidery branches igniting as Fionnuala's laughter rose above the cacophony of wind and flame.

"I dare you to come in here and do that, you *auld* bitch."

Jinks rose and took a step toward Fionnuala and the encroaching furnace, only to be hauled back by Annabelle by the scruff of his coat collar.

"You have to go; I can't feel my legs. Please."

Maggie squeezed Annabelle's hand again, her eyes imploring her friend to escape while the opportunity remained. On all sides, the wind was sweeping the furnace across the land, the wet, boggy ground lighting like dry kindling, such was its unnatural ferocity. Annabelle agonized, racking her brain for some scenario that would allow the three of them to survive. She found none and could only nod sadly in response.

"There, at the back. I've created a corridor. It will hold for a few more moments, enough time for the two of you to get through."

"But what about Fionnuala? Won't she?"

"She dare not enter this graveyard now, for she has fed here. She has angered the dead that lie beneath, disturbed their rest."

"But you..."

Words failed Annabelle as Jinks broke down beside her, sobbing uncontrollably by Maggie's side. It was heartbreaking, and Annabelle could only watch helplessly as his sister dredged every ounce of resolve she had to console the distraught boy.

"No tears, John Joseph. Come on. You're the man of the house. And worry not, you'll see me again. One way or another."

Jinks lifted his head and nodded bravely, as an unspoken exchange passed between them, one that steeled him to lean forward, kiss his sister's cold cheek, and turn away, pulling Annabelle with him. She stalled, part of her still appalled at abandoning her friend, but eventually allowed him to drag her up the hillside. They wove between the silent headstones, tripping over the uneven ground as the inferno closed in on all sides. Yet they were untouched, Maggie as good as her word, as the flames threatened but never broached the path between them and the rear of the cemetery. Reaching it with several final breathless steps, Jinks bounded over a stone wall that marked the graveyard's furthest boundary. Turning, he stretched out a hand to help Annabelle clamber over, before the two of them stumbled away, not daring to look back for fear of what they would find.

Had they looked, straining their eyes through the smoke and heat haze, they might have seen a stout, slight figure emerge from the chaotic backdrop behind Fionnuala as she savored Maggie's final moments before the blaze claimed her. A figure forgotten by so many throughout his hardworking, humble life. A career of quiet duty, no time for friends or love. Dr. Maurice Crothers had given that life to his town and its people. Only to watch it all turn to ash at the hands of the foul being that stood before him now, her head thrown back, laughing at them all.

He had watched her leave the home of the Reverend Edgar before making the grotesque discovery of the cleric's remains, shedding tears until the flames had forced him to flee the abode. Following her through the streets, he had stopped only briefly to retrieve the pistol of a fallen Constable, another victim of the dreadful sickness that, for all his medical knowledge, he had been powerless to curtail. The woman had glided through the streets, and his portly frame had struggled to keep apace, the flames licking at his ankles. When it became apparent that she was winding her way toward Friar's Bush, he had cut through a series of side streets familiar to him from his medical rounds, emerging onto the hillside mere feet from the murderer.

Crothers was a laughing stock to many of his peers, a simpering fool who lurked in the shadow of Andrew Blake, scraping and groveling at his every whim. And yet, his final moments would be his finest as he raised the pistol and, with trembling hands, pulled the trigger. The unsuspecting witch was propelled forward, the bullet passing through the back of her head. She flailed her arms like a spinning weather vane before gravity prevailed, and she toppled face-first onto the rough, stony earth of the graveyard.

Crothers stepped forward and studied the body, the gaping wound in the back of the skull satisfying his medical mind that the job was done. He began to whistle while casually reloading the pistol as the flames whipped at his feet, crackling and hissing, hungry for his flesh. Through the haze, he could have sworn he saw another young woman lying further up the hillside, but it was surely a trick of the light. His task complete, Maurice Crothers nodded in satisfaction before raising the pistol to his temple and ending his own misery.

Maggie watched the man fall, the splatter of bone and blood as he slumped to the ground, the pistol still clenched tightly in his hand. She vaguely recognized him; was he a town guardian...no, it was the doctor, one of Blake's cronies. The fires swept across the graveyard towards her, and it took what remained of her waning powers to hold them at bay. She would die here, she knew that, but so long as Jinks and Annabelle did not, she would die contented. She should have been in agony from the impact of her fall, yet felt nothing now. Her body lay twisted, stubbornly refusing to comply with even her most modest request. Yes, she would die here.

Her only solace was that so would Fionnuala, lying beneath her on the slope, a bullet having plumbed the depths of her twisted brain. They would burn together, die together, and their end would mark the end of everything that had haunted the town. The fires would cleanse Belfast of the sickness the witch had brought upon its people, and Maggie knew that. One day, the hunger would also end, allowing the survivors to start again, to build a new town, no...a city, that would rise from the ashes and stand tall and proud.

"If only the world were that simple."

Maggie started from her daydream to find herself facing a nightmare, a hellish vision that shattered the fragile hopes that had been stirring her slowing heart. Fionnuala swayed at the bottom of the hillside, the flames lapping at the trail of her gown like angry waves nibbling at a sumptuous shore. Her face was caked in mud as she smiled, revealing a bloody mouthful of tooth and gum. She took a step forward but stopped, wincing, before resuming her slow ascent of the hillside toward a stricken Maggie.

"It has not worked out quite how I planned, but I suppose we got there in the end. And what an end." Fionnuala stopped and inhaled deeply, filling her lungs with enough smoke to disable the hardiest mortal. She seemed immune to the searing heat as the flames began to gorge on the fine silk trail of her gown. Maggie watched it inch toward the main body of her skirts, willing it to consume the witch, body and soul.

"Bloody Hands no longer dogs my every step, the city is in ruins. Those not taken by hunger or sickness will be burned to an unrecognizable crisp before the day is done. Yes, all and all, a most satisfactory conclusion, don't you think?"

"A false victory, I would say," replied Maggie, using both elbows to force herself into a more upright position. Her face was coated in a sickly sweat, yet she shivered despite the wall of white-hot heat all around them. It inched ever closer; if she could only keep the witch distracted for long enough...

Fionnuala laughed as a raucous crack of lightning was immediately followed by a growl of thunder, rattling the foundations of the dour headstones and solemn monuments dotted about the graveyard. She threw her head back as a downpour ensued, spewing forth a pounding rain that hammered into the supple earth, extinguishing flames that, only seconds before, had threatened to devour all. The ground hissed and steamed, a choking smoke rising to engulf the ruined husk of Belfast.

Neither of them saw the first desiccated hand that thrust through the dark, cloying soil. It was swiftly followed by another, then another, as the ground erupted, the graves spewing forth their remaining eternal guests in a grisly harvest. A harvest that neither Fionnuala nor Maggie had anticipated but were now forced to confront.

The laughter evaporated from Fionnuala's face, a pained scowl replacing it as undead nails dug into her ankle, filthy hands clawing for purchase, low groans underpinning the roaring deluge.

"Pity the witch who dares to feed on the dead, for they shall have their vengeance," whispered Maggie as more rotting limbs emerged, sprouting from the earth in search of the woman who had condemned them to lie beneath the sullen soil, their lives cut short by her unbridled fury. It was time for them to rage, and there would be no curtailing their anger now that she had strayed into their domain.

Fionnuala screamed in frustration, twisting and turning in every direction, her futile efforts to break free to no avail as the thickening horde rose from the hallowed ground. Heads and shoulders began to emerge from the earth, their cries rising above the driving rain. Maggie shuffled backward, using what remaining strength she had to evade the deadly retribution that now held sway. She need not have worried, for the vengeful dead of Friar's Bush had no interest in the young woman who now watched mesmerized as the architect of their despair was repaid in kind.

"I curse you, Margaret Malone. I curse you and your kin, this town, this island for all eternity!"

She was on her knees now, eyes wild and fearful, no longer the imperious queen who had presided over their squalid deaths from her lofty, craggy throne. Her emerald eyes blazed with vitriol, flame-red locks thrashing in every direction as her victims dragged her ever nearer their final abodes, a damp mattress of rotting leaves and strangling weeds waiting to welcome her. Beneath the soil, there were no airs and graces, only fat, slick worms waiting to slither through her every crevice as sweet, decaying flesh sloughed off her bleached bones.

Maggie averted her eyes as an elongated scream fractured the air, focusing instead on the smoky, sodden skies. The pained cry was abruptly cut short, replaced by sounds she could not place, slapping and squelching, sounds that made her skin crawl at their unseen origins. The ferocious torrent began to ease off and then cease, coinciding with the eerie groans of the fallen. When she looked back, there was no sign of the witch or those who had risen to challenge her dark legacy. It was fitting that the two fiends who had brought such misery to so many, would meet their end at the hands of those they had slain.

Maggie witnessed many miracles that day, enough to fill the pews of every church in Belfast a hundred times over, but the greatest was yet to come. She gasped as the smoke and clouds parted, a sliver of blue sky penetrating the perpetual gloom. A spear of sunlight illuminated her raised face, its warmth a welcome reprieve from the driving rain. Maggie basked within its balmy embrace, eyes closed, relishing every second of tranquility.

"It's time, girl."

"I'm not ready yet, Mammy. I'm scared."

"No need to be scared. You're with me now."

Maggie opened an eye, and the graveyard was no longer there. Instead, she was atop the mountain again, Fionnuala's pretty cottage and garden laid out before her. Standing before them, Kate Malone smiled. She stood strong and healthy, free from the hunger and sickness that had first robbed her from them. A blue sky above, no sign of the clouds that had dogged her every waking moment back in Belfast.

Maggie swiveled to look across the lough, the sun glinting off the waters as several sleek schooners glided towards the port, a fresh breeze hastening their passage. Awaiting them, the warehouses of the docks stood tall, no sign of the fires that had earlier razed them to the ground. Maggie gasped, her eyes scanning the town's unblemished skyline. Everything was as it had been before.

"But..."

"Hush, child. Here, take my hand."

Maggie reached out without thinking, instinctively seeking the hand she had held so many times before, a hand that offered safety and reassurance. It was only as she rose to her feet that she realized the injury she had sustained in the cemetery was no more. She stood, unaided, and stared into the warm, kindly eyes of the woman who had raised her, a woman she thought she had lost forever.

"Am I dead, Mammy?"

Her mother feigned a frown, her eyes creasing. "I prefer to say, we have passed on. The dead are nowhere; they have nothing, yet here we stand upon this mountain, our mountain, looking down at our beloved town."

"Our mountain. But..."

Maggie eyed the cottage suspiciously, half expecting to find a vengeful Fionnuala storming towards her, her face ablaze with unbridled fury. It sat serenely, surrounded by a lush, verdant lawn, speckled with spectacular flower beds that dazzled with their color and diversity. A sleek butterfly busied itself with a bunch of vibrant violets, no sign of the evil that had once called this place home.

"Fionnuala will trouble us no more," explained Kate, as if reading her daughter's mind. "The curse is broken, the town is saved, and a new lady walks the mountain." She smiled, allowing the revelation to settle on her daughter's shoulders like the first flakes of snow on a wintry night. Maggie's face broke into a grin as her mother lowered into a prim curtsey, her skirts fanning out across the grass.

"I cannot reside on this mountain. What about Jinks? He will not be able to survive alone without us."

"You need not worry about your brother. He is in safe hands, your friend Annabelle will make sure of that."

Maggie relaxed slightly, but still cast an anxious eye toward her hometown. The thought of her brother living his life without her accompanying his every step filled her with unease.

"Besides, you will be watching over him. You will be watching over every soul in this town. It has faced great hardship, and it will face even greater hardship in the years ahead. Wars the like of which we can only dream about, neighbors turning on each other. These streets will run red again with the blood of the innocent. They will need you to watch over them, helping where and when you can."

"But what of heaven and hell? All the things the priests used to talk about? The Reverend Edgar?"

"These places are not our concern. All you need to know is that you are in the right place now. Now come, If I am to answer these endless questions of yours, I would much rather do it with a hot cup of tea in my hands and a freshly buttered scone to nibble on."

She held out her arm, and Maggie took it, linked together as they stepped down the sweeping hill toward their new abode. The succulent aroma of freshly baked bread wafted across the garden, causing Maggie's mouth to water.

"Perhaps I will warm to this passing over, as you call it, more than I had initially thought, Mother."

Kate Malone patted her daughter's hand and smiled.

"Perhaps you will, dear Maggie. Perhaps you will."

The Magic Of Stones And Onions

BELFAST, 1850

"**J**ohn Joseph Malone, if you don't get down these stairs now, I will feed your dinner to the dog, do you hear me?"

"Coming."

Annabelle chuckled to herself as what sounded like a herd of elephants descended from above, the boy taking the stairs three at a time. He had sprouted a foot in recent months, thriving on honest, healthy food and proper medical care. Times were still hard and the town was by no means out of the woods, but the hunger had eased, the previous two potato crops having thankfully reaped a blight-free harvest. The days of Jinks the Turnip Thief were well and truly in the past.

"What plans this evening, Annabelle?" asked a breathless Jinks, as he launched enthusiastically into his plate of potatoes, carrots, and roast beef, drowned in rich, thick gravy. The boy loved his food, burning it off at a frenetic rate. He remained slim but was filling out, his shoulders broadening, as the first signs of manhood began to emerge. Soon, thought Annabelle, he would be in need of a razor to shave off those wispy whiskers sprouting on his chin. She smiled fondly at the boy who she now regarded as a brother. His sister would be so proud of him.

"Well, I have been invited for supper at the Muldoon household." Her cheeks burned and she fought to suppress a smile. Jinks stopped, laden fork between plate and mouth, a sly expression crossing his face.

"I see. And would James Muldoon be sitting at his parent's table this evening?" Jinks fought to suppress a smirk but failed miserably.

"Possibly. Not that it's any of your concern." Annabelle rose from the table and swiped at her tormentor with a drying cloth. "Now, hurry up and eat your food."

"It most certainly is my concern, as I'll be the one walking you down the aisle some day. No man is taking the hand of Miss Annabelle Edgar without my blessing." He speared a carrot to enforce his point, fixing it with a hard stare.

"How presumptuous of you. Who says I want to marry? I do not require a man to make my way in the world. I am an independent young woman and respected member of the community, I will have you know."

Jinks groaned, as he scooped another mound of potato into his mouth. "Gets a job at the local newspaper and thinks she's lady of the manor." He guffawed at his own joke, spraying partially consumed food across the table that dominated the spacious kitchen. The untimely demise of her father had left Annabelle with a large house that she was only too happy to share with the sole remaining member of the Malone family. Yes, there had been all manner of forms to complete and hearings to attend but, in the end, it had been a formality. People were happy that they had each other, two poor orphans devastated by the terrors of Black '47.

"I'll be back no later than eleven. I'll check your homework in the morning. And don't forget you have…"

"Chores to do." groaned Jinks. "Enjoy your evening."

The door slammed shut and the gangly youth was left to finish his meal. He enjoyed the quiet, for his days were busy and he valued this time alone, away from the loose tongues of the Belfast gossips.

The Reverend Edgar had been found dead in his bed, most likely a heart attack, although the look of horror on what was left of his charred face had raised a few eyebrows. John Malone was taken by the fever, one of many that fateful day, found slumped outside his favorite watering hole. The mystery of the men who ventured up the mountain but never returned remained unsolved, although dark talk of a *Fenian* ambush grew to such an extent that many accepted it as an indisputable fact. The bodies were never recovered but they were up there somewhere, no doubt. Others whispered that the Black Lady had taken them, for daring to enter her kingdom.

Jinks was happy, however, and the idle chit-chat washed over him like a gentle wave lapping at his ankles. He rose from his chair and busied himself about the kitchen, washing the dirty dishes and ensuring the table was wiped down. Annabelle ran a tight ship and would have his hide if she returned to find their home resembling a pigsty. Home. How he loved that word. It had taken time to adjust to his new life but he felt settled now, grounded. He had his education, new friends, and a chance to live a life that had seemed beyond his reach when a resident of Carson's Court. The Reverend Edgar's pension and Annabelle's salary ensured they could lead a comfortable life.

Chores completed, Jinks retired to his first-floor bedroom overlooking the street where carriages rattled by, normality now a steadfast companion in his life. The light was good outside, a strong sun cutting a swathe across the floor to a sturdy desk that housed a small mountain of textbooks. Well, they could wait.

He dropped to his knees and ducked beneath his bed, emerging seconds later with a nondescript wooden box. He shot a wary look over his shoulder, despite knowing that there was nobody else in the house. Maggie had taught him well. Not everyone cared to understand the craft, it was a private act reserved for a select few to practice. And he was one of those precious few.

Many had remarked on his bravery at the loss of his parents to the sickness. What made him stand out, however, from the deluge of other orphaned children, was that he had also lost his sister. As with the men who went up the mountain but never returned, mystery surrounded Maggie Malone's last days. The majority consensus was that she had fled the town when suspicions were aroused that she had been dabbling in sorcery. Neighbors had accused her of casting spells and curses on them, some even went so far as to claim she had brought the fever upon the town. No wonder she had scarpered. Since then, there had been uncon-firmed sightings of her in Dublin, Liverpool, even as far afield as New York.

Jinks knew the truth. He rose and carefully carried the box to his desk, where he shoved aside the books, allowing room for his most precious possession. Setting it down, he pulled up a chair, before gently easing the lid open. He knew the contents of the box, yet never failed to be enamoured by the serene sapphire glow that greeted him.

Maggie had minded twenty six, but Jinks had no need for as many. He set them in a row on the desk, five in total, all that was required. Although he had maintained the pretense of church attendance, this was where his true faith rested. Annabelle knew, of course, and encouraged him to quietly maintain the old ways, while she protected him from the prying eyes of congregation members who always suspected there was more to the brother of the witch girl, Maggie Malone, than met the eye.

Aside from Maggie and Nell, he did not know, nor cared, where the other followers had scattered, after the demise of their beloved Black Lady. Occasionally, he would sense one of them at the fringes of his consciousness, reaching out, attempting to make contact. He could not, would not, allow that. Theirs was a web he never wished to become entangled in again, that of lost souls seeking their tainted mistress. No, he had no desire to be drawn back into that world. Instead, he focused on his stones. They were as smooth as marble, the result of decades of silent worship, rubbed and worried at, until every pit and crevice had been erased from their now flawless surfaces.

He held them every evening, head bowed and on his knees, clearing his mind of the cluttered detritus of daily life. All other petty concerns leaked from his body, entering the stones, never to return and plague his thoughts. His very own worry stones. He knew he was fortunate and thanked her for the ability to do so, while others were forced to endure the torment of carting their anxieties through their lives, weighing them down at every step, shoulders bowed, minds shackled.

"Thank you, Maggie...I mean, my Lady." He cracked an eyelid open, as a mild breeze wafted through his open window from the street outside. It tickled his nose and, try as he might, he was forced to scratch it, mindful of her gentle rebuke.

"Blessed be she who walks this mountain and watches over her people. Blessed be she who protects and sustains us. Blessed be she who is wise beyond words and kind beyond measure. Blessed be."

He set all of the stones back in the box bar one, wrapped in a crumpled sheet of paper. He removed the sheet and flattened it on the bedcovers, before raising it and planting a gentle kiss on it.

"Blessed Lady, please look over my mother, whose name I honor and entrust to you. I know she is near to you and I ask for her continued wardship."

He resealed the stone with the scrap of paper bearing Kate Malone's name, before returning it to the box with equal care. Following this, the same procedure was replicated with the other stones, each representing an individual who he cared for and offered up for protection. Annabelle and a couple of close friends he had developed in the past year and finally one Melissa Connors, a young lady who Jinks had been exchanging shy glances with across their respective pews at Rosemary Street Presbyterian Church. It passed the time while the new minister droned on from a book that no longer acted as a moral compass for Jinks. Instead, he looked to his sister, high above the city, for guidance and instruction.

She spoke to him every day and, as this new aspect of their relationship developed, Jinks had attuned his senses to the many ways in which Maggie communicated her thoughts and opinions. It could be as subtle as a certain smell or cloud formation in the sky above, meaningless to the wider population, but as obvious to him as being struck on the head with a hammer. On each occasion, it would trigger a subtle suggestion, a seemingly random thought that Jinks would cling to and mold until it formulated into a cogent idea or action for him to progress. She had never failed him yet, although he was still waiting for a firm answer as to when he would summon up the courage to speak to Miss Connors after morning service.

There was one final object, but it did not nestle in the confines of the box. Rather, it was secreted in the disused chimney breast of the room formerly occupied by the late Reverend Edgar. Not even Annabelle knew of its existence, for still too raw were the memories of her father's passing, and she never entered the room. It was the sole secret that Jinks kept from his surrogate sister, a secret intended to keep at bay a monster that still scarred his thoughts and dreams. Maggie knew its real name but would not divulge it, despite Jinks's repeated pleas that to do so would strengthen his wards against the evil that prowled the edges of his otherwise idyllic world.

Bloody Hands.

Not its real name, but that moniker would have to suffice. Scrawled on the paper, wrapped around a small onion, he hid it away up a chimney in a room that nobody visited. Nobody but John Joseph Malone. He would light the fire occasionally, just enough to ensure that the twisting smoke regularly rose to wither and shrink the onion. Wither and shrink, just as Maggie's magic had withered and shrunk the creature's black heart, ensuring that when the day came, two hundred years hence, the beast would not rise again to stalk the streets of the town that would become a city. A city that had weathered the harshest of storms and prevailed, rising from the blood-soaked ashes of its past.

The room was cloaked in every ruse and rune that Maggie had taught him. A bottle by the hearth, filled regularly with his own urine and topped with wine smuggled from the Reverend Edgar's now disused study. Nails and herbs, sage and rosemary, all designed to add layer after layer of protection. Archaic wards carved out in the wood and stone; window, door, and hearth marked to ensure the demon's spirit would never be unleashed again. Swirling circles, with no beginning or end, endless lines that would hold him for eternity, walking their endless paths, lost and without hope of reprieve or release.

Jinks busied himself lighting a small fire with paper, kindling, and turf, that he kept in a wicker basket on the hearth. He watched, eyes watering, as the gray wisps ascended from the humble flame, encasing the onion with its choking fumes. A tear trickled down his cheek, no longer grimy but freshly scrubbed with strong soap every morning, whether he liked it or not. Annabelle made sure of that. A tear, its origins partially caused by the choking smoke, but also born of hope and happiness. He rose and turned to face the solitary window that looked out over the bustling street and, beyond that, a thriving town. Beyond that, again, to the dark mountain that stood watch over both him and his fellow citizens.

He knew she was watching over them. Watching him. Always watching over him.

The sun shone more often now over Belfast, she made sure of that. It rained when it had to, for the farmers working the land needed its wet embrace as much as the heat warming their bent backs. She would stand on the mountain, looking down over the lough, as shafts of amber sunlight danced across the crests of aquamarine waves. Noisy gulls swooped low over the swell, always on the lookout for tasty morsels floating on the briny waters. Further inland, the town sprawled outwards from the docks. The market stalls were well-stocked again, shop shelves once more full. Life was still hard for many, but nobody needed to starve. New mills had opened and there was work for all. Belfast was no longer on its knees.

Maggie turned, for that was how she still wished to be addressed. Many referred to her now as their Lady, others a hateful witch, but these names meant little to her. All that mattered was that those she loved were safe and sound beneath the shadow of the mountain. The crows were her ever-watchful eyes, no longer under Fionnuala's dark thrall. They soared high above the rooftops, absorbing information that they then conveyed to their mistress at the cottage. A home she shared with her mother, who was either to be found pottering about the garden, pruning and weeding, or conjuring up mouth-watering meals in their airy kitchen.

Maggie had little recourse to walk the streets herself, but occasionally visited the town, her simple dresses and worn brogues complemented by a dark, hooded cape that concealed her features from wandering eyes. Occasionally a passer-by considered approaching the lone lady, surprised by her presence at such a late hour. They were always dissuaded from doing so, however, an uneasiness possessing them and allowing the woman to pass unimpeded. Maggie had worked hard on her fledgling powers since passing over, honing and taming them so that she could apply them in more subtle and intricate ways. Persuasion, some might even call it manipulation, but using her craft to influence others to make the right choice, walk the proper path. It could be a dream a town guardian might have the night before an important vote on workers' rights, the coming together of two sad and lonely souls on their respective daily walks, or suggesting to a well-meaning citizen that they think twice about approaching a lone lady at night as she flitted through the alleys and courtyards that she knew like the back of her hand.

She missed Jinks and Annabelle but checked on them regularly. The former was developing into a fine young man and proving a faithful follower of the old ways. They would serve him well in the years ahead, and Bloody Hands would never hunt these streets again so long as they both kept a watchful eye on the town. Annabelle was a different matter;

she had refrained from reaching out to the clergyman's daughter in the same way she had connected with her brother.

Maggie was pleased that she was courting a decent young man from an eminently respectable family, delighted that she was developing her writing talents and making an impact on a society that for too long had been governed by blinkered old men. Annabelle's articles were a breath of fresh air to a previously jaded local press, highlighting and championing social injustice and inequality. Maggie saw the young woman's future mapped out before her, and it sparkled with potential.

Yet her heart still ached at times as to what might have been. Their time together had been painfully brief, time alone together even less so, but Annabelle Edgar had been the friend that Maggie had always yearned for, but never been allowed to have, so preoccupied had she been ensuring that Jinks had food on the table. The precious handful of shared conversations and experiences between Annabelle and her had encouraged Maggie to lower her guard and expose her battered heart to the possibility of a friendship that could have blossomed into a lifelong bond. That was before Fionnuala, Bloody Hands, and all the other trials that had led her to the cemetery at Friar's Bush.

Maggie smiled ruefully; her attention taken by a wisp of smoke rising from a solitary chimney pot to the east of the sprawling town. Only one young man would see fit to light a fire on such a glorious summer's afternoon, and her chest swelled with pride at the mental image of her brother hunched over the hearth, working a flame that would keep a monster at bay.

She cast out, adding to the ward that surrounded Belfast, an impregnable shield that would be in place forever if that was required. Jinks would live his life, marry, and have children of his own. One day he would join her and their mother on the mountain and others would take his place, practicing the old ways, ensuring that life prevailed, no matter what atrocities the town would have to endure.

Maggie turned and started the long walk back along the Twelve Apostles towards home. Since the disappearance of the men on the mountain, few ventured to walk the barren mountain, the legend of the Black Lady persisting for as long as men and women had tongues in their heads. It was a burden she was willing to bear, a price she had no hesitation in paying. Witch. Ghost. Banshee. She had many names, but she did not care. For she had saved her town, saved her remaining family, and saved a dear friend. If that was the price of eternal notoriety, then it was a small one to pay.

She threw back the hood of her cape and raised her head to the flawless blue sky. Above, her faithful crows cawed noisily, sharing in her joy at what had passed and what yet lay ahead. She smiled and savored the warmth of the day on her eyelids, the aroma of fresh vegetable soup and a stacked peat hearth filling her nostrils.

"I'm on my way, Mammy. On my way home."

Acknowledgments

The Famine Witch has been very much a team effort. I just did the easy bit, writing the words. I would like to thank Cassandra L. Thompson for her unwavering belief in this story and my writing. I'd also like to thank the entire team at Quill & Crow Publishing House for their expertise and enthusiasm. Special thanks to Tiffany Putenis (editing), Alma Garcia (marketing), Melanie Whitlock (research), and William Bartlett (for first taking a chance on my horrid scribbling).

There are many, many other writers and scholars who have supported and inspired me along the way. Naming them all would involve another book, well, possibly a novella, but special thanks to Dualtach Magfhionnbhairr, Shannon Spence, Lydia Russell, Brooklynn Dean, and Catherine Fearns.

Appendix A

GLOSSARY OF TERMS

Abhartach – Irish Gaelic, meaning dwarf. The abhartach was an evil wizard in Irish folklore who was killed by a local chieftain but then rose from the dead to drink the blood of his victims.

An Bhean Dubh – Irish Gaelic, meaning The Black Lady.

Auld – Irish slang for old.

Balor – The leader of The Fomoire, a malevolent supernatural race in Irish mythology.

Banshee – A female spirit in Irish folklore who forewarned of the passing of a family member by screaming or wailing the night before the death.

Béal Feirste – The Irish spelling of Belfast, meaning 'the mouth of the sandbar.'

Bean Feasa – Irish Gaelic, meaning a woman of knowledge; a wise or cunning woman.

Cailleach – Irish Gaelic, meaning witch.

Colleen – Irish slang for a young woman or girl.

Deamhan – Irish Gaelic, meaning demon.

Shebeen – Irish slang for a drinking establishment.

Spiorad Olc – Irish Gaelic, meaning evil spirit.

The Fomoire – A malevolent supernatural race in Irish mythology.

Tuatha – The Tuatha dé Danann (translated as The Folk of the Goddess,

Danu) were a supernatural race in Irish mythology who resided in the Otherworld.

Wains – Irish slang for young children.

Appendix B

TRIGGER INDEX

- **Desecration of grave**
- **Death by execution** (hanging)
- **Extreme poverty/starvation**
- **Gore** (death/murder)
- **Implied infant death**
- **Misogyny**
- **Violence toward women** (murder, attempted murder)

About the Author

Stephen Black is a dark fantasy and horror writer from Northern Ireland. He is the author of the critically acclaimed, best-selling 'Kirkwood Scott Chronicles' series. He has also had short stories published by Quill & Crow Publishing House in their 'Grimm & Dread' and 'Haunted' anthologies, in addition to the 'Crow's Quill' online literary magazine. Stephen is married with three children. In his spare time... hang on, Stephen doesn't have any spare time.

Other Books by Stephen Black
The Kirkwood Scott Chronicles

Thank You For Reading

Thank you for reading *The Famine Witch*. We deeply appreciate our readers, and are grateful for everyone who takes the time to leave us a review. If you're interested, please visit our website to find review links. Your reviews help small presses and indie authors thrive, and we appreciate your support.

Other Titles by Quill & Crow

All the Parts of the Soul

The Quiet Stillness of Empty Houses

The Ancient Ones Trilogy